IMPACT

Fifty Short Short Stories

Fannie Safier
Secondary English Editorial Staff
Harcourt Brace Jovanovich, Publishers

Harcourt Brace Jovanovich, Publishers
Orlando   New York   Chicago   San Diego   Atlanta   Dallas

ACKNOWLEDGMENTS

For permission to reprint copyrighted material, grateful acknowledgment is made to the following sources:

American-Scandinavian Foundation: "The Eclipse" by Selma Lagerlöf, translated by Velma Swanston Howard in *American-Scandinavian Review,* December 1922.

Isaac Asimov: "The Fun They Had" from *Fifty Short Science Fiction Tales,* edited by Isaac Asimov and Groff Conklin. Copyright 1951 by NEA Service, Inc.

Julian Bach Literary Agency: "Ah Love! Ah Me!" by Max Steele from *Collier's,* Vol. 116, No. 18, Nov. 3, 1945. Copyright © 1945 by Max Steele.

Albert Bonniers Förlag AB: "Father and I" from *The Marriage Feast and Other Stories* by Pär Lagerkvist.

Curtis Brown, Ltd.: "The Rifles of the Regiment" by Eric Knight. Originally appeared in *Collier's,* Vol. 110, No. 7, August 15, 1942.

Thomas S. Brush: "Birthday Party" by Katharine Brush. Originally appeared in *The New Yorker,* March 16, 1946.

Arthur C. Clarke and Scott Meredith Literary Agency, Inc., 845 Third AV, New York, NY 10022: "Who's There?" by Arthur C. Clarke.

Don Congdon Associates, Inc.: "All Summer in a Day" by Ray Bradbury. Copyright © 1954 by Ray Bradbury; renewed 1982. "All the Years of Her Life" by Morley Callaghan. Copyright © 1936 by Morley Callaghan; renewed 1964.

Devin-Adair Publishers, Greenwich, CT: "The Trout" from *The Man Who Invented Sin and Other Stories* by Sean O'Faolain. Published by Devin-Adair Company, New York, 1949. "The Wild Duck's Nest" from *The Game Cock and Other Stories* by Michael McLaverty. Copyright 1947 by the Devin-Adair Company. Published by Devin-Adair Company, New York, 1948.

MN

iii

Contents

SETTING

POINT OF VIEW

TONE

MORE STORIES

Plot

If you were a guest at this dinner party, you could look forward to one of the most exciting and suspenseful evenings of your life.

THE DINNER PARTY

Mona Gardner

The country is India. A colonial official[1] and his wife are giving a large dinner party. They are seated with their guests—army officers and government attachés[2] and their wives, and a visiting American naturalist[3]—in their spacious dining room, which has a bare marble floor, open rafters and wide glass doors opening onto a veranda.

A spirited discussion springs up between a young girl who insists that women have outgrown the jumping-on-a-chair-at-the-sight-of-a-mouse era and a colonel who says that they haven't.

"A woman's unfailing reaction in any crisis," the colonel says, "is to scream. And while a man may feel like it, he has

---

1. **colonial official:** At this time India was a British colony.
2. **attachés** (ăt′ə-shāz′, ă-tă′shāz′): officials on the staff of a diplomatic mission.
3. **naturalist:** a person who studies animals and plants.

that ounce more of nerve control than a woman has. And that last ounce is what counts."

The American does not join in the argument but watches the other guests. As he looks, he sees a strange expression come over the face of the hostess. She is staring straight ahead, her muscles contracting slightly. With a slight gesture she summons the native boy standing behind her chair and whispers to him. The boy's eyes widen: he quickly leaves the room.

Of the guests, none except the American notices this or sees the boy place a bowl of milk on the veranda just outside the open doors.

The American comes to with a start. In India, milk in a bowl means only one thing—bait for a snake. He realizes there must be a cobra in the room. He looks up at the rafters—the likeliest place—but they are bare. Three corners of the room are empty, and in the fourth the servants are waiting to serve the next course. There is only one place left—under the table.

His first impulse is to jump back and warn the others, but he knows the commotion would frighten the cobra into striking. He speaks quickly, the tone of his voice so arresting that it sobers everyone.

"I want to know just what control everyone at this table has. I will count to three hundred—that's five minutes—and not one of you is to move a muscle. Those who move will forfeit[4] fifty rupees.[5] Ready!"

The twenty people sit like stone images while he counts. He is saying ". . . two hundred and eighty . . ." when, out of the corner of his eye, he sees the cobra emerge and make for the bowl of milk. Screams ring out as he jumps to slam the veranda doors safely shut.

---

4. **forfeit** (fôr′fĭt): surrender as a penalty.
5. **rupees** (roō-pēz′): The rupee is the basic monetary unit of India, like the dollar in the United States.

"You were right, Colonel!" the host exclaims. "A man has just shown us an example of perfect control."

"Just a minute," the American says, turning to his hostess. "Mrs. Wynnes, how did you know that cobra was in the room?"

A faint smile lights up the woman's face as she replies: "Because it was crawling across my foot."

CHECK-UP (Multiple-Choice)

1. Which of the following statements would the colonel agree with?
   a. "Women never show courage."
   b. "Men show greater self-control than women."
   c. "Men do not experience fear."
2. The naturalist knows that there is a snake in the room because
   a. he sees a strange expression on his hostess' face
   b. the native boy's eyes widen in alarm
   c. a bowl of milk is placed on the veranda
3. The naturalist gets everyone to sit still by
   a. warning them about the snake
   b. challenging the guests to test their self-control
   c. offering to pay each guest money
4. We can assume that the cobra did not strike Mrs. Wynnes because
   a. she kept her body absolutely still
   b. cobras do not attack women
   c. it wasn't hungry

FOR DISCUSSION

1. The first sentence of the story tells us that the action takes place in India. Why is this information important to the story?

2. The American is identified as a *naturalist.* How does his training as a scientist show itself in his behavior?

3. The colonel believes that men always show greater self-control than women. What do the events of the story show about his belief?

4. A situation is said to be *ironic* when the outcome of events is the opposite of what is expected or believed to be true. Why is the ending of this story ironic?

PLOT
Exposition and Conflict

1. *Plot* is the carefully worked-out sequence of related events or actions in a story. A plot has a *structure*—that is, all the individual parts of the story are arranged and inter-related in order to lead to a satisfying conclusion.

A traditional plot structure has a section of *exposition,* which gives the reader important background information. Reread the first three paragraphs of "The Dinner Party." Where does the story take place? Who are the characters? What is the subject of discussion?

2. In a short story there is generally a problem or struggle of some kind called a *conflict.* Conflict is the most important element in a plot. At the beginning of "The Dinner Party," the guests express their differences about an idea. In your own words, tell what this conflict is.

3. Conflict can be *external* or *internal.* The conflict between the naturalist and the snake is an external conflict. The naturalist's struggle to control his panic is an internal struggle. What kind of conflict or conflicts could we say the hostess experiences?

4. In a story there may be a single conflict or there may be several related conflicts. How is the conflict between the dinner guests and the snake related to the argument between the colonel and the young girl?

UNDERSTANDING THE WORDS
IN THE STORY (Multiple-Choice)

1. The *rafters* of the house are
   a. tiles decorating the walls
   b. beams that support the roof
   c. ceiling fans used to keep the room cool
2. A *veranda* is
   a. an open porch
   b. a screen door
   c. a circular staircase
3. The word *spirited* (paragraph 2) tells us that the young girl and the colonel are
   a. quarreling angrily
   b. waving their arms about
   c. having a lively conversation
4. Another word for *unfailing* (paragraph 3) is
   a. unfavorable
   b. certain
   c. unfeeling
5. When the muscles of her face *contract* (paragraph 4), the hostess
   a. smiles broadly
   b. opens her eyes in alarm
   c. draws her brows together
6. When the American "comes to with a start" (paragraph 6), he
   a. leaps out of his seat
   b. wakes up suddenly
   c. is unexpectedly startled
7. A *commotion* (paragraph 7) is
   a. noisy
   b. quiet
   c. stealthy
8. The *tone* of the American's voice refers to the
   a. speed at which he is speaking
   b. emotion and meaning of his words
   c. musical quality of his language

9. The word that tells us the American catches and holds everyone's attention is
   a. *arresting*
   b. *sobers*
   c. *control*
10. When the American sees the cobra *emerge* (paragraph 9), the snake
    a. rises up to strike
    b. becomes visible
    c. weaves across the room

FOR WRITING

1. In addition to courage and self-control, Mrs. Wynnes demonstrates that she knows a great deal about cobras. Using details in the story, show that she is familiar with the habits of cobras.
2. The snake in this story is the common cobra of India, which may reach a length of six feet and which is easily recognized by the marking on its hood. There are a number of species of cobra.

   Some Topics for Reports
   The king cobra
   The "spitting" cobra
   Antitoxins for cobra venom (Antivenines)
   Indian superstitions about cobras

3. Imagine the conversation between the colonel and the young girl *following* the events of the dinner party. Write the dialogue for that scene.
4. Write a short short story on the topic "A Narrow Escape," using real or imagined events.

*"I froze instantly, holding my breath
and trying to locate the alien sound with my ears."*

WHO'S THERE?

Arthur C. Clarke

When satellite control called me, I was writing up the
day's progress report in the Observation Bubble—the glass-
domed office that juts out from the axis of the Space Station
like the hubcap of a wheel. It was not really a good place to
work, for the view was too overwhelming. Only a few yards
away I could see the construction teams performing their
slow-motion ballet as they put the station together like a
giant jigsaw puzzle. And beyond them, twenty thousand
miles below, was the blue-green glory of the full Earth, floating against the raveled star clouds of the Milky Way.

"Station Supervisor here," I answered. "What's the trouble?"

"Our radar's showing a small echo two miles away,
almost stationary, about five degrees west of Sirius.[1] Can
you give us a visual report on it?"

Anything matching our orbit so precisely could hardly
be a meteor; it would have to be something we'd dropped—
perhaps an inadequately secured piece of equipment that
had drifted away from the station. So I assumed; but when
I pulled out my binoculars and searched the sky around

---

1. **Sirius** (sĭr′ē-əs): the "Dog Star," in the constellation Canis Major (kā′nĭs
mā′jər) in the Southern Hemisphere. It is the brightest star in the sky.

7

Orion,[2] I soon found my mistake. Though this space traveler was man-made, it had nothing to do with us.

"I've found it," I told Control. "It's someone's test satellite—cone-shaped, four antennas, and what looks like a lens system in its base. Probably U.S. Air Force, early nineteen-sixties, judging by the design. I know they lost track of several when their transmitters failed. There were quite a few attempts to hit this orbit before they finally made it."

After a brief search through the files, Control was able to confirm my guess. It took a little longer to find out that Washington wasn't in the least bit interested in our discovery of a twenty-year-old stray satellite, and would be just as happy if we lost it again.

"Well, we can't do *that,*" said Control. "Even if nobody wants it, the thing's a menace to navigation. Someone had better go out and haul it aboard."

That someone, I realized, would have to be me. I dared not detach a man from the closely knit construction teams, for we were already behind schedule—and a single day's delay on this job cost a million dollars. All the radio and TV networks on Earth were waiting impatiently for the moment when they could route their programs through us, and thus provide the first truly global service, spanning the world from Pole to Pole.

"I'll go out and get it," I answered, snapping an elastic band over my papers so that the air currents from the ventilators wouldn't set them wandering around the room. Though I tried to sound as if I was doing everyone a great favor, I was secretly not at all displeased. It had been at least two weeks since I'd been outside; I was getting a little tired of stores schedules, maintenance reports, and all the glamorous ingredients of a Space Station Supervisor's life.

---

2. **Orion** (ō-rī′ən): a constellation that the ancient Greeks named for the hunter Orion, because the stars in the constellation form the figure of a man with a belt and a sword.

The only member of the staff I passed on my way to the air lock[3] was Tommy, our recently acquired cat. Pets mean a great deal to men thousands of miles from Earth, but there are not many animals that can adapt themselves to a weightless environment. Tommy mewed plaintively at me as I clambered into my spacesuit, but I was in too much of a hurry to play with him.

At this point, perhaps I should remind you that the suits we use on the station are completely different from the flexible affairs men wear when they want to walk around on the moon. Ours are really baby spaceships, just big enough to hold one man. They are stubby cylinders, about seven feet long, fitted with low-powered propulsion jets, and have a pair of accordion-like sleeves at the upper end for the operator's arms. Normally, however, you keep your hands drawn inside the suit, working the manual controls in front of your chest.

As soon as I'd settled down inside my very exclusive spacecraft, I switched on power and checked the gauges on the tiny instrument panel. There's a magic word, "FORB," that you'll often hear spacemen mutter as they climb into their suits; it reminds them to test fuel, oxygen, radio, batteries. All my needles were well in the safety zone, so I lowered the transparent hemisphere over my head and sealed myself in. For a short trip like this, I did not bother to check the suit's internal lockers, which were used to carry food and special equipment for extended missions.

As the conveyor belt decanted[4] me into the air lock, I felt like an Indian papoose being carried along on its mother's back. Then the pumps brought the pressure down to zero, the outer door opened, and the last traces of air swept me out into the stars, turning very slowly head over heels.

---

3. **air lock:** an airtight compartment, with adjustable pressure.
4. **decanted** (dĭ-kănt′əd): unloaded.

The station was only a dozen feet away, yet I was now an independent planet—a little world of my own. I was sealed up in a tiny, mobile cylinder, with a superb view of the entire universe, but I had practically no freedom of movement inside the suit. The padded seat and safety belts prevented me from turning around, though I could reach all the controls and lockers with my hands or feet.

In space, the great enemy is the sun, which can blast you to blindness in seconds. Very cautiously, I opened up the dark filters on the "night" side of my suit, and turned my head to look out at the stars. At the same time I switched the helmet's external sunshade to automatic, so that whichever way the suit gyrated my eyes would be shielded from that intolerable glare.

Presently, I found my target—a bright fleck of silver whose metallic glint distinguished it clearly from the surrounding stars. I stamped on the jet-control pedal, and felt the mild surge of acceleration as the low-powered rockets set me moving away from the station. After ten seconds of steady thrust, I estimated that my speed was great enough, and cut off the drive. It would take me five minutes to coast the rest of the way, and not much longer to return with my salvage.

And it was at that moment, as I launched myself out into the abyss, that I knew that something was horribly wrong.

It is never completely silent inside a spacesuit; you can always hear the gentle hiss of oxygen, the faint whirr of fans and motors, the susurration[5] of your own breathing—even, if you listen carefully enough, the rhythmic thump that is the pounding of your heart. These sounds reverberate through the suit, unable to escape into the surrounding void; they are

---

5. **susurration** (soo'sə-rā'shən): soft sound, as a murmur, whisper, or rustle.

the unnoticed background of life in space, for you are aware of them only when they change.

They had changed now; to them had been added a sound which I could not identify. It was an intermittent, muffled thudding, sometimes accompanied by a scraping noise, as of metal upon metal.

I froze instantly, holding my breath and trying to locate the alien sound with my ears. The meters on the control board gave no clues; all the needles were rock-steady on their scales, and there were none of the flickering red lights that would warn of impending disaster. That was some comfort, but not much. I had long ago learned to trust my instincts in such matters; their alarm signals were flashing now, telling me to return to the station before it was too late. . . .

Even now, I do not like to recall those next few minutes, as panic slowly flooded into my mind like a rising tide, overwhelming the dams of reason and logic which every man must erect against the mystery of the universe. I knew then what it was like to face insanity; no other explanation fitted the facts.

For it was no longer possible to pretend that the noise disturbing me was that of some faulty mechanism. Though I was in utter isolation, far from any other human being or indeed any material object, I was not alone. The soundless void was bringing to my ears the faint but unmistakable stirrings of life.

In that first, heart-freezing moment it seemed that something was trying to get into my suit—something invisible, seeking shelter from the cruel and pitiless vacuum of space. I whirled madly in my harness, scanning the entire sphere of vision around me except for the blazing, forbidden cone toward the sun. There was nothing there, of course. There could not be—yet that purposeful scrabbling was clearer than ever.

Despite the nonsense that has been written about us, it is not true that spacemen are superstitious. But can you blame me if, as I came to the end of logic's resources, I suddenly remembered how Bernie Summers had died, no farther from the station than I was at this very moment?

It was one of those "impossible" accidents; it always is. Three things had gone wrong at once. Bernie's oxygen regulator had run wild and sent the pressure soaring, the safety valve had failed to blow—and a faulty joint had given way instead. In a fraction of a second, his suit was open to space.

I had never known Bernie, but suddenly his fate became of overwhelming importance to me—for a horrible idea had come into my mind. One does not talk about these things, but a damaged spacesuit is too valuable to be thrown away, even if it has killed its wearer. It is repaired, renumbered—and issued to someone else. . . .

What happens to the soul of a man who dies between the stars, far from his native world? Are you still here, Bernie, clinging to the last object that linked you to your lost and distant home?

As I fought the nightmares that were swirling around me—for now it seemed that the scratchings and soft fumblings were coming from all directions—there was one last hope to which I clung. For the sake of my sanity, I had to prove that this wasn't Bernie's suit—that the metal walls so closely wrapped around me had never been another man's coffin.

It took me several tries before I could press the right button and switch my transmitter to the emergency wave length. "Station!" I gasped. "I'm in trouble! Get records to check my suit history and——"

I never finished; they say my yell wrecked the microphone. But what man alone in the absolute isolation of a spacesuit would *not* have yelled when something patted him softly on the back of the neck?

I must have lunged forward, despite the safety harness, and smashed against the upper edge of the control panel. When the rescue squad reached me a few minutes later, I was still unconscious, with an angry bruise across my forehead.

And so I was the last person in the whole satellite relay system to know what had happened. When I came to my senses an hour later, all our medical staff was gathered around my bed, but it was quite a while before the doctors bothered to look at me. They were much too busy playing with the three cute little kittens our badly misnamed Tommy had been rearing in the seclusion of my spacesuit's Number Five Storage Locker.

CHECK-UP (True/False)

1. The narrator is an ex-astronaut.
2. The narrator has difficulty concentrating on his work.
3. The narrator's job is to look out for stray satellites.
4. Satellite Control reports a meteor in the vicinity of the Space Station.
5. The space traveler turns out to be an old test satellite.
6. The narrator leaves the Space Station to check on the construction crew.
7. The narrator doesn't bother to check the suit's internal lockers.
8. The narrator at first believes that the noise he hears is some faulty mechanism in his suit.
9. The greatest danger in outer space is being blinded by the sun.
10. The narrator is knocked unconscious by a blow from behind.

FOR DISCUSSION

1. The *exposition* of a story gives the reader important background information. Where does the action of this story take place? What details are used to create a sense of place?
2. In most stories the action develops out of a problem or situation. What is the problem the narrator must solve?
3. Why does the narrator decide that he is the person to retrieve the space traveler?
4. What preparations are necessary for using the spacesuit? What omission in the narrator's preparations has frightening consequences?
5. You have learned that the action in a story is often built around some kind of *conflict*. What is the major conflict in this story?
6. What possibilities does the narrator consider and reject in attempting to explain the noise in his spacesuit?
7. Which details are calculated to keep you guessing about the outcome of the story?
8. How does the author prepare you for the ending?

PLOT
Suspense and Foreshadowing

1. When the narrator launches himself out into deep space, he becomes aware that something is wrong inside his spacesuit. As he tries to identify the strange sounds, you want to know what the alien presence is. As he struggles to control his panic, you wonder what is going to happen to him.

In a story, *suspense* is that element that keeps you guessing about the outcome of events. The author's purpose is to keep you excited and interested so that you will read on to learn what happens next. What details in "Who's

There?" create suspense? At what point in the story did you experience the greatest suspense?

2. A writer frequently gives you hints of what is to come later in the story. This method of building in clues to the outcome of the action is called *foreshadowing*. What hints does Clarke use to prepare you for the ending of the story?

UNDERSTANDING THE WORDS IN THE STORY (Matching Columns)

1. confirm		a.	an increase in speed
2. plaintively		b.	moved in a circular path
3. clambered		c.	about to happen
4. gyrated		d.	total emptiness
5. acceleration		e.	climbed into
6. reverberate		f.	plunged forward
7. void		g.	establish as true
8. impending		h.	isolation from others
9. lunged		i.	sadly or sorrowfully
10. seclusion		j.	re-echo

FOR WRITING

1. In a paragraph, explain what must have happened inside the narrator's spacesuit. Be sure to account for all movements and sounds.
2. Clarke's story is about the possibilities of future life in outer space. Because he uses actual scientific developments and projected scientific inventions, he creates the sense of an authentic world. He is so familiar with space technology that when he describes a test satellite, he can identify its design as "early nineteen-sixties." In a brief essay, identify ten details that Clarke uses to develop a sound scientific basis for his story.

3. Investigate one of the following. Write a brief report about recent technological developments.

> Space Medicine (Aeromedicine)
> Spaceports
> Space Shuttles
> Space Stations (Platforms)

4. Write a science-fiction radio play based on Clarke's story. Determine how you will create sound effects and how you will use music to heighten dramatic action.

He had never taken the path through the cemetery—
not even in broad daylight—
but this night would be different.

THE PATH THROUGH THE CEMETERY

Leonard Q. Ross

Ivan was a timid little man—so timid that the villagers called him "Pigeon" or mocked him with the title, "Ivan the Terrible."[1] Every night Ivan stopped in at the saloon which was on the edge of the village cemetery. Ivan never crossed the cemetery to get to his lonely shack on the other side. That path would save many minutes, but he had never taken it— not even in the full light of noon.

Late one winter's night, when bitter wind and snow beat against the saloon, the customers took up the familiar mockery. "Ivan's mother was scared by a canary when she carried him." "Ivan the Terrible—Ivan the Terribly Timid One."

Ivan's sickly protest only fed their taunts, and they jeered cruelly when the young Cossack[2] lieutenant flung his horrid challenge at their quarry.

"You are a pigeon, Ivan. You'll walk all around the cemetery in this cold—but you dare not cross it."

1. **Ivan the Terrible:** Ivan IV, the first czar of Russia, was called "the Terrible" because of his cruelty and ferocity.
2. **Cossack** (kŏs′ăk): The Cossack people, from the southern Soviet Union, are noted for their courage in battle.

Ivan murmured, "The cemetery is nothing to cross, Lieutenant. It is nothing but earth, like all the other earth."

The lieutenant cried, "A challenge, then! Cross the cemetery tonight, Ivan, and I'll give you five rubles—five gold rubles!"

Perhaps it was the vodka. Perhaps it was the temptation of the five gold rubles. No one ever knew why Ivan, moistening his lips, said suddenly: "Yes, Lieutenant, I'll cross the cemetery!"

The saloon echoed with their disbelief. The lieutenant winked to the men and unbuckled his saber. "Here Ivan. When you get to the center of the cemetery, in front of the biggest tomb, stick the saber into the ground. In the morning we shall go there. And if the saber is in the ground—five gold rubles to you!"

Ivan took the saber. The men drank a toast: "To Ivan the Terrible!" They roared with laughter.

The wind howled around Ivan as he closed the door of the saloon behind him. The cold was knife-sharp. He buttoned his long coat and crossed the dirt road. He could hear the lieutenant's voice, louder than the rest, yelling after him, "Five rubles, pigeon! *If you live!*"

Ivan pushed the cemetery gate open. He walked fast. "Earth, just earth . . . like any other earth." But the darkness was a massive dread. "Five gold rubles . . ." The wind was cruel and the saber was like ice in his hands. Ivan shivered under the long, thick coat and broke into a limping run.

He recognized the large tomb. He must have sobbed— that was the sound that was drowned in the wind. And he kneeled, cold and terrified, and drove the saber through the crust into the hard ground. With all his strength, he pushed it down to the hilt. It was done. The cemetery . . . the challenge . . . five gold rubles.

Ivan started to rise from his knees. But he could not move. Something held him. Something gripped him in an unyielding and implacable hold. Ivan tugged and lurched and pulled—gasping in his panic, shaken by a monstrous fear. But something held Ivan. He cried out in terror, then made senseless gurgling noises.

They found Ivan, next morning, on the ground in front of the tomb that was in the center of the cemetery. He was frozen to death. The look on his face was not that of a frozen man, but of a man killed by some nameless horror. And the lieutenant's saber was in the ground where Ivan had pounded it—through the dragging folds of his long coat.

CHECK-UP (True/False)

1. The action of the story takes place one winter night in a small European village.
2. Ivan was called "the Terrible" because he had a violent temper.
3. The villagers admired Ivan.
4. In calling Ivan "a pigeon," the lieutenant implied that Ivan was meek.
5. Ivan at first refused to accept the lieutenant's challenge.
6. The purpose of the saber was to protect Ivan from danger.
7. Ivan agreed to drive the saber into the ground in front of the biggest tomb in the cemetery.
8. No one in the saloon believed that Ivan would succeed in meeting the challenge.
9. Ivan drove the sword through the folds of his long coat.
10. The conclusion of the story leads us to believe that Ivan died of fright.

FOR DISCUSSION

1. The exposition of a story gives the reader important background information. What do you learn about Ivan's character at the opening of the story? Why is this information crucial to the story?

2. In a short story there may be a single conflict or several related conflicts. What is the conflict between Ivan and the lieutenant? How is this conflict related to the conflict between Ivan and the villagers? In what way are both of these conflicts related to Ivan's internal struggle with fear?

3. At what point in the story did you experience the greatest suspense?

4. How is the ending of the story foreshadowed? Locate specific details.

PLOT
Climax and Resolution

1. In "The Path Through the Cemetery," Ivan's cowardice—a conflict within his own mind—is established in the very first sentence. Ivan is called "Pigeon" because to be "pigeon-hearted" or "pigeon-livered" is to be easily frightened. The lieutenant's challenge sets into motion Ivan's attempt to master his fear.

Once the major conflict is established, the action of a story generally moves toward a *climax,* the point of greatest intensity. The climax determines how the story will turn out. What do you consider the climax, or most exciting moment, of the story?

2. The final part of a story is its *resolution,* which makes clear the outcome of events. In the resolution of "The Path Through the Cemetery," you learn what happened to Ivan. What rational explanation is given for Ivan's panic? Why does this information increase the story's impact?

UNDERSTANDING THE WORDS
IN THE STORY (Matching Columns)

1. protest
2. taunts
3. jeered
4. quarry
5. saber
6. massive
7. dread
8. implacable
9. lurched
10. senseless

a. terror
b. not giving way
c. staggered
d. scornful remarks
e. meaningless
f. sword
g. ridiculed
h. objection
i. unusually large
j. victim

FOR WRITING

1. No one knew why Ivan accepted the lieutenant's challenge. Give your explanation of his action.
2. Were the lieutenant and the villagers guilty of causing Ivan's death, or was Ivan the victim of his own character? Use details from the story to defend your answer.
3. Write a short story on the topic "A Dare," using real or imagined events.

"What galled him was the oft-repeated
warning, 'you can't take it with you.'
After all, it was all his."

YOU
CAN'T TAKE
IT WITH YOU

Eva-Lis Wuorio

There was no denying two facts. Uncle Basil was rich.
Uncle Basil was a miser.

The family were unanimous about that. They had used
up all the words as their temper and their need of ready
money dictated. Gentle Aunt Clotilda, who wanted a new
string of pearls because the one she had was getting old, had
merely called him Scrooge[1] Basil. Percival, having again
smashed his Aston Martin[2] for which he had not paid, had
declared Uncle Basil a skinflint, a miser, tightwad, churl,
and usurer with colorful adjectives added. The rest had used
up all the other words in the dictionary.

"He doesn't have to be so parsimonious,[3] that's true,
with all he has," said Percival's mother. "But you shouldn't
use rude words, Percival. They might get back to him."

"He can't take it with him," said Percival's sister Letitia,
combing her golden hair. "I need a new fur but he said,
'Why? it's summer.' Well! He's mingy,[4] that's what he is."

---

1. **Scrooge:** the most famous miser in literature. He appears in Charles
   Dickens' "A Christmas Carol."
2. **Aston Martin:** a very expensive sports car.
3. **parsimonious** (pär'sə-mō'nē-əs): stingy.
4. **mingy** (mĭn'jē): mean and stingy.

22

"He can't take it with him" was a phrase the family used so often it began to slip out in front of Uncle Basil as well.

"You can't take it with you, Uncle Basil," they said. "Why don't you buy a sensible house out in the country, and we could all come and visit you? Horses. A swimming pool. The lot. Think what fun you'd have, and you can certainly afford it. You can't take it with you, you know."

Uncle Basil had heard all the words they called him because he wasn't as deaf as he made out. He knew he was a mingy, stingy, penny-pinching screw, scrimp, scraper, pinchfist, hoarder, and curmudgeon[5] (just to start with). There were other words, less gentle, he'd also heard himself called. He didn't mind. What galled him was the oft-repeated warning, "You can't take it with you." After all, it was all his.

He'd gone to the Transvaal[6] when there was still gold to be found if one knew where to look. He'd found it. They said he'd come back too old to enjoy his fortune. What did they know? He enjoyed simply having a fortune. He enjoyed also saying no to them all. They were like circus animals, he often thought, behind the bars of their thousand demands of something for nothing.

Only once had he said yes. That was when his sister asked him to take on Verner, her somewhat slow-witted eldest son. "He'll do as your secretary," his sister Maud had said. Verner didn't do at all as a secretary, but since all he wanted to be happy was to be told what to do, Uncle Basil let him stick around as an all-around handyman.

Uncle Basil lived neatly in a house very much too small for his money, the family said, in an unfashionable suburb. It was precisely like the house where he had been born. Verner looked after the small garden, fetched the papers from

5. **curmudgeon** (kər-mŭj′ən): ill-tempered, disagreeable person.
6. **Transvaal** (trăns-väl, trănz-): a province of the Republic of South Africa, formerly known as South African Republic.

the corner tobacconist, and filed his nails when he had time. He had nice nails. He never said to Uncle Basil, "You can't take it with you," because it didn't occur to him.

Uncle Basil also used Verner to run messages to his man of affairs, the bank, and such, since he didn't believe either in the mails or the telephone. Verner got used to carrying thick envelopes back and forth without ever bothering to question what was in them. Uncle Basil's lawyers, accountants, and bank managers also got used to his somewhat unorthodox business methods. He did have a fortune, and he kept making money with his investments. Rich men have always been allowed their foibles.

Another foible of Uncle Basil's was that, while he still was in excellent health he had Verner drive him out to an old-fashioned carpenter shop where he had himself measured for a coffin. He wanted it roomy, he said.

The master carpenter was a dour countryman of the same generation as Uncle Basil, and he accepted the order matter-of-factly. They consulted about woods and prices, and settled on a medium-price, unlined coffin. A lined one would have cost double.

"I'll line it myself," Uncle Basil said. "Or Verner can. There's plenty of time. I don't intend to pop off tomorrow. It would give the family too much satisfaction. I like enjoying my fortune."

Then one morning, while in good humor and sound mind, he sent Verner for his lawyer. The family got to hear about this, and there were in-fights, out-fights, and general quarreling while they tried to find out to whom Uncle Basil had decided to leave his money. To put them out of their misery, he said, he'd tell them the truth. He didn't like scattering money about. He liked it in a lump sum. Quit bothering him about it.

That happened a good decade before the morning his housekeeper, taking him his tea, found him peacefully asleep forever. It had been a good decade for him. The family hadn't dared to worry him, and his investments had risen steadily.

Only Percival, always pressed for money, had threatened to put arsenic in his tea, but when the usual proceedings were gone through Uncle Basil was found to have died a natural death. "A happy death," said the family. "He hadn't suffered."

They began to remember loudly how nice they'd been to him and argued about who had been the nicest. It was true too. They had been attentive, the way families tend to be to rich and stubborn elderly relatives. They didn't know he'd heard all they'd said out of his hearing, as well as the flattering drivel they'd spread like soft butter on hot toast in his hearing. Everyone, recalling his own efforts to be thoroughly nice, was certain that he and only he would be the heir to the Lump Sum.

They rushed to consult the lawyer. He said that he had been instructed by Uncle Basil in sane and precise terms. The cremation was to take place immediately after his death, and they would find the coffin ready in the garden shed. Verner would know where it was.

"Nothing else?"

"Well," said the lawyer in the way lawyers have, "he left instructions for a funeral repast to be sent in from Fortnum and Mason.[7] Everything of the best. Goose and turkey, venison and beef, oysters and lobsters, and wines of good vintage plus plenty of whiskey. He liked to think of a good sendoff, curmudgeon though he was, he'd said."

The family was a little shaken by the use of the word "curmudgeon." How did Uncle Basil know about that? But they were relieved to hear that the lawyer also had an enve-

---

7. **Fortnum and Mason:** a well-known British store that supplies food for parties.

lope, the contents of which he did not know, to read to them at the feast after the cremation.

They all bought expensive black clothes, since black was the color of that season anyway, and whoever inherited would share the wealth. That was only fair.

Only Verner said that couldn't they buy Uncle Basil a smarter coffin? The one in the garden shed was pretty tatty, since the roof leaked. But the family hardly listened to him. After all, it would only be burned, so what did it matter?

So, duly and with proper sorrow, Uncle Basil was cremated.

The family returned to the little house as the housekeeper was leaving. Uncle Basil had given her a generous amount of cash, telling her how to place it so as to have a fair income for life. In gratitude she'd spread out the Fortnum and Mason goodies, but she wasn't prepared to stay to do the dishes.

They were a little surprised, but not dismayed, to hear from Verner that the house was now in his name. Uncle Basil had also given him a small sum of cash and told him how to invest it. The family taxed[8] him about it, but the amount was so nominal they were relieved to know Verner would be off their hands. Verner himself, though mildly missing the old man because he was used to him, was quite content with his lot. He wasn't used to much, so he didn't need much.

The storm broke when the lawyer finally opened the envelope.

There was only one line in Uncle Basil's scrawl.

"I did take it with me."

Of course there was a great to-do. What about the fortune? The millions and millions!

Yes, said the men of affairs, the accountants, and even

8. **taxed:** expressed disapproval of; criticized.

the bank managers, who finally admitted, yes, there had been a very considerable fortune. Uncle Basil, however, had drawn large sums in cash, steadily and regularly, over the past decade. What had he done with it? That the men of affairs, the accountants, and the bank managers did not know. After all, it had been Uncle Basil's money, ergo,[9] his affair.

Not a trace of the vast fortune ever came to light.

No one thought to ask Verner, and it didn't occur to Verner to volunteer that for quite a long time he had been lining the coffin, at Uncle Basil's behest, with thick envelopes he brought back from the banks. First he'd done a thick layer of these envelopes all around the sides and bottom of the coffin. Then, as Uncle Basil wanted, he'd tacked on blue sailcloth.

He might not be so bright in his head but he was smart with his hands.

He'd done a neat job.

9. **ergo** (ûr′gō, âr′-): therefore.

CHECK-UP (Completion)

1. Uncle Basil's family urged him to ___spend___ his money.
   (spend, invest, save)

2. Uncle Basil had made his fortune in the Transvaal mining ___gold___.
   (tin, diamonds, gold)

3. Verner was Basil's ___handyman___.
   (accountant, handyman, lawyer)

4. Uncle Basil ordered and had himself measured for ___coffin___.
   (a coffin, evening clothes, a business suit)

5. Uncle Basil died of ___natural___.
   (poisoning, overeating, natural causes)

6. Uncle Basil left instructions with his lawyer for a ___funeral ceremony___.
   (funeral ceremony, feast, charity ball)

7. Verner wanted the family to give Uncle Basil a ___nicer coffin___.
   (new suit, nicer coffin, funeral wreath)

8. Verner inherited the ___house___.
   (house, bulk of the fortune, fine china)

9. Uncle Basil's money wound up in large, thick ___envelopes___.
   (mattresses, bookcases, envelopes)

10. Uncle Basil's fortune was _____.
    (stolen, lost, burned)

FOR DISCUSSION

1. What is Uncle Basil's conflict with his family? What is his plan for resolving this conflict? What part does Verner play in this plan?
2. At one point in the story, Uncle Basil's plan is nearly prevented. Where does this occur? How do the greed

and selfishness of the family make them play into Uncle
Basil's hands?
3. Why do you suppose Uncle Basil provides for Verner
and for the housekeeper?
4. The end of a story is satisfying when it grows out of
events in the story. What hints foreshadow the story's
ending?
5. Would the title "Getting Even" be appropriate for this
story? Tell why or why not.

PLOT
The Ironic Ending

When the ending of a story turns out to be the opposite
of what a character or the reader expects, it is said to be
ironic. All of the stories you have read so far end ironically.
For example, in "Who's There?" (page 7), the narrator
thinks his spacesuit is haunted, but the alien presence turns
out to be a litter of kittens. In "The Dinner Party" (page 1),
the characters and the reader have been led to agree with
the colonel's assertion that men have greater nerve control
than women. To everyone's surprise, a woman shows even
greater self-control and courage than the naturalist.

In what way is the ending of "The Path Through the
Cemetery" (page 17) ironic? Why is the ending of "You
Can't Take It with You" ironic?

An ironic ending is effective when the outcome is unexpected, yet completely logical. Given Uncle Basil's character, his attitude toward money, his distaste for his relatives,
and the various hints dropped about his unusual business
methods, his plan to outwit his family fits the facts.

Examine the endings of "The Dinner Party" and "The
Path Through the Cemetery." Why is the ending of each
story unpredictable, yet logical?

UNDERSTANDING THE WORDS
IN THE STORY (Fill in the Blanks)

Answer each of the questions in this exercise with a word
from the following list. Use each word only once.

unanimous	decade
skinflint	drivel
usurer	heir
suburb	venison
foibles	repast

1. What do we call a period of ten years?

   decade

2. What kind of decision has everyone's approval?

   _____

3. What do we call someone who is stingy or miserly?

   _____

4. What do we call someone who lends money at outrageous rates of interest?

   usurer

5. What do we call the person who inherits an estate?

   _____

6. What word refers to food and drink for a meal?

   _____

7. What is the name for trivial weaknesses of character?

   _____

8. What do we call the flesh of deer that is used for food?

   _____

9. What is the outlying residential area of a city called?

   _____

10. What is silly, stupid talk that is childish nonsense?

    _____

(Matching Columns)

1. ready	a. not traditional
2. dictated	b. earnest request
3. churl	c. required
4. galled	d. burning of a corpse
5. unorthodox	e. properly
6. dour	f. minimal
7. cremation	g. miserly person
8. duly	h. gloomy
9. nominal	i. immediately available
10. behest	j. irritated

FOR WRITING

1. Give a step-by-step account of Uncle Basil's plan to keep his fortune. Indicate how Verner, the carpenter, and the lawyer each play a part.
2. Throughout history, people have wished to take their worldly possessions with them after death. The pharaohs of ancient Egypt, for example, had their tombs filled with jewelry, furniture, tools, hunting weapons, and food and drink for the hereafter. Viking heroes had their armor, swords, shields, drinking horns, gold ornaments and other riches buried in grave mounds. Find out about these burial customs by consulting an encyclopedia, and write a brief report explaining what you have learned.
3. Write an original story with the title, "You *Can* Take It with You."

*The children were bored
with stories about good little girls—
until they heard the story of Bertha.*

THE STORYTELLER

Saki (H. H. Munro)

It was a hot afternoon, and the railway carriage was correspondingly sultry, and the next stop was at Temple-combe, nearly an hour ahead. The occupants of the carriage were a small girl, and a smaller girl, and a small boy. An aunt belonging to the children occupied one corner seat, and the further corner seat on the opposite side was occupied by a bachelor who was a stranger to their party, but the small girls and the small boy emphatically occupied the compartment. Both the aunt and the children were conversational in a limited, persistent way, reminding one of the attentions of a housefly that refused to be discouraged. Most of the aunt's remarks seemed to begin with "Don't," and nearly all of the children's remarks began with "Why?" The bachelor said nothing out loud.

"Don't, Cyril, don't," exclaimed the aunt, as the small boy began smacking the cushions of the seat, producing a cloud of dust at each blow.

"Come and look out of the window," she added.

The child moved reluctantly to the window. "Why are those sheep being driven out of that field?" he asked.

"I expect they are being driven to another field where there is more grass," said the aunt weakly.

"But there is lots of grass in that field," protested the boy; "there's nothing else but grass there, Aunt, there's lots of grass in that field."

"Perhaps the grass in the other field is better," suggested the aunt fatuously.[1]

"Why is it better?" came the swift, inevitable question.

"Oh, look at those cows!" exclaimed the aunt. Nearly every field along the line had contained cows or bullocks, but she spoke as though she were drawing attention to a rarity.

"Why is the grass in the other field better?" persisted Cyril.

The frown on the bachelor's face was deepening to a scowl. He was a hard, unsympathetic man, the aunt decided in her mind. She was utterly unable to come to any satisfactory decision about the grass in the other field.

The smaller girl created a diversion by beginning to recite "On the Road to Mandalay."[2] She only knew the first line, but she put her limited knowledge to the fullest possible use. She repeated the line over and over again in a dreamy but resolute and very audible voice; it seemed to the bachelor as though someone had had a bet with her that she could not repeat the line aloud two thousand times without stopping. Whoever it was who had made the wager was likely to lose his bet.

"Come over here and listen to a story," said the aunt, when the bachelor had looked twice at her and once at the communication cord.[3]

The children moved listlessly towards the aunt's end of

1. **fatuously** (făch′ŏo-əs-lē): foolishly.
2. **"On the Road to Mandalay":** a poem by Rudyard Kipling, in which a British soldier thinks back on Mandalay, a city in Burma. The opening line of the poem is: "By the old Moulmein Pagoda, lookin' eastward to the sea."
3. **communication cord:** signal used in an emergency to call for the conductor of the train.

the carriage. Evidently her reputation as a storyteller did not rank high in their estimation.

In a low, confidential voice, interrupted at frequent intervals by loud, petulant questions from her listeners, she began an unenterprising and deplorably uninteresting story about a little girl who was good, and made friends with everyone on account of her goodness, and was finally saved from a mad bull by a number of rescuers who admired her moral character.

"Wouldn't they have saved her if she hadn't been good?" demanded the bigger of the small girls. It was exactly the question that the bachelor had wanted to ask.

"Well, yes," admitted the aunt lamely, "but I don't think they would have run quite so fast to help her if they had not liked her so much."

"It's the stupidest story I've ever heard," said the bigger of the small girls, with immense conviction.

"I didn't listen after the first bit, it was so stupid," said Cyril.

The smaller girl made no actual comment on the story, but she had long ago recommenced a murmured repetition of her favorite line.

"You don't seem to be a success as a storyteller," said the bachelor suddenly from his corner.

The aunt bristled in instant defense at this unexpected attack.

"It's a very difficult thing to tell stories that children can both understand and appreciate," she said stiffly.

"I don't agree with you," said the bachelor.

"Perhaps *you* would like to tell them a story," was the aunt's retort.

"Tell us a story," demanded the bigger of the small girls.

"Once upon a time," began the bachelor, "there was a little girl called Bertha, who was extraordinarily good."

The children's momentarily aroused interest began at once to flicker; all stories seemed dreadfully alike, no matter who told them.

"She did all that she was told, she was always truthful, she kept her clothes clean, ate milk puddings as though they were jam tarts, learned her lessons perfectly, and was polite in her manners."

"Was she pretty?" asked the bigger of the small girls.

"Not as pretty as any of you," said the bachelor, "but she was horribly good."

There was a wave of reaction in favor of the story; the word *horrible* in connection with goodness was a novelty that commended itself. It seemed to introduce a ring of truth that was absent from the aunt's tales of infant life.

"She was so good," continued the bachelor, "that she won several medals for goodness, which she always wore, pinned on to her dress. There was a medal for obedience, another medal for punctuality, and a third for good behavior. They were large metal medals and they clinked against one another as she walked. No other child in the town where she lived had as many as three medals, so everybody knew that she must be an extra good child."

"Horribly good," quoted Cyril.

"Everybody talked about her goodness, and the Prince of the country got to hear about it, and he said that as she was so very good she might be allowed once a week to walk in his park, which was just outside the town. It was a beautiful park, and no children were ever allowed in it, so it was a great honor for Bertha to be allowed to go there."

"Were there any sheep in the park?" demanded Cyril.

"No," said the bachelor, "there were no sheep."

"Why weren't there any sheep?" came the inevitable question arising out of that answer.

The aunt permitted herself a smile, which might almost have been described as a grin.

"There were no sheep in the park," said the bachelor, "because the Prince's mother had once had a dream that her son would either be killed by a sheep or else by a clock falling on him. For that reason the Prince never kept a sheep in his park or a clock in his palace."

The aunt suppressed a gasp of admiration.

"Was the Prince killed by a sheep or by a clock?" asked Cyril.

"He is still alive, so we can't tell whether the dream will come true," said the bachelor unconcernedly; "anyway, there were no sheep in the park, but there were lots of little pigs running all over the place."

"What color were they?"

"Black with white faces, white with black spots, black all over, gray with white patches, and some were white all over."

The storyteller paused to let a full idea of the park's treasures sink into the children's imaginations; then he resumed:

"Bertha was rather sorry to find that there were no flowers in the park. She had promised her aunts, with tears in her eyes, that she would not pick any of the kind Prince's flowers, and she had meant to keep her promise, so of course it made her feel silly to find that there were no flowers to pick."

"Why weren't there any flowers?"

"Because the pigs had eaten them all," said the bachelor promptly. "The gardeners had told the Prince that you couldn't have pigs and flowers, so he decided to have pigs and no flowers."

There was a murmur of approval at the excellence of the Prince's decision; so many people would have decided the other way.

"There were lots of other delightful things in the park. There were ponds with gold and blue and green fish in them, and trees with beautiful parrots that said clever things at a moment's notice, and hummingbirds that hummed all the popular tunes of the day. Bertha walked up and down and enjoyed herself immensely, and thought to herself: 'If I were not so extraordinarily good I should not have been allowed to come into this beautiful park and enjoy all that there is to be seen in it,' and her three medals clinked against one another as she walked and helped to remind her how very good she really was. Just then an enormous wolf came prowling into the park to see if it could catch a fat little pig for its supper."

"What color was it" asked the children, amid an immediate quickening of interest.

"Mud color all over, with a black tongue and pale gray eyes that gleamed with unspeakable ferocity. The first thing that it saw in the park was Bertha; her pinafore was so spotlessly white and clean that it could be seen from a great distance. Bertha saw the wolf and saw that it was stealing towards her, and she began to wish that she had never been allowed to come into the park. She ran as hard as she could, and the wolf came after her with huge leaps and bounds. She managed to reach a shrubbery of myrtle bushes and she hid herself in one of the thickest of the bushes. The wolf came sniffing among the branches, its black tongue lolling out of its mouth and its pale gray eyes glaring with rage. Bertha was terribly frightened, and thought to herself: 'If I had not been so extraordinarily good I should have been safe in the town at this moment.' However, the scent of the myrtle was so strong that the wolf could not sniff out where Bertha was hiding, and the bushes were so thick that he might have hunted about in them for a long time without catching sight of her, so he thought he might as well go off and catch a little pig instead. Bertha was trembling very much at having the wolf prowling and sniffing so near her, and as she trembled the medal for obedience clinked against the medals for good conduct and punctuality. The wolf was just moving away when he heard the sound of the medals clinking and stopped to listen; they clinked again in a bush quite near him. He dashed into the bush, his pale gray eyes gleaming with ferocity and triumph, and dragged Bertha out and devoured her to the last morsel. All that was left of her were her shoes, bits of clothing, and the three medals for goodness."

"Were any of the little pigs killed?"

"No, they all escaped."

"The story began badly," said the smaller of the small girls, "but it had a beautiful ending."

"It is the most beautiful story that I ever heard," said the bigger of the small girls, with immense decision.

"It is the *only* beautiful story I have ever heard," said Cyril.

A dissentient[4] opinion came from the aunt.

"A most improper story to tell to young children! You have undermined the effect of years of careful teaching."

"At any rate," said the bachelor, collecting his belongings preparatory to leaving the carriage, "I kept them quiet for ten minutes, which was more than you were able to do."

"Unhappy woman!" he observed to himself as he walked down the platform of Templecombe station; "for the next six months or so those children will assail her in public with demands for an improper story!"

4. **dissentient** (dĭ-sĕn′shənt): not agreeing.

CHECK-UP (True/False)

1. The children in the railway carriage are bored and restless.
2. The bachelor is annoyed because the aunt cannot keep the children quiet.
3. The aunt tells the children a story about a little girl who is nearly drowned.
4. The aunt believes that stories told to children should show goodness rewarded.
5. The children are entertained and fascinated by the aunt's story.
6. The bachelor's story is about a little girl who is horribly good.
7. The Prince allows Bertha to walk in his park because she has promised not to pick his flowers.
8. Of all the treasures in the Prince's park, the children are most impressed by the pigs.
9. Bertha is gobbled up by a wolf.
10. The children are pleased by the ending of the bachelor's story.

FOR DISCUSSION

1. What similarities are there in the stories told by the aunt and by the bachelor? What differences are there?
2. Compare the bachelor's technique of answering the children's questions with the aunt's technique. Why is he more successful than she?
3. From the children's point of view, why is the phrase "horribly good" an accurate description of Bertha?
4. According to the aunt, what characteristics make a story "proper"? Why does she consider the bachelor's story "improper"?
5. Is the conflict in this story between two people or two ideas? Give reasons for your answer.

PLOT
The Story Within a Story

Sometimes a short story will contain one narrative within the framework of another—a story within a story. One of the characters in the story may tell a completely separate story to another character or group of characters. Very often the two stories will be related in some way.

"The Storyteller" contains two stories. In the outer story, or *frame story,* we are introduced to the aunt, the children, the bachelor, and the situation that gives rise to the *inner story,* the story of Bertha.

In what way are the frame story and the inner story related? How does the inner story influence the outcome of the frame story?

UNDERSTANDING THE WORDS
IN THE STORY (Multiple-Choice)

1. A *sultry* day is
   a. cloudy and cool
   b. mild and pleasant
   c. uncomfortably hot
2. To speak *emphatically* is to speak
   a. decisively
   b. hesitantly
   c. calmly
3. To take directions *reluctantly* is to
   a. act unwillingly
   b. misbehave
   c. obey quickly
4. An *inevitable* question is
   a. embarrassing to answer
   b. certain to be asked
   c. often repeated

5. A *bullock* is a
   a. sheep
   b. steer
   c. goat
6. A *scowl* is a
   a. smile
   b. puzzled look
   c. frown
7. To create a *diversion* is to
   a. cause a distraction
   b. become a nuisance
   c. come up with an original idea
8. A *resolute* character is
   a. weak
   b. unyielding
   c. unsympathetic
9. An *audible* voice is
   a. loud enough to be heard
   b. pleasant and clear
   c. deafening
10. A *wager* is a
    a. promise
    b. loan
    c. bet

(Matching Columns)

1. listlessly
2. estimation
3. petulant
4. unenterprising
5. deplorably
6. moral
7. lamely
8. conviction
9. recommenced
10. bristled

a. began again
b. irritable
c. unimaginative
d. right
e. got ready to fight back
f. strong belief
g. unenthusiastically
h. badly
i. judgment
j. weakly

(Completion)

Choose one of the words in the following list to complete each of the sentences below. A word may be used once.

retort
novelty
suppressed
resumed
unspeakable

lolling
devoured
improper
undermine
assail

1. A terrible crime might be described as _____.

2. That which is stopped is said to be _____.

3. Something that is new is a _____.

4. Conduct that is unbecoming is _____.

5. Another word for *attack* is _____.

6. A quick, sharp reply is known as a _____.

7. An animal's tongue that hangs loosely is _____.

8. Irregular habits can _____ one's health.

9. Work continued after an interruption is _____.

10. Food that is gulped down greedily is _____.

FOR WRITING

1. Saki tells us that the children react favorably to the elements of *novelty* in the bachelor's story of Bertha. Discuss these "new" elements and tell why they hold the children's interest.
2. Suppose the aunt were telling the story of Bertha. What changes would she make? Write the version of the story that the aunt would very likely tell.
3. Write a new ending for a children's classic such as "Snow White" or "Goldilocks and the Three Bears."

Character

*The old man claimed that there was one thing
on his land that was not his to sell.*

GENTLEMAN
OF RÍO EN MEDIO

Juan A. A. Sedillo

It took months of negotiation to come to an understanding with the old man. He was in no hurry. What he had the most of was time. He lived up in Río en Medio, where his people had been for hundreds of years. He tilled the same land they had tilled. His house was small and wretched, but quaint. The little creek ran through his land. His orchard was gnarled and beautiful.

The day of the sale he came into the office. His coat was old, green and faded. I thought of Senator Catron,[1] who had been such a power with these people up there in the mountains. Perhaps it was one of his old Prince Alberts.[2] He also wore gloves. They were old and torn and his fingertips showed through them. He carried a cane, but it was only the skeleton of a worn-out umbrella. Behind him walked one of

1. **Senator Catron:** Thomas Benton Catron, Senator from New Mexico (1912–1917).
2. **Prince Alberts:** The Prince Albert was a long, double-breasted coat named after the English Prince Albert, who later became Edward VII.

his innumerable kin—a dark young man with eyes like a gazelle.

The old man bowed to all of us in the room. Then he removed his hat and gloves, slowly and carefully. Chaplin[3] once did that in a picture, in a bank—he was the janitor. Then he handed his things to the boy, who stood obediently behind the old man's chair.

There was a great deal of conversation, about rain and about his family. He was very proud of his large family. Finally we got down to business. Yes, he would sell, as he had agreed, for twelve hundred dollars, in cash. We would buy, and the money was ready. "Don[4] Anselmo," I said to him in Spanish, "we have made a discovery. You remember that we sent that surveyor, that engineer, up there to survey your land so as to make the deed. Well, he finds that you own more than eight acres. He tells us that your land extends across the river and that you own almost twice as much as you thought." He didn't know that. "And now, Don Anselmo," I added, "these Americans are *buena gente,* they are good people, and they are willing to pay you for the additional land as well, at the same rate per acre, so that instead of twelve hundred dollars you will get almost twice as much, and the money is here for you."

The old man hung his head for a moment in thought. Then he stood up and stared at me. "Friend," he said, "I do not like to have you speak to me in that manner." I kept still and let him have his say. "I know these Americans are good people, and that is why I have agreed to sell my house to them. But I do not care to be insulted. I have agreed to sell my house and land for twelve hundred dollars and that is the price."

3. **Chaplin:** Charlie Chaplin, known for his great comic performances in silent movies.
4. **Don:** a title of respect, formerly used for Spaniards of high rank, now used as a title of courtesy.

I argued with him but it was useless. Finally he signed the deed and took the money but refused to take more than the amount agreed upon. Then he shook hands all around, put on his ragged gloves, took his stick and walked out with the boy behind him.

A month later my friends had moved into Río en Medio. They had replastered the old adobe house, pruned the trees, patched the fence, and moved in for the summer. One day they came back to the office to complain. The children of the village were overrunning their property. They came every day and played under the trees, built little play fences around them, and took blossoms. When they were spoken to they only laughed and talked back good-naturedly in Spanish.

I sent a messenger up to the mountains for Don Anselmo. I took a week to arrange another meeting. When he arrived he repeated his previous preliminary performance. He wore the same faded cutaway,[5] carried the same stick and was accompanied by the boy again. He shook hands all around, sat down with the boy behind his chair, and talked about the weather. Finally I broached the subject. "Don Anselmo, about the ranch you sold to these people. They are good people and want to be your friends and neighbors always. When you sold to them you signed a document, a deed, and in that deed you agreed to several things. One thing was that they were to have the complete possession of the property. Now, Don Anselmo, it seems that every day the children of the village overrun the orchard and spend most of their time there. We would like to know if you, as the most respected man in the village, could not stop them from doing so in order that these people may enjoy their new home more in peace."

---

5. **cutaway:** a long coat used for formal occasions, so named because part of its lower front is cut away.

Don Anselmo stood up. "We have all learned to love these Americans," he said, "because they are good people and good neighbors. I sold them my property because I knew they were good people, but I did not sell them the trees in the orchard."

This was bad. "Don Anselmo," I pleaded, "when one signs a deed and sells real property one sells also everything that grows on the land, and those trees, every one of them, are on the land and inside the boundaries of what you sold."

"Yes, I admit that," he said. "You know," he added, "I am the oldest man in the village. Almost everyone there is my relative and all the children of Río en Medio are my *sobrinos* and *nietos,*[6] my descendants. Every time a child has been born in Río en Medio since I took possession of that house from my mother I have planted a tree for that child. The trees in that orchard are not mine, *Señor,* they belong to the children of the village. Every person in Río en Medio born since the railroad came to Santa Fe owns a tree in that orchard. I did not sell the trees because I could not. They are not mine."

There was nothing we could do. Legally we owned the trees but the old man had been so generous, refusing what amounted to a fortune for him. It took most of the following winter to buy the trees, individually, from the descendants of Don Anselmo in the valley of Río en Medio.

6. *sobrinos* (sō-brē′nōs) **and** *nietos* (nyĕ′tōs): Spanish for "nephews and nieces" and "grandchildren."

CHECK-UP (True/False)

1. Don Anselmo does not have any intention of selling his land.
2. Don Anselmo demands an outrageous price for his land.
3. Good manners are important to Don Anselmo.
4. The lawyer tries to cheat Don Anselmo and the Americans.
5. Don Anselmo is a shrewd and practical businessman.
6. Don Anselmo lives in the mountains.
7. The children of the village are rude to the new owners of the orchard.
8. Every day the children play under the trees and pick flowers.
9. Don Anselmo offers to keep the children out of the orchard.
10. The owners feel they have been tricked by Don Anselmo.

FOR DISCUSSION

1. Describe the way Don Anselmo is dressed when he appears for the first time in the story. How does his behavior contrast with his physical appearance?
2. Look up the origin of the word *gentleman* in a dictionary. In what way is the word *gentleman* an accurate description of Don Anselmo's character and manners?
3. Don Anselmo lives by a code that the Americans find surprising. Why does he refuse to accept more money for his property? Why does he believe that he does not own the trees in the orchard?
4. Are the descendants of Don Anselmo entitled to the money they receive for the trees? Give reasons for your answer.

CHARACTER
Direct and Indirect Characterization

Although a short story may focus on several characters, most of the time there is one main character who is at the center of the story. In "Gentleman of Río en Medio," the main character, or *protagonist,* is Don Anselmo.

The way a writer presents a character in a story is known as *characterization.* A writer may tell you *directly* what a character is like. For example, at one point in the story you have just read, Don Anselmo is identified as "the most respected man in the village." Later on, he is described as "generous." These are direct comments revealing Don Anselmo's character.

It is more common, however, for a writer to develop a character *indirectly.* The writer allows you to draw your own conclusions about a character by

describing the character's physical appearance
showing the character's actions and words
revealing the character's thoughts
showing how the character is treated by others

A writer may, of course, use both direct and indirect methods of characterization in presenting a character.

In "Gentleman of Río en Medio," we are not told directly that Don Anselmo is a person of great dignity. The writer reveals that trait indirectly in describing Don Anselmo's manners:

The old man bowed to all of us in the room. Then he removed his hat and gloves, slowly and carefully. . . . Then he handed his things to the boy, who stood obediently behind the old man's chair.

Find other passages in the story that develop the character of Don Anselmo indirectly. In each case, tell what conclusion you have drawn.

UNDERSTANDING THE WORDS IN THE STORY (Multiple-Choice)

1. If you succeed in *negotiation,* you
   a. get a raise
   b. reach an agreement
   c. sign a contract
2. A house that is described as *quaint* is most likely to appear
   a. strange and ugly
   b. dingy and shabby
   c. unusual but pleasing
3. Trees that are *gnarled* are
   a. knotty and twisted
   b. straight and tall
   c. decayed and rotten
4. Which of the following might best be described as *innumerable?*
   a. stars
   b. elements
   c. continents
5. Another word for *kin* is
   a. children
   b. parents
   c. relatives
6. To *survey* land is to
   a. determine its boundaries
   b. establish ownership
   c. estimate its value
7. To restore an *adobe* building, you would use
   a. earthenware tile
   b. sun-dried brick
   c. sand and gravel
8. A *preliminary* event
   a. is the main event
   b. leads up to the main event
   c. follows the main event

9. When the lawyer *broached* the subject, he
   a. summarized it
   b. avoided it
   c. introduced it
10. Which of the following would not be considered *real property?*
    a. cars
    b. trees
    c. houses

FOR WRITING

1. In a brief essay, compare Don Anselmo's ideas about money and property with those of the lawyer and his clients.
2. Defend or refute this statement in a brief essay: "Gentleman of Río en Medio" is a story that emphasizes character rather than events.

*"How she loved sitting here,
watching it all! It was like a play."*

MISS BRILL

Katherine Mansfield

Although it was so brilliantly fine—the blue sky powdered with gold and great spots of light like white wine splashed over the Jardins Publiques[1]—Miss Brill was glad that she had decided on her fur. The air was motionless, but when you opened your mouth, there was just a faint chill, like a chill from a glass of iced water before you sip, and now and again a leaf came drifting—from nowhere, from the sky. Miss Brill put up her hand and touched her fur. Dear little thing! It was nice to feel it again. She had taken it out of its box that afternoon, shaken out the moth powder, given it a good brush, and rubbed the life back into the dim little eyes. "What has been happening to me?" said the sad little eyes. Oh, how sweet it was to see them snap at her again from the red eiderdown![2] . . . But the nose, which was of some black composition, wasn't at all firm. It must have had a knock, somehow. Never mind—a little dab of black sealing wax when the time came—when it was absolutely necessary . . . Little rogue! Yes, she really felt like that about it. Little rogue biting its tail just by her left ear. She could have taken it off and laid it on her lap and stroked it. She felt a tingling in her hands and arms, but that came from walking, she supposed. And when she breathed, something light and sad—no, not sad, exactly—something gentle seemed to move in her bosom.

1. **Jardins Publiques** (zhär-däɴ′ poō-blēk′): French for "Public Gardens."
2. **eiderdown:** bed quilt stuffed with down from an eider duck.

51

There were a number of people out this afternoon, far more than last Sunday. And the band sounded louder and gayer. That was because the Season had begun. For although the band played all the year round on Sundays, out of season it was never the same. It was like someone playing with only the family to listen; it didn't care how it played if there weren't any strangers present. Wasn't the conductor wearing a new coat, too? She was sure it was new. He scraped with his foot and flapped his arms like a rooster about to crow, and the bandsmen sitting in the green ro-tunda[3] blew out their cheeks and glared at the music. Now there came a little "flutey" bit—very pretty!—a little chain of bright drops. She was sure it would be repeated. It was; she lifted her head and smiled.

Only two people shared her "special" seat: a fine old man in a velvet coat, his hands clasped over a huge carved walking stick, and a big old woman, sitting upright, with a roll of knitting on her embroidered apron. They did not speak. This was disappointing, for Miss Brill always looked forward to the conversation. She had become really quite expert, she thought, at listening as though she didn't listen, at sitting in other people's lives just for a minute while they talked round her.

She glanced, sideways, at the old couple. Perhaps they would go soon. Last Sunday, too, hadn't been as interesting as usual. An Englishman and his wife, he wearing a dreadful Panama hat and she button boots. And she'd gone on the whole time about how she ought to wear spectacles; she knew she needed them; but that it was no good getting any; they'd be sure to break and they'd never keep on. And he'd been so patient. He'd suggested everything—gold rims, the kind that curved round your ears, little pads inside the bridge. No, nothing would please her. "They'll always be slid-

---

3. **rotunda** (rō-tŭn′də): a circular structure, usually covered by a dome.

ing down my nose!" Miss Brill had wanted to shake her.

The old people sat on the bench, still as statues. Never mind, there was always the crowd to watch. To and fro, in front of the flower beds and the band rotunda, the couples and groups paraded, stopped to talk, to greet, to buy a handful of flowers from the old beggar who had his tray fixed to the railings. Little children ran among them, swooping and laughing; little boys with big white silk bows under their chins, little girls, little French dolls, dressed up in velvet and lace. And sometimes a tiny staggerer came suddenly rocking into the open from under the trees, stopped, stared, as suddenly sat down "flop," until its small high-stepping mother, like a young hen, rushed scolding to its rescue. Other people sat on the benches and green chairs, but they were nearly always the same, Sunday after Sunday, and—Miss Brill had often noticed—there was something funny about nearly all of them. They were odd, silent, nearly all old, and from the way they stared they looked as though they'd just come from dark little rooms or even—even cupboards!

Behind the rotunda the slender trees with yellow leaves down drooping, and through them just a line of sea, and beyond the blue sky with gold-veined clouds.

Tum-tum-tum tiddle-um! tiddle-um! tum tiddley-um tum ta! blew the band.

Two young girls in red came by and two young soldiers in blue met them, and they laughed and paired and went off arm in arm. Two peasant women with funny straw hats passed, gravely, leading beautiful smoke-colored donkeys. A cold, pale nun hurried by. A beautiful woman came along and dropped her bunch of violets, and a little boy ran after to hand them to her, and she took them and threw them away as if they'd been poisoned. Dear me! Miss Brill didn't know whether to admire that or not! And now an ermine toque[4]

4. **toque** (tōk): a close-fitting hat.

and a gentleman in gray met just in front of her. He was tall, stiff, dignified, and she was wearing the ermine toque she'd bought when her hair was yellow. Now everything, her hair, her face, even her eyes, was the same color as the shabby ermine, and her hand, in its cleaned glove, lifted to dab her lips, was a tiny yellowish paw. Oh, she was so pleased to see him—delighted! She rather thought they were going to meet that afternoon. She described where she'd been—everywhere, here, there, along by the sea. The day was so charming—didn't he agree? And wouldn't he, perhaps? . . . But he shook his head, lighted a cigarette, slowly breathed a great deep puff into her face, and, even while she was still talking and laughing, flicked the match away and walked on. The ermine toque was alone; she smiled more brightly than ever. But even the band seemed to know what she was feeling and played more softly, played tenderly, and the drum beat, "The Brute! The Brute!" over and over. What would she do? What was going to happen now? But as Miss Brill wondered, the ermine toque turned, raised her hand as though she'd seen someone else, much nicer, just over there, and pattered away. And the band changed again and played more quickly, more gayly than ever, and the old couple on Miss Brill's seat got up and marched away, and such a funny old man with long whiskers hobbled along in time to the music and was nearly knocked over by four girls walking abreast.

Oh, how fascinating it was! How she enjoyed it! How she loved sitting here, watching it all! It was like a play. It was exactly like a play. Who could believe the sky at the back wasn't painted? But it wasn't till a little brown dog trotted on solemn and then slowly trotted off, like a little "theater" dog, a little dog that had been drugged, that Miss Brill discovered what it was that made it so exciting. They were all on the stage. They weren't only the audience, not only looking on; they were acting. Even she had a part and came every Sunday. No doubt somebody would have noticed if she hadn't been there; she was part of the performance after all. How strange she'd never thought of it like that before! And yet it explained why she made such a point of starting from home at just the same time each week—so as not to be late for the performance—and it also explained why she had quite a queer, shy feeling at telling her English pupils how she spent her Sunday afternoons. No wonder! Miss Brill nearly laughed out loud. She was on the stage. She thought of the old invalid gentleman to whom she read the newspaper four afternoons a week while he slept in the garden. She had got quite used to the frail head on the cotton pillow, the hollowed eyes, the open mouth and the high pinched nose. If he'd been dead she mightn't have noticed for weeks; she wouldn't have minded. But suddenly he knew he was having the paper read to him by an actress! "An actress!" The old head lifted; two points of light quivered in the old eyes. "An actress—are ye?" And Miss Brill smoothed the newspaper as though it were the manuscript of her part and said gently: "Yes, I have been an actress for a long time."

The band had been having a rest. Now they started again. And what they played was warm, sunny, yet there was just a faint chill—a something, what was it?—not sadness—no, not sadness—a something that made you want to sing. The tune lifted, lifted, the light shone; and it seemed to Miss Brill that in another moment all of them, all the whole company, would begin singing. The young ones, the laughing ones who were moving together, they would begin, and the men's voices, very resolute and brave, would join them. And then she too, she too, and the others on the benches—they would come in with a kind of accompaniment—something low, that scarcely rose or fell, something so beautiful—moving . . . And Miss Brill's eyes filled with tears and she looked smiling at all the other members of the company. Yes, we understand, we understand, she thought—though what they understood she didn't know.

Just at that moment a boy and a girl came and sat down where the old couple had been. They were beautifully dressed; they were in love. The hero and heroine, of course, just arrived from his father's yacht. And still soundlessly singing, still with that trembling smile, Miss Brill prepared to listen.

"No, not now," said the girl. "Not here, I can't."

"But why? Because of that stupid old thing at the end there?" asked the boy. "Why does she come here at all—who wants her? Why doesn't she keep her silly old mug at home?"

"It's her fu-fur which is so funny," giggled the girl. "It's exactly like a fried whiting."[5]

"Ah, be off with you!" said the boy in an angry whisper. Then: "Tell me, ma petite chérie[6]—"

"No, not here," said the girl. "Not *yet*."

On her way home she usually bought a slice of honey-cake at the baker's. It was her Sunday treat. Sometimes there was an almond in her slice, sometimes not. It made a great difference. If there was an almond it was like carrying home a tiny present—a surprise—something that might very well not have been there. She hurried on the almond Sundays and struck the match for the kettle in quite a dashing way.

But today she passed the baker's by, climbed the stairs, went into the little dark room—her room like a cupboard—and sat down on the red eiderdown. She sat there for a long time. The box that the fur came out of was on the bed. She unclasped the necklet quickly; quickly, without looking, laid it inside. But when she put the lid on she thought she heard something crying.

5. **whiting:** a fish.
6. **ma petite chérie** (mȧ pǝ-tēt′ shâ-rē′): French for "my little darling."

CHECK-UP (Multiple-Choice)

1. Miss Brill is best described as a
   a. rich, old busybody
   b. cheerful, friendly person
   c. lonely, pitiful woman
2. We can infer that Miss Brill
   a. leads a quiet and uneventful life
   b. has had many exciting experiences
   c. knows a great many people
3. Miss Brill goes to the park every Sunday in order to
   a. make new acquaintances
   b. eavesdrop on other people's lives
   c. get exercise
4. Miss Brill thinks of herself as
   a. an actress in a play
   b. the star performer in a play
   c. the director of a play
5. To the young lovers, Miss Brill is
   a. a welcome visitor to the park
   b. an unwanted intruder on their privacy
   c. someone they wish to confide in

FOR DISCUSSION

1. Miss Brill cherishes her fur wrap. How do you know that it is quite old and unbecoming?
2. Miss Brill observes people and listens in to their conversations. What does this reveal about her life?
3. Miss Brill observes that some people sitting on benches and chairs look as though they had come from cupboards. In what way is she one of them?
4. Why is Miss Brill pleased at the thought of being part of the performance every Sunday?
5. What insight into herself does Miss Brill get from the remarks of the young boy and girl?
6. How does the author develop sympathy for Miss Brill?

CHARACTER
Methods of Characterization

The way an author presents a character in a short story is called *characterization.* Sometimes an author tells you directly what a character is like. More often, the author lets you draw your own conclusions about a character from information in the story.

Katherine Mansfield uses several *methods of characterization* to reveal what Miss Brill is like.

1. *Details of Physical Appearance.* Katherine Mansfield chooses to focus on one item of Miss Brill's apparel—her fox fur. This fur piece is obviously a precious possession. Miss Brill keeps it carefully wrapped in its box and touches it lovingly when she takes it out. To other eyes, however, this fur piece is quite worn and unattractive. At the end of the story it is compared to a "fried whiting." What conclusion about Miss Brill can you draw from these details?

2. *What a Character Thinks.* Most of this story lets you know what is going on in Miss Brill's mind. During her visit to the park, she speaks to no one and she does nothing. Her imagination, however, is active, and she identifies with what is going on all around her. How do her reactions to what she sees reveal the emptiness of her life?

3. *What Other Characters Think.* Miss Brill, who has been imagining herself an important part of the park scene, an "actress" in the performance, finds out what others think of her when she overhears the insulting comments of the young boy and girl. How does this scene convey the pitiful nature of her life?

4. *How the Character Behaves.* At the end of the story, Miss Brill bypasses the honeycake, her Sunday treat, and returns to her "cupboard" of a room. It is clear that she is crying as she puts away her fur. What does this action reveal about Miss Brill? Do you think something has changed for her?

UNDERSTANDING THE WORDS
IN THE STORY (Multiple-Choice)

Choose the best synonym for each italicized word.

1. ". . . the blue sky *powdered* with gold . . ."
   a. mixed   b. sprinkled   c. smeared

2. "The air was *motionless* . . ."
   a. still   b. cold   c. stirring

3. ". . . the nose, which was of some black *composition,* wasn't . . . firm."
   a. combination of materials
   b. writing paper
   c. rough cloth

4. "Little *rogue* biting its tail just by her left ear."
   a. animal   b. pet   c. rascal

5. ". . . his hands *clasped* over a huge carved walking stick . . ."
   a. held together   b. stretched   c. moved

6. ". . . a big old woman, sitting *upright* . . ."
   a. erect   b. firmly   c. uncomfortably

7. ". . . sometimes a tiny *staggerer* came suddenly rocking into the open . . ."
   a. beggar   b. totterer   c. singer

8. "Two peasant women . . . passed, *gravely* . . ."
   a. swiftly   b. seriously   c. quietly

9. "Now everything . . . was the same color as the *shabby* ermine . . ."
   a. ugly   b. stylish   c. worn-out

10. ". . . the ermine toque . . . *pattered* away."
    a. chattered
    b. moved lightly and quickly
    c. strolled leisurely

(Completion)

Choose one of the words in the following list to complete each of the sentences below. A word may be used only once.

hobbled	hollowed
abreast	pinched
solemn	quivered
invalid	resolute
frail	dashing

1. The prisoner took a (an) _____ vow to avenge the wrongs he had suffered.

2. The hero of the play was a smiling, _____ cavalry officer.

3. The beggar's face was _____ from hunger and cold.

4. The cheerleaders, walking four _____, entered the stadium.

5. Because her shoes were too tight, the woman _____ along.

6. The _____ eyes of the sick man followed the doctor's movements anxiously.

7. The leaves on the sycamore trees _____ in the breeze.

8. The crystal was too _____ to be shipped and had to be carried by hand.

9. Although she is confined to a wheelchair, the patient does not think of herself as a(an) _____.

10. Once I make up my mind to do something, you will find me _____.

FOR WRITING

1. Sometimes a story ends with a dramatic *revelation* that reveals something important to the main character. Write a brief essay describing the moment of illumination in "Miss Brill" and its probable effect on the main character.

2. Do you think Miss Brill will ever return to the park? Support your answer with what you know about Miss Brill's character.

"When I get through with you, sir,
you are going to remember
Mrs. Luella Bates Washington Jones."

THANK YOU, M'AM

Langston Hughes

She was a large woman with a large purse that had everything in it but hammer and nails. It had a long strap and she carried it slung across her shoulder. It was about eleven o'clock at night, and she was walking alone, when a boy ran up behind her and tried to snatch her purse. The strap broke with the single tug the boy gave it from behind. But the boy's weight, and the weight of the purse combined caused him to lose his balance so, instead of taking off full blast as he had hoped, the boy fell on his back on the sidewalk, and his legs flew up. The large woman simply turned around and kicked him right square in his blue-jeaned sitter. Then she reached down, picked the boy up by his shirt front, and shook him until his teeth rattled.

After that the woman said, "Pick up my pocketbook, boy, and give it here."

She still held him. But she bent down enough to permit him to stoop and pick up her purse. Then she said, "Now ain't you ashamed of yourself?"

Firmly gripped by his shirt front, the boy said, "Yes'm."

The woman said, "What did you want to do it for?"

The boy said, "I didn't aim to."

62

She said, "You a lie!"

By that time two or three people passed, stopped, turned to look, and some stood watching.

"If I turn you loose, will you run?" asked the woman.

"Yes'm," said the boy.

"Then I won't turn you loose," said the woman. She did not release him.

"I'm very sorry, lady, I'm sorry," whispered the boy.

"Um-hum! And your face is dirty. I got a great mind to wash your face for you. Ain't you got nobody home to tell you to wash your face?"

"No'm," said the boy.

"Then it will get washed this evening," said the large woman starting up the street, dragging the frightened boy behind her.

He looked as if he were fourteen or fifteen, frail and willow-wild, in tennis shoes and blue jeans.

The woman said, "You ought to be my son. I would teach you right from wrong. Least I can do right now is to wash your face. Are you hungry?"

"No'm," said the being-dragged boy. "I just want you to turn me loose."

"Was I bothering *you* when I turned that corner?" asked the woman.

"No'm."

"But you put yourself in contact with *me*," said the woman. "If you think that that contact is not going to last awhile, you got another thought coming. When I get through with you, sir, you are going to remember Mrs. Luella Bates Washington Jones."

Sweat popped out on the boy's face and he began to struggle. Mrs. Jones stopped, jerked him around in front of her, put a half nelson about his neck, and continued to drag him up the street. When she got to her door, she dragged the boy inside, down a hall, and into a large kitchenette-furnished room at the rear of the house. She switched on the light and left the door open. The boy could hear other roomers laughing and talking in the large house. Some of their doors were open, too, so he knew he and the woman were not alone. The woman still had him by the neck in the middle of her room.

She said, "What is your name?"

"Roger," answered the boy.

"Then, Roger, you go to that sink and wash your face," said the woman, whereupon she turned him loose—at last. Roger looked at the door—looked at the woman—looked at the door—*and went to the sink.*

"Let the water run until it gets warm," she said. "Here's a clean towel."

"You gonna take me to jail?" asked the boy, bending over the sink.

"Not with that face, I would not take you nowhere," said the woman.

"Here I am trying to get home to cook me a bite to eat and you snatch my pocketbook! Maybe you ain't been to your supper either, late as it be. Have you?"

"There's nobody home at my house," said the boy.

"Then we'll eat," said the woman. "I believe you're hungry—or been hungry—to try to snatch my pocketbook."

"I wanted a pair of blue suede shoes," said the boy.

"Well, you didn't have to snatch *my* pocketbook to get some suede shoes," said Mrs. Luella Bates Washington Jones. "You could of asked me."

"M'am?"

The water dripping from his face, the boy looked at her. There was a long pause. A very long pause. After he had dried his face and not knowing what else to do dried it again, the boy turned around, wondering what next. The door was open. He could make a dash for it down the hall. He could run, run, run, run, *run!*

The woman was sitting on the daybed. After awhile she said, "I were young once and I wanted things I could not get."

There was another long pause. The boy's mouth opened. Then he frowned, but not knowing he frowned.

The woman said, "Um-hum! You thought I was going to say *but*, didn't you? You thought I was going to say, *but I didn't snatch people's pocketbooks*. Well, I wasn't going to say that." Pause. Silence. "I have done things, too, which I would not tell you, son—neither tell God, if he didn't already know. So you set down while I fix us something to eat. You might run that comb through your hair so you will look presentable."

In another corner of the room behind a screen was a gas plate and an icebox. Mrs. Jones got up and went behind the screen. The woman did not watch the boy to see if he was going to run now, nor did she watch her purse which she left behind her on the daybed. But the boy took care to sit on the far side of the room where he thought she could easily see him out of the corner of her eye, if she wanted to. He did not trust the woman *not* to trust him. And he did not want to be mistrusted now.

"Do you need somebody to go to the store," asked the boy, "maybe to get some milk or something?"

"Don't believe I do," said the woman, "unless you just want sweet milk yourself. I was going to make cocoa out of this canned milk I got here."

"That will be fine," said the boy.

She heated some lima beans and ham she had in the icebox, made the cocoa, and set the table. The woman did not ask the boy anything about where he lived, or his folks, or anything else that would embarrass him. Instead, as they ate, she told him about her job in a hotel beauty shop that stayed open late, what the work was like, and how all kinds of women came in and out, blondes, redheads, and Spanish.

Then she cut him a half of her ten-cent cake.

"Eat some more, son," she said.

When they were finished eating she got up and said, "Now, here, take this ten dollars and buy yourself some blue suede shoes. And next time, do not make the mistake of latching onto *my* pocketbook *nor nobody else's*—because shoes come by devilishly like that will burn your feet. I got to get my rest now. But I wish you would behave yourself, son, from here on in."

She led him down the hall to the front door and opened it. "Goodnight! Behave yourself, boy!" she said, looking out into the street.

The boy wanted to say something else other than, "Thank you, m'am," to Mrs. Luella Bates Washington Jones, but he couldn't do so as he turned at the barren stoop and looked back at the large woman in the door. He barely managed to say, "Thank you," before she shut the door. And he never saw her again.

CHECK-UP (Putting Events in Order)

Arrange the following events in the order in which they occur in the story.

The woman drags the boy up the street.
The boy washes his face.
The woman turns the boy loose.
The boy snatches the woman's purse.
The boy thanks the woman.
The woman grabs the boy by his shirt front.
The woman gives the boy money to buy a pair of
   blue suede shoes.
The woman cooks dinner.
The boy offers to go to the store.
The woman tells the boy about her job in a hotel
   beauty shop.

FOR DISCUSSION

1. After the boy tries to steal her purse, Mrs. Jones refuses to release him. Why does she take the boy home with her instead of calling the police?
2. After she releases Roger, Mrs. Jones leaves her door open and her purse on the bed. Why does she do this? Why doesn't Roger take the purse and run?
3. What is Mrs. Jones's purpose in talking to Roger about herself? Why do you think she gives him the ten dollars?
4. At one point Mrs. Jones tells the boy, "You ought to be my son. I would teach you right from wrong." Do you think she succeeds in teaching Roger the difference?
5. This story begins with a conflict between a boy and a woman. How is this conflict resolved?

CHARACTER
Credibility, Consistency, and Motivation

In fairy tales and stories written for children, it is common for characters to be one-sided and simple. The wicked witch is always evil; the selfish sister is always mean; the good and obedient child never has a temper tantrum. Real people, of course, are a good deal more complicated. They are neither all good nor all bad, and they cannot be reduced to a single trait.

In order for the characters in a story to have *credibility*, or believability, they must behave like real people. We need to feel that they are true to life.

To be believable, characters must behave with *consistency.* If a character undergoes a change, there must be sufficient reason to explain it. A character who is presented as shy and awkward cannot suddenly turn into a bold, confident individual unless there is some crucial experience that makes change possible.

There must be *motivation,* or reason, to account for a character's actions. People can be motivated by outside forces or by their inner needs.

1. How does Langston Hughes make Mrs. Jones a "true-to-life" character?
2. While he is in Mrs. Jones's apartment, Roger has an opportunity to steal her purse and run, but he does not do so. Is his behavior consistent? Give reasons for your answer.
3. Why does Mrs. Jones take Roger into her home? Why does she cook for him and give him money? Are her motives believable? Give reasons for your answer.

FOR WRITING

1. Do you think Mrs. Jones is right or wrong not to report Roger to the police? Write a brief essay in which you attempt to persuade other readers to agree with you.
2. Write a brief essay showing how Hughes develops the character of Mrs. Jones through direct and indirect methods of characterization.

*"He wanted to sound like a swaggering, big guy . . .
yet the old, childish hope was in him,
the longing that someone at home
would come and help him."*

ALL
THE YEARS
OF HER LIFE

Morley Callaghan

They were closing the drugstore, and Alfred Higgins,
who had just taken off his white jacket, was putting on his
coat and getting ready to go home. The little gray-haired
man, Sam Carr, who owned the drugstore, was bending
down behind the cash register, and when Alfred Higgins
passed him, he looked up and said softly, "Just a moment,
Alfred. One moment before you go."

The soft, confident, quiet way in which Sam Carr spoke
made Alfred start to button his coat nervously. He felt sure
his face was white. Sam Carr usually said, "Good night,"
brusquely, without looking up. In the six months he had
been working in the drugstore Alfred had never heard his
employer speak softly like that. His heart began to beat so
loud it was hard for him to get his breath. "What is it, Mr.
Carr?" he asked.

"Maybe you'd be good enough to take a few things out of
your pocket and leave them here before you go," Sam Carr
said.

"What things? What are you talking about?"

"You've got a compact and a lipstick and at least two tubes of toothpaste in your pockets, Alfred."

"What do you mean? Do you think I'm crazy?" Alfred blustered. His face got red and he knew he looked fierce with indignation. But Sam Carr, standing by the door with his blue eyes shining brightly behind his glasses and his lips moving underneath his gray mustache, only nodded his head a few times, and then Alfred grew very frightened and he didn't know what to say. Slowly he raised his hand and dipped it into his pocket, and with his eyes never meeting Sam Carr's eyes, he took out a blue compact and two tubes of toothpaste and a lipstick, and he laid them one by one on the counter.

"Petty thieving, eh, Alfred?" Sam Carr said. "And maybe you'd be good enough to tell me how long this has been going on."

"This is the first time I ever took anything."

"So now you think you'll tell me a lie, eh? What kind of a sap do I look like, huh? I don't know what goes on in my own store, eh? I tell you you've been doing this pretty steady," Sam Carr said as he went over and stood behind the cash register.

Ever since Alfred had left school he had been getting into trouble wherever he worked. He lived at home with his mother and his father, who was a printer. His two older brothers were married and his sister had got married last year, and it would have been all right for his parents now if Alfred had only been able to keep a job.

While Sam Carr smiled and stroked the side of his face very delicately with the tips of his fingers, Alfred began to feel that familiar terror growing in him that had been in him every time he had got into such trouble.

"I liked you," Sam Carr was saying. "I liked you and would have trusted you, and now look what I got to do." While Alfred watched with his alert, frightened blue eyes,

Sam Carr drummed with his fingers on the counter. "I don't like to call a cop in point-blank," he was saying as he looked very worried. "You're a fool, and maybe I should call your father and tell him you're a fool. Maybe I should let them know I'm going to have you locked up."

"My father's not at home. He's a printer. He works nights," Alfred said.

"Who's at home?"

"My mother, I guess."

"Then we'll see what she says." Sam Carr went to the phone and dialed the number. Alfred was not so much ashamed, but there was that deep fright growing in him, and he blurted out arrogantly, like a strong, full-grown man, "Just a minute. You don't need to draw anybody else in. You don't need to tell her." He wanted to sound like a swaggering, big guy who could look after himself, yet the old, childish hope was in him, the longing that someone at home would come and help him. "Yeah, that's right, he's in trouble," Mr. Carr was saying. "Yeah, your boy works for me. You'd better come down in a hurry." And when he was finished Mr. Carr went over to the door and looked out at the street and watched the people passing in the late summer night. "I'll keep my eye out for a cop," was all he said.

Alfred knew how his mother would come rushing in; she would rush in with her eyes blazing, or maybe she would be crying, and she would push him away when he tried to talk to her, and make him feel her dreadful contempt; yet he longed that she might come before Mr. Carr saw the cop on the beat passing the door.

While they waited—and it seemed a long time—they did not speak, and when at last they heard someone tapping on the closed door, Mr. Carr, turning the latch, said crisply, "Come in, Mrs. Higgins." He looked hard-faced and stern.

Mrs. Higgins must have been going to bed when he telephoned, for her hair was tucked in loosely under her hat, and her hand at her throat held her light coat tight across her chest so her dress would not show. She came in, large and plump, with a little smile on her friendly face. Most of the store lights had been turned out and at first she did not see Alfred, who was standing in the shadow at the end of the counter. Yet as soon as she saw him she did not look as Alfred thought she would look: she smiled, her blue eyes never wavered, and with a calmness and dignity that made them forget that her clothes seemed to have been thrown on her, she put out her hand to Mr. Carr and said politely, "I'm Mrs. Higgins. I'm Alfred's mother."

Mr. Carr was a bit embarrassed by her lack of terror and her simplicity, and he hardly knew what to say to her, so she asked, "Is Alfred in trouble?"

"He is. He's been taking things from the store. I caught him red-handed. Little things like compacts and toothpaste and lipsticks. Stuff he can sell easily," the proprietor said.

As she listened Mrs. Higgins looked at Alfred sometimes and nodded her head sadly, and when Sam Carr had finished she said gravely, "Is it so, Alfred?"

"Yes."

"Why have you been doing it?"

"I been spending money, I guess."

"On what?"

"Going around with the guys, I guess," Alfred said.

Mrs. Higgins put out her hand and touched Sam Carr's arm with an understanding gentleness, and speaking as though afraid of disturbing him, she said, "If you would only listen to me before doing anything." Her simple earnestness made her shy; her humility made her falter and look away, but in a moment she was smiling gravely again, and she said with a kind of patient dignity, "What did you intend to do, Mr. Carr?"

"I was going to get a cop. That's what I ought to do."

"Yes, I suppose so. It's not for me to say, because he's my

son. Yet I sometimes think a little good advice is the best thing for a boy when he's at a certain period in his life," she said.

Alfred couldn't understand his mother's quiet composure, for if they had been at home and someone had suggested that he was going to be arrested, he knew she would be in a rage and would cry out against him. Yet now she was standing there with that gentle, pleading smile on her face, saying, "I wonder if you don't think it would be better just to let him come home with me. He looks like a big fellow, doesn't he? It takes some of them a long time to get any sense," and they both stared at Alfred, who shifted away with a bit of light shining for a moment on his thin face and the tiny pimples over his cheekbone.

But even while he was turning away uneasily Alfred was realizing that Mr. Carr had become aware that his mother was really a fine woman; he knew that Sam Carr was puzzled by his mother, as if he had expected her to come in and plead with him tearfully, and instead he was being made to feel a bit ashamed by her vast tolerance. While there was only the sound of the mother's soft, assured voice in the store, Mr. Carr began to nod his head encouragingly at her. Without being alarmed, while being just large and still and simple and hopeful, she was becoming dominant there in the dimly lit store. "Of course, I don't want to be harsh," Mr. Carr was saying. "I'll tell you what I'll do. I'll just fire him and let it go at that. How's that?" and he got up and shook hands with Mrs. Higgins, bowing low to her in deep respect.

There was such warmth and gratitude in the way she said, "I'll never forget your kindness," that Mr. Carr began to feel warm and genial himself.

"Sorry we had to meet this way," he said. "But I'm glad I got in touch with you. Just wanted to do the right thing, that's all," he said.

"It's better to meet like this than never, isn't it?" she said.

Suddenly they clasped hands as if they liked each other, as if they had known each other a long time. "Good night, sir," she said.

"Good night, Mrs. Higgins. I'm truly sorry," he said.

The mother and son walked along the street together, and the mother was taking a long, firm stride as she looked ahead with her stern face full of worry. Alfred was afraid to speak to her, he was afraid of the silence that was between them, so he only looked ahead too, for the excitement and relief was still pretty strong in him; but in a little while, going along like that in silence made him terribly aware of the strength and the sternness in her; he began to wonder what she was thinking of as she stared ahead so grimly; she seemed to have forgotten that he walked beside her; so when they were passing under the Sixth Avenue elevated[1] and the rumble of the train seemed to break the silence, he said in his old, blustering way, "Thank God it turned out like that. I certainly won't get in a jam like that again."

"Be quiet. Don't speak to me. You've disgraced me again and again," she said bitterly.

"That's the last time. That's all I'm saying."

"Have the decency to be quiet," she snapped. They kept on their way, looking straight ahead.

When they were at home and his mother took off her coat, Alfred saw that she was really only half-dressed, and she made him feel afraid again when she said, without even looking at him, "You're a bad lot. God forgive you. It's one thing after another and always has been. Why do you stand there stupidly? Go to bed, why don't you?" When he was going, she said, "I'm going to make myself a cup of tea. Mind, now, not a word about tonight to your father."

While Alfred was undressing in his bedroom, he heard

---

1. **elevated:** a railway that runs above street level.

his mother moving around the kitchen. She filled the kettle and put it on the stove. She moved a chair. And as he listened there was no shame in him, just wonder and a kind of admiration of her strength and repose. He could still see Sam Carr nodding his head encouragingly to her; he could hear her talking simply and earnestly, and as he sat on his bed he felt a pride in her strength. "She certainly was smooth," he thought. "Gee, I'd like to tell her she sounded swell."

And at last he got up and went along to the kitchen, and when he was at the door he saw his mother pouring herself a cup of tea. He watched and he didn't move. Her face, as she sat there, was a frightened, broken face utterly unlike the face of the woman who had been so assured a little while ago in the drugstore. When she reached out and lifted the kettle to pour hot water in her cup, her hand trembled and the water splashed on the stove. Leaning back in the chair, she sighed and lifted the cup to her lips, and her lips were groping loosely as if they would never reach the cup. She swallowed the hot tea eagerly, and then she straightened up in relief, though her hand holding the cup still trembled. She looked very old.

It seemed to Alfred that this was the way it had been every time he had been in trouble before, that this trembling had really been in her as she hurried out half-dressed to the drugstore. He understood why she had sat alone in the kitchen the night his young sister had kept repeating doggedly that she was getting married. Now he felt all that his mother had been thinking of as they walked along the street together a little while ago. He watched his mother, and he never spoke, but at that moment his youth seemed to be over; he knew all the years of her life by the way her hand trembled as she raised the cup to her lips. It seemed to him that this was the first time he had ever looked upon his mother.

CHECK-UP (Multiple-Choice)

1. Alfred Higgins has been working for Sam Carr
   a. since he left school
   b. for six months
   c. for a few weeks
2. When he is questioned by his employer, Alfred
   a. at first denies that he has anything in his pockets
   b. calls Mr. Carr a liar
   c. immediately returns the stolen items
3. Alfred is guilty of
   a. robbery
   b. burglary
   c. petty theft
4. From evidence in the story we know that Alfred
   a. is bored with his job
   b. enjoys getting into trouble
   c. can't keep a job
5. From Mr. Carr's actions we can conclude that he
   a. is hesitant to call the police
   b. is eager to have Alfred locked up
   c. will let Alfred have his job back
6. Alfred expects his mother to
   a. rush into the drugstore in a rage
   b. beg Mr. Carr to give her son another chance
   c. urge Mr. Carr to call the police
7. Mrs. Higgins surprises both Alfred and Mr. Carr by
   a. her calm manner
   b. her stern looks
   c. the way she is dressed
8. Mrs. Higgins convinces Mr. Carr that
   a. she will punish Alfred severely
   b. Alfred is innocent
   c. what Alfred needs is good advice
9. Alfred's reaction to the incident is
   a. anger at Mr. Carr
   b. admiration for his mother's strength
   c. shame and guilt

10. At the end of the story, Alfred realizes that his mother
    is
    a. fatally ill
    b. filled with self-pity
    c. broken in spirit

FOR DISCUSSION

1. Although Alfred is a big boy, he has not completely grown up. How does his behavior reveal that he is immature and irresponsible?
2. How does Mr. Carr show that he is really concerned about Alfred? Why is he reluctant to call the police?
3. Alfred is surprised by his mother's behavior in the drugstore. What has he come to expect? What do you think accounts for this change in his mother's attitude?
4. How does Mrs. Higgins win Mr. Carr's respect and confidence? How do both adults show an effort to help Alfred?
5. When Alfred leaves the drugstore with his mother, he is relieved. At what point in the story does he become aware of the consequences of his actions?
6. What does Alfred finally realize about his mother? How is he changed by this new understanding?
7. Is the major conflict in this story external or internal? Support your answer with evidence from the story.

CHARACTER
Static and Dynamic Characters

Some characters in short stories do not change in any meaningful way. At the end of their stories, they have essentially the same personalities that they had at the beginning. Such characters are referred to as *static*. Mrs. Jones in Langston Hughes's "Thank You, M'am" (page 62) is a static character. She does not undergo any visible change as a result of her encounter with Roger.

Characters who undergo some important change are referred to as *dynamic.* In "All the Years of Her Life," Alfred experiences an important change. How does his understanding of his mother cause Alfred to change? Find the passage that tells you.

Is Miss Brill (page 51) a static or dynamic character? Give reasons for your answer.

UNDERSTANDING THE WORDS IN THE STORY (Multiple-Choice)

1. When one speaks *brusquely,* one
   a. hesitates over each word
   b. shouts angrily
   c. is blunt to the point of rudeness
2. The person most likely to *bluster* is
   a. an infant
   b. a bully
   c. a librarian
3. *Indignation* results from
   a. anger at some injustice
   b. jealousy over possessions
   c. rivalry in sports
4. Something that is *blurted out* is
   a. spoken before thinking
   b. expressed calmly
   c. whispered brokenly
5. To behave *arrogantly* is to
   a. pay attention to other people's ideas
   b. act superior to other people
   c. submit willingly to criticism
6. To *swagger* is to
   a. drink thirstily
   b. stagger along
   c. show off

7. One feels *contempt* for someone or something
   that is
   a. despised
   b. far away
   c. precious
8. When one speaks *crisply,* one's words are
   a. harsh and angry
   b. short and forceful
   c. gentle and flattering
9. Eyes that *waver*
   a. stare fixedly at an object
   b. grow tearful
   c. show indecision
10. The *proprietor* of a store is
    a. its owner
    b. a merchant
    c. the salesperson

(Matching Columns)

1. gravely	a. respect for others' beliefs
2. humility	b. stubbornly
3. falter	c. calmness
4. composure	d. seriously
5. tolerance	e. hesitate
6. assured	f. reaching for uncertainly
7. dominant	g. quietness
8. repose	h. most important
9. groping	i. confident
10. doggedly	j. modesty

FOR WRITING

1. A writer may present a character in a short story *directly*
   by telling you what the character is like. A writer may
   also present a character *indirectly* by using any of these

methods: describing the character's physical appearance; showing the character's actions and words; revealing the character's thoughts; and showing what other characters think. Using specific reference to "All the Years of Her Life," show how Morley Callaghan develops the character of Mrs. Higgins or Alfred Higgins through both direct and indirect methods.

2. Do you expect Alfred Higgins to turn over a new leaf? Examine the evidence in the story before you state your opinion.

3. We are told that Mrs. Higgins' behavior in the drugstore is different from her reactions to similar incidents in the past. In a brief essay, explain the difference in her behavior and suggest what might have caused this change.

*This story takes place in France
during World War II, two weeks after
British troops had been evacuated from
the seaport of Dunkirk.*

THE
RIFLES OF
THE REGIMENT

Eric Knight

Colonel Heathergall has become a bit of a regimental
legend already. In the mess[1] of the Loyal Rifles, they say,
"Ah, but old Glass-eye! He was a one for one. A pukka sahib![2]
I'll never forget once . . ."

Then off they go on some story or other about "Old
Glass-eye."

But the regiment doesn't know the finest and truest
story of all: when he fought all night with Fear—and won.

Colonel Heathergall met Fear in a little shack atop a cliff
near the French village of Ste. Marguerite-en-Vaux.[3] He had
never met Fear before—not on the Somme[4] nor in India nor
in Palestine—because he was the type brought up not to

---

1. **mess:** the place where soldiers eat meals together.
2. **pukka sahib:** In Anglo-Indian, *pukka* means "genuine or good." *Sahib* is
   a respectful title formerly used by Indians in addressing Europeans.
3. **Ste. Marguerite-en-Vaux** (săn mär′gə-rēt′-äN-vō).
4. **Somme** (sôm): a river in northern France. A major battle was fought
   there during World War I. The French and British tried to break through
   the German line along the Somme River. They lost over half a million
   men.

81

know Fear. Fear is a cad—you just don't recognize the bounder.

The system has its points. Not being even on nodding acquaintance with Fear had allowed the colonel to keep the Loyal Rifle Regiment going in France long after all other British troops had gone—they were still fighting, working their way westward toward the Channel,[5] nearly two weeks after Dunkirk[6] was all over.

The men—those that were left—were drunk with fatigue. When they marched between fights, they slept. When they rested, they went into a sort of coma, and the sergeants had to slap them to waken them.

"They're nearly done," the adjutant[7] said. "Shouldn't we jettison[8] equipment?"

"All right," the colonel said, finally. "Equipment can be destroyed and left behind. But not rifles! Regiment's never failed to carry its rifles in—and carry 'em out. We'll take our rifles with us—every last single rifle."

The adjutant saluted.

"Er—and tell 'em we'll cut through soon," the colonel added. "Tell 'em I say we'll find a soft spot and cut through soon."

But the Loyal Rifles never did cut through. For there was then no British Army left in France to cut through to. But the regiment didn't know that. It marched west and north and attacked, and went west and north again. Each

5. **Channel:** The English Channel, which lies between England and France.
6. **Dunkirk** (dŭn'kûrk'): a seaport in northern France. In May of 1940, the British army was trapped at Dunkirk by Hitler's armies. English civilians sent their boats across the English Channel to help evacuate the British troops.
7. **adjutant** (ăj'ōō-tənt): officer who serves as an assistant to a commanding officer.
8. **jettison** (jĕt'ĭ-sən, -zən): cast off (unwanted articles), generally in an emergency.

time it brought out its rifles and left its dead. First the sergeants were carrying two rifles, and then the men, and then the officers.

The Loyal Rifles went on until—they could go no farther. For they had reached the sea. It was on a headland looking out over the Channel, beside the fishing port of Ste. Marguerite-en-Vaux.

In the late afternoon the colonel used the regiment's last strength in an attempt to take Ste. Marguerite, for there might be boats there, fishing smacks,[9] something that could carry them all back to England. He didn't find boats. He found the enemy with tanks and artillery, and the regiment withdrew. They left their dead, but they left no rifles.

The colonel sent out scouts. They brought him the report. They were cut off by the Germans—ringed about with their backs to the sea; on a cliff top with a two-hundred-foot drop to the beach below.

The regiment posted pickets, and dug foxholes,[10] and fought until darkness came. Then they waited through the night for the last attack that was sure to come.

And it was that night, in his headquarters at the cliff top shack, that Colonel Heathergall, for the first time in his well-bred, British, military life, met Fear.

Fear had a leprous face. Its white robes were damp, and it smelled of stale sweat.

Colonel Heathergall, who had not heard the door close, saw the figure standing there in the darkness.

"Who—who is it?"

Fear bowed and said, "You know me, really, Colonel. All

9. **smacks:** boats, also called *well smacks,* used to transport live fish to market.
10. **foxholes:** shallow pits dug in the ground for shelter against enemy gunfire.

your arrogant, aristocratic, British life you've snubbed me and pretended you didn't know me, but really you do, don't you? Let us be friends."

The colonel adjusted his monocle.[11] "What do you want?" he asked.

"I've come to tell you," Fear said, "that it's time for you to surrender the regiment. You're finished."

"You're a slimy brute," the colonel said. "I won't surrender. There must be some way out! That R.A.F.[12] plane this morning! I'm sure it saw us—the way the chap waggled[13] his wings. He'd go get help. The navy—they'll come!"

Fear laughed. "And if they come, then what? How would you get down that cliff? . . . You *can't* get down—and you know it!"

"We could cut south and find a better spot—the men still have fight left," the colonel said desperately.

"The men," Fear said, "they'll leave their broken bodies wherever you choose. They've got the stuff. And oh, yes, you, too, have courage, in your way. The huntin'-shootin'-fishin' sort of courage. The well-bred polo-field kind of courage. But that's got nothing to do with *this* kind of war. You haven't the right to ask your men to die to preserve that sort of record. Have you?"

The colonel sat still, not answering.

Fear spoke again. "The enemy will be here soon. Your men are exhausted. They can't do any more. Really, you'd be saving their lives if you surrender. No one would blame you. . . ."

The colonel shook his head. "No," he said. "We can't do that. You see—we never have done that. And we can't now. Perhaps we are outmoded. I and my kind may be out-of-

---

11. **monocle** (mŏn′ə-kəl): an eyeglass for one eye.
12. **R.A.F.**: Royal Air Force.
13. **waggled** (wăg′əld): moved rapidly up and down.

date—incompetent—belonging to a bygone day. But . . ." He looked around him as if for help. Then he went on desperately: "But—we've brought out all the rifles."

"Is that all?" mocked Fear.

"All?" the colonel echoed. "Is that all?"

Then at last he squared his shoulders. "All? Why, you bloody civilian, it's everything! I may die—and my men may die—but the regiment! It doesn't. The regiment goes on living. It's bigger than me—it's bigger than the men. Why, you slimy dugout king of a base-wallah[14]—it's bigger than you!"

And exactly as he said that, Fear fled. And there came a rap on the door, and the adjutant's voice sounded.

"Come in," the colonel said quietly.

"Are you alone, sir?" the adjutant asked.

"Yes," the colonel said. "Quite alone. What is it?"

"Report from the signal officer, sir. He has carried an ordinary torch with him, and he feels the colonel will be interested to know that he's in visual communication with the navy—destroyers or something. They say they're ready to put off boats to take us off."

"Tell him my thanks to C.O.[15] of whatever naval force there is there. Message to company commanders: Withdraw pickets quietly. Rendezvous[16] cliff top north of this H.Q.[17] at three-fifty-five ack emma.[18] Er—pretty good chaps in the navy—I've heard."

"Indeed, sir," the adjutant said.

So they assembled the men of the Loyal Rifle Regiment on the cliff top, where they could see out and below them the

14. **wallah:** Anglo-Indian for someone who is associated with a particular occupation or function.
15. **C.O.:** Commanding Officer.
16. **Rendezvous** (rän′dä-vōo′, rän′də-): Assemble troops.
17. **H.Q.:** Headquarters.
18. **ack emma:** A.M.

brief dots and dashes of light that winked.[19] And there, too, in the night wind, they could feel the space and know the vast drop to the beach. Some of the men lay flat and listened for the sound of the sailors two hundred feet below them.

The officers waited, looking toward the colonel. It was the major who spoke: "But—how on earth are we going to get down there, Colonel?"

Colonel Heathergall smiled privately within himself. "The rifles," he said softly. "The rifles, of course. I think we'll just about have enough."

And that's how the regiment escaped. They made a great chain of linked rifle slings, and went down it one at a time. The colonel came last, of course, as custom dictated.

Below, they picked up the rifles, whole and shattered, that they had thrown from the cliff top, and wading out into the sea, carried them to the boats.

By this time the Germans were awake, and they let loose with everything they had. The sailors used fine naval language, and said that Dunkirk was a picnic compared to this so-and-so bloody mess. But they got the men into the boats. The navy got in and got them out.

That's the way the Loyal Rifle Regiment came home nearly two weeks after the last troops from Dunkirk had landed in Blighty.[20] . . .

In the mess they still talk of the colonel. "Old Glass-eye," they say. "Ah, there was a colonel for you. Saved the outfit, he did. Knew the only way it'd ever get out would be down a cliff—so he made 'em carry all the rifles halfway across France. Knew he'd need the slings for that cliff. Foresight, eh? . . . Great Chap, Old Glass-eye. Never knew the meaning of Fear."

19. **dots . . . winked:** The message was transmitted in Morse code.
20. **Blighty:** British slang for "England."

CHECK-UP (True/False)

1. Colonel Heathergall has only one eye.
2. The colonel will not permit the regiment to get rid of its equipment.
3. The regiment is trapped on a cliff beside the English Channel.
4. The men use the rifles to escape from the Germans.
5. The British troops are rescued by American soldiers.

FOR DISCUSSION

1. How did Colonel Heathergall get the nickname "Old Glass-eye"? Does this name show the men's affection or disrespect for their leader? Explain your answer.
2. We are told early in the story that Colonel Heathergall was the "type brought up not to know Fear." Explain what this statement means, using what you learn about the colonel's background, education, and military career.
3. The colonel insists that the men carry out all their rifles. What does this tell you about his feeling for army traditions?
4. At what point does the colonel first experience fear? Why do you think the author represents the colonel's inner conflict as a conversation between two characters? How does the colonel master his fear?
5. How is the colonel's escape solution logical and consistent with his character?

CHARACTER
Stock Characters

Some characters appear in literature so often that they are recognized immediately as *types.* Instead of existing as individual or original creations, they conform to a set pattern. For example, in fairy tales, a familiar character type is the wicked stepmother. Her behavior is predictable because it is based on a pattern that remains the same from one story to another. Other familiar character types are the lawman in Westerns, the "hard-boiled" private investigator, and the absent-minded professor. These characters are known as *stock characters* or *stereotypes* (stĕr'ē-ə-tīps', stîr'-).

Sometimes a writer will choose to individualize a stock character, creating a new personality out of a familiar pattern. The colonel in Knight's story has many of the stock characteristics associated with the British officer who prizes devotion to duty above all else. One conventional feature of this type is keeping a "stiff upper lip," that is, refraining from showing fear or discouragement. This character type typically is efficient and unemotional. No breaches in discipline or military regulations are tolerated. Even the physical detail of the monocle establishes the type.

In his confrontation with Fear, however, the colonel becomes a human being who experiences great misgivings about his principles and his judgment. What details in the story make the colonel's experience of fear vivid and persuasive? How does the colonel show his desperation? What doubts does he express about his own abilities as a leader?

Personification

In the story Knight represents an emotion—fear—as a person who converses with the colonel. The presentation of an abstract quality or idea as a human being is called *personification* (pər-sŏn'ə-fĭ-kā'shən).

This technique is sometimes used to intensify the importance of some event or condition. What physical characteristics are given to Fear? How do these characteristics suggest a nightmare vision? How does the personification of Fear make the colonel's experience of terror convincing?

UNDERSTANDING THE WORDS IN THE STORY (Multiple-Choice)

1. A *cad* is
   a. a carrier of golf clubs
   b. an ill-mannered person
   c. a military cadet
2. A *bounder* is
   a. coarse and offensive
   b. simple and earnest
   c. agile and quick
3. A *headland* is a
   a. narrow strip of land along the sea
   b. cliff projecting into water
   c. peninsula
4. A *leprous* face suggests
   a. tigerish ferocity
   b. unrestrained anger
   c. disease and decay
5. An *arrogant* attitude is
   a. modest
   b. forgiving
   c. scornful
6. An *aristocratic* person is
   a. a member of a privileged class
   b. an officer in the British army
   c. someone who runs for public office
7. *Outmoded* ideas
   a. never grow old
   b. are out of fashion
   c. constantly change

8. An *incompetent* worker
   a. is unintelligent
   b. has no understanding of a situation
   c. lacks ability or skill for a job
9. A *bygone* time
   a. lies in the past
   b. occupies the present
   c. is in the future
10. *Foresight* is necessary to
    a. understand an event after it happens
    b. plan for the future
    c. read small print on a page

FOR WRITING

1. Discuss the colonel's escape plan for his regiment, and tell whether or not you think it is believable.
2. To what degree is Uncle Basil in "You Can't Take It with You" (page 22) a stereotype of a miser? To what degree is he an individual? In your essay, refer to specific evidence in the story.

Setting

*"The silence was so immense and unbelievable
that you felt your ears had been stuffed or you
had lost your hearing altogether."*

ALL
SUMMER
IN A DAY

Ray Bradbury

"Ready?"

"Ready."

"Now?"

"Soon."

"Do the scientists really know? Will it happen today, will
it?"

"Look, look; see for yourself!"

The children pressed to each other like so many roses,
so many weeds, intermixed, peering out for a look at the
hidden sun.

It rained.

It had been raining for seven years; thousands upon
thousands of days compounded and filled from one end to
the other with rain, with the drum and gush of water, with
the sweet crystal fall of showers and the concussion of
storms so heavy they were tidal waves come over the islands.

A thousand forests had been crushed under the rain and grown up a thousand times to be crushed again. And this was the way life was forever on the planet Venus, and this was the schoolroom of the children of the rocket men and women who had come to a raining world to set up civilization and live out their lives.

"It's stopping, it's stopping!"

"Yes, yes!"

Margot stood apart from them, from these children who could never remember a time when there wasn't rain and rain and rain. They were all nine years old, and if there had been a day, seven years ago, when the sun came out for an hour and showed its face to the stunned world, they could not recall. Sometimes, at night, she heard them stir, in remembrance, and she knew they were dreaming and remembering gold or a yellow crayon or a coin large enough to buy the world with. She knew they thought they remembered a warmness, like a blushing in the face, in the body, in the arms and legs and trembling hands. But then they always awoke to the tatting drum, the endless shaking down of clear bead necklaces upon the roof, the walk, the gardens, the forests, and their dreams were gone.

All day yesterday they had read in class about the sun. About how like a lemon it was, and how hot. And they had written small stories or essays or poems about it:

> *I think the sun is a flower,*
> *That blooms for just one hour.*

That was Margot's poem, read in a quiet voice in the still classroom while the rain was falling outside.

"Aw, you didn't write that!" protested one of the boys.

"I did," said Margot. "I did."

"William!" said the teacher.

But that was yesterday. Now the rain was slackening, and the children were crushed in the great thick windows.

"Where's teacher?"

"She'll be back."

"She'd better hurry, we'll miss it!"

They turned on themselves, like a feverish wheel, all tumbling spokes.

Margot stood alone. She was a very frail girl who looked as if she had been lost in the rain for years and the rain had washed out the blue from her eyes and the red from her mouth and the yellow from her hair. She was an old photograph dusted from an album, whitened away, and if she spoke at all her voice would be a ghost. Now she stood, separate, staring at the rain and the loud wet world beyond the huge glass.

"What're *you* looking at?" said William.

Margot said nothing.

"Speak when you're spoken to." He gave her a shove. But she did not move; rather she let herself be moved only by him and nothing else.

They edged away from her, they would not look at her. She felt them go away. And this was because she would play no games with them in the echoing tunnels of the underground city. If they tagged her and ran, she stood blinking after them and did not follow. When the class sang songs about happiness and life and games her lips barely moved. Only when they sang about the sun and the summer did her lips move as she watched the drenched windows.

And then, of course, the biggest crime of all was that she had come here only five years ago from Earth, and she remembered the sun and the way the sun was and the sky was when she was four in Ohio. And they, they had been on Venus all their lives, and they had been only two years old when last the sun came out and had long since forgotten the color and heat of it and the way it really was. But Margot remembered.

"It's like a penny," she said once, eyes closed.

"No, it's not!" the children cried.

"It's like a fire," she said, "in the stove."

"You're lying, you don't remember!" cried the children.

But she remembered and stood quietly apart from all of them and watched the patterning[1] windows. And once, a month ago, she had refused to shower in the school shower rooms, had clutched her hands to her ears and over her head, screaming the water mustn't touch her head. So after that, dimly, dimly, she sensed it, she was different and they knew her difference and kept away.

There was talk that her father and mother were taking her back to Earth next year; it seemed vital to her that they do so, though it would mean the loss of thousands of dollars to her family. And so, the children hated her for all these reasons of big and little consequence. They hated her pale snow face, her waiting silence, her thinness, and her possible future.

"Get away!" The boy gave her another push. "What're you waiting for?"

Then, for the first time, she turned and looked at him. And what she was waiting for was in her eyes.

"Well, don't wait around here!" cried the boy savagely. "You won't see nothing!"

Her lips moved.

"Nothing!" he cried. "It was all a joke, wasn't it?" He turned to the other children. "Nothing's happening today. *Is* it?"

They all blinked at him and then, understanding, laughed and shook their heads. "Nothing, nothing!"

"Oh, but," Margot whispered, her eyes helpless. "But this is the day, the scientists predict, they say, they *know*, the sun . . ."

---

1. **patterning** (păt′ər-nĭng): forming a pattern (of raindrops).

"All a joke!" said the boy, and seized her roughly. "Hey, everyone, let's put her in a closet before teacher comes!"

"No," said Margot, falling back.

They surged about her, caught her up and bore her, protesting, and then pleading, and then crying, back into a tunnel, a room, a closet, where they slammed and locked the door. They stood looking at the door and saw it tremble from her beating and throwing herself against it. They heard her muffled cries. Then, smiling, they turned and went out and back down the tunnel, just as the teacher arrived.

"Ready, children?" She glanced at her watch.

"Yes!" said everyone.

"Are we all here?"

"Yes!"

The rain slackened still more.

They crowded to the huge door.

The rain stopped.

It was as if, in the midst of a film concerning an avalanche, a tornado, a hurricane, a volcanic eruption, something had, first, gone wrong with the sound apparatus, thus muffling and finally cutting off all noise, all of the blasts and repercussions and thunders, and then, second, ripped the film from the projector and inserted in its place a peaceful tropical slide which did not move or tremor. The world ground to a standstill. The silence was so immense and unbelievable that you felt your ears had been stuffed or you had lost your hearing altogether. The children put their hands to their ears. They stood apart. The door slid back and the smell of the silent, waiting world came in to them.

The sun came out.

It was the color of flaming bronze and it was very large. And the sky around it was a blazing blue tile color. And the jungle burned with sunlight as the children, released from their spell, rushed out, yelling, into the springtime.

"Now, don't go too far," called the teacher after them.

"You've only two hours, you know. You wouldn't want to get caught out!"

But they were running and turning their faces up to the sky and feeling the sun on their cheeks like a warm iron; they were taking off their jackets and letting the sun burn their arms.

"Oh, it's better than the sunlamps, isn't it?"

"Much, much better!"

They stopped running and stood in the great jungle that covered Venus, that grew and never stopped growing, tumultuously, even as you watched it. It was a nest of octopi, clustering up great arms of fleshlike weed, wavering, flowering in this brief spring. It was the color of rubber and ash, this jungle, from the many years without sun. It was the color of stones and white cheeses and ink, and it was the color of the moon.

The children lay out, laughing, on the jungle mattress, and heard it sigh and squeak under them, resilient and alive. They ran among the trees, they slipped and fell, they pushed each other, they played hide-and-seek and tag, but most of all they squinted at the sun until tears ran down their faces, they put their hands up to that yellowness and that amazing blueness and they breathed of the fresh, fresh air and listened and listened to the silence which suspended them in a blessed sea of no sound and no motion. They looked at everything and savored everything. Then, wildly, like animals escaped from their caves, they ran and ran in shouting circles. They ran for an hour and did not stop running.

And then——

In the midst of their running one of the girls wailed.

Everyone stopped.

The girl, standing in the open, held out her hand.

"Oh, look, look," she said, trembling.

They came slowly to look at her opened palm.

In the center of it, cupped and huge, was a single raindrop.

She began to cry, looking at it.

They glanced quietly at the sky.

"Oh. Oh."

A few cold drops fell on their noses and their cheeks and their mouths. The sun faded behind a stir of mist. A wind blew cool around them. They turned and started to walk back toward the underground house, their hands at their sides, their smiles vanishing away.

A boom of thunder startled them and like leaves before a new hurricane, they tumbled upon each other and ran. Lightning struck ten miles away, five miles away, a mile, a half mile. The sky darkened into midnight in a flash.

They stood in the doorway of the underground for a moment until it was raining hard. Then they closed the door and heard the gigantic sound of the rain falling in tons and avalanches, everywhere and forever.

"Will it be seven more years?"

"Yes. Seven."

Then one of them gave a little cry.

"Margot!"

"What?"

"She's still in the closet where we locked her."

"Margot."

They stood as if someone had driven them, like so many stakes, into the floor. They looked at each other and then looked away. They glanced out at the world that was raining now and raining and raining steadily. They could not meet each other's glances. Their faces were solemn and pale. They looked at their hands and feet, their faces down.

"Margot."

One of the girls said, "Well . . . ?"

No one moved.

"Go on," whispered the girl.

They walked slowly down the hall in the sound of cold rain. They turned through the doorway to the room in the sound of the storm and thunder, lightning on their faces, blue and terrible. They walked over to the closet door slowly and stood by it.

Behind the closet door was only silence.

They unlocked the door, even more slowly, and let Margot out.

CHECK-UP (Multiple-Choice)

1. The author of this story imagines the planet Venus to be
   a. covered with forests and lakes
   b. a wetter place than Earth
   c. pitted with craters
2. The other children in the class resent Margot because she
   a. is the teacher's pet
   b. is a crybaby
   c. was born on Earth
3. The events of the story suggest that Margot probably will
   a. never adjust to life on Venus
   b. get even with her classmates
   c. make friends with the other children
4. The children lock Margot in the closet
   a. to frighten her
   b. to keep her from seeing the sun
   c. as a game
5. At the end of the story, the children feel
   a. ashamed of their behavior
   b. affection for Margot
   c. angry at their teacher

FOR DISCUSSION

1. What are the climatic conditions the author imagines to exist on the planet Venus? What area of Earth's surface does the planet Venus most closely resemble?
2. Although this story takes place on an alien world, the characters behave pretty much the way human beings behave on Earth. Why do the children pick on Margot? In what ways is she different from them?
3. Why do you suppose Margot makes no effort to join the children in their games or to respond to their taunts?
4. How are the children affected by their first experience of the sun?
5. Do you think that the children have a better understanding of Margot at the end of the story? Explain your answer.

SETTING
Background in a Story

A painting or a photograph is said to have a *foreground* and a *background.* The foreground is that part of the scene that is nearest to you, the viewer, and therefore most noticeable. The background is that part of the scene that is toward the back and that forms the surroundings for the images in the foreground.

A short story, too, may be said to have a foreground and a background. The main characters and the actions, which are of greatest interest to the reader, form the foreground. The background of the story—the time and place of the events and the circumstances that surround these events— is known as its *setting.*

Setting is an important element in many short stories. Clearly, the action of Ray Bradbury's story depends upon its physical background. The events he describes are tied to the setting.

Find details in the story that describe the climatic conditions and environment Bradbury imagines to exist on the planet Venus. How does the author make the setting convincing?

UNDERSTANDING THE WORDS IN THE STORY (Multiple-Choice)

1. concussion
2. consequence
3. muffling
4. repercussions
5. resilient
6. savored
7. slackening
8. solemn
9. suspended
10. tumultuously

a. reflections of sound
b. enjoyed
c. slowing down
d. held in position
e. importance
f. serious
g. leaping back
h. disturbance
i. in a riotous way
j. deadening

FOR WRITING

1. Imagine Margot's first day back on Earth in Ohio. Write a story telling what she experiences and how she feels.
2. What do scientists know about surface conditions on Venus? What do they conjecture about the existence of life forms on the planet? Consult a recently published reference book for answers to these questions. Present your findings in a brief essay.

*"His face was the face of a student—
thin and ascetic, but his eyes had
the cold gleam of the fanatic."*

THE
SNIPER

Liam O'Flaherty

The long June twilight faded into night. Dublin lay
enveloped in darkness but for the dim light of the moon
that shone through fleecy clouds, casting a pale light as of
approaching dawn over the streets and the dark waters of
the Liffey. Around the beleaguered Four Courts the heavy
guns roared. Here and there through the city machine guns
and rifles broke the silence of the night, spasmodically,[1] like
dogs barking on lone farms. Republicans and Free Staters
were waging civil war.[2]

On a rooftop near O'Connell Bridge, a Republican
sniper lay watching. Beside him lay his rifle and over his
shoulders were slung a pair of field glasses. His face was the
face of a student—thin and ascetic, but his eyes had the cold
gleam of the fanatic. They were deep and thoughtful, the
eyes of a man who is used to looking at death.

He was eating a sandwich hungrily. He had eaten nothing since morning. He had been too excited to eat. He fin-

---

1. **spasmodically** (spăz-mŏd′ĭk-lē): fitfully; happening at irregular intervals.
2. **civil war:** Civil war followed the founding of the Irish Free State in 1921.
   The Free State forces supported dominion status in the British Empire.
   The Republicans aimed at overthrowing English rule in Ireland.

ished the sandwich, and taking a flask of whiskey from his pocket, he took a short draft. Then he returned the flask to his pocket. He paused for a moment, considering whether he should risk a smoke. It was dangerous. The flash might be seen in the darkness and there were enemies watching. He decided to take the risk. Placing a cigarette between his lips, he struck a match, inhaled the smoke hurriedly and put out the light. Almost immediately, a bullet flattened itself against the parapet of the roof. The sniper took another whiff and put out the cigarette. Then he swore softly and crawled away to the left.

Cautiously he raised himself and peered over the parapet. There was a flash and a bullet whizzed over his head. He dropped immediately. He had seen the flash. It came from the opposite side of the street.

He rolled over the roof to a chimney stack in the rear, and slowly drew himself up behind it, until his eyes were level with the top of the parapet. There was nothing to be seen—just the dim outline of the opposite housetop against the blue sky. His enemy was under cover.

Just then an armored car came across the bridge and advanced slowly up the street. It stopped on the opposite side of the street fifty yards ahead. The sniper could hear the dull panting of the motor. His heart beat faster. It was an enemy car. He wanted to fire, but he knew it was useless. His bullets would never pierce the steel that covered the gray monster.

Then round the corner of a side street came an old woman, her head covered by a tattered shawl. She began to talk to the man in the turret of the car. She was pointing to the roof where the sniper lay. An informer.

The turret opened. A man's head and shoulders appeared, looking towards the sniper. The sniper raised his rifle and fired. The head fell heavily on the turret wall. The woman darted toward the side street. The sniper fired again.

The woman whirled round and fell with a shriek into the gutter.

Suddenly from the opposite roof a shot rang out and the sniper dropped his rifle with a curse. The rifle clattered to the roof. The sniper thought the noise would wake the dead. He stopped to pick the rifle up. He couldn't lift it. His forearm was dead. "I'm hit," he muttered.

Dropping flat onto the roof, he crawled back to the parapet. With his left hand he felt the injured right forearm. The blood was oozing through the sleeve of his coat. There was no pain—just a deadened sensation, as if the arm had been cut off.

Quickly he drew his knife from his pocket, opened it on the breastwork[3] of the parapet and ripped open the sleeve. There was a small hole where the bullet had entered. On the other side there was no hole. The bullet had lodged in the bone. It must have fractured it. He bent the arm below the wound. The arm bent back easily. He ground his teeth to overcome the pain.

Then, taking out his field dressing, he ripped open the packet with his knife. He broke the neck of the iodine bottle and let the bitter fluid drip into the wound. A paroxysm[4] of pain swept through him. He placed the cotton wadding over the wound and wrapped the dressing over it. He tied the end with his teeth.

Then he lay still against the parapet, and closing his eyes, he made an effort of will to overcome the pain.

In the street beneath all was still. The armored car had retired speedily over the bridge, with the machine gunner's head hanging lifeless over the turret. The woman's corpse lay still in the gutter.

The sniper lay for a long time nursing his wounded arm

3. **breastwork** (brĕst′wûrk′): a low wall.
4. **paroxysm** (păr′ək-sĭz′əm): sudden attack or spasm.

and planning escape. Morning must not find him wounded on the roof. The enemy on the opposite roof covered his escape. He must kill that enemy and he could not use his rifle. He had only a revolver to do it. Then he thought of a plan.

Taking off his cap, he placed it over the muzzle of his rifle. Then he pushed the rifle slowly upwards over the parapet, until the cap was visible from the opposite side of the street. Almost immediately there was a report,[5] and a bullet pierced the center of the cap. The sniper slanted the rifle forward. The cap slipped down into the street. Then, catching the rifle in the middle, the sniper dropped his left hand over the roof and let it hang, lifelessly. After a few moments he let the rifle drop to the street. Then he sank to the roof, dragging his hand with him.

Crawling quickly to the left, he peered up at the corner of the roof. His ruse had succeeded. The other sniper, seeing the cap and rifle fall, thought that he had killed his man. He was now standing before a row of chimney pots, looking across, with his head clearly silhouetted[6] against the western sky.

The Republican sniper smiled and lifted his revolver above the edge of the parapet. The distance was about fifty yards—a hard shot in the dim light, and his right arm was paining him like a thousand devils. He took a steady aim. His hand trembled with eagerness. Pressing his lips together, he took a deep breath through his nostrils and fired. He was almost deafened with the report and his arm shook with the recoil.

Then, when the smoke cleared, he peered across and uttered a cry of joy. His enemy had been hit. He was reeling over the parapet in his death agony. He struggled to keep his

---

5. **report:** an explosive noise.
6. **silhouetted** (sĭl′o͞o-ĕt′əd): outlined.

feet, but he was slowly falling forward, as if in a dream. The rifle fell from his grasp, hit the parapet, fell over, bounded off the pole of a barber's shop beneath and then cluttered[7] onto the pavement.

Then the dying man on the roof crumpled up and fell forward. The body turned over and over in space and hit the ground with a dull thud. Then it lay still.

The sniper looked at his enemy falling and he shuddered. The lust of battle died in him. He became bitten by remorse. The sweat stood out in beads on his forehead. Weakened by his wound and the long summer day of fasting and watching on the roof, he revolted from the sight of the shattered mass of his dead enemy. His teeth chattered. He began to gibber[8] to himself, cursing the war, cursing himself, cursing everybody.

He looked at the smoking revolver in his hand and with an oath he hurled it to the roof at his feet. The revolver went off with the concussion, and the bullet whizzed past the sniper's head. He was frightened back to his senses by the shock. His nerves steadied. The cloud of fear scattered from his mind and he laughed.

Taking the whiskey flask from his pocket, he emptied it at a draft. He felt reckless under the influence of the spirits. He decided to leave the roof and look for his company commander to report. Everywhere around was quiet. There was not much danger in going through the streets. He picked up his revolver and put it in his pocket. Then he crawled down through the skylight to the house underneath.

When the sniper reached the laneway on the street level, he felt a sudden curiosity as to the identity of the enemy sniper whom he had killed. He wondered if he knew him. Perhaps he had been in his own company before the split in

---

7. **cluttered:** clattered.
8. **gibber** (jĭb'ər, gĭb'-): talk senselessly.

the army. He decided to risk going over to have a look at him. He peered around the corner into O'Connell Street. In the upper part of the street there was heavy firing, but around here all was quiet.

The sniper darted across the street. A machine gun tore up the ground around him with a hail of bullets, but he escaped. He threw himself face downwards beside the corpse. The machine gun stopped.

Then the sniper turned over the dead body and looked into his brother's face.

CHECK-UP (Putting Events in Order)

Arrange the following events in the order in which they occur in the story.

> The sniper is wounded.
> The sniper crawls down through the skylight.
> The sniper eats a sandwich.
> An armored car advances up the street.
> The sniper strikes a match.
> The sniper shoots the informer.
> The sniper turns over the dead body of his enemy.
> The sniper kills the machine gunner.
> The sniper lets his rifle drop to the street.
> The sniper feels remorse.

FOR DISCUSSION

1. From details in the story, give the exact time and place of the action.
2. In this story O'Flaherty gives us a realistic account of the fighting in the Irish Civil War. What impressions can you draw about the war from the events in the story?

3. The sniper is referred to as a *fanatic*. How do his actions show that he is obsessed with a cause? How does he show courage? How does he show cunning?
4. What change becomes apparent in the sniper after he succeeds in killing his opponent? How do you explain this change?
5. What is the ironic twist at the end of the story? Do you consider this ending a logical outcome of the events? Explain.
6. The characters in this story are not identified by name, but by function. The old woman wearing a shawl is referred to as an informer. The central character is known only as the sniper. What do you think is O'Flaherty's purpose in making his characters anonymous?
7. What do the events of the story lead you to conclude about the author's attitude toward war?

SETTING
Verisimilitude

In the story "All Summer in a Day" (page 91), Ray Bradbury imaginatively creates the climatic conditions and environment of the planet Venus. Bradbury's fictional world is so well realized that while we read his story we are convinced that Venus is a raining world where the sun comes out for an hour once every seven years.

A short story may be given a setting that is true to a specific time and place. This appearance of reality in fiction is called *verisimilitude* (věr′ə-sĭm-ĭl′ə-tōōd′, -tyōōd′). "The Sniper" takes place in a real city, Dublin, during the period of the Irish Civil War. O'Flaherty's story shows accurately how this war was fought in small skirmishes on rooftops and in the streets, often between members of the same family.

Identify at least five details that establish the historical setting of "The Sniper."

UNDERSTANDING THE WORDS IN THE STORY (Completion)

1. A person who gives information against others for pay is a(an) _____. (informer, fanatic)

2. To stagger or sway is to _____. (revolt, reel)

3. Regret for one's past actions is _____. (agony, remorse)

4. To deny oneself comforts is to be _____. (reckless, ascetic)

5. A low protective structure is a _____. (turret, parapet)

6. The kick of a gun when it's fired is known as its _____. (recoil, concussion)

7. To look intently is to _____. (bound, peer)

8. To besiege with an army is to _____ the enemy. (envelop, beleaguer)

9. An action intended to mislead someone is a _____. (ruse, recoil)

10. The light in someone's eyes is a _____. (ruse, gleam)

FOR WRITING

1. In a paragraph, describe the physical background of "The Sniper," emphasizing those details that contribute to the story's verisimilitude.
2. In a short essay, analyze the plot of "The Sniper." Include a discussion of the exposition, conflict, climax, and resolution.
3. Is the sniper in this story a fully developed character or a stereotype? Defend your answer in a short essay, using evidence from the story.

*"Two weeks we had been moving
when we picked up Mary, who had run away
from somewhere that she wouldn't tell."*

TOO
SOON
A WOMAN

Dorothy M. Johnson

We left the home place behind, mile by slow mile, heading for the mountains, across the prairie where the wind blew forever.

At first there were four of us with the one-horse wagon and its skimpy load. Pa and I walked, because I was a big boy of eleven. My two little sisters romped and trotted until they got tired and had to be boosted up into the wagon bed.

That was no covered Conestoga,[1] like Pa's folks came West in, but just an old farm wagon, drawn by one weary horse, creaking and rumbling westward to the mountains, toward the little woods town where Pa thought he had an old uncle who owned a little two-bit sawmill.

Two weeks we had been moving when we picked up Mary, who had run away from somewhere that she wouldn't tell. Pa didn't want her along, but she stood up to him with no fear in her voice.

"I'd rather go with a family and look after kids," she said,

---

1. **Conestoga** (kŏn′ĭ-stō′gə): a covered wagon with broad wheels, used by American pioneers in crossing the prairies.

109

"but I ain't going back. If you won't take me, I'll travel with any wagon that will."

Pa scowled at her, and her wide blue eyes stared back.

"How old are you?" he demanded.

"Eighteen," she said. "There's teamsters come this way sometimes. I'd rather go with you folks. But I won't go back."

"We're prid'near out of grub," my father told her. "We're clean out of money. I got all I can handle without taking anybody else." He turned away as if he hated the sight of her. "You'll have to walk," he said.

So she went along with us and looked after the little girls, but Pa wouldn't talk to her.

On the prairie, the wind blew. But in the mountains, there was rain. When we stopped at little timber claims along the way, the homesteaders said it had rained all summer. Crops among the blackened stumps were rotted and spoiled. There was no cheer anywhere, and little hospitality. The people we talked to were past worrying. They were scared and desperate.

So was Pa. He traveled twice as far each day as the wagon, ranging through the woods with his rifle, but he never saw game. He had been depending on venison.[2] But we never got any except as a grudging gift from the homesteaders.

He brought in a porcupine once, and that was fat meat and good. Mary roasted it in chunks over the fire, half crying with the smoke. Pa and I rigged up the tarp[3] sheet for shelter to keep the rain from putting the fire clean out.

The porcupine was long gone, except for some of the tried-out fat[4] that Mary had saved, when we came to an old,

2. **venison** (vĕn'ə-sən, -zən): deer meat.
3. **tarp:** tarpaulin (tär-pô'lĭn, tär'pə-lĭn), waterproof canvas.
4. **tried-out fat:** fat that is rendered, or melted down.

empty cabin. Pa said we'd have to stop. The horse was wore out, couldn't pull anymore up those grades on the deep-rutted roads in the mountains.

At the cabin, at least there was shelter. We had a few potatoes left and some corn meal. There was a creek that probably had fish in it, if a person could catch them. Pa tried it for half a day before he gave up. To this day I don't care for fishing. I remember my father's sunken eyes in his gaunt, grim face.

He took Mary and me outside the cabin to talk. Rain dripped on us from branches overhead.

"I think I know where we are," he said. "I calculate to get to old John's and back in about four days. There'll be grub in the town, and they'll let me have some whether old John's still there or not."

He looked at me. "You do like she tells you," he warned. It was the first time he had admitted Mary was on earth since we picked her up two weeks before.

"You're my pardner," he said to me, "but it might be she's got more brains. You mind what she says."

He burst out with bitterness. "There ain't anything good left in the world, or people to care if you live or die. But I'll get grub in the town and come back with it."

He took a deep breath and added, "If you get too all-fired hungry, butcher the horse. It'll be better than starvin'."

He kissed the little girls goodbye and plodded off through the woods with one blanket and the rifle.

The cabin was moldy and had no floor. We kept a fire going under a hole in the roof, so it was full of blinding smoke, but we had to keep the fire so as to dry out the wood.

The third night we lost the horse. A bear scared him. We heard the racket, and Mary and I ran out, but we couldn't see anything in the pitch-dark.

In gray daylight I went looking for him, and I must have

walked fifteen miles. It seemed like I had to have that horse at the cabin when Pa came or he'd whip me. I got plumb[5] lost two or three times and thought maybe I was going to die there alone and nobody would ever know it, but I found the way back to the clearing.

That was the fourth day, and Pa didn't come. That was the day we ate up the last of the grub.

The fifth day, Mary went looking for the horse. My sisters whimpered, huddled in a quilt by the fire, because they were scared and hungry.

I never did get dried out, always having to bring in more damp wood and going out to yell to see if Mary would hear me and not get lost. But I couldn't cry like the little girls did, because I was a big boy, eleven years old.

It was near dark when there was an answer to my yelling, and Mary came into the clearing.

Mary didn't have the horse—we never saw hide nor hair of that old horse again—but she was carrying something big and white that looked like a pumpkin with no color to it.

She didn't say anything, just looked around and saw Pa wasn't there yet, at the end of the fifth day.

"What's that thing?" my sister Elizabeth demanded.

"Mushroom," Mary answered. "I bet it hefts[6] ten pounds."

"What are you going to do with it now?" I sneered. "Play football here?"

"Eat it—maybe," she said, putting it in a corner. Her wet hair hung over her shoulders. She huddled by the fire.

My sister Sarah began to whimper again. "I'm hungry!" she kept saying.

"Mushrooms ain't good eating," I said. "They can kill you."

5. **plumb** (plŭm): completely.
6. **hefts:** weighs.

"Maybe," Mary answered. "Maybe they can. I don't set up to know all about everything, like some people."

"What's that mark on your shoulder?" I asked her. "You tore your dress on the brush."

"What do you think it is?" she said, her head bowed in the smoke.

"Looks like scars," I guessed.

" 'Tis scars. They whipped me. Now mind your own business. I want to think."

Elizabeth whimpered, "Why don't Pa come back?"

"He's coming," Mary promised. "Can't come in the dark. Your pa'll take care of you soon's he can."

She got up and rummaged around in the grub box.

"Nothing there but empty dishes," I growled. "If there was anything, we'd know it."

Mary stood up. She was holding the can with the porcupine grease. "I'm going to have something to eat," she said coolly. "You kids can't have any yet. And I don't want any squalling, mind."

It was a cruel thing, what she did then. She sliced that big, solid mushroom and heated grease in a pan.

The smell of it brought the little girls out of their quilt, but she told them to go back in so fierce a voice that they obeyed. They cried to break your heart.

I didn't cry. I watched, hating her.

I endured the smell of the mushroom frying as long as I could. Then I said, "Give me some."

"Tomorrow," Mary answered. "Tomorrow, maybe. But not tonight." She turned to me with a sharp command: "Don't bother me! Just leave me be."

She knelt there by the fire and finished frying the slice of mushroom.

If I'd had Pa's rifle, I'd have been willing to kill her right then and there.

She didn't eat right away. She looked at the brown, fried

slice for a while and said, "By tomorrow morning, I guess you can tell whether you want any."

The little girls stared at her as she ate. Sarah was chewing an old leather glove.

When Mary crawled into the quilts with them, they moved away as far as they could get.

I was so scared that my stomach heaved, empty as it was.

Mary didn't stay in the quilts long. She took a drink out of the water bucket and sat down by the fire and looked through the smoke at me.

She said in a low voice, "I don't know how it will be if it's poison. Just do the best you can with the girls. Because your pa will come back, you know. . . . You better go to bed. I'm going to sit up."

And so would you sit up. If it might be your last night on earth and the pain of death might seize you at any moment, you would sit up by the smoky fire, wide-awake, remembering whatever you had to remember, savoring life.

We sat in silence after the girls had gone to sleep. Once I asked, "How long does it take?"

"I never heard," she answered. "Don't think about it."

I slept after a while, with my chin on my chest. Maybe Peter[7] dozed that way at Gethsemane[8] as the Lord knelt praying.

Mary's moving around brought me wide-awake. The black of night was fading.

"I guess it's all right," Mary said. "I'd be able to tell by now, wouldn't I?"

I answered gruffly, "I don't know."

---

7. **Peter:** one of the twelve apostles, also called Simon Peter or Saint Peter.
8. **Gethsemane** (gĕth-sĕm′ə-nē): The garden outside Jerusalem where Jesus was arrested (Matthew 26:36–57).

Mary stood in the doorway for a while, looking out at the dripping world as if she found it beautiful. The she fried slices of the mushroom while the little girls danced with anxiety.

We feasted, we three, my sisters and I, until Mary ruled, "That'll hold you," and would not cook any more. She didn't touch any of the mushroom herself.

That was a strange day in the moldy cabin. Mary laughed and was gay; she told stories, and we played "Who's Got the Thimble?" with a pine cone.

In the afternoon we heard a shout, and my sisters screamed and I ran ahead of them across the clearing.

The rain had stopped. My father came plunging out of the woods leading a pack horse—and well I remember the treasures of food in that pack.

He glanced at us anxiously as he tore at the ropes that bound the pack.

"Where's the other one?" he demanded.

Mary came out of the cabin then, walking sedately. As she came toward us, the sun began to shine.

My stepmother was a wonderful woman.

CHECK-UP (Short Answer)

1. Why doesn't Pa want to have Mary travel with the family?
2. Why does the group stop at the cabin?
3. Where does Pa go when he leaves Mary and the children at the cabin?
4. Why does Mary refuse at first to give any of the mushroom to the children?
5. How do you know that Mary stays on with the family?

FOR DISCUSSION

1. Pa makes it clear that he doesn't want to take anyone else along on the trip. Why, then, does he allow Mary to join the family?
2. How does Mary save the children from starving?
3. How does Mary show that she has a strong will and courage? How does she show that she can be gentle?
4. At the end of the story, what change occurs in the family's attitude toward Mary?
5. Explain the title of the story.

SETTING
Setting and Plot

In some stories, setting is incidental to the characters and action. The story "You Can't Take It with You" (page 22) would be effective if it were set in a large city or small town, or at any season of the year. The plot of that story depends upon the vices and follies of human beings, and not upon their environment. In other stories, setting is a crucial element. "The Dinner Party" (page 1), for example, would not be believable if the action were set in England rather than in India, for the cobra is not native to Great Britain.

The events in "Too Soon a Woman" take place in a setting unique to American history. Although no specific time or place is mentioned in the story, we know that the background is the Old West and that the characters are pioneers. References to the prairie, to homesteaders, to the great distances traveled, and to the hardships endured by the settlers are typical in Western stories. The main action of the story tells of the desperate courage that was necessary for survival in this vast, uninhabited land.

Find at least five details in the story that give you a sense of what life was like on the frontier.

UNDERSTANDING THE WORDS
IN THE STORY (Matching Columns)

1. scowled
2. gaunt
3. grim
4. whimpered
5. rummaged
6. squalling
7. savoring
8. gruffly
9. anxiety
10. sedately

a. cried softly
b. roughly
c. loud crying
d. calmly
e. frowned
f. eagerness
g. thin
h. searched thoroughly
i. enjoying
j. severe

FOR WRITING

1. Conflict, as you have seen, can be external or internal, and there may be more than one kind of conflict in a story. What is the primary conflict in "Too Soon a Woman"? Present your opinion in a short essay.
2. Examine the role of the land in this story. Is it an enemy or a friend? Support your answer with references to the story.
3. In most Western stories, the main character is a man. In this story, the central character is a woman. In a short essay discuss the heroic qualities that Mary possesses.

*"Colm was delighted. He looked around
and saw no one. The nest was his."*

THE
WILD
DUCK'S NEST

Michael McLaverty

The sun was setting, spilling gold light on the low western hills of Rathlin Island.[1] A small boy walked jauntily along a hoof-printed path that wriggled between the folds of these hills and opened out into a craterlike valley on the clifftop. Presently he stopped as if remembering something, then suddenly he left the path, and began running up one of the hills. When he reached the top he was out of breath and stood watching streaks of light radiating from golden-edged clouds, the scene reminding him of a picture he had seen of the Transfiguration.[2] A short distance below him was the cow standing at the edge of a reedy lake. Colm[3] ran down to meet her waving his stick in the air, and the wind rumbling in his ears made him give an exultant whoop which splashed upon the hills in a shower of echoed sound. A flock of gulls lying on the short grass near the lake rose up languidly, drifting like blown snowflakes over the rim of the cliff.

The lake faced west and was fed by a stream, the drain-

---

1. **Rathlin Island:** an island a few miles off the northern coast of Ireland.
2. **the Transfiguration:** an event in the life of Jesus Christ, told in Matthew 17:1–8.
3. **Colm** (kŭl′əm).

ings of the semicircling hills. One side was open to the winds from the sea and in winter a little outlet trickled over the cliffs making a black vein in their gray sides. The boy lifted stones and began throwing them into the lake, weaving web after web on its calm surface. Then he skimmed the water with flat stones, some of them jumping the surface and coming to rest on the other side. He was delighted with himself and after listening to his echoing shouts of delight he ran to fetch his cow. Gently he tapped her on the side and reluctantly she went towards the brown-mudded path that led out of the valley. The boy was about to throw a final stone into the lake when a bird flew low over his head, its neck astrain, and its orange-colored legs clear in the soft light. It was a wild duck. It circled the lake twice, thrice, coming lower each time and then with a nervous flapping of wings it skidded along the surface, its legs breaking the water into a series of silvery arcs. Its wings closed, it lit silently, gave a slight shiver, and began pecking indifferently at the water.

Colm with dilated eyes eagerly watched it making for the farther end of the lake. It meandered[4] between tall bulrushes[5], its body black and solid as stone against the graying water. Then as if it had sunk it was gone. The boy ran stealthily along the bank looking away from the lake, pretending indifference. When he came opposite to where he had last seen the bird he stopped and peered through the sighing reeds whose shadows streaked the water in a maze of black strokes. In front of him was a soddy islet guarded by the spears of sedge[6] and separated from the bank by a narrow channel of water. The water wasn't too deep—he could wade across with care.

Rolling up his short trousers he began to wade, his arms

---

4. **meandered** (mē-ăn′dərd): wandered aimlessly, without a set direction.
5. **bulrushes** (bool′rŭsh′ĭz): grasslike plants.
6. **sedge**: a grasslike plant with pointed leaves.

outstretched, and his legs brown and stunted in the mountain water. As he drew near the islet, his feet sank in the cold mud and bubbles winked up at him. He went more carefully and nervously. Then one trouser fell and dipped into the water; the boy dropped his hands to roll it up, he unbalanced, made a splashing sound, and the bird arose with a squawk and whirred away over the cliffs. For a moment the boy stood frightened. Then he clambered onto the wet-soaked sod of land, which was spattered with sea gulls' feathers and bits of wind-blown rushes.

Into each hummock[7] he looked, pulling back the long grass. At last he came on the nest, facing seawards. Two flat rocks dimpled the face of the water and between them was a neck of land matted with coarse grass containing the nest. It was untidily built of dried rushes, straw and feathers, and in it lay one solitary egg. Colm was delighted. He looked around and saw no one. The nest was his. He lifted the egg, smooth and green as the sky, with a faint tinge of yellow like the reflected light from a buttercup; and then he felt he had done wrong. He put it back. He knew he shouldn't have touched it and he wondered would the bird forsake the nest. A vague sadness stole over him and he felt in his heart he had sinned. Carefully smoothing out his footprints he hurriedly left the islet and ran after his cow. The sun had now set and the cold shiver of evening enveloped him, chilling his body and saddening his mind.

In the morning he was up and away to school. He took the grass rut that edged the road for it was softer on the bare feet. His house was the last on the western headland and after a mile or so he was joined by Paddy McFall; both boys dressed in similar hand-knitted blue jerseys and gray trousers carried homemade schoolbags. Colm was full of the nest and as soon as he joined his companion he said eagerly:

---

7. **hummock** (hŭm′ək): a small mound of earth.

"Paddy, I've a nest—a wild duck's with one egg."

"And how do you know it's a wild duck's?" asked Paddy slightly jealous.

"Sure I saw her with my own two eyes, her brown speckled back with a crow's patch on it, and her yellow legs——"

"Where is it?" interrupted Paddy in a challenging tone.

"I'm not going to tell you, for you'd rob it!"

"Aach! I suppose it's a tame duck's you have or maybe an old gull's."

Colm put out his tongue at him. "A lot you know!" he said, "for a gull's egg has spots and this one is greenish-white, for I had it in my hand."

And then the words he didn't want to hear rushed from Paddy in a mocking chant, "You had it in your hand! . . . She'll forsake it! She'll forsake it! She'll forsake it!" he said, skipping along the road before him.

Colm felt as if he would choke or cry with vexation.

His mind told him that Paddy was right, but somehow he couldn't give in to it and he replied: "She'll not forsake it! She'll not! I know she'll not!"

But in school his faith wavered. Through the windows he could see moving sheets of rain—rain that dribbled down the panes filling his mind with thoughts of the lake creased and chilled by wind; the nest sodden and black with wetness; and the egg cold as a cave stone. He shivered from the thoughts and fidgeted with the inkwell cover, sliding it backwards and forwards mechanically. The mischievous look had gone from his eyes and the school day dragged on interminably. But at last they were out in the rain, Colm rushing home as fast as he could.

He was no time at all at his dinner of potatoes and salted fish until he was out in the valley now smoky with drifts of slanting rain. Opposite the islet he entered the water. The wind was blowing into his face, rustling noisily the rushes heavy with the dust of rain. A moss cheeper,[8] swaying on a reed like a mouse, filled the air with light cries of loneliness.

The boy reached the islet, his heart thumping with excitement, wondering did the bird forsake. He went slowly, quietly onto the strip of land that led to the nest. He rose on his toes, looking over the ledge to see if he could see her. And then every muscle tautened.[9] She was on, her shoulders hunched up, and her bill lying on her breast as if she were asleep. Colm's heart hammered wildly in his ears. She hadn't forsaken. He was about to turn stealthily away. Something happened. The bird moved, her neck straightened, twitching nervously from side to side. The boy's head swam with lightness. He stood transfixed. The wild duck with a panicky flapping, rose heavily, and flew off towards the sea. . . . A guilty silence enveloped the boy. . . . He turned to go away, hesitated, and glanced back at the bare nest; it'd be no harm to have a look. Timidly he approached it, standing straight, and gazing over the edge. There in the nest lay two eggs. He drew in his breath with delight, splashed quickly from the island, and ran off whistling in the rain.

8. **moss cheeper:** a songbird.
9. **tautened** (tôt′nd): grew tense.

CHECK-UP (Multiple-Choice)

1. The period of time covered by this story is
   a. a little more than a week
   b. approximately twenty-four hours
   c. one afternoon and one evening
2. Colm follows the bird in order to
   a. catch and tame it
   b. rob its nest
   c. discover its nesting place
3. Paddy is Colm's
   a. cousin
   b. older brother
   c. schoolmate
4. Colm's chief fear is that
   a. the bird will desert its nest
   b. Paddy will steal the duck's egg
   c. the rain will destroy the nest
5. Colm is relieved when
   a. the bird moves on the nest
   b. he sees a second egg in the nest
   c. the wild duck flies off toward the sea

FOR DISCUSSION

1. In the first part of the story, we get a sense that Colm lives in harmony with nature. Which details express his delight in the beauty and wonder of nature?
2. Colm is unusually sensitive to the natural world. Why, then, does he pursue the wild duck and lift its egg from the nest?
3. You have seen that in some stories the central conflict is internal. Although Colm comes into brief conflict with Paddy, the most important conflict in the story is the psychological conflict within Colm. Explain why he is torn by guilt.

4. How is Colm's conflict resolved at the end of the story?
5. Do you think Colm will visit the nest again? Give reasons for your answer.

SETTING
Setting and Character

Setting which is presented effectively tends to make us believe in fictional characters and events. The realistic and recognizable streets of Dublin, described so vividly in "The Sniper" (page 101), help make the actions and individuals of that story credible. The wholly imaginary setting of the planet Venus in "All Summer in a Day" (page 91) is rendered so convincingly that we are willing to accept the existence of that alien world.

Setting may do more than create an illusion of reality. Setting may also be a means of revealing character to us. The environment in which a character lives may help us understand that character's motives and behavior. In stories where the primary conflict is internal, rather than external, details of setting may indicate a character's states of mind.

In "The Wild Duck's Nest," the setting is a key to Colm's thoughts and feelings. At the opening of the story, we know how happy and carefree Colm is by his response to the setting. His race to the top of a hill where he watches a radiant sunset, his "exultant whoop," his delight in the lake and in the wild duck, all show us how sensitive Colm is to the beauty and wonder of nature. After he lifts the egg and feels that he has sinned against nature, the setting changes dramatically, signaling a change in Colm's state of mind. The "cold shiver of evening" surrounds him.

How does the setting reflect Colm's inner conflict on the following day? Find descriptive details that mirror his sadness and concern.

UNDERSTANDING THE WORDS IN THE STORY (Multiple-Choice)

1. Colm walked *jauntily* along the path.
   a. carefully
   b. boldly
   c. cheerfully
2. He let out a cry that was *exultant.*
   a. terrifying
   b. joyful
   c. wild
3. The gulls rose into the air *languidly.*
   a. actively
   b. quickly
   c. lazily
4. The flat stones *skimmed* the water.
   a. bounced along the surface of
   b. passed over
   c. caused ripples in
5. The cow went out of the valley *reluctantly.*
   a. unwillingly
   b. slowly
   c. nervously
6. The wild duck pecked *indifferently* at the water in the lake.
   a. hungrily
   b. without interest
   c. in rapid, skillful movements
7. Colm watched the bird with *dilated* eyes.
   a. half-closed
   b. wide-open
   c. tear-filled
8. The shadows of the reeds formed a *maze* of black streaks.
   a. complicated network
   b. simple pattern
   c. pleasing arrangement

9. Colm waded to the *islet.*
   a. isthmus
   b. small island
   c. peninsula
10. Frightened, the bird *whirred* away over the cliff.
    a. flew in a circular motion
    b. moved quickly and softly
    c. flew quickly with a swishing sound .

(Matching Columns)

1. clambered	a. thickly covered
2. spattered	b. completely soaked
3. matted	c. made motionless
4. forsake	d. climbed with difficulty
5. vague	e. endlessly
6. vexation	f. became unsure
7. wavered	g. spotted
8. sodden	h. indefinite
9. interminably	i. desert
10. transfixed	j. annoyance

FOR WRITING

1. In a short essay give a summary of the plot of "The Wild Duck's Nest." Include a discussion of the conflict, climax, and resolution of the story.
2. Show how McLaverty uses direct and indirect methods of characterization in presenting his main character. Be sure to include the role of setting in revealing character.

"It was all so creepy.
Nothing was real, nothing was natural,
all seemed a mystery."

FATHER
AND I

Pär Lagerkvist°

I remember one Sunday afternoon when I was about ten
years old, Daddy took my hand and we went for a walk in the
woods to hear the birds sing. We waved goodbye to mother,
who was staying at home to prepare supper, and so couldn't
go with us. The sun was bright and warm as we set out
briskly on our way. We didn't take this bird singing too seriously, as though it was something special or unusual. We
were sensible people, Daddy and I. We were used to the
woods and the creatures in them, so we didn't make any fuss
about it. It was just because it was Sunday afternoon and
Daddy was free. We went along the railway line where other
people aren't allowed to go, but Daddy belonged to the railway and had a right to. And in this way we came direct into
the woods and did not need to take a roundabout way. Then
the bird song and all the rest began at once. They chirped in
the bushes; hedge sparrows, thrushes, and warblers; and we
heard all the noises of the little creatures as we came into the
woods. The ground was thick with anemones,[1] the birches
were dressed in their new leaves, and the pines had young,
green shoots. There was such a pleasant smell everywhere.

° **Pär Lagerkvist** (pâr lä′gûr-kvĭst).
1. **anemones** (ə-nĕm′ə-nēz): plants with colorful cup-shaped flowers.

The mossy ground was steaming a little, because the sun was shining upon it. Everywhere there was life and noise; bumblebees flew out of their holes, midges circled where it was damp. The birds shot out of the bushes to catch them and then dived back again. All of a sudden a train came rushing along and we had to go down the embankment.[2] Daddy hailed the driver with two fingers to his Sunday hat: the driver saluted and waved his hand. Everything seemed on the move. As we went on our way along the sleepers[3] which lay and oozed tar in the sunshine, there was a smell of everything, machine oil and almond blossom, tar and heather, all mixed. We took big steps from sleeper to sleeper so as not to step among the stones, which were rough to walk on, and wore your shoes out. The rails shone in the sunshine. On both sides of the line stood the telephone poles that sang as we went by them. Yes! That was a fine day! The sky was absolutely clear. There wasn't a single cloud to be seen: there just couldn't be any on a day like this, according to what Daddy said. After a while we came to a field of oats on the right side of the line, where a farmer, whom we knew, had a clearing. The oats had grown thick and even; Daddy looked at it knowingly, and I could feel that he was satisfied. I didn't understand that sort of thing much, because I was born in town. Then we came to the bridge over the brook that mostly hadn't much water in it, but now there was plenty. We took hands so that we shouldn't fall down between the sleepers. From there it wasn't far to the railway gatekeeper's little place, which was quite buried in green. There were apple trees and gooseberry bushes right close to the house. We went in there, to pay a visit, and they offered us milk. We looked at the pigs, the hens, and the fruit trees, which were

2. **embankment** (ĕm-băngk′mənt): a pile of earth heaped up to support the ties and rails of the railroad.
3. **sleepers:** ties supporting the railroad track.

in full blossom, and then we went on again. We wanted to go
to the river, because there it was prettier than anywhere else.
There was something special about the river, because higher
upstream it flowed past Daddy's old home. We never liked
going back before we got to it, and, as usual, this time we got
there after a fair walk. It wasn't far to the next station; but we
didn't go on there. Daddy just looked to see whether the signals were right. He thought of everything. We stopped by the
river, where it flowed broad and friendly in the sunshine,
and the thick leafy trees on the banks mirrored themselves in
the calm water. It was all so fresh and bright. A breeze came
from the little lakes higher up. We climbed down the bank,
went a little way along the very edge. Daddy showed me the
fishing spots. When he was a boy he used to sit there on the
stones and wait for perch all day long. Often he didn't get a
single bite, but it was a delightful way to spend the day. Now
he never had time. We played about for some time by the
side of the river, and threw in pieces of bark that the current
carried away, and we threw stones to see who could throw
farthest. We were, by nature, very merry and cheerful,
Daddy and I. After a while we felt a bit tired. We thought we
had played enough, so we started off home again.

Then it began to get dark. The woods were changed. It
wasn't quite dark yet, but almost. We made haste. Maybe
mother was getting anxious, and waiting supper. She was
always afraid that something might happen, though nothing
had. This had been a splendid day. Everything had been just
as it should, and we were satisfied with it all. It was getting
darker and darker, and the trees were so queer. They stood
and listened for the sound of footsteps, as though they didn't
know who we were. There was a glowworm under one of
them. It lay down there in the dark and stared at us. I held
Daddy's hand tight, but he didn't seem to notice the strange
light: he just went on. It was quite dark when we came to the

bridge over the stream. It was roaring down underneath us as if it wanted to swallow us up, as the ground seemed to open under us. We went along the sleepers carefully, holding hands tight so that we shouldn't fall in. I thought Daddy would carry me over, but he didn't say anything about it. I suppose he wanted me to be like him, and not think anything of it. We went on. Daddy was so calm in the darkness, walking with even steps without speaking. He was thinking his own thoughts. I couldn't understand how he could be so calm when everything was so ghostly. I looked round scared. It was nothing but darkness everywhere. I hardly dared to breathe deeply, because then the darkness comes into one, and that was dangerous, I thought. One must die soon. I remember quite well thinking so then. The railway embankment was very steep. It finished in black night. The telephone posts stood up ghostlike against the sky, mumbling deep inside as though someone were speaking, way down in the earth. The white china hats sat there scared, cowering with fear, listening. It was all so creepy. Nothing was real, nothing was natural, all seemed a mystery. I went closer to Daddy, and whispered: "Why is it so creepy when it's dark?"

"No, child, it isn't creepy," he said, and took my hand.

"Oh, yes, but it is, Daddy."

"No, you mustn't think that. We know there is a God don't we?" I felt so lonely, so abandoned. It was queer that it was only me that was frightened, and not Daddy. It was queer that we didn't feel the same about it. And it was queerer still that what he said didn't help, didn't stop me being frightened. Not even what he said about God helped. The thought of God made one feel creepy too. It was creepy to think that He was everywhere here in the darkness, down there under the trees, and in the telephone posts that mumbled so—probably that was Him everywhere. But all the same one could never see Him.

We went along silently, each of us thinking his own thoughts. My heart felt cramped as though the darkness had come in and was squeezing it.

Then, when we were in a bend, we suddenly heard a great noise behind us. We were startled out of our thoughts. Daddy pulled me down the embankment and held me tight, and a train rushed by; a black train. The lights were out in all the carriages, as it whizzed past us. What could it be? There shouldn't be any train now. We looked at it, frightened. The furnace roared in the big engine, where they shovelled in coal, and the sparks flew out into the night. It was terrible. The driver stood so pale and immovable, with such a stony look in the glare. Daddy didn't recognize him—didn't know who he was. He was just looking ahead as though he was driving straight into darkness, far into darkness, which had no end.

Startled and panting with fear I looked after the wild thing. It was swallowed up in the night. Daddy helped me up onto the line, and we hurried home. He said, "That was strange! What train was that I wonder? And I didn't know the driver either." Then he didn't say any more.

I was shaking all over. That had been for me—for my sake. I guessed what it meant. It was all the fear which would come to me, all the unknown; all that Daddy didn't know about, and couldn't save me from. That was how the world would be for me, and the strange life I should live; not like Daddy's, where everyone was known and sure. It wasn't a real world, or a real life—it just rushed burning into the darkness which had no end.

CHECK-UP (True/False)

1. The child and his father set out one Sunday afternoon to inspect the railway line.
2. The father shows the child how to fish for perch.
3. In the dark the child begins to feel that nothing is natural.
4. The father pulls the child down the embankment to save him from a speeding train.
5. The child concludes that it is dangerous to walk along the railway line.

FOR DISCUSSION

1. The child narrates that his father "belonged to the railway." What special privileges does this entitle them to? What are the unforeseen consequences of these privileges?
2. During the first half of the story, the child feels completely secure in his father's company. At what point does his sense of trust begin to fail him?
3. At the end of the story, the child realizes that his father cannot protect him from life—the great unknown that lies ahead. In what way does the incident of the unscheduled train make this clear to him?

SETTING
Setting and Mood

Setting is an important element in creating or evoking mood in short stories. In "Father and I," the physical world and the child's inner world are related. In the first half of the story, the child's sense of security and well-being seems to be a reflection of the peace and order in nature. Sights, sounds, and smells are all delightful. The child feels protected by his father and comforted by the familiar surroundings.

The mood of the story changes as night descends. The world of nature becomes mysterious, and the child feels frightened and isolated. His uncertainty and terror build to a climax in the unscheduled appearance of a train that almost kills them.

Find details in the description of the landscape that reveal the harmony and pleasures of nature. Find details that register the child's growing fear of the physical world.

UNDERSTANDING THE WORDS
IN THE STORY (Matching Columns)

1. briskly	a. steadfast
2. hailed	b. energetically
3. oozed	c. crouching in fear
4. mirrored	d. blinding light
5. anxious	e. leaked out
6. cowering	f. unfeeling
7. abandoned	g. greeted
8. immovable	h. worried
9. stony	i. showed a reflection
10. glare	j. deserted

FOR WRITING

1. In a brief essay tell how the contrasting settings in the story mirror the child's thoughts and feelings.
2. Consider the characterization of children in "All Summer in a Day" (page 91), "The Wild Duck's Nest" (page 118), and "Father and I." Which of these stories do you think depicts children most believably? Give reasons for your answer.

Point of View

*"It is impossible to say how first
the idea entered my brain; but once conceived,
it haunted me day and night."*

THE
TELL-TALE
HEART

Edgar Allan Poe

True!—nervous—very, very dreadfully nervous I had been and am; but why *will* you say that I am mad? The disease had sharpened my senses—not destroyed—not dulled them. Above all was the sense of hearing acute. I heard all things in the heaven and in the earth. I heard many things in hell. How, then, am I mad? Hearken![1] and observe how healthily—how calmly I can tell you the whole story.

It is impossible to say how first the idea entered my brain; but once conceived, it haunted me day and night. Object there was none. Passion there was none. I loved the old man. He had never wronged me. He had never given me insult. For his gold I had no desire. I think it was his eye! yes, it was this! One of his eyes resembled that of a vulture—a pale blue eye, with a film over it. Whenever it fell upon me,

1. **Hearken** (här′kən): listen.

my blood ran cold; and so by degrees—very gradually—I made up my mind to take the life of the old man, and thus rid myself of the eye forever.

Now this is the point. You fancy[2] me mad. Madmen know nothing. But you should have seen *me.* You should have seen how wisely I proceeded—with what caution— with what foresight—with what dissimulation[3] I went to work! I was never kinder to the old man than during the whole week before I killed him. And every night, about midnight, I turned the latch of his door and opened it—oh, so gently! And then, when I had made an opening sufficient for my head, I put in a dark lantern,[4] all closed, closed, so that no light shone out, and then I thrust in my head. Oh, you would have laughed to see how cunningly I thrust it in! I moved it slowly—very, very slowly, so that I might not disturb the old man's sleep. It took me an hour to place my whole head within the opening so far that I could see him as he lay upon his bed. Ha!—would a madman have been so wise as this? And then, when my head was well in the room, I undid the lantern cautiously–oh, so cautiously—cautiously (for the hinges creaked)—I undid it just so much that a single thin ray fell upon the vulture eye. And this I did for seven long nights—every night just at midnight—but I found the eye always closed; and so it was impossible to do the work; for it was not the old man who vexed me, but his Evil Eye. And every morning, when the day broke, I went boldly into the chamber, and spoke courageously to him, calling him by name in a hearty tone, and inquiring how he had passed the night. So you see he would have been a very profound old man, indeed, to suspect that every night, just at twelve, I looked in upon him while he slept.

Upon the eighth night I was more than usually cautious

2. **fancy** (făn′sē): imagine; suppose.
3. **dissimulation** (dĭ-sĭm′yə-lā′shən): concealment of intentions.
4. **dark lantern:** a lantern with a panel or shutter to block its light.

in opening the door. A watch's minute hand moves more quickly than did mine. Never before that night had I *felt* the extent of my own powers—of my sagacity.[5] I could scarcely contain my feelings of triumph. To think that there I was, opening the door, little by little, and he not even to dream of my secret deeds or thoughts. I fairly chuckled at the idea; and perhaps he heard me; for he moved on the bed suddenly, as if startled. Now you may think that I drew back—but no. His room was as black as pitch with the thick darkness (for the shutters were close fastened, through fear of robbers), and so I know that he could not see the opening of the door, and I kept pushing it on steadily, steadily.

I had my head in, and was about to open the lantern, when my thumb slipped upon the tin fastening, and the old man sprang up in the bed, crying out—"Who's there?"

I kept quite still and said nothing. For a whole hour I did not move a muscle, and in the meantime I did not hear him lie down. He was still sitting up in the bed listening—just as I have done, night after night, hearkening to the death-watches[6] in the wall.

Presently I heard a slight groan, and I knew it was the groan of mortal terror. It was not a groan of pain or of grief—oh, no!—it was the low stifled sound that arises from the bottom of the soul when overcharged with awe. I knew the sound well. Many a night, just at midnight, when all the world slept, it has welled up from my own bosom, deepening, with its dreadful echo, the terrors that distracted me. I say I knew it well. I knew what the old man felt, and pitied him, although I chuckled at heart. I knew that he had been lying awake ever since the first slight noise, when he had turned in the bed. His fears had been ever since growing

---

5. **sagacity** (sǝ-găs'ǝ-tē): shrewdness.
6. **deathwatches** (dĕth'wŏch'ǝs): beetles that make a clicking sound when they strike their heads against wood. According to superstition, they are a forewarning of death.

upon him. He had been trying to fancy them causeless, but could not. He had been saying to himself—"It is nothing but the wind in the chimney—it is only a mouse crossing the floor," or "It is merely a cricket which has made a single chirp." Yes, he had been trying to comfort himself with these suppositions;[7] but he had found all in vain. *All in vain;* because Death, in approaching him, had stalked with his black shadow before him, and enveloped the victim. And it was the mournful influence of the unperceived[8] shadow that caused him to feel—although he neither saw nor heard—to *feel* the presence of my head within the room.

When I had waited a long time, very patiently, without hearing him lie down, I resolved to open a little—a very, very little crevice[9] in the lantern. So I opened it—you cannot imagine how stealthily, stealthily—until, at length, a single dim ray, like the thread of the spider, shot from out the crevice and full upon the vulture eye.

It was open—wide, wide open—and I grew furious as I gazed upon it. I saw it with perfect distinctness—all a dull blue, with a hideous veil over it that chilled the very marrow in my bones; but I could see nothing else of the old man's face or person: for I had directed the ray as if by instinct, precisely upon the damned spot.

And now have I not told you that what you mistake for madness is but overacuteness of the senses?—now, I say, there came to my ears a low, dull, quick sound, such as a watch makes when enveloped in cotton. I knew *that* sound well too. It was the beating of the old man's heart. It increased my fury, as the beating of a drum stimulates the soldier into courage.

But even yet I refrained and kept still. I scarcely breathed. I held the lantern motionless. I tried how steadily I

7. **suppositions** (sŭp'ə-zĭsh'əns): ideas accepted without proof.
8. **unperceived** (ŭn'pər-sēvd'): unseen and unheard.
9. **crevice** (krĕv'ĭs): an opening.

could maintain the ray upon the eye. Meantime the hellish tattoo[10] of the heart increased. It grew quicker and quicker, and louder and louder every instant. The old man's terror *must* have been extreme! It grew louder, I say, louder every moment!—do you mark[11] me well? I have told you that I am nervous: so I am. And now at the dead hour of the night, amid the dreadful silence of that old house, so strange a noise as this excited me to uncontrollable terror. Yet, for some minutes longer I refrained and stood still. But the beating grew louder, louder! I thought the heart must burst. And now a new anxiety seized me—the sound would be heard by a neighbor! The old man's hour had come! With a loud yell, I threw open the lantern and leaped into the room. He shrieked once—once only. In an instant I dragged him to the floor, and pulled the heavy bed over him. I then smiled gaily, to find the deed so far done. But, for many minutes, the heart beat on with a muffled sound. This, however, did not vex me; it would not be heard through the wall. At length it ceased. The old man was dead. I removed the bed and examined the corpse. Yes, he was stone, stone dead. I placed my hand upon the heart and held it there many minutes. There was no pulsation. He was stone dead. His eye would trouble me no more.

If still you think me mad, you will think so no longer when I describe the wise precautions I took for the concealment of the body. The night waned,[12] and I worked hastily, but in silence. First of all I dismembered the corpse. I cut off the head and the arms and the legs.

I then took up three planks from the flooring of the chamber, and deposited all between the scantlings.[13] I then

10. **tattoo** (tă-tōo′): a continuous, even beating.
11. **mark** (märk): pay attention to.
12. **waned** (wānd): drew to an end.
13. **scantlings** (skănt′lĭngz): small upright pieces beneath the floorboards.

replaced the boards so cleverly, so cunningly, that no human eye—not even *his*—could have detected anything wrong. There was nothing to wash out—no stain of any kind—no blood spot whatever. I had been too wary for that. A tub had caught all—ha! ha!

When I had made an end of these labors, it was four o'clock—still dark as midnight. As the bell sounded the hour, there came a knocking at the street door. I went down to open it with a light heart—for what had I *now* to fear? There entered three men, who introduced themselves, with perfect suavity,[14] as officers of the police. A shriek had been heard by a neighbor during the night; suspicion of foul play had been aroused; information had been lodged at the police office, and they (the officers) had been deputed[15] to search the premises.

I smiled—for *what* had I to fear? I bade the gentlemen welcome. The shriek, I said, was my own in a dream. The old man, I mentioned, was absent in the country. I took my visitors all over the house. I bade them search—search *well*. I led them, at length, to *his* chamber. I showed them his treasures, secure, undisturbed. In the enthusiasm of my confidence, I brought chairs into the room, and desired them *here* to rest from their fatigues, while I myself, in the wild audacity[16] of my perfect triumph, placed my own seat upon the very spot beneath which reposed the corpse of the victim.

The officers were satisfied. My *manner* had convinced them. I was singularly at ease. They sat, and while I answered cheerily, they chatted familiar things. But, ere long, I felt myself getting pale and wished them gone. My head ached, and I fancied a ringing in my ears: but still they sat and still chatted. The ringing became more distinct; I talked

---

14. **suavity** (swäv′ə-tē, swāv-): graciousness, refinement.
15. **deputed** (dĭ-pyōō′təd): assigned.
16. **audacity** (ô-dăs′ə-tē): boldness.

more freely to get rid of the feelings, but it continued and gained definitiveness—until, at length, I found that the noise was *not* within my ears.

No doubt I now grew *very* pale—but I talked more fluently, and with a heightened voice. Yet the sound increased—and what could I do? It was *a low, dull, quick sound—much such a sound as a watch makes when enveloped in cotton.* I gasped for breath—and yet the officers heard it not. I talked more quickly—more vehemently;[17] but the noise steadily increased. I arose and argued about trifles, in a high key and with violent gesticulations,[18] but the noise steadily increased. Why *would* they not be gone? I paced the floor to and fro with heavy strides, as if excited to fury by the observation of the men—but the noise steadily increased. Oh what *could* I do? I foamed—I raved—I swore! I swung the chair upon which I had been sitting, and grated it upon the boards, but the noise arose over all and continually increased. It grew louder—louder—*louder!* And still the men chatted pleasantly, and smiled. Was it possible they heard not? No, no! They heard!—they suspected!—they *knew!* they were making a mockery of my horror!—this I thought, and this I think. But anything was better than this agony! Anything was more tolerable than this derision![19] I could bear those hypocritical smiles no longer! I felt that I must scream or die!—and now—again!—hark! louder! louder! louder! *louder!*—

"Villains!" I shrieked, "dissemble[20] no more! I admit the deed!—tear up the planks!—here, here!—it is the beating of his hideous heart!"

17. **vehemently** (vē′ə-mənt-lē): forcefully.
18. **gesticulations** (jĕ-stĭk′yə-lā′shənz): vigorous movements of the limbs or body.
19. **derision** (dĭ-rĭzh′ən): ridicule.
20. **dissemble** (dĭ-sĕm′bəl): pretend.

CHECK-UP (Multiple-Choice)

1. The narrator claims that his keenest sense is his sense of
   a. smell   b. touch   c. hearing

2. The narrator admits to being
   a. mad   b. nervous   c. depressed

3. His object in killing the old man is
   a. to possess his gold
   b. to revenge an insult
   c. to get rid of an obsession

4. The narrator is most pleased by his own
   a. cleverness   b. strength   c. courage

5. The sight of the old man's eye arouses the narrator's
   a. fear   b. fury   c. curiosity

6. Before he kills the old man, the narrator is aware of
   a. the ticking of a clock
   b. the sound of a drum
   c. the beating of a human heart

7. The narrator hides the body in
   a. the old man's room
   b. the parlor
   c. the bathroom

8. A neighbor reports hearing a
   a. loud shriek
   b. drumbeat
   c. ringing noise

9. When the police first arrive, the narrator feels
   a. vaguely uneasy
   b. very angry
   c. completely confident

10. The narrator suspects the police of
    a. brutality   b. cunning   c. hypocrisy

FOR DISCUSSION

1. At the opening of the story, the narrator is trying to convince someone of his sanity. What examples does he use to demonstrate his sanity? To whom do you think he is speaking?
2. The narrator claims that his sense of hearing is extremely sharp. What instances does he give of his sensitivity to sound? How do these instances reveal that he is insane?
3. What is the narrator's motive for killing the old man? Why does he wait until the eighth night to commit the murder?
4. What causes the narrator to lose control at the end of the story?

POINT OF VIEW
First-Person Point of View

The person who tells a story is called the *narrator,* and the angle from which the story is told is called its *point of view.* A story can be told by someone who is a character in the story or by an outside observer.

"The Tell-Tale Heart" is told from the inside, through the words of the main character. This point of view, in which the narrator speaks as "I," is known as the *first-person point of view.*

The first-person point of view has the advantage of adding immediacy to a story—we get the story directly from one of its characters. The first-person point of view also has its limitations. The reader sees the events from the vantage point of only one character. That character can reveal his or her feelings, thoughts, and observations, but cannot get into the minds of other characters. As a result, the reader must determine whether the narrator's impressions are to be trusted.

Poe gives his readers sufficient clues to indicate that the narrator of "The Tell-Tale Heart" is mad, and therefore unreliable as a narrator. However, much of the interest of the story arises from the operations of the madman's mind.

At what points in the story did your interpretations of the action differ from that of the narrator?

Point out several instances of dramatic irony, when you were aware of things that the narrator did not perceive.

UNDERSTANDING THE WORDS IN THE STORY (Multiple-Choice)

1. The narrator claims that his sense of hearing is *acute.*
   a. serious
   b. sharp
   c. painful
2. Once the idea of murder was *conceived,* he was haunted by it.
   a. imagined
   b. declared
   c. confided
3. He opened the door and *thrust* his head into the room.
   a. slipped
   b. poked
   c. crammed
4. He was *vexed* by the Evil Eye.
   a. delayed
   b. irritated
   c. enchanted
5. Only a *profound* person could have suspected his plan.
   a. suspicious
   b. highly intelligent
   c. sane

6. The old man *stifled* a groan.
   a. smothered
   b. grumbled
   c. uttered
7. The narrator often felt his soul filled with *awe.*
   a. grief and pain
   b. rage and jealousy
   c. wonder and fear
8. Dreadful sounds would *well up* from his soul at midnight.
   a. come
   b. fall
   c. rise
9. He was *distracted* by terrors.
   a. confused
   b. entertained
   c. frightened
10. The victim tried to imagine that all his fears were *causeless.*
    a. unnecessary
    b. unfounded
    c. silly

(Matching Columns)

1. stalked	a. showing grief
2. enveloped	b. cut into pieces
3. mournful	c. very careful
4. resolved	d. held back
5. refrained	e. care taken beforehand
6. precaution	f. covered or surrounded
7. dismembered	g. set down
8. deposited	h. cleverly
9. cunningly	i. approached secretly
10. wary	j. determined

(Completion)

Choose one of the words in the following list to complete each of the sentences below. A word may be used once.

lodged	grated
premises	mockery
reposed	agony
fluently	tolerable
heightened	hypocritical

1. At first the narrator spoke _____ while the police sat and listened.

2. The police made a search of the _____.

3. A neighbor had _____ a complaint with the police.

4. He believed that the police knew the truth and were making a (an) _____ of his feelings.

5. He _____ a chair against the floor.

6. The remains of the victim _____ under the planks.

7. He was unable to endure the _____ any longer.

8. He spoke with a (an) _____ voice.

9. He could not bear their false, _____ smiles.

10. Anything would be more _____ than their pretense.

FOR WRITING

1. Imagine that you are one of the police officers sent to investigate suspicion of foul play. Write an eyewitness account of what you observe.

2. To whom is the narrator telling this story? Is he talking to the police? to his lawyer? to a doctor? to a cell mate? Or is he ranting to himself? Write a short paper giving your opinion of the circumstances.

It became obvious that this was a special occasion
and that she had planned a surprise.

BIRTHDAY PARTY

Katharine Brush

They were a couple in their late thirties, and they looked
unmistakably married. They sat on the banquette[1] opposite
us in a little narrow restaurant, having dinner. The man had
a round, self-satisfied face, with glasses on it; the woman
was fadingly pretty, in a big hat. There was nothing conspicuous about them, nothing particularly noticeable, until the
end of their meal, when it suddenly became obvious that this
was an Occasion—in fact, the husband's birthday, and the
wife had planned a little surprise for him.

It arrived, in the form of a small but glossy birthday
cake, with one pink candle burning in the center. The head-
waiter brought it in and placed it before the husband, and
meanwhile the violin-and-piano orchestra played "Happy
Birthday to You," and the wife beamed with shy pride over
her little surprise, and such few people as there were in the
restaurant tried to help out with a pattering of applause. It
became clear at once that help was needed, because the husband was not pleased. Instead, he was hotly embarrassed,
and indignant at his wife for embarrassing him.

You looked at him and you saw this and you thought,
"Oh, now, don't be like that!" But he was like that, and as

---

1. **banquette** (băng-kĕt'): an upholstered bench, usually along a wall in a
   restaurant.

147

soon as the little cake had been deposited on the table, and the orchestra had finished the birthday piece, and the general attention had shifted from the man and the woman, I saw him say something to her under his breath—some punishing thing, quick and curt and unkind. I couldn't bear to look at the woman then, so I stared at my plate and waited for quite a long time. Not long enough, though. She was still crying when I finally glanced over there again. Crying quietly and heartbrokenly and hopelessly, all to herself, under the gay big brim of her best hat.

CHECK-UP (True/False)

1. The action of this story takes place in an expensive, fashionable restaurant.
2. The man and his wife are an unusually attractive and interesting couple.
3. The woman expects her husband to be pleased by her surprise.
4. The husband shows his anger and embarrassment by yelling at his wife.
5. The narrator feels sympathy for the woman.

FOR DISCUSSION

1. In this brief story, a single incident throws light on the relationship between a husband and wife. What does the phrase "unmistakably married" in the opening paragraph imply about the couple? What detail hints at the husband's unpleasantness? What has happened to the wife's looks?
2. What impression do you get of the restaurant? Is it a romantic or unromantic setting? Explain your answer.
3. What does the phrase "shy pride" tell you about the wife? How does the husband squelch her pleasure?

4. How does the narrator arouse sympathy for the woman?

POINT OF VIEW
First-Person Observer

A story may be told by someone who is an observer of the action rather than a main character. In "Birthday Party," the *I* is not the main character, like the narrator in Poe's "The Tell-Tale Heart" (page 135). The *I* is an observer who is seated in the restaurant, watching the interaction between the main characters. We call this point of view *first-person observer.*

This point of view creates distance from the characters. The narrator cannot see into the characters' minds and read their thoughts. The narrative must be restricted to what can be seen and what can be inferred. However, the narrator is free to comment on the action and does not have to be an objective witness. In "Birthday Party" the narrator clearly is in sympathy with the wife's feelings.

Point out instances where the narrator's comments control the reader's reaction to events in the story.

UNDERSTANDING THE WORDS
IN THE STORY (Matching Columns)

1. conspicuous
2. glossy
3. beamed
4. pattering
5. indignant
6. deposited
7. shifted
8. punishing
9. quick
10. curt

a. smiled radiantly
b. changed; moved
c. set down
d. having a shiny surface
e. brief and abrupt
f. offended; angry
g. harsh; rough
h. hasty and sharp
i. striking; obvious
j. light, sharp sounds

FOR WRITING

1. Write the story from the point of view of the husband or wife. Have your character reveal his or her feelings, thoughts, and observations.
2. Show how Katharine Brush develops the characters of the husband and wife through direct and indirect methods of characterization. (See the exercise on page 58.)

*"Zlateh trusted human beings.
She knew that they always fed her
and never did her any harm."*

ZLATEH
THE GOAT

Isaac Bashevis Singer

At Hanukkah[1] time the road from the village to the town
is usually covered with snow, but this year the winter had
been a mild one. Hanukkah had almost come, yet little snow
had fallen. The sun shone most of the time. The peasants
complained that because of the dry weather there would be a
poor harvest of winter grain. New grass sprouted, and the
peasants sent their cattle out to pasture.

For Reuven the furrier it was a bad year, and after long
hesitation he decided to sell Zlateh the goat. She was old and
gave little milk. Feyvel the town butcher had offered eight
gulden[2] for her. Such a sum would buy Hanukkah candles,
potatoes and oil for pancakes, gifts for the children, and
other holiday necessaries for the house. Reuven told his oldest boy Aaron to take the goat to town.

Aaron understood what taking the goat to Feyvel meant,
but he had to obey his father. Leah, his mother, wiped the
tears from her eyes when she heard the news. Aaron's
younger sisters, Anna and Miriam, cried loudly. Aaron put
on his quilted jacket and a cap with earmuffs, bound a rope

1. **Hanukkah** (ĸʜä′nŏŏ-kə): a Jewish holiday, usually falling in December,
   that is celebrated for eight days.
2. **gulden** (gŏŏl′dən): coins used in several European countries.

around Zlateh's neck, and took along two slices of bread with cheese to eat on the road. Aaron was supposed to deliver the goat by evening, spend the night at the butcher's, and return the next day with the money.

While the family said goodbye to the goat, and Aaron placed the rope around her neck, Zlateh stood as patiently and good-naturedly as ever. She licked Reuven's hand. She shook her small white beard. Zlateh trusted human beings. She knew that they always fed her and never did her any harm.

When Aaron brought her out on the road to town, she seemed somewhat astonished. She'd never been led in that direction before. She looked back at him questioningly, as if to say, "Where are you taking me?" But after a while she seemed to come to the conclusion that a goat shouldn't ask questions. Still, the road was different. They passed new fields, pastures, and huts with thatched roofs. Here and there a dog barked and came running after them, but Aaron chased it away with his stick.

The sun was shining when Aaron left the village. Suddenly the weather changed. A large black cloud with a bluish center appeared in the east and spread itself rapidly over the sky. A cold wind blew in with it. The crows flew low, croaking. At first it looked as if it would rain, but instead it began to hail as in summer. It was early in the day, but it became dark as dusk. After a while the hail turned to snow.

In his twelve years Aaron had seen all kinds of weather, but he had never experienced a snow like this one. It was so dense it shut out the light of the day. In a short time their path was completely covered. The wind became as cold as ice. The road to town was narrow and winding. Aaron no longer knew where he was. He could not see through the snow. The cold soon penetrated his quilted jacket.

At first Zlateh didn't seem to mind the change in weather. She too was twelve years old and knew what winter meant. But when her legs sank deeper and deeper into the snow, she began to turn her head and look at Aaron in wonderment. Her mild eyes seemed to ask, "Why are we out in such a storm?" Aaron hoped that a peasant would come along with his cart, but no one passed by.

The snow grew thicker, falling to the ground in large, whirling flakes. Beneath it Aaron's boots touched the softness of a plowed field. He realized that he was no longer on the road. He had gone astray. He could no longer figure out which was east or west, which way was the village, the town. The wind whistled, howled, whirled the snow about it in eddies.[3] It looked as if white imps were playing tag on the fields. A white dust rose above the ground. Zlateh stopped. She could walk no longer. Stubbornly she anchored her cleft hooves in the earth and bleated as if pleading to be taken home. Icicles hung from her white beard, and her horns were glazed with frost.

Aaron did not want to admit the danger, but he knew just the same that if they did not find shelter they would freeze to death. This was no ordinary storm. It was a mighty blizzard. The snowfall had reached his knees. His hands were numb, and he could no longer feel his toes. He choked when he breathed. His nose felt like wood, and he rubbed it with snow. Zlateh's bleating began to sound like crying. Those humans in whom she had so much confidence had dragged her into a trap. Aaron began to pray to God for himself and for the innocent animal.

Suddenly he made out the shape of a hill. He wondered what it could be. Who had piled snow into such a huge heap? He moved toward it, dragging Zlateh after him. When he came near it, he realized that it was a large haystack which the snow had blanketed.

Aaron realized immediately that they were saved. With

3. **eddies** (ĕd′ēz): An *eddy* is a current of air or water moving circularly.

great effort he dug his way through the snow. He was a village boy and knew what to do. When he reached the hay, he hollowed out a nest for himself and the goat. No matter how cold it may be outside, in the hay it is always warm. And hay was food for Zlateh. The moment she smelled it she became contented and began to eat. Outside the snow continued to fall. It quickly covered the passageway Aaron had dug. But a boy and an animal need to breathe, and there was hardly any air in their hideout. Aaron bored a kind of window through the hay and snow and carefully kept the passage clear.

Zlateh, having eaten her fill, sat down on her hind legs and seemed to have regained her confidence in man. Aaron ate his two slices of bread and cheese, but after the difficult journey he was still hungry. He looked at Zlateh and noticed her udders were full. He lay down next to her, placing himself so that when he milked her he could squirt the milk into his mouth. It was rich and sweet. Zlateh was not accustomed to being milked that way, but she did not resist. On the contrary, she seemed eager to reward Aaron for bringing her to a shelter whose very walls, floor, and ceiling were made of food.

Through the window Aaron could catch a glimpse of the chaos outside. The wind carried before it whole drifts of snow. It was completely dark, and he did not know whether night had already come or whether it was the darkness of the storm. Thank God that in the hay it was not cold. The dried hay, grass, and field flowers exuded the warmth of the summer sun. Zlateh ate frequently; she nibbled from above, below, from the left and right. Her body gave forth an animal warmth, and Aaron cuddled up to her. He had always loved Zlateh, but now she was like a sister. He was alone, cut off from his family, and wanted to talk. He began to talk to Zlateh. "Zlateh, what do you think about what has happened to us?" he asked.

"Maaaa," Zlateh answered.

"If we hadn't found this stack of hay, we would both be frozen stiff by now," Aaron said.

"Maaaa," was the goat's reply.

"If the snow keeps on falling like this, we may have to stay here for days," Aaron explained.

"Maaaa," Zlateh bleated.

"What does 'Maaaa' mean?" Aaron asked. "You'd better speak up clearly."

"Maaaa, Maaaa," Zlateh tried.

"Well, let it be 'Maaaa' then," Aaron said patiently. "You can't speak, but I know you understand. I need you and you need me. Isn't that right?"

"Maaaa."

Aaron became sleepy. He made a pillow out of some hay, leaned his head on it, and dozed off. Zlateh too fell asleep.

When Aaron opened his eyes, he didn't know whether it was morning or night. The snow had blocked up his window. He tried to clear it, but when he had bored through to the length of his arm, he still hadn't reached the outside. Luckily he had his stick with him and was able to break through to the open air. It was still dark outside. The snow continued to fall and the wind wailed, first with one voice and then with many. Sometimes it had the sound of devilish laughter. Zlateh too awoke, and when Aaron greeted her, she answered, "Maaaa." Yes, Zlateh's language consisted of only one word, but it meant many things. Now she was saying, "We must accept all that God gives us—heat, cold, hunger, satisfaction, light, and darkness."

Aaron had awakened hungry. He had eaten up his food, but Zlateh had plenty of milk.

For three days Aaron and Zlateh stayed in the haystack. Aaron had always loved Zlateh, but in these three days he loved her more and more. She fed him with her milk and helped him keep warm. She comforted him with her patience. He told her many stories, and she always cocked her ears and listened. When he patted her, she licked his hand and his face. Then she said, "Maaaa," and he knew it meant, I love you too.

The snow fell for three days, though after the first day it was not as thick and the wind quieted down. Sometimes Aaron felt that there could never have been a summer, that the snow had always fallen, ever since he could remember. He, Aaron, never had a father or mother or sisters. He was a snow child, born of the snow, and so was Zlateh. It was so quiet in the hay that his ears rang in the stillness. Aaron and Zlateh slept all night and a good part of the day. As for Aaron's dreams, they were all about warm weather. He dreamed of green fields, trees covered with blossoms, clear brooks, and singing birds. By the third night the snow had stopped, but Aaron did not dare to find his way home in the darkness. The sky became clear and the moon shone, casting silvery nets on the snow. Aaron dug his way out and looked at the world. It was all white, quiet, dreaming dreams of heavenly splendor. The stars were large and close. The moon swam in the sky as in a sea.

On the morning of the fourth day Aaron heard the ringing of sleigh bells. The haystack was not far from the road. The peasant who drove the sleigh pointed out the way to him—not to the town and Feyvel the butcher, but home to the village. Aaron had decided in the haystack that he would never part with Zlateh.

Aaron's family and their neighbors had searched for the boy and the goat but had found no trace of them during the storm. They feared they were lost. Aaron's mother and sisters cried for him; his father remained silent and gloomy. Suddenly one of the neighbors came running to their house with the news that Aaron and Zlateh were coming up the road.

There was great joy in the family. Aaron told them how he had found the stack of hay and how Zlateh had fed him with her milk. Aaron's sisters kissed and hugged Zlateh and gave her a special treat of chopped carrots and potato peels, which Zlateh gobbled up hungrily.

Nobody ever again thought of selling Zlateh, and now that the cold weather had finally set in, the villagers needed the services of Reuven the furrier once more. When Hanukkah came, Aaron's mother was able to fry pancakes every evening, and Zlateh got her portion too. Even though Zlateh had her own pen, she often came to the kitchen, knocking on the door with her horns to indicate that she was ready to visit, and she was always admitted. In the evening Aaron, Miriam, and Anna played dreidel.[4] Zlateh sat near the stove watching the children and the flickering of the Hanukkah candles.

Once in a while Aaron would ask her, "Zlateh, do you remember the three days we spent together?"

And Zlateh would scratch her neck with a horn, shake her white bearded head and come out with the single sound which expressed all her thoughts, and all her love.

---

4. **dreidel** (drā′dəl): a game played with a four-sided top called a dreidel.

CHECK-UP (Short Answer)

1. What kind of work does Reuven do?
2. Why does Reuven decide to sell Zlateh?
3. How old is Aaron?
4. How long is Aaron lost?
5. What decision does Aaron come to in the haystack?

FOR DISCUSSION

1. In what way are Reuven and his family dependent on nature for their livelihood? Why is Reuven forced to sell the goat?
2. Aaron and the goat almost perish in the snowstorm. How does the storm ironically turn out to be a godsend for the family?
3. At one point in the story, Singer interprets Zlateh's thoughts: "We must accept all that God gives us." In what way does the story show that all the characters are in God's hands?
4. How are the bonds of the family strengthened by their hardships?

OMNISCIENT POINT OF VIEW

The standpoint from which a writer tells a story is called *point of view.* The *first-person point of view,* as you have seen, tells everything from the standpoint of a narrator who is one of the characters in the story. This point of view is limited to what one character sees, thinks, and feels.

A story can be told from the *third-person point of view,* by an outside observer who does not play a role in the events. The narrator tells the story from the vantage point of "he" or "she." The third-person narrator may be an *omniscient* (ŏm-nĭsh′ənt), or all-knowing, observer, who knows what *all* the characters can see, hear, think, and feel, and who comments on the action.

"Zlateh the Goat" is told from the omniscient point of view. We are allowed to know what all the characters, including Zlateh, think and feel:

> Aaron did not want to admit the danger, but he knew just the same that if they did not find shelter they would freeze to death.

> Zlateh trusted human beings. She knew that they always fed her and never did her any harm.

> Nobody ever again thought of selling Zlateh . . .

The author also comments on and interprets the events:

> Yes, Zlateh's language consisted of only one word, but it meant many things. Now she was saying "We must accept all that God gives us—heat, cold, hunger, satisfaction, light, and darkness."

Find three other passages in the story that demonstrate Singer's use of the omniscient point of view.

UNDERSTANDING THE WORDS IN THE STORY (Matching Columns)

1. necessaries
2. dense
3. penetrated
4. wonderment
5. astray
6. imp
7. glazed
8. chaos
9. exuded
10. wailed

a. devilish spirit
b. gave off
c. coated
d. thick
e. cried
f. surprise
g. disorder
h. essential items
i. out of the right way
j. got through

FOR WRITING

1. Sometimes the setting of a story is crucial to the action. This story takes place during the winter in a small European village. In what way is nature, in the story, both an enemy and a friend? Write a short essay, citing passages that support your position.
2. Select one of the episodes in the story and retell it in first person from Aaron's point of view.
3. Hanukkah is often called the Festival of Lights. Consult a reference book for information about this holiday. Write a short essay telling what the festival commemorates and how it is celebrated.

*"Opening the glass doors onto the snowy
gardens, she thought that it was
like the end of a film."*

THE
FIRST DEATH
OF HER LIFE

Elizabeth Taylor

Suddenly tears poured from her eyes. She rested her forehead against her mother's hand and let the tears soak into the counterpane.[1]

Dear Mr. Wilcox, she began; for her mind was always composing letters. I shall not be at the shop for the next four days, as my mother has passed away and I shall not be available until after the funeral. My mother passed away very peacefully. . . .

The nurse came in. She took her patient's wrist for a moment, replaced it, removed a jar of forced lilac from beside the bed as if this were no longer necessary, and went out again.

The girl kneeling by the bed had looked up.

Dear Mr. Wilcox, she resumed, her face returning to the counterpane. My mother has died. I shall come back to work the day after tomorrow. Yours sincerely, Lucy Mayhew.

Her father was late. She imagined him hurrying from work, bicycling through the darkening streets, dogged,

---

1. **counterpane** (koun′tər-pān′): bedspread or coverlet.

161

hunched up, slush thrown up by his wheels. Her mother did not move. She stroked her hand with its loose gold ring, the callused palms, the fine long fingers. Then she stood up stiffly, her knees bruised from the waxed floor, and went to the window.

Snowflakes turned idly, drifting down over the hospital gardens. It was four o'clock in the afternoon, and already the day seemed over. So few sounds came from this muffled and discolored world. In the hospital itself there was a deep silence.

Her thoughts came to her in words, as if her mind spoke them first, understood them later. She tried to think of her childhood: little scenes she selected to prove how they loved each other. Other scenes, especially last week's quarrel, she chose to forget, not knowing that in this moment she sent them away forever. Only loving kindness remained.

But all the same, intolerable pictures broke through— her mother at the sink; her mother ironing; her mother standing between the lace curtains, staring out at the dreary street with a wounded look in her eyes; her mother tying the same lace curtains with yellow ribbons; attempts at lightness, gaiety, which came to nothing; her mother gathering her huge black cat to her, burying her face in its fur, and a great shivering sigh—of despair, boredom—escaping her.

She no longer sighed. She lay very still and sometimes took a little sip of air. He arms were neatly at her sides. Her eyes, which all day long had been turned to the white lilac, were closed. Her cheekbones rose sharply from her bruised, exhausted face. She smelled faintly of wine.

A small lilac flower floated on a glass of champagne, now discarded on the table at her side.

The champagne, with which they hoped to stretch out the thread of her life minute by minute; the lilac; the room of her own, coming to her at the end of a life of drabness and denial, just as, all along the mean street where they lived, the dying and the dead might claim a lifetime's savings from the bereaved.

She is no longer there, Lucy thought, standing beside the bed.

All day her mother had stared at the white lilac; now she had sunk away. Outside, beyond the hospital gardens, mist settled over the town, blurred the street lamps.

The nurse returned with the matron. Ready to be on her best behavior, Lucy tautened.[2] In her heart she trusted her mother to die without frightening her, and when the matron, deftly drawing Lucy's head to rest on her own shoulder, said in her calm voice, "She has gone," she felt she had met this happening halfway.

A little bustle began, quick footsteps along the empty passages, and for a moment she was left alone with her dead mother. She laid her hand timidly on her soft dark hair, so often touched, played with when she was a little girl, standing on a stool behind her mother's chair while she sewed.

There was still the smell of wine and the hospital smell. It was growing dark in the room. She went to the dressing table and took her mother's handbag, very worn and shiny, and a book, a library book which she had chosen carefully for her, believing she would read it.

Then she had a quick sip from the glass on the table, a mouthful of champagne, which she had never tasted before, and, looking wounded and aloof, walked down the middle of the corridor, feeling the nurses falling away to the left and right.

Opening the glass doors onto the snowy gardens, she thought that it was like the end of a film. But no music rose up and engulfed her. Instead there was her father turning in at the gates. He propped his bicycle up against the wall and began to run clumsily across the wet gravel.

---

2. **tautened** (tôt′nd): grew tense.

CHECK-UP (True/False)

1. The action of this story takes place in a hospital on an afternoon in winter.
2. At the opening of the story, Lucy is composing a letter to her employer.
3. Lucy blames her father for being late.
4. Lucy's memories of her mother are mostly cheerful.
5. Lucy's mother regains consciousness at the end of the story.

FOR DISCUSSION

1. This story allows us to read the thoughts of a young girl at the bedside of her dying mother. When we first meet her, she has just started to cry. What has evoked this outburst?
2. Compare the two versions of the letter Lucy is composing mentally to her employer. Which of the two is more emotional? Which is more restrained? What do you think is responsible for the change in the second version?
3. Lucy tries to think of pleasant memories of her mother, but "intolerable pictures" keep breaking through. What do these "intolerable pictures" reveal about her mother's life?
4. When the nurse returns, Lucy gets ready to be on her "best behavior." How does she behave? What evidence is there in the story that Lucy is concerned with the impression she makes on others?
5. Lucy trusts her mother to die without "frightening her." What do you think Lucy fears?
6. As she leaves the hospital, Lucy imagines the scene as "the end of a film." In what way is the first death of her life a sobering experience, less satisfying and less dramatic than the movies?

LIMITED THIRD-PERSON POINT OF VIEW

A story may be told in the third person by a narrator who is all-knowing, or omniscient. This kind of observer is free to enter into the minds and feelings of all the characters, and to comment on or interpret events. Sometimes an author tells a story in the third person from the point of view of only *one* character. Instead of learning what all the characters see, feel, and think, we get our information filtered through one character's viewpoint. This *limited third-person point of view* brings us close to a character: we are allowed to feel that we are inside that character's mind.

"The First Death of Her Life" is told from the limited third-person point of view. This point of view enables us to focus on Lucy's inner and outer lives. We do not know what the nurse thinks or feels; we see her as Lucy sees her, externally. We do not know what the dying woman may be feeling or thinking; we have only Lucy's impressions of her mother.

Find several key passages in the story that give you insight into Lucy's thoughts and feelings about her mother and about herself.

UNDERSTANDING THE WORDS IN THE STORY (Multiple-Choice)

1. Lucy *resumed* the letter she had been composing in her mind.
   a. reviewed
   b. began again
   c. completed
2. She pictured the *dogged* figure of her father bicycling to the hospital.
   a. determined
   b. tired
   c. angry

3. The sounds in the hospital were *muffled.*
   a. deadened
   b. soothing
   c. disturbing
4. Everything in the hospital looked *discolored.*
   a. old
   b. faded
   c. dirty
5. Thoughts of her mother brought back *intolerable* memories.
   a. pleasant
   b. kind
   c. unbearable
6. The glass of champagne on the table had been *discarded.*
   a. disappointing
   b. rejected
   c. given away
7. The street they lived on was drab and *mean* in appearance.
   a. shabby
   b. cold
   c. frightening
8. The matron, who had returned with the nurse, *deftly* drew Lucy's head to her shoulder.
   a. gently
   b. thoughtlessly
   c. expertly
9. Lucy walked down the hospital corridor looking *aloof.*
   a. cool and reserved
   b. bitter and angry
   c. sad and pitiful
10. When Lucy opened the doors to the gardens, she expected to be *engulfed* by emotion.
    a. weakened
    b. overcome
    c. shaken

FOR WRITING

1. Imagine Lucy as the narrator of this story. Select a passage and retell it from the first-person point of view.
2. Although the story focuses on Lucy's thoughts and feelings, the reader learns a great deal about Lucy's mother. Write a short essay revealing what you learn about her mother from Lucy's memories.

" 'Do you know what, Monk?'
he announced in a few moments. 'I can make
you two guys do anything I want.' "

A
GAME
OF CATCH

Richard Wilbur

Monk and Glennie were playing catch on the side lawn
of the firehouse when Scho caught sight of them. They were
good at it, for seventh-graders, as anyone could see right
away. Monk, wearing a catcher's mitt, would lean easily
sidewise and back, with one leg lifted and his throwing hand
almost down to the grass, and then lob the white ball
straight up into the sunlight. Glennie would shield his eyes
with his left hand and, just as the ball fell past him, snag it
with a little dart of his glove. Then he would burn the ball
straight toward Monk, and it would spank into the round
mitt and sit, like a still-life apple on a plate,[1] until Monk
flipped it over into his right hand and, with a negligent flick
of his hanging arm, gave Glennie a fast grounder.

They were going on and on like that, in a kind of slow,
mannered,[2] luxurious dance in the sun, their faces perfectly
blank and entranced, when Glennie noticed Scho dawdling
along the other side of the street and called hello to him.

---

1. **still-life . . . plate:** A still life is a painting that uses objects such as fruit
   or flowers as its subject.
2. **mannered** (măn'ərd): having specified movements.

168

Scho crossed over and stood at the front edge of the lawn, near an apple tree, watching.

"Got your glove?" asked Glennie after a time. Scho obviously hadn't.

"You could give me some easy grounders," said Scho. "But don't burn 'em."

"All right," Glennie said. He moved off a little, so the three of them formed a triangle, and they passed the ball around for about five minutes, Monk tossing easy grounders to Scho, Scho throwing to Glennie, and Glennie burning them in to Monk. After a while, Monk began to throw them back to Glennie once or twice before he let Scho have his grounder, and finally Monk gave Scho a fast, bumpy grounder that hopped over his shoulder and went into the brake on the other side of the street.

"Not so hard," called Scho as he ran across to get it.

"You should've had it," Monk shouted.

It took Scho a little while to find the ball among the ferns and dead leaves, and when he saw it, he grabbed it up and threw it toward Glennie. It struck the trunk of the apple tree, bounced back at an angle, and rolled steadily and stupidly onto the cement apron in front of the firehouse, where one of the trucks was parked. Scho ran hard and stopped it just before it rolled under the truck, and this time he carried it back to his former position on the lawn and threw it carefully to Glennie.

"I got an idea," said Glennie. "Why don't Monk and I catch for five minutes more, and then you can borrow one of our gloves?"

"That's all right with me," said Monk. He socked his fist into his mitt, and Glennie burned one in.

"All right," Scho said, and went over and sat under the tree. There in the shade he watched them resume their skillful play. They threw lazily fast or lazily slow—high, low, or wide—and always handsomely, their expressions serene, changeless and forgetful. When Monk missed a low back-hand catch, he walked indolently after the ball and, hardly even looking, flung it sidearm for an imaginary putout. After a good while of this, Scho said, "Isn't it five minutes yet?"

"One minute to go," said Monk, with a fraction of a grin.

Scho stood up and watched the ball slap back and forth for several minutes more, and then he turned and pulled himself up into the crotch of the tree.

"Where you going?" Monk asked.

"Just up the tree," Scho said.

"I guess he doesn't want to catch," said Monk.

Scho went up and up through the fat light-gray branches until they grew slender and bright and gave under him. He found a place where several supple branches were knit to make a dangerous chair, and sat there with his head coming out of the leaves into the sunlight. He could see the two other boys down below, the ball going back and forth between them as if they were bowling on the grass, and Glennie's crew-cut head looking like a sea urchin.

"I found a wonderful seat up here," Scho said loudly. "If I don't fall out." Monk and Glennie didn't look up or comment, and so he began jouncing gently in his chair of branches and singing "Yo-ho, heave ho" in an exaggerated way.

"Do you know what, Monk?" he announced in a few minutes. "I can make you two guys do anything I want. Catch that ball, Monk! Now you catch it, Glennie!"

"I was going to catch it anyway," Monk suddenly said. "You're not making anybody do anything when they're already going to do it anyway."

"I made you say what you just said," Scho replied joyfully.

"No, you didn't," said Monk, still throwing and catching but now less serenely absorbed in the game.

"That's what I wanted you to say," Scho said.

The ball bounded off the rim of Monk's mitt and plowed into a gladiolus bed beside the firehouse, and Monk ran to get it while Scho jounced in his treetop and sang, "I wanted you to miss that. Anything you do is what I wanted you to do."

"Let's quit for a minute," Glennie suggested.

"We might as well, until the peanut gallery[3] shuts up," Monk said.

They went over and sat cross-legged in the shade of the tree. Scho looked down between his legs and saw them on the dim, spotty ground, saying nothing to one another. Glennie soon began abstractedly spinning his glove between his palms; Monk pulled his nose and stared out across the lawn.

"I want you to mess around with your nose, Monk," said Scho, giggling. Monk withdrew his hand from his face.

"Do that with your glove, Glennie," Scho persisted. "Monk, I want you to pull up hunks of grass and chew on it."

Glennie looked up and saw a self-delighted, intense face staring down at him through the leaves. "Stop being a dope and come down and we'll catch for a few minutes," he said.

Scho hesitated, and then said, in a tentatively mocking voice, "That's what I wanted you to say."

"All right, then, nuts to you," said Glennie.

"Why don't you keep quiet and stop bothering people?" Monk asked.

"I made you say that," Scho replied, softly.

"Shut up," Monk said.

---

3. **peanut gallery:** the topmost section of the balcony in a theater, where the cheaper seats are found.

"I made you say that, and I want you to be standing there looking sore. And I want you to climb up the tree. I'm making you do it!"

Monk was scrambling up through the branches, awkward in his haste, and getting snagged on twigs. His face was furious and foolish, and he kept telling Scho to shut up, shut up, shut up, while the other's exuberant and panicky voice poured down upon his head.

"*Now* you shut up or you'll be sorry," Monk said, breathing hard as he reached up and threatened to shake the cradle of slight branches in which Scho was sitting.

"I *want*——" Scho screamed as he fell. Two lower branches broke his rustling, crackling fall, but he landed on his back with a deep thud and lay still, with a strangled look on his face and his eyes clenched. Glennie knelt down and asked breathlessly, "Are you O.K., Scho? Are you O.K.?" while Monk swung down through the leaves crying that honestly he hadn't even touched him, the crazy guy just let go. Scho doubled up and turned over on his right side, and now both the other boys knelt beside him, pawing at his shoulder and begging to know how he was.

Then Scho rolled away from them and sat partly up, still struggling to get his wind but forcing a species of smile onto his face.

"I'm sorry, Scho," Monk said. "I didn't mean to make you fall."

Scho's voice came out weak and gravelly, in gasps. "I meant—you to do it. You—had to. You can't do—anything—unless—I want—you to."

Glennie and Monk looked helplessly at him as he sat there, breathing a bit more easily and smiling fixedly, with tears in his eyes. Then they picked up their gloves and the ball, walked over to the street, and went slowly away down the sidewalk, Monk punching his fist into the mitt, Glennie juggling the ball between glove and hand.

From under the apple tree, Scho, still bent over a little for lack of breath, croaked after them in triumph and misery, "I want you to do whatever you're going to do for the whole rest of your life!"

CHECK-UP (Putting Events in Order)

Arrange the following events in the order in which they occur in the story.

Scho begins singing in an exaggerated way.
Monk and Glennie kneel beside Scho, asking how he is.
Scho falls from the tree and lands on his back.
Monk throws a bumpy grounder to Scho.
Monk begins to climb the apple tree.
Glennie asks Scho if he has his glove.
Scho stands on the lawn watching Monk and Glennie play catch.
Scho throws a ball that strikes the trunk of the apple tree and bounces onto the sidewalk in front of the firehouse.
Scho pulls himself up into the apple tree.
Monk and Glennie stop the game and sit down under the apple tree.

FOR DISCUSSION

1. The game of catch between Monk and Glennie is described as a kind of "dance in the sun." What features of dancing does the narrator have in mind?
2. What problem does Scho's presence introduce? Why do you suppose Monk and Glennie ease Scho out of the game?

3. Some people react to rejection by withdrawing or showing anger. How does Scho get even with the other boys? What makes his "game" effective?
4. At the end of the story, is the conflict between Scho and the other boys resolved? Or does it take another form?
5. Why do children's games often end in conflicts or broken friendships? What insight does this story offer into the relationships and motivations of young people?

OBJECTIVE POINT OF VIEW

Sometimes a writer tells a story from the point of view of an observer who witnesses the action but offers no commentary or interpretation of the events. This observer tells us what the characters say and do, but does not reveal their thoughts and feelings. We must draw our own conclusions about the characters from their dialogue and actions. This point of view is called the *objective* (or *dramatic*) *point of view* because the narrator maintains distance from the story in much the same way as the playwright does, letting the dialogue and action speak for themselves.

Wilbur uses the objective point of view in "A Game of Catch." His observer records external details with the fidelity of a camera. We see what the boys are doing, we hear their dialogue, but we do not enter their thoughts. We do not know what the author thinks of this incident—whether he is sympathetic or unsympathetic—whether he blames any of the boys or none of them. Wilbur does not take sides and he does not ask the reader to do so. By using the objective point of view, he remains detached. Instead of engaging our sympathies for a specific character, he allows us to experience the situation as a whole.

What do you think is gained by the objective point of view in this story? Do you think that the action requires direct commentary and interpretation, or are such conclusions better left to the individual reader?

UNDERSTANDING THE WORDS
IN THE STORY (Multiple-Choice)

1. When Monk would *lob* the ball, he would
   a. throw it in a high, arching curve
   b. bounce it along the ground
   c. pass it overhand
2. Glennie would *snag* the ball by
   a. pretending to drop it
   b. tossing it carefully to his partner
   c. catching it quickly
3. When he would *burn* the ball, he would
   a. catch the ball on the fly
   b. throw it very hard
   c. pitch the ball in a curve
4. When the ball would *spank* into the round mitt, it would
   a. make a sharp, explosive sound
   b. drop with a slapping sound
   c. land without a sound
5. A *negligent* movement is
   a. unskillful
   b. careless
   c. dangerous
6. The boys' game is described as a *luxurious* dance because it is
   a. extremely pleasurable
   b. what rich people do
   c. not necessary to life or health
7. The boys' faces are *blank* because the boys
   a. are untroubled
   b. are too stupid to think
   c. have lost interest in the game
8. They are *entranced,* or
   a. competing with one another
   b. enclosed on all sides
   c. filled with delight

9. Glennie notices Scho *dawdling,* or
   a. smiling
   b. idling
   c. moving restlessly
10. The *brake* is
   a. an area covered with bushes
   b. a recess from the game
   c. a wall around the firehouse

(Matching Columns)

1. apron
2. resume
3. serene
4. changeless
5. indolently
6. putout
7. supple
8. jouncing
9. absorbed
10. abstractedly

a. calm; peaceful
b. a baseball play
c. bending easily
d. completely involved in
e. to begin again
f. absent-mindedly
g. constant
h. area in front of a building
i. lazily
j. bouncing

(Synonyms and Antonyms)

persisted   awkward
intense   exuberant
tentatively   clenched
mocking   species
scrambling   croak

Choose a word from the above list that means

1. the opposite of *opened wide*
2. the same as *clumsy*
3. the opposite of *stopped*
4. the same as *kind*

5. the opposite of *miserable*
6. the same as *to speak in a low, hoarse voice*
7. the opposite of *with certainty*
8. the same as *moving hastily*
9. the opposite of *weak*
10. the same as *scornful*

FOR WRITING

1. Rewrite a part of this story in the first person, from the point of view of one of its characters—Monk, Glennie, or Scho. Have your narrator reveal his thoughts and feelings.
2. Choose a game that you know well and describe one of its plays. For example, you might describe a scrimmage in football, a serve in tennis, or a pass in basketball.

Tone

The child was at work on a marvelous palace,
but the work was never completed.

THE
STORY OF
MUHAMMAD DIN

Rudyard Kipling

The polo-ball[1] was an old one, scarred, chipped, and dinted. It stood on the mantelpiece among the pipe-stems which Imam Din, *khitmatgar*,[2] was cleaning for me.

'Does the Heaven-born want this ball?' said Imam Din, deferentially.[3]

The Heaven-born set no particular store by it; but of what use was a polo-ball to a *khitmatgar*?

'By Your Honour's favour, I have a little son. He has seen this ball, and desires it to play with. I do not want it for myself.'

No one would for an instant accuse portly old Imam Din

---

1. **polo** (pō'lō) **ball:** used in a game played by two teams of players on horseback. The players use a long-handled mallet (a kind of hammer) to drive a small wooden ball into the opponents' goal.
2. **khitmatgar:** A man's personal servant. This story takes place in colonial India.
3. **deferentially** (děf'ə-rěn'shə-lē): respectfully.

of wanting to play with polo-balls. He carried out the battered thing into the verandah; and there followed a hurricane of joyful squeaks, a patter of small feet, and the *thud-thud-thud* of the ball rolling along the ground. Evidently the little son had been waiting outside the door to secure his treasure. But how had he managed to see that polo-ball?

Next day, coming back from office half an hour earlier than usual, I was aware of a small figure in the dining-room—a tiny, plump figure in a ridiculously inadequate shirt which came, perhaps, half-way down the tubby stomach. It wandered around the room, thumb in mouth, crooning to itself as it took stock of the pictures. Undoubtedly this was the 'little son.'

He had no business in my room, of course; but was so deeply absorbed in his discoveries that he never noticed me in the doorway. I stepped into the room and startled him nearly into a fit. He sat down on the ground with a gasp. His eyes opened, and his mouth followed suit. I knew what was coming, and fled, followed by a long, dry howl which reached the servants' quarters far more quickly than any command of mine had ever done. In ten seconds Imam Din was in the dining-room. Then despairing sobs arose, and I returned to find Imam Din admonishing[4] the small sinner who was using most of his shirt as a handkerchief.

'This boy,' said Imam Din, judicially, 'is a *budmash*[5]—a big *budmash*. He will, without doubt, go to the *jail-khana*[6] for his behaviour.' Renewed yells from the penitent, and an elaborate apology to myself from Imam Din.

'Tell the baby,' said I, 'that the *Sahib*[7] is not angry, and take him away.' Imam Din conveyed my forgiveness to the offender, who had now gathered all his shirt around his

---

4. **admonishing** (ăd-mŏn′ĭsh-əng): mildly criticizing.
5. **budmash:** a bad character.
6. **jail-khana:** prison.
7. **Sahib** (sä′ĭb): a title used by Indians in addressing Europeans.

neck, stringwise, and the yell subsided into a sob. The two
set off for the door. 'His name,' said Imam Din, as though the
name were part of the crime, 'is Muhammad Din, and he is a
budmash.' Freed from present danger, Muhummad Din
turned round in his father's arms, and said gravely, 'It is true
that my name is Muhammad Din, *Tahib,*[8] but I am not a
budmash. I am a *man!*'

From that day dated my acquaintance with Muhummad
Din. Never again did he come into my dining-room, but on
the neutral ground of the garden we greeted each other with
much state, though our conversation was confined to *'Talaam, Tahib'* from his side, and *'Salaam,*[9] *Muhummad Din'*
from mine. Daily on my return from office, the little white
shirt and fat little body used to rise from the shade of the
creeper-covered trellis where they had been hid; and daily I
checked my horse here, that my salutation might not be
slurred over or given unseemly.

Muhammad Din never had any companions. He used to
trot about the compound, in and out of the castor-oil bushes,
on mysterious errands of his own. One day I stumbled upon
some of his handiwork far down the grounds. He had half
buried the polo-ball in dust, and stuck six shrivelled old
marigold flowers in a circle round it. Outside that circle
again was a rude square, traced out in bits of red brick alter-
nating with fragments of broken china; the whole bounded
by a little bank of dust. The water-man from the well-curb[10]
put in a plea for the small architect, saying that it was only
the play of a baby and did not much disfigure my garden.

Heaven knows that I had no intention of touching the
child's work then or later; but, that evening, a stroll through

---

8. **Tahib:** the child's mispronunciation of *Sahib.*
9. **Salaam** (sə-läm′): a Moslem greeting performed by bending low and
   placing the right palm on the forehead. The word *salaam* means
   "peace" in Arabic.
10. **well-curb:** raised edging around a well.

the garden brought me unawares full on it; so that I trampled, before I knew, marigold-heads, dust-bank, and fragments of broken soap-dish into confusion past all hope of mending. Next morning, I came upon Muhammad Din crying softly to himself over the ruin I had wrought. Someone had cruelly told him that the *Sahib* was very angry with him for spoiling the garden, and had scattered his rubbish, using bad language the while. Muhammad Din laboured for an hour at effacing every trace of the dust-bank and pottery fragments, and it was with a tearful and apologetic face that he said '*Talaam, Tahib,*' when I came home from office. A hasty inquiry resulted in Imam Din informing Muhammad Din that, by my singular favour, he was permitted to disport himself[11] as he pleased. Whereat the child took heart and fell to tracing the ground-plan of an edifice which was to eclipse the marigold-polo-ball creation.

For some months the chubby little eccentricity[12] revolved in his humble orbit among the castor-oil bushes and in the dust; always fashioning magnificent palaces from stale flowers thrown away by the bearer, smooth water-worn pebbles, bits of broken glass, and feathers pulled, I fancy, from my fowls—always alone, and always crooning to himself.

A gaily-spotted sea-shell was dropped one day close to the last of his little buildings; and I looked that Muhammad Din should build something more than ordinarily splendid on the strength of it. Nor was I disappointed. He meditated for the better part of an hour, and his crooning rose to a jubilant song. Then he began tracing in the dust. It would certainly be a wondrous palace, this one, for it was two yards long and a yard broad in ground-plan. But the palace was never completed.

---

11. **disport** (dĭs-pôrt′, -pōrt′) **himself:** play.
12. **eccentricity** (ĕk′sĕn-trĭs′ə-tē): oddity; a person that is unusual.

Next day there was no Muhammad Din at the head of the carriage drive, and no *'Talaam, Tahib'* to welcome my return. I had grown accustomed to the greeting, and its omission troubled me. Next day Imam Din told me that the child was suffering slightly from fever and needed quinine.[13] He got the medicine, and an English Doctor.

'They have no stamina, these brats,' said the Doctor, as he left Imam Din's quarters.

A week later, though I would have given much to have avoided it, I met on the road to the Mussulman[14] burying-ground Imam Din, accompanied by one other friend, carrying in his arms, wrapped in a white cloth, all that was left of little Muhammad Din.

13. **quinine** (kwī'nīn'): a bitter substance used in drugs to treat malaria.
14. **Mussulman** (mŭs'əl-mən): Moslem.

CHECK-UP (Multiple-Choice)

1. Muhammad Din must have seen the polo ball
   a. in the garden when he was playing in the bushes
   b. when the narrator was using it in a game
   c. while he was exploring the dining room, uninvited
2. The narrator's reaction to finding the little boy in his house is
   a. annoyance
   b. gentle amusement
   c. intense interest
3. The narrator takes care to
   a. show respect for Muhammad Din's feelings
   b. provide Muhammad Din with playmates
   c. warn the gardener to watch the child
4. Muhammad Din fashions his little buildings from
   a. fragments he finds in the garden
   b. materials that the gardener gives him
   c. objects he steals from the dining room

5. When the narrator calls Muhammad Din's buildings "magnificent palaces," he indicates that he
   a. believes the child is a gifted architect
   b. thinks the child has foolish ideas
   c. appreciates the power of the child's imagination

FOR DISCUSSION

1. This story focuses on the relationship between the narrator (the person telling the story) and a little boy. How does the narrator know at their first meeting that the child wishes to be treated with dignity and respect?
2. After their first meeting, the man and the boy always greet each other formally. How do their actions and words show this mutual courtesy?
3. The narrator's interest in the child grows during the months that he sees the child playing in the garden. What do you think is the reason for his interest? How does he encourage Muhammad Din in his play?
4. Compare the attitudes of the narrator and of the English doctor toward the child's illness. What is the purpose of this contrast?
5. What does the last paragraph of the story reveal about the narrator's feelings for the child?

TONE
Recognizing Tone

Tone is the attitude a writer takes toward the subject, characters, and readers of a literary work. Tone shows the writer's mood. To give you some examples, tone can be solemn, humorous, romantic, mocking, compassionate, bitter. If you have read Morley Callaghan's "All the Years of Her Life" (page 69), you remember that the tone of that story is serious. If you have read Saki's "The Storyteller" (page 32), you recall that the tone of that story is humorous. A writer's tone can sometimes shift within a work. It is not uncommon for a writer to shift from a comic mood to a serious mood or to express individual attitudes toward different characters in a story. Generally, however, a story has a predominant tone.

It is important to recognize the tone of a story. If you fail to recognize tone, you may misunderstand the author's intention. If you were to take the tale of Bertha and her medals as a tragedy, you would miss the ironic point of Saki's story.

An important element that contributes to the overall tone of a story is the writer's choice of words. Kipling uses the word *crooning* to describe Muhammad Din's singing. *To croon* is to make a soft, pleasant, lulling sound. Consider the difference in tone had Kipling used the word *moan*.

Kipling's story is emotionally moving in a quiet way. We might use the words *touching* or *poignant* to describe its tone.

Despite the formal and dignified relationship between the narrator and Muhammad Din, we are aware that the narrator finds the child charming. Find examples in the story that show the narrator's interest in the child.

How does Kipling convey the joyful innocence of Muhammad Din?

Read the last paragraph of the story aloud. How does Kipling manage to show both strong emotion and restraint?

UNDERSTANDING THE WORDS IN THE STORY (Multiple-Choice)

1. The polo ball was old and *dinted.*
   a. scarred
   b. dented
   c. dirty

2. The narrator *set no store by* the polo ball.
   a. did not value
   b. had no need for
   c. was not using
3. Imam Din was too *portly* to play polo.
   a. old
   b. stout
   c. weary
4. The child had been waiting to *secure* the ball.
   a. get possession of
   b. ensure
   c. protect
5. The child's *inadequate* shirt was
   a. too large for him
   b. just the right size
   c. too small for him
6. The child was *crooning.*
   a. sobbing quietly
   b. howling
   c. singing softly
7. Muhammad Din *took stock of* the pictures.
   a. put away
   b. valued
   c. examined
8. The child was too *absorbed* in his discoveries to notice
   the narrator.
   a. active
   b. fully occupied
   c. inattentive
9. The child let out a *gasp.*
   a. wild shriek
   b. long, dry howl
   c. sudden catch of breath
10. The child was so startled that his eyes opened and his
    mouth *followed suit.*
    a. also opened
    b. began making noises
    c. trembled

(Matching Columns)

1. quarters		a.	enclosed group of residences
2. penitent		b.	to lessen
3. convey		c.	supporting frame
4. subside		d.	in poor taste
5. state		e.	communicate
6. trellis		f.	place to live in
7. salutation		g.	person's work
8. unseemly		h.	greeting
9. compound		i.	one who is sorry
10. handiwork		j.	grand style

(Fill in the Blanks)

eclipse	rude
disfigure	edifice
alternating	meditated
singular	effacing
orbit	bounded

1. Muhammad Din had built a(an) _____ square.

2. Bits of brick were _____ with bits of broken china.

3. The construction was _____ by a bank of dust.

4. The child's work did not _____ the garden.

5. Muhammad Din spent an hour _____ all his work.

6. Imam Din told the child that by the _____ favor of the Sahib, he would be allowed to play in the garden.

7. The child planned a new _____ to build.

8. The beauty of the new work would _____ the old work.

9. The child's _____ was among the castor-oil bushes.

10. Before starting, the child _____ for an hour.

FOR WRITING

1. Review the methods of direct and indirect characterization (see pages 48 and 58). Show how Kipling develops the character of Muhammad Din by a combination of methods.

2. Setting, as you have seen, is the physical background for a story. "The Story of Muhammad Din" takes place in colonial India. Show how Kipling gives the reader a feeling for the setting through details of description, speech, and action.

3. In the collection of stories where "The Story of Muhammad Din" first appeared, it was accompanied by the following quotation:

> Who is the happy man? He that sees in his own house at home, little children crowned with dust, leaping and falling and crying.
>
> *Munichandra*
> translated by Professor Peterson

Explain what relationship this quotation has to Kipling's tale.

*"See the look in that horse's eyes?
You know, I think those two share a secret."*

A
SECRET
FOR TWO

Quentin Reynolds

Montreal is a very large city, but, like all large cities, it has some very small streets. Streets, for instance, like Prince Edward Street, which is only four blocks long, ending in a cul-de-sac.[1] No one knew Prince Edward Street as well as did Pierre Dupin, for Pierre had delivered milk to the families on the street for thirty years now.

During the past fifteen years the horse which drew the milk wagon used by Pierre was a large white horse named Joseph. In Montreal, especially in that part of Montreal which is very French, the animals, like children, are often given the names of saints. When the big white horse first came to the Provincale Milk Company he didn't have a name. They told Pierre that he could use the white horse henceforth. Pierre stroked the softness of the horse's neck; he stroked the sheen of its splendid belly and he looked into the eyes of the horse.

"This is a kind horse, a gentle and a faithful horse," Pierre said, "and I can see a beautiful spirit shining out of the eyes of the horse. I will name him after good St. Joseph,

1. **cul-de-sac** (kŭl′dĭ-săk′): dead-end street.

189

who was also kind and gentle and faithful and a beautiful spirit."

Within a year Joseph knew the milk route as well as Pierre. Pierre used to boast that he didn't need reins—he never touched them. Each morning Pierre arrived at the stables of the Provincale Milk Company at five o'clock. The wagon would be loaded and Joseph hitched to it. Pierre would call *"Bon jour, vieille ami,"*[2] as he climbed into his seat and Joseph would turn his head and the other drivers would smile and say that the horse would smile at Pierre. Then Jacques, the foreman, would say, "All right, Pierre, go on," and Pierre would call softly to Joseph, *"Avance, mon ami,"*[3] and this splendid combination would stalk proudly down the street.

The wagon, without any direction from Pierre, would roll three blocks down St. Catherine Street, then turn right two blocks along Roslyn Avenue; then left, for that was Prince Edward Street. The horse would stop at the first house, allow Pierre perhaps thirty seconds to get down from his seat and put a bottle of milk at the front door and would then go on, skipping two houses and stopping at the third. So down the length of the street. Then Joseph, still without any direction from Pierre, would turn around and come back along the other side. Yes, Joseph was a smart horse.

Pierre would boast at the stable of Joseph's skill. "I never touch the reins. He knows just where to stop. Why, a blind man could handle my route with Joseph pulling the wagon."

So it went on for years—always the same. Pierre and Joseph both grew old together, but gradually, not suddenly.

---

2. *"Bon jour, vieille ami"* (bōn zhōōr′ vyā ȧ-mē′): French for "Good morning, old friend."
3. *"Avance, mon ami"* (ȧ-väns′ mōn ȧ-mē′): French for "Go ahead, my friend."

Pierre's huge walrus mustache was pure white now and Joseph didn't lift his knees so high or raise his head quite as much. Jacques, the foreman of the stables, never noticed that they were both getting old until Pierre appeared one morning carrying a heavy walking stick.

"Hey, Pierre," Jacques laughed. "Maybe you got the gout, hey?"

"*Mais oui,*[4] *Jacques,*" Pierre said a bit uncertainly. "One grows old. One's legs get tired."

"You should teach that horse to carry the milk to the front door for you," Jacques told him. "He does everything else."

He knew every one of the forty families he served on Prince Edward Street. The cooks knew that Pierre could neither read nor write, so instead of following the usual custom of leaving a note in an empty bottle if an additional quart of milk was needed they would sing out when they heard the rumble of his wagon wheels over the cobbled street, "Bring an extra quart this morning, Pierre."

"So you have company for dinner tonight," he would call back gaily.

Pierre had a remarkable memory. When he arrived at the stable he'd always remember to tell Jacques, "The Paquins took an extra quart this morning; the Lemoines bought a pint of cream."

Jacques would note these things in a little book he always carried. Most of the drivers had to make out the weekly bills and collect the money, but Jacques, liking Pierre, had always excused him from this task. All Pierre had to do was to arrive at five in the morning, walk to his wagon, which was always in the same spot at the curb, and deliver his milk. He returned some two hours later, got down stiffly

---

4. *"Mais oui"* (mā wē′): French for "But of course."

from his seat, called a cheery *"Au 'voir"*[5] to Jacques and then limped slowly down the street.

One morning the president of the Provincale Milk Company came to inspect the early morning deliveries. Jacques pointed Pierre out to him and said: "Watch how he talks to that horse. See how the horse listens and how he turns his head toward Pierre? See the look in that horse's eyes? You know, I think those two share a secret. I have often noticed it. It is as though they both sometimes chuckle at us as they go off on their route. Pierre is a good man, Monsieur[6] President, but he gets old. Would it be too bold of me to suggest that he be retired and be given perhaps a small pension?" he added anxiously.

"But of course," the president laughed. "I know his record. He has been on this route now for thirty years and never once has there been a complaint. Tell him it is time he rested. His salary will go on just the same."

But Pierre refused to retire. He was panic-stricken at the thought of not driving Joseph every day. "We are two old men," he said to Jacques. "Let us wear out together. When Joseph is ready to retire—then I, too, will quit."

Jacques, who was a kind man, understood. There was something about Pierre and Joseph which made a man smile tenderly. It was as though each drew some hidden strength from the other. When Pierre was sitting in his seat, and when Joseph was hitched to the wagon, neither seemed old. But when they finished their work, then Pierre would limp down the street slowly, seeming very old indeed, and the horse's head would drop and he would walk very wearily to his stall.

Then one morning Jacques had dreadful news for Pierre when he arrived. It was a cold morning and still pitch-dark.

---

5. *"Au 'voir"*: "Au revoir" (ō' rə-vwär'), French for "Until we meet again."
6. **Monsieur** (mə-syœ'): a French title equivalent to "Mister" or "Sir."

The air was like iced wine that morning and the snow which had fallen during the night glistened like a million diamonds piled together.

Jacques said, "Pierre, your horse, Joseph, did not wake up this morning. He was very old, Pierre, he was twenty-five and that is like being seventy-five for a man."

"Yes," Pierre said, slowly. "Yes. I am seventy-five. And I cannot see Joseph again."

"Of course you can," Jacques soothed. "He is over in his stall, looking very peaceful. Go over and see him."

Pierre took one step forward then turned. "No . . . no . . . you don't understand, Jacques."

Jacques clapped him on the shoulder. "We'll find another horse just as good as Joseph. Why, in a month you'll teach him to know your route as well as Joseph did. We'll . . ."

The look in Pierre's eyes stopped him. For years Pierre had worn a heavy cap, the peak of which came low over his eyes, keeping the bitter morning wind out of them. Now Jacques looked into Pierre's eyes and he saw something which startled him. He saw a dead, lifeless look in them. The eyes were mirroring the grief that was in Pierre's heart and his soul. It was as though his heart and soul had died.

"Take today off, Pierre," Jacques said, but already Pierre was hobbling off down the street, and had one been near one would have seen tears streaming down his cheeks and have heard half-smothered sobs. Pierre walked to the corner and stepped into the street. There was a warning yell from the driver of a huge truck that was coming fast and there was the scream of brakes, but Pierre apparently heard neither.

Five minutes later an ambulance driver said, "He's dead. Was killed instantly."

Jacques and several of the milk-wagon drivers had arrived and they looked down at the still figure.

"I couldn't help it," the driver of the truck protested, "he walked right into my truck. He never saw it, I guess. Why, he walked into it as though he were blind."

The ambulance doctor bent down, "Blind? Of course the man was blind. See those cataracts? This man has been blind for five years." He turned to Jacques, "You say he worked for you? Didn't you know he was blind?"

"No . . . no . . ." Jacques said, softly. "None of us knew. Only one knew—a friend of his named Joseph. . . . It was a secret, I think, just between those two."

CHECK-UP (True/False)

1. This story takes place in Canada.
2. The main character is a foreman.
3. Joseph is named for the driver's brother.
4. Pierre Dupin works as a deliveryman for a milk company.
5. Pierre's customers leave notes for their orders in empty bottles.
6. Pierre works for six hours a day.
7. Pierre agrees to retire after the president offers him a pension.
8. The horse dies on a summer night.
9. Pierre is deaf as well as blind.
10. The secret in this story is shared by a man and his horse.

FOR DISCUSSION

1. What does the "secret" in the title of the story refer to? Why are the two friends able to keep this secret from others?
2. What details in the story foreshadow Pierre's blindness?

3. Did you find the story believable? Explain your answer.
4. How do you know that the author has a warmhearted view of his characters?

TONE
Sentimentalism

Short stories can arouse different feelings in readers. Some stories, like "Who's There?" (page 7), can cause us to experience suspense and excitement. Some stories, like "The Tell-Tale Heart" (page 135), can make us experience horror. Other stories, like "Miss Brill" (page 51), can make us feel sad. Still other stories, like "The Storyteller" (page 32), can make us laugh. Some stories, like "Father and I" (page 127), shift in tone so that we first experience feelings of happiness, then feelings of anxiety.

When the term *sentimentalism* is used of literature, it refers to the expression of gentle or tender feelings. Quentin Reynolds' tone in "A Secret for Two" is *sentimental.* His feelings toward his characters are warm and tender. He has affection for his characters and wants the reader to feel kindly and sympathetic toward them.

Note how Reynolds focuses on the relationship of Pierre and his horse. How does he develop the sense of a special bond between man and animal?

Note the reactions of other characters in the story. How do their comments and actions create sympathy for Pierre and Joseph?

Note the direct comments of the narrator. Find several examples that reveal his attitude toward the different characters.

How does the final episode of the story make you feel?

UNDERSTANDING THE WORDS
IN THE STORY (Completion)

Choose one of the words in the following list to complete each of the sentences below. A word may be used only once.

hobbling	route
stalk	boast
protested	apparently
sheen	soothed
glistened	stall

1. When Pierre first saw the big white horse, he stroked the _____ of the horse's belly.

2. The horse was as familiar with the milk _____ as Pierre was.

3. After the wagon was loaded, the man and animal would _____ down the street.

4. At the stable Pierre used to _____ of his horse's ability.

5. When they returned, Joseph would be put in his _____.

6. The snow that had fallen during the night _____ like diamonds.

7. Jacques _____ Pierre with the news that Joseph was looking peaceful.

8. After he left the stable, Pierre began _____ down the street.

9. Although the driver called a warning, Pierre _____ heard nothing.

10. The truck driver _____ that the accident was unavoidable.

FOR WRITING

1. "A Secret for Two" ends with the death of the horse and shortly thereafter the death of the old man. Did you feel that this was an appropriate ending for the story? Explain your reaction briefly.
2. Think of another story or novel that focuses on the relationship between a person and an animal. Some examples are "Weep No More, My Lady" by James Street; "My Friend Flicka" by Mary O'Hara; "Lassie Come Home" by Eric Knight; *National Velvet* by Enid Bagnold. In a brief essay, describe the relationship and tell how it affects the outcome of the narrative.

Alan could hardly believe his ears.
The effects of the potion would be permanent.

THE
CHASER

John Collier

Alan Austen, as nervous as a kitten, went up certain dark and creaky stairs in the neighborhood of Pell Street, and peered about for a long time on the dim landing before he found the name he wanted written obscurely on one of the doors.

He pushed open this door, as he had been told to do, and found himself in a tiny room, which contained no furniture but a plain kitchen table, a rocking chair, and an ordinary chair. On one of the dirty buff-colored walls were a couple of shelves, containing in all perhaps a dozen bottles and jars.

An old man sat in the rocking chair, reading a newspaper. Alan, without a word, handed him the card he had been given. "Sit down, Mr. Austen," said the old man politely. "I am glad to make your acquaintance."

"Is it true," asked Alan, "that you have a certain mixture that has—er—quite extraordinary effects?"

"My dear sir," replied the old man, "my stock in trade is not very large—I don't deal in laxatives and teething mixtures—but, such as it is, it is varied. I think nothing I sell has effects which could be precisely described as ordinary."

"Well, the fact is—" began Alan.

"Here, for example," interrupted the old man, reaching

for a bottle from the shelf. "Here is a liquid as colorless as water, almost tasteless, quite imperceptible[1] in coffee, milk, wine, or any other beverage. It is also quite imperceptible to any known method of autopsy."

"Do you mean it is a poison?" cried Alan, very much horrified.

"Call it cleaning fluid if you like," said the old man indifferently. "Lives need cleaning. Call it a spot remover. 'Out, damned spot!' Eh? 'Out, brief candle!' "[2]

"I want nothing of that sort," said Alan.

"Probably it is just as well," said the old man. "Do you know the price of this? For one teaspoonful, which is sufficient, I ask five thousand dollars. Never less. Not a penny less."

"I hope all your mixtures are not as expensive," said Alan apprehensively.[3]

"Oh, dear, no," said the old man. "It would be no good charging that sort of price for a love potion, for example. Young people who need a love potion very seldom have five thousand dollars. If they had they would not need a love potion."

"I'm glad to hear you say so," said Alan.

"I look at it like this," said the old man. "Please a customer with one article, and he will come back when he needs another. Even if it *is* more costly. He will save up for it, if necessary."

"So," said Alan, "you really do sell love potions?"

"If I did not sell love potions," said the old man, reaching for another bottle, "I should not have mentioned the other

1. **imperceptible** (ĭm′pər-sĕp′tə-bəl): not noticeable.
2. " **'Out damned . . . candle!'** ": Two famous quotations from *Macbeth*, a tragedy by William Shakespeare; the first referring to the guilt of murder, which can never be cleansed away, the second to the brevity of life.
3. **apprehensively** (ăp′rĭ-hĕn′sĭv-lē): anxiously; uneasily.

matter to you. It is only when one is in a position to oblige that one can afford to be so confidential."

"And these potions," said Alan. "They are not just—just—er—"

"Oh, no," said the old man. "Their effects are permanent, and extend far beyond the mere carnal impulse. But they include it. Oh, yes, they include it. Bountifully. Insistently. Everlastingly."

"Dear me!" said Alan, attempting a look of scientific detachment. "How very interesting!"

"But consider the spiritual side," said the old man.

"I do, indeed," said Alan.

"For indifference," said the old man, "they substitute devotion. For scorn, adoration. Give one tiny measure of this to the young lady—its flavor is imperceptible in orange juice, soup, or cocktails—and however gay and giddy she is, she will change altogether. She'll want nothing but solitude, and you."

"I can hardly believe it," said Alan. "She is so fond of parties."

"She will not like them anymore," said the old man. "She'll be afraid of the pretty girls you may meet."

"She'll actually be jealous?" cried Alan in a rapture. "Of me?"

"Yes, she will want to be everything to you."

"She is, already. Only she doesn't care about it."

"She will, when she has taken this. She will care intensely. You will be her sole interest in life."

"Wonderful!"

"She'll want to know all you do," said the old man. "All that has happened to you during the day. Every word of it. She'll want to know what you are thinking about, why you smile suddenly, why you are looking sad."

"That is love!" cried Alan.

"Yes," said the old man. "How carefully she'll look after you! She'll never allow you to be tired, to sit in a draft, to neglect your food. If you are an hour late, she'll be terrified. She'll think you are killed, or that some siren[4] has caught you."

"I can hardly imagine Diana like that!" cried Alan, overwhelmed with joy.

"You will not have to use your imagination," said the old man. "And, by the way, since there are always sirens, if by any chance you *should*, later on, slip a little, you need not worry. She will forgive you, in the end. She'll be terribly hurt, of course, but she'll forgive you—in the end."

"That will not happen," said Alan fervently.

"Of course not," said the old man. "But if it does, you need not worry. She'll never divorce you. Oh, no! And, of course, she herself will never give you the least, the very least, grounds for—not divorce, of course—but even uneasiness."

"And how much," said Alan, "how much is this wonderful mixture?"

"It is not so dear," said the old man, "as the spot remover, as I think we agreed to call it. No. That is five thousand dollars; never a penny less. One has to be older than you are to indulge in that sort of thing. One has to save up for it."

"But the love potion?" said Alan.

"Oh, that," said the old man, opening the drawer in the kitchen table and taking out a tiny, rather dirty-looking phial. "That is just a dollar."

"I can't tell you how grateful I am," said Alan, watching him fill it.

"I like to oblige," said the old man. "Then customers

---

4. **siren** (sī′rən): a temptress.

come back, later in life, when they are rather better off, and want more expensive things. Here you are. You will find it very effective."

"Thank you again," said Alan. "Goodbye."

"Au revoir," said the old man.

CHECK-UP (True/False)

1. At the opening of the story, Alan is feeling bold and confident.
2. The old man keeps a shop on the ground floor of a building in an elegant street.
3. Alan is amazed to see rows of bottles and jars on the shelves.
4. The old man is eager to oblige his customers.
5. Alan and the old man have met at a party.
6. The old man's spot remover is a poison.
7. The old man's mixtures are colorless and tasteless.
8. The love potion costs five thousand dollars.
9. Alan wants the potion to have a permanent effect on Diana.
10. The old man's customers frequently come back for other mixtures.

FOR DISCUSSION

1. How does the opening description capture your interest?
2. Instead of referring to his mixture as a poison, the old man calls it a "cleaning fluid." An inoffensive word or phrase substituted for one that is disagreeable or harsh is called a *euphemism* (yōō′fə-mĭz′əm). Why do you think the old man prefers this indirect use of language?

3. Alan is interested in a love potion. Why does the old man tell him about the spot remover? Why does he keep referring to it?
4. Alan believes that he will be happy by the transformation in Diana after she takes the love potion. What do you think is going to happen?
5. When Alan leaves, the old man says *"au revoir"* instead of "goodbye." What is the significance of this parting phrase?
6. A *chaser* is something mild, such as water or ginger ale, taken after a strong alcoholic drink. What do you think the *chaser* of the title refers to?

TONE
Irony

You have seen that a story can have ironic elements (see pages 4, 29, and 107). Sometimes the tone of an entire story is ironic.

Irony involves a difference or contrast between appearance and reality—that is a discrepancy between what appears to be true and what really is true. Irony reminds us that life is unpredictable and that what we expect to happen or wish to have happen does not always have the intended result. Irony can make us smile or wince. Irony can be genial or bitter.

In "The Chaser" there are three kinds of irony:

1. *Irony of situation,* in which there is a contrast between what is expected to happen and what actually happens. Alan Austen is in love and thinks that all he needs to be happy is to be loved in return. It is clear that the love potion will fulfill his expectations, but that something unexpected will happen as well. How will giving the love potion to Diana bring about results that are the opposite of what he wishes for?

2. *Dramatic irony,* in which the reader knows something that a character in the story does not know. Alan believes that he is interested only in the love potion. The reader is led to believe that Alan will return at a later time for the spot remover. How is this outcome suggested in the story?

3. *Verbal Irony,* in which a character says one thing and means something entirely different. Alan takes the old man's speeches at face value, never grasping the sinister meaning of his words. What is he predicting will happen eventually to Alan's love? Refer to specific passages in your answer.

UNDERSTANDING THE WORDS IN THE STORY (Multiple-Choice)

1. To *peer* at something is to
   a. stare blankly without recognizing it
   b. take quick glances on the sly
   c. look closely in order to see it clearly
2. A name written *obscurely*
   a. is easy to read
   b. is difficult to make out
   c. has an odd spelling
3. Effects that are *extraordinary* are
   a. remarkable
   b. painful
   c. expected
4. A merchant's *stock in trade* consists of
   a. goods available for sale
   b. cattle for branding
   c. raw materials for industry
5. An *autopsy* is conducted to
   a. check one's financial records
   b. diagnose a patient's illness
   c. find the cause of death

6. When one is said to speak or behave *indifferently*, one
   a. seems annoyed
   b. shows interest
   c. appears unconcerned
7. A *sufficient* quantity is
   a. enough
   b. inadequate
   c. plentiful
8. A *potion* is something one
   a. shares
   b. drinks
   c. eats
9. When you *oblige* someone, you make a special effort to be
   a. distant
   b. helpful
   c. demanding
10. The opposite of *carnal* is
    a. spiritual
    b. earthly
    c. physical

(Matching Columns)

1. bountifully	a.	overcome
2. detachment	b.	small bottle
3. scorn	c.	eagerly
4. giddy	d.	contempt
5. solitude	e.	give in to an urge
6. rapture	f.	aloneness
7. overwhelm	g.	generously
8. fervently	h.	flighty
9. indulge	i.	separation
10. phial	j.	extreme joy

FOR WRITING

1. Choose one of the three kinds of irony described on pages 203–204. In a brief essay, show how John Collier makes use of that form of irony in "The Chaser."
2. Transform "The Chaser" into a short radio play, adding sound effects where they would be effective. Write the script, adapting the action and dialogue for presentation on the air.
3. One of the most famous stories in English literature, "The Strange Case of Dr. Jekyll and Mr. Hyde" by Robert Louis Stevenson, makes use of a magic potion, which changes personality. If you have read the story, tell how that potion was created and what its effects were.

*"The Princess smiled and walked up to the table
and picked up the present she liked the most."*

THE PRINCESS AND THE TIN BOX

James Thurber

Once upon a time, in a far country, there lived a king
whose daughter was the prettiest princess in the world. Her
eyes were like the cornflower, her hair was sweeter than the
hyacinth, and her throat made the swan look dusty.

From the time she was a year old, the princess had been
showered with presents. Her nursery looked like Cartier's[1]
window. Her toys were all made of gold or platinum or diamonds or emeralds. She was not permitted to have wooden
blocks or china dolls or rubber dogs or linen books, because
such materials were considered cheap for the daughter of a
king.

When she was seven, she was allowed to attend the wedding of her brother and throw real pearls at the bride instead
of rice. Only the nightingale, with his lyre of gold, was permitted to sing for the princess. The common blackbird, with
his boxwood flute, was kept out of the palace grounds. She
walked in silver-and-samite[2] slippers to a sapphire-and-

---

1. **Cartier's** (kär-tyāz′): a store in New York City that sells very expensive
   jewelry.
2. **samite** (sā′mīt′): a heavy fabric of silk, often with silver or gold threads
   interwoven.

topaz bathroom and slept in an ivory bed inlaid with rubies.

On the day the princess was eighteen, the king sent a royal ambassador to the courts of five neighboring kingdoms to announce that he would give his daughter's hand in marriage to the prince who brought her the gift she liked the most.

The first prince to arrive at the palace rode a swift white stallion and laid at the feet of the princess an enormous apple made of solid gold which he had taken from a dragon who had guarded it for a thousand years. It was placed on a long ebony table set up to hold the gifts of the princess's suitors. The second prince, who came on a gray charger, brought her a nightingale made of a thousand diamonds, and it was placed beside the golden apple. The third prince, riding on a black horse, carried a great jewel box made of platinum and sapphires, and it was placed next to the diamond nightingale. The fourth prince, astride a fiery yellow horse, gave the princess a gigantic heart made of rubies and pierced by an emerald arrow. It was placed next to the platinum-and-sapphire jewel box.

Now the fifth prince was the strongest and handsomest of all the five suitors, but he was the son of a poor king whose realm had been overrun by mice and locusts and wizards and mining engineers so that there was nothing much of value left in it. He came plodding up to the palace of the princess on a plow horse and he brought her a small tin box filled with mica and feldspar and hornblende[3] which he had picked up on the way.

The other princes roared with disdainful laughter when they saw the tawdry gift the fifth prince had brought to the princess. But she examined it with great interest and

---

3. **mica** (mī′kə) . . . **feldspar** (fĕld′spär′, fĕl′) . . . **hornblende** (hôrn′blĕnd′): common mineral substances found in rocks.

squealed with delight, for all her life she had been glutted with precious stones and priceless metals, but she had never seen tin before or mica or feldspar or hornblende. The tin box was placed next to the ruby heart pierced with an emerald arrow.

"Now," the king said to his daughter, "you must select the gift you like best and marry the prince that brought it."

The princess smiled and walked up to the table and picked up the present she liked the most. It was the platinum-and-sapphire jewel box, the gift of the third prince.

"The way I figure it," she said, "is this. It is a very large and expensive box, and when I am married, I will meet many admirers who will give me precious gems with which to fill it to the top. Therefore, it is the most valuable of all the gifts my suitors have brought me and I like it the best."

The princess married the third prince that very day in the midst of great merriment and high revelry. More than a hundred thousand pearls were thrown at her and she loved it.

Moral: All those who thought the princess was going to select the tin box filled with worthless stones instead of one of the other gifts will kindly stay after class and write one hundred times on the blackboard "I would rather have a hunk of aluminum silicate than a diamond necklace."

CHECK-UP (True/False)

1. The princess's toys were all made of precious metals and gems.
2. She had a pet blackbird that sang to her in the palace.
3. She was allowed to throw rice at her brother's wedding.
4. All the suitors' gifts were placed on the princess's ivory bed.
5. The first of the princess's suitors brought an enormous golden apple.
6. One of the gifts was a bird made of a thousand diamonds.
7. The princess received a heart made of rubies with an emerald arrow.
8. The fifth prince was the strongest and handsomest of the suitors but brought nothing.
9. The princess made her choice on the basis of what was most valuable.
10. The princess in this story believes that is better to give than to receive.

FOR DISCUSSION

1. In fairy tales the beautiful princess and the handsome prince fall in love, marry, and live happily ever after. What has replaced the importance of love in Thurber's story?
2. Why does the princess choose the jewel box? What does this choice reveal about her values?
3. Do you think Thurber admires the princess, or do you think he is poking fun at her? Support your opinion with evidence from the story.
4. How does Thurber show a keen understanding of human nature in this story?

TONE
Satire

Sometimes a humorous story, such as Thurber's "The Princess and the Tin Box," mocks or ridicules certain weaknesses, follies, or vices in human nature and society. A literary work that pokes fun at some failing of human behavior is called *satire.* Satire is generally of two kinds: it can be gentle, amusing, and lighthearted, or it can be biting, bitter, even savage. Thurber's story is of the genial variety. This satiric work is not intended to insult or hurt anyone, but to point out the foolishness of certain attitudes and beliefs.

In a traditional fairy tale, the plot might go like this. The princess would prefer the poor but handsome prince above the other suitors and would choose his insignificant gift. As a reward, the prince would drop his disguise and announce that he assumed a humble appearance in order to test her, that in reality he is the richest prince in all the neighboring kingdoms.

Thurber's princess, however, is not an idealist who has noble spiritual goals and principles. She is a materialist who believes that wealth and pleasure are the chief goals and values to be concerned with.

Thurber seems to be saying that both extremes are laughable. The princess who would choose a "hunk of aluminum silicate" over a diamond necklace would be unbelievably foolish. The princess in the story comes in for her share of ridicule, too. She is what is commonly referred to as a "gold digger," a woman whose chief interest in men is to get money and gifts from them. By exposing her for what she is, Thurber gets us to laugh at her and her shallow values.

One way Thurber achieves a satiric tone in this story is by using *exaggeration.* Note, for example, Thurber's account of the privileged childhood of the princess. Which details are particularly absurd?

Another technique Thurber uses is *incongruity* (ĭn'kŏng-groo'ə-tē, ĭn'kən-), the pairing of opposites to create an unexpected contrast. Note the princess's manner of speaking in Thurber's story. How is her speech *incongruous,* or inconsistent, with the traditional image of a storybook princess?

UNDERSTANDING THE WORDS IN THE STORY (Multiple-Choice)

1. The *hyacinth* is a
   a. small, furry animal
   b. plant with sweet-smelling flowers
   c. precious gem
2. The *lyre* is used to
   a. make music
   b. weave precious cloth
   c. house birds
3. An *ambassador* is
   a. a representative of one country to another
   b. an official who arranges royal weddings
   c. a servant in charge of palace expenses
4. The color of an *ebony* table is
   a. silvery
   b. dark or black
   c. pale blue
5. One rides a *charger*
   a. on a racecourse
   b. into battle
   c. to deliver mail
6. One rides *astride* when one sits
   a. with one leg on each side of a horse
   b. with both legs on one side of a saddle
   c. on a horse with no saddle
7. One is *disdainful* when feeling
   a. ill at ease in someone's presence
   b. talkative and friendly
   c. superior to someone or something

8. An example of *tawdry* jewelry is a
   a. string of cultured pearls
   b. rope of flashy glass beads
   c. diamond engagement ring
9. To be *glutted* is to
   a. have just enough to be satisfied
   b. experience hunger
   c. be filled beyond the point of satisfaction
10. One expects *revelry* during a
    a. feast
    b. concert
    c. test

FOR WRITING

1. Some readers think that "The Princess and the Tin Box" is critical of certain values in our society. Other readers believe that Thurber is having fun with the make-believe world of fairy tales. What do you think? Express your opinion in a brief essay.
2. Write a satirical version of a well-known fairy tale, such as "Hansel and Gretel," "Cinderella," or "Little Red Ridinghood," using elements of exaggeration and incongruity to provide humor.

*"I'd never taken a litho-bromide and
I didn't know that the tablets were supposed
to be dropped into a glass of water where
they would fizz while dissolving."*

AH LOVE!
AH ME!

Max Steele

It happened six years ago—when I was in my junior
year at high school—that I saw Sara Nell Workman for the
first time and—not to be sentimental—I liked the girl. I liked
her so much, in fact, that I would go to the library and read
the cards in the back of the books to find the ones she had
borrowed. I would take these out and read them carefully,
including one called *Needlepoint and Needlecraft*.

"It's for my sister," I said hoarsely to the librarian who
was looking at me curiously. There were some penciled
notes in the margins about hemstitching, and whether Sara
made these notes or not, I don't know. At the time I liked to
imagine that she did, and I read them over and over: "Two
skeins of black, two orange, one yellow, and the tulip stencil.
Mother's Day, 17 days."

But when you're sixteen, you can't keep reading mar-
ginal notes over and over. At least I couldn't. And so the time
came that I decided to ask Sara for a date. That day at school
I couldn't find her by herself, and juniors in high school
don't just up and ask a girl for a date in front of everybody.

214

At home that night I went out into the hall where the phone was and shut the door behind me. I wrote Sara's number on the pad and then one sentence: "Sara—*Jezebel* is on Friday night and I was just wondering if you'd like to see it with me."

That sounded casual and easy enough to say, but when I heard the operator ringing the number, I got excited and crumpled the paper in my hand. For a second I considered hanging up, but then someone said, "Hello."

"Oh," I said. "May I speak to Sara Workman?"

"This is she," she said, rather impatiently it seemed.

"Oh, Sara," I said, "uh, this is Dave . . ."

"Yes," she said.

"Do you know what our history assignment is for tomorrow?" I asked hopelessly.

"Just a minute," she said. She got her book and gave me the assignment. I thanked her and hung up. Then I untwisted the phone wire and went back to my room to brood.

About an hour later I decided that the thing to do was to jump up suddenly without thinking, rush into the hall, and phone her before I had a chance to become flustered. I jumped up quickly, but then I turned back to the dresser and brushed my hair before rushing out of the room.

When Sara answered the phone, I blurted out, "Would you like to go to the show with me Friday night? This is Dave."

"Well, I don't know," Sara said very slowly and coolly. "What's on?"

"I don't know," I said. "I thought maybe we'd just go mess around uptown."

"What?" she asked.

"I mean I don't know," I said. "*Lucy Belle* or something like that." I really couldn't remember.

"*Jezebel!*" she said. "Bette Davis. Yeah! I'd love to see it."

"Okay," I said. "Goodbye."

The next day I avoided meeting Sara alone. In the line at cafeteria she leaned against two people and said to me, "That was you last night, wasn't it?"

"Yeah," I said.

She smiled and for a moment I was afraid that she was going to laugh but she didn't.

Friday night at eight o'clock when we were leaving Sara's house, Mr. Workman, who looked like John L. Lewis,[1] asked, "Who's driving?"

"I am," I said.

"You got a license?"

"Yes, sir."

"Well," he hollered, as we went down the walk, "just see to it that you get Sara back here safe. And before eleven o'clock."

"Yes, sir," I said.

"Eleven o'clock, Sara," he screamed.

She was embarrassed, but she hollered back, "Yes, sir."

At the theater we had to stand in line, and when finally we did get seats they were in the third row. My neck was hurting before the newsreel was over, but Sara didn't seem to mind looking straight up at the screen.

When the picture was almost over, she caught me looking at her. "Whatsa matter?" she whispered.

"Headache," I said. "I think it's from looking straight . . ."

"Shhhh . . ." she whispered. On the screen Bette Davis

---

1. **John L. Lewis:** a labor leader (1880–1969), whose bushy eyebrows made him look stern.

was risking death by yellow fever to be with her man and nurse him.

Sara was very quiet when we came out of the show. As we walked down Main Street, I said, "Do you think she should have stayed with him? She probably caught yellow fever, too."

"It's not a matter of what you should or shouldn't do," Sara said. "For when you love a man, nothing can tear you away."

"Good gosh!" I said. Above us a neon light flickered off and on and buzzed as though it would explode.

We stood in front of Shaeffer's drugstore for a minute. It was ten-fifteen then, and Sara was worried about getting home.

"Just something to drink," she said, "we haven't time to eat."

She ordered a chocolate milk, and I wanted one, too, but I thought it would look kind of sophisticated to order something for my headache. I couldn't remember ammonia and Coke, so I asked the waiter what he had for a headache.

"Aspirin, epsom salts, litho-bromide, anything you want," he said.

"Bring me a litho-bromide," I said, trying to sound weary, "and a Coke."

"Still hurts?" Sara asked softly.

I smiled at her without answering.

John Bowerman and two other seniors came in and took the booth next to ours. All of the booths and tables were filling with the crowd from the movie.

The waiter brought the order. My Coke was in one glass, two litho-bromide tablets were in the bottom of an empty glass, and there was a big glass of water.

I'd never taken a litho-bromide and I didn't know that the tablets were supposed to be dropped into a glass of water where they would fizz while dissolving. I just shook the tablets out into my hand, popped them in my mouth, and swallowed them one at a time as though they were aspirin. Then I drank half the Coke while Sara tasted her milkshake.

Before I had time to say anything, the litho-bromide started bubbling noisily in my stomach.

I drank the rest of the Coke and tried to pretend that nothing was happening. Sara put down her glass and stared at me, terrified. I sounded like somebody gargling under a barrel.

"It always does this," I said bravely. But by then the rumblings from the mixture were too ominous to be ignored by me or the people in the other booths. Everyone was staring at my stomach.

"Everybody's looking at you," Sara whispered. She was so red that I was afraid she was going to cry.

"Sounds like somebody churning buttermilk," John Bowerman said, coming around to our booth.

"He's effervescing!"[2] the waiter announced happily to the astonished customers. "Just listen to him fizz!"

"Sara," I said, and I was going to tell her to get me out of there, but I was afraid to open my mouth to say anything else. The rumbling just sounded deeper when I did, like drumming on a hollow log.

"Doc Shaeffer!" John Bowerman called out when Sara told him what I had done.

Doc Shaeffer climbed over the prescription counter. "Stand back!" he said to the crowd that was gathering around our booth.

They stepped back as though they expected me to explode.

"It's nothing serious," Doc Shaeffer said. "Get his head lower than his stomach. Give me a hand with him."

---

2. **effervescing** (ĕf'ər-vĕs'ĭng): bubbling up; foaming.

"He says it always does this," Sara said.

"That's pretty hard to believe," Doc said, as John Bowerman and the two seniors picked me up and carried me to the prescription counter. They stretched me out and let my head hang off with my mouth open. A dogfight couldn't have attracted more attention. Doc Shaeffer brought a wet towel from the back of the drugstore. Sara stood beside me and rubbed my forehead with it.

"Sara," I said, and I suppose now I must have sounded rather melodramatic[3] to the other people, "you won't leave me, will you?"

"Oh, my goodness!" Sara said. "What time is it?"

"Ten till eleven," John Bowerman said.

Sara dropped the wet towel in my face. "I've got to be home by eleven!" she said.

"I'll take you," John said.

I took the towel off my face in time to see them stopping by the booth for Sara's pocketbook. She didn't even look back at me.

The four or five people who were standing by me went back to their tables. I lay quietly on the counter and watched the light above swaying gently in the noisy room.

Gradually, two by two, the people left, and the noise of the dishes being stacked grew quieter and quieter. I watched the waiter turn the chairs upside down on the tables and felt sorry for him and for myself and for the whole pitiful world.

---

3. **melodramatic** (mĕl′ə-drə-măt′ĭk): overly emotional and exaggerated.

CHECK-UP (Putting Events in Order)

Arrange the following events in the order in which they occur in the story.

>   The waiter brings the order.
>   Dave telephones Sara and asks for a homework assignment.
>   A crowd gathers around the booth where Dave and Sara are sitting.
>   Dave checks out a library book on needlepoint.
>   Dave watches the waiter turn the chairs upside down.
>   Mr. Workman asks Dave if he has a license.
>   Sara drops the towel and leaves.
>   Two seniors pick Dave up and carry him to the prescription counter.
>   Dave's stomach begins to make rumbling noises.
>   Dave gets a headache.

FOR DISCUSSION

1. In spite of carefully planning what he will say to Sara on the phone, Dave loses his nerve when he hears Sara's voice. Why does he have such a difficult time asking for a date?
2. Why does Dave think Sara will be impressed by his ordering a litho-bromide for his headache?
3. At the end of the story, John Bowerman, a senior, takes Sara home. Why does this event make Dave feel even sorrier for himself?
4. The movie that Dave and Sara see is a romantic melodrama in which a woman risks "death by yellow fever to be with her man and nurse him." In what way is the episode in the drugstore a comic parallel to the movie?

TONE
Humor

In Steele's story there are ironic elements. Events turn out to be the opposite of what is intended. Dave, who tries so hard to impress Sara, succeeds only in embarrassing her and in making a fool of himself. The story also satirizes Dave's pretensions at being mature and worldly. The overall tone of the story, however, is not ironic or satirical; it is humorous. The tone is warm and genial rather than critical. We laugh at Dave's predicament, but we also sympathize with him. Everyone has embarrassing moments; they are a natural part of growing up.

One source of the story's humor lies in the amusing contrast between the movie romance and the real-life romance. Unlike the heroine in the film, Sara will not risk anything, and surely not her father's anger, to stay at Dave's side. She drops the wet towel in his face and leaves with an "older man," the senior John Bowerman.

Reread the passage describing Dave's phone call to Sara. Why is this episode so funny?

UNDERSTANDING THE WORDS
IN THE STORY (Matching Columns)

1. sentimental
2. casual
3. brood
4. flustered
5. blurted
6. flickering
7. sophisticated
8. dissolving
9. ominous
10. churning

a. to think deeply
b. threatening
c. unplanned
d. shaking vigorously
e. said suddenly without thinking
f. passing into solution
g. worldly
h. giving off light unsteadily
i. showing tender feelings
j. nervous

FOR WRITING

1. Write a dialogue in which Sara tells a friend about her date with Dave. Be sure to use quotation marks to enclose the speakers' exact words.
2. Sometimes a story is built around an *anecdote,* a humorous or entertaining incident from personal experience. Choose an episode from your own life that might be expanded into a humorous story. You might follow Steele's example and choose to tell about an embarrassing moment.

Theme

*"None of the Emperor's clothes
had ever met with such a success."*

THE
EMPEROR'S
NEW CLOTHES

Hans Christian Andersen

Many years ago there lived an Emperor who was so exceedingly fond of fine new clothes that he spent all his money on being elaborately dressed. He took no interest in his soldiers, no interest in the theater, nor did he care to drive about in his state coach, unless it were to show off his new clothes. He had different robes for every hour of the day, and just as one says of a King that he is in his Council Chamber, people always said of him, "The Emperor is in his wardrobe!"

The great city in which he lived was full of gaiety. Strangers were always coming and going. One day two swindlers arrived; they made themselves out to be weavers, and said they knew how to weave the most magnificent fabric that one could imagine. Not only were the colors and patterns unusually beautiful, but the clothes that were made of this material had the extraordinary quality of becoming invisible to everyone who was either unfit for his post, or inexcusably stupid.

"What useful clothes to have!" thought the Emperor. "If I had some like that, I might find out which of the people in my Empire are unfit for their posts. I should also be able to distinguish the wise from the fools. Yes, that material must be woven for me immediately!" Then he gave the swindlers large sums of money so that they could start work at once.

Quickly they set up two looms and pretended to weave, but there was not a trace of anything on the frames. They made no bones about demanding the finest silk and the purest gold thread. They stuffed everything into their bags, and continued to work at the empty looms until late into the night.

"I'm rather anxious to know how much of the material is finished," thought the Emperor, but to tell the truth, he felt a bit uneasy, remembering that anyone who was either a fool or unfit for his post would never be able to see it. He rather imagined that he need not have any fear for himself, yet he thought it wise to send someone else first to see how things were going. Everyone in the town knew about the exceptional powers of the material, and all were eager to know how incompetent or how stupid their neighbors might be.

"I will send my honest old Chamberlain[1] to the weavers," thought the Emperor. "He will be able to judge the fabric better than anyone else, for he has brains, and nobody fills his post better than he does."

So the nice old Chamberlain went into the hall where the two swindlers were sitting working at the empty looms.

1. **Chamberlain** (chām′bər-lĭn): a high official at court.

"Upon my life!" he thought, opening his eyes very wide, "I can't see anything at all!" But he didn't say so.

Both the swindlers begged him to be good enough to come nearer, and asked how he liked the unusual design and the splendid colors. They pointed to the empty looms, and the poor old Chamberlain opened his eyes wider and wider, but he could see nothing, for there was nothing. "Heavens above!" he thought, "could it possibly be that I am stupid? I have never thought that of myself, and not a soul must know it. Could it be that I am not fit for my post? It will never do for me to admit that I can't see the material!"

"Well, you don't say what you think of it," said one of the weavers.

"Oh, it's delightful—most exquisite!" said the old Chamberlain, looking through his spectacles. "What a wonderful design and what beautiful colors! I shall certainly tell the Emperor that I am enchanted with it."

"We're very pleased to hear that," said the two weavers, and they started describing the colors and the curious pattern. The old Chamberlain listened carefully in order to repeat, when he came home to the Emperor, exactly what he had heard, and he did so.

The swindlers now demanded more money, as well as more silk and gold thread, saying that they needed it for weaving. They put everything into their pockets and not a thread appeared upon the looms, but they kept on working at the empty frames as before.

Soon after this, the Emperor sent another nice official to see how the weaving was getting on, and to inquire whether the stuff would soon be ready. Exactly the same thing happened to him as to the Chamberlain. He looked and looked, but as there was nothing to be seen except the empty looms, he could see nothing.

"Isn't it a beautiful piece of material?" said the swindlers, showing and describing the pattern that did not exist at all.

"Stupid I certainly am not," thought the official; "then I must be unfit for my excellent post, I suppose. That seems rather funny—but I'll take great care that nobody gets wind of it." Then he praised the material he could not see, and assured them of his enthusiasm for the gorgeous colors and the beautiful pattern. "It's simply enchanting!" he said to the Emperor.

The whole town was talking about the splendid material.

And now the Emperor was curious to see it for himself while it was still upon the looms.

Accompanied by a great number of selected people, among whom were the two nice old officials who had already been there, the Emperor went forth to visit the two wily swindlers. They were now weaving madly, yet without a single thread upon the looms.

"Isn't it magnificent?" said the two nice officials. "Will your Imperial Majesty deign to look at this splendid pattern and these glorious colors?" Then they pointed to the empty looms, for each thought that the others could probably see the material.

"What on earth can this mean?" thought the Emperor. "I don't see anything! This is terrible. Am I stupid? Am I unfit to be Emperor? That would be the most disastrous thing that could possibly befall me.—Oh, it's perfectly wonderful!" he said. "It quite meets with my Imperial approval." And he nodded appreciatively and stared at the empty looms—he would not admit that he saw nothing. His whole suite looked and looked, but with as little result as the others; nevertheless, they all said, like the Emperor, "It's perfectly wonderful!" They advised him to have some new clothes made from this splendid stuff and to wear them for the first time in the next great procession.

"Magnificent!" "Excellent!" "Prodigious!"[2] went from mouth to mouth, and everyone was exceedingly pleased. The Emperor gave each of the swindlers a decoration to wear in his buttonhole, and the title of "Knight of the Loom."

Before the procession they worked all night, burning more than sixteen candles. People could see how busy they were finishing the Emperor's new clothes. They pretended to take the material from the looms, they slashed the air with great scissors, they sewed with needles without any thread, and finally they said, "The Emperor's clothes are ready!"

Then the Emperor himself arrived with his most distinguished courtiers, and each swindler raised an arm as if he were holding something, and said, "These are Your Imperial Majesty's knee breeches. This is Your Imperial Majesty's robe. This is Your Imperial Majesty's mantle," and so forth. "It is all as light as a spider's web, one might fancy one had nothing on, but that is just the beauty of it!"

"Yes, indeed," said all the courtiers, but they could see nothing, for there was nothing to be seen.

"If Your Imperial Majesty would graciously consent to take off your clothes," said the swindlers, "we could fit on the new ones in front of the long glass."

So the Emperor laid aside his clothes, and the swindlers pretended to hand him, piece by piece, the new ones they were supposed to have made, and they fitted him round the waist, and acted as if they were fastening something on—it was the train;[3] and the Emperor turned round and round in front of the long glass.

"How well the new robes suit Your Imperial Majesty! How well they fit!" they all said. "What a splendid design! What gorgeous colors! It's all magnificently regal!"

"The canopy which is to be held over Your Imperial

2. **prodigious** (prə-dĭj'əs): amazing.
3. **train:** the part of the robe that trails behind.

Majesty in the procession is waiting outside," announced the Lord High Chamberlain.

"Well, I suppose I'm ready," said the Emperor. "Don't you think they are a nice fit?" And he looked at himself again in the glass, first on one side and then the other, as if he really were carefully examining his handsome attire.

The courtiers who were to carry the train groped about on the floor with fumbling fingers, and pretended to lift it; they walked on, holding their hands up in the air; nothing would have induced them to admit that they could not see anything.

And so the Emperor set off in the procession under the beautiful canopy, and everybody in the streets and at the windows said, "Oh! how superb the Emperor's new clothes are! What a gorgeous train! What a perfect fit!" No one would acknowledge that he didn't see anything, so proving that he was not fit for his post, or that he was very stupid.

None of the Emperor's clothes had ever met with such a success.

"But he hasn't got any clothes on!" gasped out a little child.

"Good heavens! Hark at the little innocent!" said the father, and people whispered to one another what the child had said. "But he hasn't got any clothes on! There's a little child saying he hasn't got any clothes on!"

"But he hasn't got any clothes on!" shouted the whole town at last. The Emperor had a creepy feeling down his spine, because it began to dawn upon him that the people were right. "All the same," he thought to himself, "I've got to go through with it as long as the procession lasts."

So he drew himself up and held his head higher than before, and the courtiers held on to the train that wasn't there at all.

CHECK-UP (True/False)

1. The swindlers in this story take advantage of the Emperor's vanity.
2. The swindlers claim that their fabric is invisible to anyone who is dishonest or cowardly.
3. The old Chamberlain pretends to admire the fabric because he wishes to trap the swindlers.
4. The only honest person in the story is a little child.
5. At the end of the story, the Emperor realizes that he has been tricked.

FOR DISCUSSION

1. What does the Emperor's overriding interest in fine clothes reveal about his character?
2. Why are the swindlers able to dupe the Emperor, the Chamberlain, the courtiers, and the people watching the procession?
3. How does the child's innocence expose the folly and deceitfulness of the other people in the story?
4. At the end of the story, the Emperor realizes that he has been tricked. Why does he decide, nevertheless, to go through with the procession?
5. The swindlers claim that people who cannot see the cloth are stupid or unfit for their posts. How do the events of the story show, ironically, that this judgment is true?

UNDERSTANDING THEME

Is "The Emperor's New Clothes" really about clothes? Although "clothes"—real or imaginary—are the focus in the story, we sense that the events of the story are meant to illustrate something about human nature. The Emperor and all his subjects are willing to spread an outrageous falsehood rather than risk being accused of stupidity or incompetence. The clothes in the story are central to the underlying notion that people need a flattering image of themselves. This is the central idea, or *theme,* that is developed in the story.

Not every story can be said to have a theme. Mysteries and adventure stories are told mainly for entertainment, and theme is generally of little or no significance in them. Theme is an important element in those stories that offer insight into human beings.

Sometimes theme is expressed directly in a story. Most of the time, however, the theme must be inferred from other elements in the story.

UNDERSTANDING THE WORDS IN THE STORY (Completion)

Choose one of the words in the following list to complete each of the sentences below. A word may be used only once.

suite	induced
wily	exquisite
dawn	attire
imperial	deign
regal	acknowledge

1. The old Chamberlain told the two swindlers that their work was _____.

2. The Emperor finally went in person to see what the two _____ swindlers had woven.

3. They asked if the Emperor would _____ to examine the cloth.

4. The Emperor nodded and said that the fabric had his _____ approval.

5. The Emperor's entire _____ looked at the empty looms and said that the material was wonderful.

6. The courtiers praised the splendor of the _____ robes.

7. The Emperor looked at himself in the mirror, admiring his _____ .

8. The courtiers could not be _____ to admit that they could not see the cloth.

9. The people watching the procession would not _____ that they couldn't see the Emperor's new clothes.

10. Finally, it began to _____ upon the Emperor that he had been swindled.

FOR WRITING

1. In a paragraph tell why the people in this story allow themselves to be cheated by the two swindlers.
2. Do you think the Emperor gets what he deserves? Give your opinion in a short essay.
3. Try your hand at a modern-day version of "The Emperor's New Clothes."

"Is it possible in this world to be without teeth and claws—to be such a nincompoop?"

A NINCOMPOOP

Anton Chekhov°

A few days ago I asked my children's governess, Julia Vassilyevna,[1] to come into my study.

"Sit down, Julia Vassilyevna," I said. "Let's settle our accounts. Although you most likely need some money, you stand on ceremony and won't ask for it yourself. Now then, we agreed on thirty rubles a month. . . ."

"Forty."

"No, thirty. I made a note of it. I always pay the governess thirty. Now then, you've been here two months, so . . ."

"Two months and five days."

"Exactly two months. I made a specific note of it. That means you have sixty rubles coming to you. Subtract nine Sundays . . . you know you didn't work with Kolya[2] on Sundays, you only took walks. And three holidays . . ."

Julia Vassilyevna flushed a deep red and picked at the flounce of her dress, but—not a word.

"Three holidays, therefore take off twelve rubles. Four days Kolya was sick and there were no lessons, as you were occupied only with Vanya.[3] Three days you had a toothache and my wife gave you permission not to work after lunch.

° **Chekhov** (chĕk′ôf′).
1. **Vassilyevna** (vä-sēl′yĕv-nä).
2. **Kolya** (kōl′yä).
3. **Vanya** (vän′yä).

Twelve and seven—nineteen. Subtract . . . that leaves . . .
hmm . . . forty-one rubles. Correct?"

Julia Vassilyevna's left eye reddened and filled with
moisture. Her chin trembled; she coughed nervously and
blew her nose, but—not a word.

"Around New Year's you broke a teacup and saucer:
take off two rubles. The cup cost more, it was an heirloom,
but—let it go. When didn't I take a loss! Then, due to your
neglect, Kolya climbed a tree and tore his jacket: take away
ten. Also due to your heedlessness the maid stole Vanya's
shoes. You ought to watch everything! You get paid for it.
So, that means five more rubles off. The tenth of January I
gave you ten rubles. . . ."

"You didn't," whispered Julia Vassilyevna.

"But I made a note of it."

"Well . . . all right."

"Take twenty-seven from forty-one—that leaves fourteen."

Both eyes filled with tears. Perspiration appeared on the
thin, pretty little nose. Poor girl!

"Only once was I given any money," she said in a trembling voice, "and that was by your wife. Three rubles, nothing more."

"Really? You see now, and I didn't make a note of it!
Take three from fourteen . . . leaves eleven. Here's your
money, my dear. Three, three, three, one and one. Here it
is!"

I handed her eleven rubles. She took them and with
trembling fingers stuffed them into her pocket.

"*Merci*,"[4] she whispered.

I jumped up and started pacing the room. I was overcome with anger.

---

4. *Merci* (mâr-sē′): French for "Thank you." During the nineteenth century
in czarist Russia, French was spoken by the upper classes.

"For what, this—*'merci'*?" I asked.

"For the money."

"But you know I've cheated you—robbed you! I have actually stolen from you! *Why* this *'merci'*?"

"In my other places they didn't give me anything at all."

"They didn't give you anything? No wonder! I played a little joke on you, a cruel lesson, just to teach you. . . . I'm going to give you the entire eighty rubles! Here they are in an envelope all ready for you. . . . Is it really possible to be so spineless? Why don't you protest? Why be silent? Is it possible in this world to be without teeth and claws—to be such a nincompoop?"

She smiled crookedly and I read in her expression: "It is possible."

I asked her pardon for the cruel lesson and, to her great surprise, gave her the eighty rubles. She murmured her little *"merci"* several times and went out. I looked after her and thought: "How easy it is to crush the weak in this world!"

a statement talk about theme

CHECK-UP (True/False)

1. The person telling the story is Julia Vassilyevna's employer.
2. He wishes to cheat the girl.
3. Julia Vassilyevna works as a maid.
4. She is used to being cheated.
5. At the end of the story, she decides to leave her job.

FOR DISCUSSION

1. What is the relationship of the two characters?
2. Why is the speaker "overcome with anger" at the girl's passive acceptance of the eleven rubles?
3. The speaker says he wants to teach the girl "a cruel lesson." What is the lesson he wishes her to learn?
4. In your opinion, does the girl learn the lesson? Give reasons for your answer.
5. Do you think the speaker learns another lesson from this episode? Explain your answer.
6. Why does the speaker refer to the girl as a "nincompoop"? Does this word create derision or sympathy for her?

EXPLICIT THEME

A theme is the controlling idea behind a story. It expresses a point of view about life or gives us insight into human behavior. Sometimes an author makes the theme of a story *explicit,* or plain, through direct statement. The last sentence of "A Nincompoop" leaves no doubt about the meaning of Chekhov's story. His tale of the pathetic governess, who can be so easily bullied, dramatizes his compassion for weak and defenseless creatures in society.

Cite specific passages in the story that help to create sympathy for Julia Vassilyevna.

UNDERSTANDING THE WORDS
IN THE STORY (Matching Columns)

1. governess
2. ceremony
3. flushed
4. flounce
5. heirloom
6. heedlessness
7. spineless
8. protest
9. nincompoop
10. expression

a. turned red
b. object to
c. look
d. precious possession
e. cowardly
f. fool
g. ruffle
h. instructor
i. carelessness
j. formal act

FOR WRITING

1. In a short story there is generally a problem or struggle of some kind called a *conflict.* In a brief essay, tell what the conflict in this story is.
2. It is often said of Chekhov's stories that they express both the comic and the serious aspects of human nature. In a brief essay, show how "A Nincompoop" combines both comic and serious moods.

*During the Spanish Civil War (1936–1939),
the Loyalists supported the government
of Spain. The Fascists were led by
General Francisco Franco.*

OLD MAN AT THE BRIDGE

Ernest Hemingway

An old man with steel-rimmed spectacles and very dusty clothes sat by the side of the road. There was a pontoon bridge[1] across the river and carts, trucks, and men, women and children were crossing it. The mule-drawn carts staggered up the steep bank from the bridge with soldiers helping push against the spokes of the wheels. The trucks ground up and away heading out of it all and the peasants plodded along in the ankle-deep dust. But the old man sat there without moving. He was too tired to go any farther.

It was my business to cross the bridge, explore the bridgehead beyond and find out to what point the enemy had advanced. I did this and returned over the bridge. There were not so many carts now and very few people on foot, but the old man was still there.

"Where do you come from?" I asked him.

"From San Carlos," he said, and smiled.

That was his native town and so it gave him pleasure to mention it and he smiled. *he proud where he come from*

---

1. **pontoon** (pŏn-tōon′) **bridge:** a temporary floating bridge using floats called *pontoons* for support.

"I was taking care of animals," he explained.

"Oh," I said, not quite understanding.

"Yes," he said, "I stayed, you see, taking care of animals. I was the last one to leave the town of San Carlos."

He did not look like a shepherd nor a herdsman and I looked at his black dusty clothes and his gray dusty face and his steel-rimmed spectacles and said, "What animals were they?"

"Various animals," he said, and shook his head. "I had to leave them."

I was watching the bridge and the African-looking country of the Ebro[2] Delta and wondering how long now it would be before we would see the enemy, and listening all the while for the first noises that would signal that ever mysterious event called contact, and the old man still sat there.

"What animals were they?" I asked.

"There were three animals altogether," he explained. "There were two goats and a cat and then there were four pairs of pigeons."

"And you had to leave them?" I asked.

"Yes. Because of the artillery. The captain told me to go because of the artillery."

"And you have no family?" I asked, watching the far end of the bridge where a few last carts were hurrying down the slope of the bank.

"No," he said, "only the animals I stated. The cat, of course, will be all right. A cat can look out for itself, but I cannot think what will become of the others."

"What politics have you?" I asked.

"I am without politics," he said. "I am seventy-six years old. I have come twelve kilometers now and I think now I can go no further."

---

2. **Ebro** (ē′brō): the longest river in Spain. It rises in the north and flows southeast into the Mediterranean Sea.

"This is not a good place to stop," I said. "If you can make it, there are trucks up the road where it forks for Tortosa."

"I will wait a while," he said, "and then I will go. Where do the trucks go?"

"Towards Barcelona," I told him.

"I know no one in that direction," he said, "but thank you very much. Thank you again very much."

He looked at me very blankly and tiredly, then said, having to share his worry with someone, "The cat will be all right, I am sure. There is no need to be unquiet about the cat. But the others. Now what do you think about the others?"

"Why they'll probably come through it all right."

"You think so?"

"Why not," I said, watching the far bank where now there were no carts.

"But what will they do under the artillery when I was told to leave because of the artillery?"

"Did you leave the dove cage unlocked?" I asked.

"Yes."

"Then they'll fly."

"Yes, certainly they'll fly. But the others. It's better not to think about the others," he said.

"If you are rested I would go," I urged. "Get up and try to walk now."

"Thank you," he said and got to his feet, swayed from side to side and then sat down backwards in the dust.

"I was taking care of animals," he said dully, but no longer to me. "I was only taking care of animals."

There was nothing to do about him. It was Easter Sunday and the Fascists were advancing toward the Ebro. It was a gray overcast day with a low ceiling so their planes were not up. That and the fact that cats know how to look after themselves was all the good luck that old man would ever have.

CHECK-UP (True/False)

1. The old man is a farmer.
2. The narrator is a Fascist who is in revolt against the republic.
3. The old man wishes to go in the direction of Barcelona.
4. The old man is in favor of the Loyalist forces.
5. The old man was the last one to leave his native town.

FOR DISCUSSION

1. In this story the old man represents the innocent people who are the victims of war. How does Hemingway convey the sadness of the old man's situation?
2. The old man is worried about what will happen to the animals. In what way is his own fate mirrored in that of the animals he can no longer care for?
3. How does the old man's statement "I am without politics" emphasize the central meaning of the story?
4. What ironic significance is there to this action taking place on Easter Sunday?

IMPLIED THEME

The theme of a short story is seldom expressed directly. Most of the time, the theme of a story is *implied*—that is, readers have to work out the theme on their own.

Sometimes a single sentence or a key passage will point the way to the theme. In Hemingway's story, the old man's statement "I am without politics" focuses our attention on the central meaning of the story. The victims of war are often innocent and helpless people who are caught in the struggle for political power.

What does the narrator expect will happen to the old man and to the animals? How do you know?

FOR WRITING

1. Show how Hemingway develops the character of the old man through direct and indirect methods of characterization.
2. Compare the treatment of war in this story with that in "The Sniper" (page 101). Do you think the authors are making a similar statement or a different statement about war?

*"Ladies and gentlemen, this is the thrilling
moment the world has breathlessly awaited."*

THE PHOENIX°

Sylvia Townsend Warner

Lord Strawberry, a nobleman, collected birds. He had
the finest aviary[1] in Europe, so large that eagles did not find
it uncomfortable, so well laid out that both humming-birds
and snow-buntings had a climate that suited them perfectly.
But for many years the finest set of apartments remained
empty, with just a label saying: "PHOENIX. *Habitat: Arabia.*"

Many authorities on bird life had assured Lord Strawberry that the phoenix is a fabulous bird, or that the breed
was long extinct. Lord Strawberry was unconvinced: his
family had always believed in phoenixes. At intervals he
received from his agents (together with statements of their
expenses) birds which they declared were the phoenix but
which turned out to be orioles, macaws, turkey buzzards
dyed orange, etc., or stuffed cross-breeds, ingeniously assembled from various plumages. Finally Lord Strawberry
went himself to Arabia, where, after some months, he found
a phoenix, won its confidence, caught it, and brought it
home in perfect condition.

It was a remarkably fine phoenix, with a charming character—affable to the other birds in the aviary and much

° **Phoenix** (fē′nĭks): in Egyptian mythology, a bird of remarkable beauty,
  the only one of its kind. After 500 years, it would set itself on fire, and
  then rise renewed from its own ashes.
1. **aviary** (ā′vē-ĕr′ē): an enclosure for live birds.

attached to Lord Strawberry. On its arrival in England it made a great stir among ornithologists,[2] journalists, poets, and milliners, and was constantly visited. But it was not puffed up by these attentions, and when it was no longer in the news, and the visits fell off, it showed no pique or rancour. It ate well, and seemed perfectly contented.

It costs a great deal of money to keep up an aviary. When Lord Strawberry died he died penniless. The aviary came on the market. In normal times the rarer birds, and certainly the phoenix, would have been bid for by the trustees of Europe's great zoological societies, or by private persons in the U.S.A.; but as it happened Lord Strawberry died just after a world war, when both money and bird-seed were hard to come by (indeed the cost of bird-seed was one of the things which had ruined Lord Strawberry). The London *Times* urged in a leader[3] that the phoenix be bought for the London Zoo, saying that a nation of bird-lovers had a moral right to own such a rarity; and a fund, called the Strawberry Phoenix Fund, was opened. Students, naturalists, and schoolchildren contributed according to their means; but their means were small, and there were no large donations. So Lord Strawberry's executors (who had the death duties[4] to consider) closed with the higher offer of Mr. Tancred Poldero, owner and proprietor of Poldero's Wizard Wonderworld.

For quite a while Mr. Poldero considered his phoenix a bargain. It was a civil and obliging bird, and adapted itself readily to its new surroundings. It did not cost much to feed, it did not mind children; and though it had no tricks, Mr. Poldero supposed it would soon pick up some. The publicity

2. **ornithologists** (ô′nə-thŏl′ə-jĭsts): scientists who make a study of birds.
3. **leader:** the main editorial in a newspaper.
4. **death duties:** inheritance taxes.

of the Strawberry Phoenix Fund was now most helpful. Almost every contributor now saved up another half-crown[5] in order to see the phoenix. Others, who had not contributed to the fund, even paid double to look at it on the five-shilling days.

But then business slackened. The phoenix was as handsome as ever, and as amiable; but, as Mr. Poldero said, it hadn't got Udge. Even at popular prices the phoenix was not really popular. It was too quiet, too classical. So people went instead to watch the antics of the baboons, or to admire the crocodile who had eaten the woman.

One day Mr. Poldero said to his manager, Mr. Ramkin:

"How long since any fool paid to look at the phoenix?"

"Matter of three weeks," replied Mr. Ramkin.

"Eating his head off," said Mr. Poldero. "Let alone the insurance. Seven shillings a week it costs me to insure that bird, and I might as well insure the Archbishop of Canterbury."

"The public don't like him. He's too quiet for them, that's the trouble. Won't mate nor nothing. And I've tried him with no end of pretty pollies, ospreys, and Cochin-Chinas,[6] and the Lord knows what. But he won't look at them."

"Wonder if we could swap him for a livelier one," said Mr. Poldero.

"Impossible. There's only one of him at a time."

"Go on!"

"I mean it. Haven't you ever read what it says on the label?"

They went to the phoenix's cage. It flapped its wings politely, but they paid no attention. They read:

---

5. **half-crown:** a British coin worth two shillings and sixpence.
6. **Cochin** (kō′chĭn, kŏch′ĭn) **-Chinas:** large domestic fowls from Asia.

"PANSY. *Phoenix phoenixissima formosissima arabiana.*[7] This rare and fabulous bird is UNIQUE. The World's Old Bachelor. Has no mate and doesn't want one. When old, sets fire to itself and emerges miraculously reborn. Specifically imported from the East."

"I've got an idea," said Mr. Poldero, "How old do you suppose that bird is?"

"Looks in its prime to me," said Mr. Ramkin.

"Suppose," continued Mr. Poldero, "we could somehow get him alight? We'd advertise it beforehand, of course, work up interest. Then we'd have a new bird, and a bird with some romance about it, a bird with a life-story. We could sell a bird like that."

Mr. Ramkin nodded.

"I've read about it in a book," he said. "You've got to give them scented woods and what not, and they build a nest and sit down on it and catch fire spontaneous. But they won't do it till they're old. That's the snag."

"Leave that to me," said Mr. Poldero. "You get those scented woods, and I'll do the ageing."

It was not easy to age the phoenix. Its allowance of food was halved, and halved again, but though it grew thinner its eyes were undimmed and its plumage glossy as ever. The heating was turned off; but it puffed out its feathers against the cold, and seemed none the worse. Other birds were put into its cage, birds of a peevish and quarrelsome nature. They pecked and chivied[8] it; but the phoenix was so civil and amiable that after a day or two they lost their animosity. Then Mr. Poldero tried alley cats. These could not be won by good manners, but the phoenix darted above their heads and flapped its gold wings in their faces, and daunted them.

---

7. ***Phoenix . . . arabiana:*** The most beautiful Arabian phoenix of phoenixes.
8. **chivied** (chĭv′ēd): irritated, harassed.

Mr. Poldero turned to a book on Arabia, and read that the climate was dry. "Aha!" said he. The phoenix was moved to a small cage that had a sprinkler in the ceiling. Every night the sprinkler was turned on. The phoenix began to cough. Mr. Poldero had another good idea. Daily he stationed himself in front of the cage to jeer at the bird and abuse it.

When spring was come, Mr. Poldero felt justified in beginning a publicity campaign about the ageing phoenix. The old public favourite, he said, was nearing its end. Meanwhile he tested the bird's reactions every few days by putting a few tufts of foul-smelling straw and some strands of rusty barbed wire into the cage, to see if it were interested in nesting yet. One day the phoenix began turning over the straw. Mr. Poldero signed a contract for the film rights. At last the hour seemed ripe. It was a fine Saturday evening in May. For some weeks the public interest in the ageing phoenix had been working up, and the admission charge had risen to five shillings. The enclosure was thronged. The lights and the cameras were trained on the cage, and a loudspeaker proclaimed to the audience the rarity of what was about to take place.

"The phoenix," said the loud-speaker, "is the aristocrat of bird-life. Only the rarest and most expensive specimens of oriental woods, drenched in exotic perfumes, will tempt him to construct his strange love-nest."

Now a neat assortment of twigs and shavings, strongly scented, was shoved into the cage.

"The phoenix," the loud-speaker continued, "is as capricious as Cleopatra,[9] as luxurious as la du Barry,[10] as heady

---

9. **Cleopatra** (klē'ə-păt'rə, -pā'trə, -pä'trə): Queen of Egypt who lived from 69 to 30 B.C. She is often depicted as fascinating and unpredictable.
10. **du Barry** (dо̄о̄ băr'ē, dyо̄о̄): French countess (1746?–1793), favorite of King Louis XV. She lived in great splendor.

as a strain of wild gypsy music. All the fantastic pomp and passion of the ancient East, its languorous magic, its subtle cruelties . . ."

"Lawks!" cried a woman in the crowd. "He's at it!"

A quiver stirred the dulled plumage. The phoenix turned its head from side to side. It descended, staggering, from its perch. Then wearily it began to pull about the twigs and shavings.

The cameras clicked, the lights blazed full on the cage. Rushing to the loud-speaker Mr. Poldero exclaimed:

"Ladies and gentlemen, this is the thrilling moment the world has breathlessly awaited. The legend of centuries is materializing before our modern eyes. The phoenix . . ."

The phoenix settled on its pyre and appeared to fall asleep.

The film director said:

"Well, if it doesn't evaluate more than this, mark it instructional."

At that moment the phoenix and the pyre burst into flames. The flames streamed upwards, leaped out on every side. In a minute or two everything was burned to ashes, and some thousand people, including Mr. Poldero, perished in the blaze.

CHECK-UP (Multiple-Choice)

1. Mr. Poldero becomes the owner of the phoenix
   a. because he operates a zoo
   b. by buying it
   c. since he is Lord Strawberry's heir
2. Visitors lose interest in the phoenix because
   a. it hasn't any tricks
   b. the price is too high
   c. it doesn't like children

3. Mr. Poldero succeeds in aging the phoenix by
   a. turning off the heat
   b. cutting down its food allowance
   c. putting a sprinkler in its cage
4. Mr. Poldero knows that the phoenix is ready to build its nest when it
   a. begins coughing
   b. pulls at the twigs and shavings
   c. falls asleep on its perch

FOR DISCUSSION

1. The phoenix has two owners: first Lord Strawberry and then Mr. Poldero. Why is each man eager to possess the bird? How are their attitudes toward the phoenix contrasted?
2. Why do the people who come to the carnival prefer the baboons and the crocodile to the phoenix? What does this preference suggest about the public's taste?
3. How does Mr. Poldero plan to exploit the phoenix for his own profit? What do his methods reveal about him as a businessman? as a human being?
4. Mr. Poldero is hoping for a media event. How do his plans misfire?
5. A *satire* is a work that points out certain weaknesses or vices in human nature. What is the author satirizing in this story?

THEME AND SYMBOL

In "The Phoenix" Sylvia Townsend Warner gives us an unflattering image of our age. Her theme is that the commercial spirit of our time, with its overwhelming regard for profit, exploits and destroys those very elements which are of inestimable value. Central to Warner's theme is the symbol of the phoenix.

A *symbol* is a person, object, or event that has meaning in itself and that also stands for something else. An eagle, for example, is a bird of prey. That is its *literal* meaning. But an eagle also has a *symbolic* meaning. It is often used to represent our nation.

There are many conventional symbols. A dove symbolizes peace; snow symbolizes innocence or purity; light symbolizes spiritual inspiration or knowledge.

In a short story, a character, setting, or action may have both literal and symbolic meaning. In Hemingway's story "Old Man at the Bridge" (page 237), the animals clearly have a symbolic function. Their fate is symbolic of the fate of the old man; they are all innocent victims of war.

In Warner's story, the phoenix *literally* is a rare and wonderful bird. *Symbolically,* the phoenix stands for certain qualities: classical beauty, dignity, and nobility. These qualities are not compatible with the tastes of the age. The public begins to show interest when the phoenix becomes a media event. In other words, they need to be stimulated by sensationalism and violence.

In what way is Poldero's Wizard Wonderworld symbolic? How does it contribute to Warner's theme?

UNDERSTANDING THE WORDS IN THE STORY (Matching Columns)

1. fabulous
2. affable
3. pique
4. rancor
5. executor
6. proprietor
7. civil
8. slacken
9. antics
10. unique

a. ill will
b. polite
c. owner of a business
d. resentment
e. funny acts
f. legendary
g. slow down
h. alone of its kind
i. pleasant
j. someone who carries out the provisions of a will

(Multiple-Choice)

1. Mr. Ramkin told Mr. Poldero that the phoenix was in its *prime.*
   a. youth
   b. ideal period of life
   c. middle age
2. A *spontaneous* action occurs
   a. of its own accord
   b. on request
   c. with regularity
3. Birds of a *peevish* nature were placed in the phoenix's cage.
   a. friendly
   b. calm
   c. irritable
4. The birds soon lost their *animosity.*
   a. interest
   b. curiosity
   c. hostility
5. The phoenix's pleasant nature would *daunt* them.
   a. upset
   b. discourage
   c. frighten
6. People began to *throng* into the enclosure.
   a. crowd
   b. climb
   c. rush
7. The loudspeaker claimed that the wood had been scented with *exotic* perfumes.
   a. unusual
   b. expensive
   c. overpowering
8. The bird was compared to the *capricious* queen of Egypt.
   a. enchanting
   b. unpredictable
   c. beautiful

9. The *luxurious* du Barry lived in great splendor.
   a. pleasure-loving
   b. unhappy
   c. famous
10. The ancient East was associated with *languorous* magic.
    a. mysterious
    b. romantic
    c. dreamy

FOR WRITING

1. A *satire* mocks or ridicules certain weaknesses or vices in human nature and society (see page 211). Discuss "The Phoenix" as a satire. What is the object of Warner's satire? How does she use irony and incongruity to make her point?
2. Imagine that you are the publicist conducting the campaign about the aging phoenix. Write an ad to be placed in newspapers and magazines to attract the public.
3. Choose one of the following mythical creatures as the subject of a report. In your essay describe the creature and tell what special legends were associated with it.

   Cerberus
   Chimera
   Hydra
   Pegasus
   unicorn

THE
SPIDER'S
THREAD

Akutagawa Ryûnosuke

1

One day the Buddha[1] was strolling alone on the brink of
the lotus pond of Paradise.

The lotus flowers in bloom in the pond were all as white
as pearls, and the golden pistils and stamens in their centers
ceaselessly filled all the air with ineffable fragrance.

It was morning in Paradise.

Presently the Buddha stood still on the brink of the
pond, and through an opening among the leaves which
covered the face of the water, suddenly beheld the scene
below.

As the floor of Hell lay directly beneath the lotus pond of
Paradise, the River of the Threefold Path to eternal darkness
and the piercing peaks of the Needle Mountain were dis-
tinctly visible through the crystal water, as through a stereopticon.[2]

Then his eye fell on a man named Kandata, who was
squirming with the other sinners in the bottom of Hell.

---

1. **Buddha** (bōō'də, bōōd'ə): title of Gautama Siddhartha (563?–483? B.C.),
   Indian philosopher and teacher, the founder of Buddhism. He stands for
   divine wisdom and goodness.
2. **stereopticon** (stĕr'ē-ŏp'tĭ-kŏn', stîr'-): a projector for showing pictures
   from transparent slides.

This Kandata was a great robber who had done many evil things, murdering and setting fire to houses, but he had to his credit one good action. Once while on his way through a deep forest, he had noticed a little spider creeping along beside the road.

So quickly lifting his foot, he was about to trample it to death, when he suddenly thought: "No, no, as small as this thing is, it too has a soul. It would be rather a shame to kill it inconsiderately," and he spared the spider's life.

As he looked down into Hell, the Buddha remembered how this Kandata had spared the spider's life. And in return for that good deed, he thought, if possible he would like to deliver him out of Hell. Fortunately, when he looked around, he saw a spider of Paradise spinning a beautiful silvery thread on the lotus leaves.

The Buddha quietly took up the spider's thread in his hand. And he let it straight down to the bottom of Hell far below through the opening among the pearly-white lotus flowers.

2

Here Kandata had been rising and sinking with the other sinners in the Pool of Blood on the floor of Hell.

It was pitch black everywhere, and when at times a glimpse was caught of something rising from that darkness, it turned out to be the gleam of the peaks of the dread Needle Mountain. The stillness of the grave reigned everywhere, and the only thing that could be heard now and then was the faint sighing of the sinners. This was because such sinners as had come down to this spot had already been worn out by the other manifold tortures of Hell and had lost even the strength to cry aloud.

So, great robber though he was, Kandata, choking with the blood, could do nothing but struggle in the pool like a dying frog.

But his time came. On this day, when Kandata lifted his head by chance and looked up at the sky above the Pool of Blood, he saw a silver spider's thread slipping down toward him from the high, high heavens, glittering slightly in the silent darkness just as if it feared the eyes of man.

When he saw this, his hands clapped themselves for joy. If, clinging to this thread, he climbed as far as it went, he could surely escape from Hell. Nay, if all went well, he might even enter Paradise. Then he would never be driven on to the Needle Mountain or sunk in the Pool of Blood.

As soon as these thoughts came into his mind, he grasped the thread tightly in his two hands and began to climb up and up with all his might. Because he was a great robber, he had long been thoroughly familiar with such things.

But Hell is nobody knows how many myriads[3] of miles removed from Paradise, and strive as he might, he could not easily get out. After climbing for a while, he was finally exhausted and could not ascend an inch higher.

Since he could do nothing else, he stopped to rest, and hanging to the thread, looked far, far down below him. Now since he had climbed with all his might, the Pool of Blood where he had just been was already, much to his surprise, hidden deep down in the darkness. And the dread Needle Mountain glittered dimly under him. If he went up at this rate, he might get out of Hell more easily than he had thought.

With his hand twisted into the spider's thread, Kandata laughed and exulted in a voice such as he had not uttered during all the years since coming here: "Success! Success!"

But suddenly he noticed that below on the thread, countless sinners were climbing eagerly after him, up and

3. **myriads** (mîr'ē-əds): vast numbers.

up, like a procession of ants.

When he saw this, Kandata simply blinked his eyes for a moment, with his big mouth hanging foolishly open in surprise and terror.

How could that slender spider's thread, which seemed as if it must break even with him alone, ever support the weight of all those people?

If it should break in midair, even he himself, after all his effort in reaching this spot, would have to fall headlong back into Hell.

But meanwhile hundreds and thousands of sinners were squirming out of the dark Pool of Blood and climbing with all their might in a line up the slender, glittering thread. If he did not do something quickly, the thread was sure to break in two and fall. So Kandata cried out in a loud voice:

"Hey, you sinners! This spider's thread is mine. Who gave *you* permission to come up it? Get down! Get down!"

Just at that moment, the spider's thread, which had shown no sign of breaking up to that time, suddenly broke with a snap at the point where Kandata was hanging. Without even time to utter a cry, he shot down and fell headlong into the darkness, spinning swiftly around and around like a top.

Afterward, only the spider's thread of Paradise, glittering and slender, hung short in the moonless and starless sky.

3

Standing on the brink of the lotus pond of Paradise, the Buddha had watched closely all that had happened, and when Kandata sank like a stone to the bottom of the Pool of Blood, he began to walk again with a sad expression on his face.

Doubtless Kandata's cold heart that would have saved only himself, and his fall back into Hell, had appeared to the

Buddha's eyes most pitiful. But the lotuses in the lotus pond of Paradise cared nothing at all about such things.

The pearly-white flowers were swaying about the Buddha's feet. As they swayed, from the golden pistils in their centers, their ineffable fragrance filled all the air.

It was near noon in Paradise.

CHECK-UP (Putting Events in Order)

Arrange the following events in the order in which they occur in the story.

Kandata sees the silver spider's thread.
The Buddha remembers that Kandata spared a spider's life.
Kandata is exhausted by his climb toward Paradise.
Kandata sinks to the bottom of the Pool of Blood.
The Buddha decides to give Kandata a chance to leave Hell.
Kandata orders the sinners to get down.
The Buddha lets the spider's thread down to the bottom of Hell.
The Buddha looks at the sinners squirming in Hell.
Kandata sees a procession of sinners climbing after him.
The spider's thread snaps.

FOR DISCUSSION

1. What was Kandata's single good deed on earth? How does that deed become the means of rescuing him from Hell?
2. Why does the Buddha choose a spider's thread in order to test Kandata?

3. What evil in his own nature causes Kandata to fail the test?
4. Why is the Buddha saddened by Kandata's fate?
5. "The Spider's Thread" is an *exemplum,* a short narrative that illustrates some lesson about human conduct. In your own words, state the moral, or point, of the story.
6. What is the relationship of Part 2 to the opening and closing parts of the story?

THEME AND MORAL

A theme, as you have seen, is the underlying meaning of a story. It is some insight or generalization about life. Sometimes theme is expressed directly in a key passage of a story. Sometimes it is revealed indirectly.

Not every story has a theme. The purpose of a story like "The Dinner Party" (page 1) is to carry its readers through a series of suspenseful incidents and to surprise them with an ironic ending, rather than to illuminate character and relationships.

Sometimes, instead of expressing a theme, a story carries a *moral* that is intended to teach some rule of conduct about life. In the Middle Ages, preachers often inserted a tale into a sermon in order to illustrate a moral. Wishing to teach the text "Greed is the root of all evil," a preacher might insert a story about people who are destroyed by their greedy desires. The narrative was known as an *exemplum* (ĕg-zĕm'pləm), the Latin word for *example.* Although such a tale was entertaining, its primary purpose was to teach some timeless bit of wisdom about human conduct.

In "The Spider's Thread," the teachings of Buddha are conveyed through a story. Buddha emphasized the necessity of kindness, pity, and patience for salvation. How does "The Spider's Thread" illustrate the wisdom of Buddha?

UNDERSTANDING THE WORDS
IN THE STORY (Multiple-Choice)

Choose the best synonym for each of the following italicized words.

1. ". . . the Buddha was strolling alone on the *brink* of the lotus pond . . ."
   a. sands   b. edge   c. pebbles

2. "The lotus flowers . . . filled all the air with *ineffable* fragrance."
   a. indescribable   b. sweet   c. heavy

3. ". . . if possible he would like to *deliver* him out of Hell."
   a. release   b. carry   c. send

4. ". . . sinners . . . had already been worn out by the other *manifold* tortures of Hell . . ."
   a. cruel   b. unlimited   c. varied

5. ". . . *strive* as he might, he could not easily get out."
   a. cry   b. struggle   c. complain

6. ". . . he was finally exhausted and could not *ascend* an inch higher."
   a. see   b. move   c. climb

7. ". . . Kandata laughed and *exulted* . . ."
   a. rejoiced   b. wept   c. shouted

8. ". . . Kandata laughed . . . in a voice such as he had not *uttered* during all the years since coming here . . ."
   a. heard   b. used   c. spoken

9. ". . . countless sinners were climbing . . . like a *procession* of ants."
   a. long line   b. party   c. colony

10. ". . . he shot down and fell *headlong* into the darkness, spinning swiftly around . . ."
    a. tumbling   b. with great speed   c. slowly

FOR WRITING

1. "The Spider's Thread" is divided into three parts. In a brief essay, explain the purpose of this structure.
2. Write an original exemplum illustrating one of these sayings or another of your own choosing:

   The love of money is the root of evil.
   Virtue is its own reward.
   The only way to have a friend is to be one.
   A small leak will sink a great ship.

Total Effect

"There was something unnatural, uncanny,
in meeting this man."

AUGUST HEAT

William Fryer Harvey

PENISTONE ROAD, CLAPHAM,
20*th August*, 190—.

I have had what I believe to be the most remarkable day in my life, and while the events are still fresh in my mind, I wish to put them down on paper as clearly as possible.

Let me say at the outset that my name is James Clarence Withencroft.

I am forty years old, in perfect health, never having known a day's illness.

By profession I am an artist, not a very successful one, but I earn enough money by my black-and-white work to satisfy my necessary wants.

My only near relative, a sister, died five years ago, so that I am independent.

I breakfasted this morning at nine, and after glancing through the morning paper I lighted my pipe and proceeded to let my mind wander in the hope that I might chance upon some subject for my pencil.

The room, though door and windows were open, was

261

oppressively hot, and I had just made up my mind that the coolest and most comfortable place in the neighborhood would be the deep end of the public swimming bath, when the idea came.

I began to draw. So intent was I on my work that I left my lunch untouched, only stopping work when the clock of St. Jude's struck four.

The final result, for a hurried sketch, was, I felt sure, the best thing I had done.

It showed a criminal in the dock[1] immediately after the judge had pronounced sentence. The man was fat—enormously fat. The flesh hung in rolls about his chin; it creased his huge, stumpy neck. He was cleanshaven (perhaps I should say a few days before he must have been cleanshaven) and almost bald. He stood in the dock, his short, clumsy fingers clasping the rail, looking straight in front of him. The feeling that his expression conveyed was not so much one of horror as of utter, absolute collapse.

There seemed nothing in the man strong enough to sustain that mountain of flesh.

I rolled up the sketch, and without quite knowing why, placed it in my pocket. Then with the rare sense of happiness which the knowledge of a good thing well done gives, I left the house.

I believe that I set out with the idea of calling upon Trenton, for I remember walking along Lytton Street and turning to the right along Gilchrist Road at the bottom of the hill where the men were at work on the new tram[2] lines.

From there onwards I have only the vaguest recollection of where I went. The one thing of which I was fully conscious was the awful heat, that came up from the dusty asphalt pavement as an almost palpable wave. I longed for the thun-

---

1. **dock** (dŏk): in English criminal courts, the place where a defendant sits or stands.
2. **tram** (trăm): streetcar.

der promised by the great banks of copper-colored cloud that hung low over the western sky.

I must have walked five or six miles, when a small boy roused me from my reverie by asking the time.

It was twenty minutes to seven.

When he left me I began to take stock of my bearings. I found myself standing before a gate that led into a yard bordered by a strip of thirsty earth, where there were flowers, purple stock and scarlet geranium. Above the entrance was a board with the inscription:

CHAS. ATKINSON
MONUMENTAL MASON
WORKER IN ENGLISH AND ITALIAN MARBLES

From the yard itself came a cheery whistle, the noise of hammer blows, and the cold sound of steel meeting stone.

A sudden impulse made me enter.

A man was sitting with his back towards me, busy at work on a slab of curiously veined marble. He turned round as he heard my steps and I stopped short.

It was the man I had been drawing, whose portrait lay in my pocket.

He sat there, huge and elephantine,[3] the sweat pouring from his scalp, which he wiped with a red silk handkerchief. But though the face was the same, the expression was absolutely different.

He greeted me smiling, as if we were old friends, and shook my hand.

I apologized for my intrusion.

"Everything is hot and glary outside," I said. "This seems an oasis in the wilderness."

"I don't know about the oasis," he replied, "but it certainly is hot. Take a seat, sir!"

---

3. **elephantine** (ĕl′ə-făn′tĭn, -tēn′, -tīn′): huge and heavy-footed.

He pointed to the end of the gravestone on which he was at work, and I sat down.

"That's a beautiful piece of stone you've got hold of," I said.

He shook his head. "In a way it is," he answered; "the surface here is as fine as anything you could wish, but there's a big flaw at the back, though I don't expect you'd ever notice it. I could never make really a good job of a bit of marble like that. It would be all right in a summer like this; it wouldn't mind the blasted heat. But wait till the winter comes. There's nothing quite like frost to find out the weak points in stone."

"Then what's it for?" I asked.

The man burst out laughing.

"You'd hardly believe me if I was to tell you it's for an exhibition, but it's the truth. Artists have exhibitions: so do grocers and butchers; we have them too. All the latest little things in headstones, you know."

He went on to talk of marbles, which sort best withstood wind and rain; and which were easiest to work; then of his garden and a new sort of carnation he had bought. At the end of every other minute he would drop his tools, wipe his shining head, and curse the heat.

I said little, for I felt uneasy. There was something unnatural, uncanny, in meeting this man.

I tried at first to persuade myself that I had seen him before, that his face, unknown to me, had found a place in some out-of-the-way corner of my memory, but I knew that I was practicing little more than a plausible piece of self-deception.

Mr. Atkinson finished his work, spat on the ground, and got up with a sigh of relief.

"There! What do you think of that?" he said, with an air of evident pride.

The inscription which I read for the first time was this:

SACRED TO THE MEMORY
OF
JAMES CLARENCE WITHENCROFT.
BORN JAN. 18TH, 1860.

HE PASSED AWAY VERY SUDDENLY
ON AUGUST 20TH, 190—

"In the midst of life we are in death."

For some time I sat in silence. Then a cold shudder ran down my spine. I asked him where he had seen the name.

"Oh, I didn't see it anywhere," replied Mr. Atkinson. "I wanted some name, and I put down the first that came into my head. Why do you want to know?"

"It's a strange coincidence, but it happens to be mine."

He gave a long, low whistle.

"And the dates?"

"I can only answer for one of them, and that's correct."

"It's a rum go!"[4] he said.

But he knew less than I did. I told him of my morning's work. I took the sketch from my pocket and showed it to him. As he looked, the expression of his face altered until it became more and more like that of the man I had drawn.

"And it was only the day before yesterday," he said, "that I told Maria there were no such things as ghosts!"

Neither of us had seen a ghost, but I knew what he meant.

"You probably heard my name," I said.

"And you must have seen me somewhere and have forgotten it! Were you at Clacton-on-Sea last July?"

I had never been to Clacton in my life. We were silent for

---

4. **rum go:** British slang with the general meaning of "It's a strange business."

some time. We were both looking at the same thing, the two dates on the gravestone, and one was right.

"Come inside and have some supper, " said Mr. Atkinson.

His wife is a cheerful little woman, with the flaky red cheeks of the country-bred. Her husband introduced me as a friend of his who was an artist. The result was unfortunate, for after the sardines and watercress had been removed, she brought out a Doré[5] Bible, and I had to sit and express my admiration for nearly half an hour.

I went outside, and found Atkinson sitting on the gravestone smoking.

We resumed the conversation at the point we had left off.

"You must excuse my asking," I said, "but do you know of anything you've done for which you could be put on trial?"

He shook his head.

"I'm not a bankrupt, the business is prosperous enough. Three years ago I gave turkeys to some of the guardians[6] at Christmas, but that's all I can think of. And they were small ones, too," he added as an afterthought.

He got up, fetched a can from the porch, and began to water the flowers. "Twice a day regular in the hot weather," he said, "and then the heat sometimes gets the better of the delicate ones. And ferns, they could never stand it. Where do you live?"

I told him my address. It would take an hour's quick walk to get back home.

"It's like this, " he said. "We'll look at the matter straight. If you go back home tonight, you take your chance of accidents. A cart may run over you, and there's always banana

5. **Doré:** (Paul) Gustave Doré (dô-rā′), a French artist and illustrator.
6. **guardians:** members of a board that cares for the poor within a parish or district.

skins and orange peel, to say nothing of fallen ladders."

He spoke of the improbable with an intense seriousness that would have been laughable six hours before. But I did not laugh.

"The best thing we can do," he continued, "is for you to stay here till twelve o'clock. We'll go upstairs and smoke; it may be cooler inside."

To my surprise I agreed.

We are sitting now in a long, low room beneath the eaves. Atkinson has sent his wife to bed. He himself is busy sharpening some tools at a little oilstone, smoking one of my cigars the while.

The air seems charged with thunder. I am writing this at a shaky table before the open window. The leg is cracked, and Atkinson, who seems a handy man with his tools, is going to mend it as soon as he has finished putting an edge on his chisel.

It is after eleven now. I shall be gone in less than an hour.

But the heat is stifling.

It is enough to send a man mad.

CHECK-UP (Putting Events in Order)

Arrange the following events in the order in which they occur in the story.

> Withencroft hears the noise of hammer blows.
> Atkinson greets Withencroft with a smile.
> Withencroft draws a sketch of a criminal.
> Atkinson waters his flowers.
> Withencroft goes for a walk.
> Atkinson sharpens his chisel.
> Withencroft sees the inscription on the monument.
> Mrs. Atkinson shows Withencroft an illustrated Bible.
> A boy asks Withencroft the time.
> Atkinson invites Withencroft to supper.

FOR DISCUSSION

1. This story takes place during the *dog days,* the hot, uncomfortable part of summer between mid-July and September. The ancients reckoned this period from the rising of Sirius, the Dog Star. During this time, dogs were supposed to be especially apt to go mad. What is the connection between this belief and the events of the story?

2. The narrator says that a "sudden impulse" makes him enter the yard. What evidence is there that the characters have no control over what is taking place?

3. What rational explanations do the two men offer for the strange coincidences of the story? Why are these explanations rejected?

4. Judging from clues in the last part of the story, what do you think will be the final outcome?

5. The background of this story is ordinary and familiar. There are references to the asphalt pavement, streetcars, the front yard and garden of a house. Why does this naturalistic setting make the events of the story more terrifying?

TOTAL EFFECT

The total effect of a story is the central impression or impact it makes on its readers. "August Heat" clearly is intended to arouse suspense and terror. All the elements in the story contribute to the total effect of chilling horror.

The story presents a fascinating mystery that has no rational explanation. The reader responds to the mounting horror of coincidence and irony. A murder is about to be committed. Both the victim and the murderer have an uncanny foreknowledge of each other and are drawn together by some mysterious power. Yet, ironically, they remain ignorant of what is going to happen.

The narrator tells the story in a completely serious and naturalistic manner. How does he convince us that the events he records are true? How does the setting make the action believable? Can you explain why these realistic details contribute to the effect of horror?

UNDERSTANDING THE WORDS IN THE STORY (Completion)

1. The *outset* of something is its _____.
   (beginning, middle, end)

2. An *oppressively* hot day is _____.
   (rainy, unbearable, pleasant)

3. An *intent* gaze is _____.
   (earnest, curious, angry)

4. *Stumpy* fingers are _____.
   (thick, graceful, bony)

5. An *utter* surprise is _____.
   (total, expected, imaginative)

6. To *sustain* something is to _____ it.
   (distrust, support, surrender)

7. A *recollection* is a _____.
   (memory, fund, book)

8. Something that is *palpable* is experienced by the

_____.
(senses, mind, unconscious)

9. When one is *roused,* one _____.
(sleeps, dreams, stirs)

10. To be lost in *reverie* is to _____.
(forget, travel, daydream)

(Matching Columns)

1. inscription
2. intrusion
3. flaw
4. uncanny
5. plausible
6. coincidence
7. prosperous
8. improbable
9. eaves
10. stifling

a. not likely
b. well-off
c. weird; mysterious
d. writing on a surface
e. edges of a roof
f. smothering
g. uninvited entry
h. seemingly true
i. chance occurrence
j. defect

FOR WRITING

1. Imagine that you are the detective who is called in to investigate the murder. Reconstruct the circumstances of the crime, including the motive, and write a report telling what happened.
2. The weather has often been cited as having an influence on human behavior. For example, the Santa Ana, a California wind, is believed to have a troubling effect on people. What scientific evidence is there that weather affects how we behave? Investigate *one* aspect of this question and write a report summarizing your research.

*"God grant that the child
may become a blessing to you!"*

THE FATHER

Björnstjerne Björnson°

The man whose story is here to be told was the wealthiest and most influential person in his parish; his name was Thord Överaas. He appeared in the parson's study one day, tall and earnest.

"I have gotten a son," said he, "and I wish to present him for baptism."

"What shall his name be?"

"Finn—after my father."

"And the sponsors?"

They were mentioned, and proved to be the best men and women of Thord's relations in the parish.

"Is there anything else?" inquired the parson, and looked up. The peasant hesitated a little.

"I should like very much to have him baptized by himself," said he, finally.

"That is to say on a weekday?"

"Next Saturday, at twelve o'clock noon."

"Is there anything else?" inquired the parson.

"There is nothing else;" and the peasant twirled his cap, as though he were about to go.

Then the parson rose. "There is yet this, however," said he, and walking toward Thord, he took him by the hand and

---

° **Björnstjerne Björnson** (byûrn′styĕrn-ə byûrn′sōn).

looked gravely into his eyes: "God grant that the child may become a blessing to you!"

One day sixteen years later, Thord stood once more in the parson's study.

"Really, you carry your age astonishingly well, Thord," said the parson; for he saw no change whatever in the man.

"That is because I have no troubles," replied Thord.

To this the parson said nothing, but after a while he asked: "What is your pleasure this evening?"

"I have come this evening about that son of mine who is to be confirmed tomorrow."

"He is a bright boy."

"I did not wish to pay the parson until I heard what number the boy would have when he takes his place in the church tomorrow."

"He will stand number one."

"So I have heard; and here are ten dollars for the parson."

"Is there anything else I can do for you?" inquired the parson, fixing his eyes on Thord.

"There is nothing else."

Thord went out.

Eight years more rolled by, and then one day a noise was heard outside of the parson's study, for many men were approaching, and at their head was Thord, who entered first.

The parson looked up and recognized him.

"You come well attended this evening, Thord," said he.

"I am here to request that the banns[1] may be published for my son: he is about to marry Karen Storliden, daughter of Gudmund, who stands here beside me."

---

1. **banns** (bănz): the announcement in church of an intended marriage.

"Why, that is the richest girl in the parish."

"So they say," replied the peasant, stroking back his hair with one hand.

The parson sat awhile as if in deep thought, then entered the names in his book, without making any comments, and the men wrote their signatures underneath. Thord laid three dollars on the table.

"One is all I am to have," said the parson.

"I know that very well; but he is my only child; I want to do it handsomely."

The parson took the money.

"This is now the third time, Thord, that you have come here on your son's account."

"But now I am through with him," said Thord, and folding up his pocketbook he said farewell and walked away.

The men slowly followed him.

A fortnight later, the father and son were rowing across the lake, one calm, still day, to Storliden to make arrangements for the wedding.

"This thwart is not secure," said the son, and stood up to straighten the seat on which he was sitting.

At the same moment the board he was standing on slipped from under him; he threw out his arms, uttered a shriek, and fell overboard.

"Take hold of the oar!" shouted the father, springing to his feet and holding out the oar.

But when the son had made a couple of efforts he grew stiff.

"Wait a moment!" cried the father, and began to row toward his son.

Then the son rolled over on his back, gave his father one long look, and sank.

Thord could scarcely believe it; he held the boat still, and stared at the spot where his son had gone down, as though he must surely come to the surface again. There rose some bubbles, then some more, and finally one large one that burst; and the lake lay there as smooth and bright as a mirror again.

For three days and three nights people saw the father rowing round and round the spot, without taking either food or sleep; he was dragging the lake for the body of his son. And toward morning of the third day he found it, and carried it in his arms up over the hills to his gard.[2]

It might have been about a year from that day, when the parson, late one autumn evening, heard someone in the passage outside of the door, carefully trying to find the latch. The parson opened the door, and in walked a tall, thin man, with bowed[3] form and white hair. The parson looked long at him before he recognized him. It was Thord.

"Are you out walking so late?" said the parson, and stood still in front of him.

"Ah, yes! it is late," said Thord, and took a seat.

The parson sat down also, as though waiting. A long, long silence followed. At last Thord said:

"I have something with me that I should like to give to the poor; I want it to be invested as a legacy in my son's name."

He rose, laid some money on the table, and sat down again. The parson counted it.

"It is a great deal of money," said he.

"It is half the price of my gard. I sold it today."

The parson sat in long silence. At last he asked, but gently:

"What do you propose to do now, Thord?"

"Something better."

They sat there for a while, Thord with downcast eyes,

---

2. **gard** (gärd): a farm.
3. **bowed** (boud); bent or stooped.

the parson with his eyes fixed on Thord. Presently the parson said, slowly and softly:

"I think your son has at last brought you a true blessing."

"Yes, I think so myself," said Thord, looking up, while two big tears coursed slowly down his cheeks.

CHECK-UP (True/False)

1. The events in this story cover about twenty-five years.
2. We learn that Finn's mother has died in childbirth.
3. On his second visit to the pastor, Thord's appearance has changed greatly.
4. Finn dies in a fishing accident.
5. At the end of the story, Thord donates half of his wealth to the poor.

FOR DISCUSSION

1. This story consists of five scenes. Identify each one.
2. On his first appearance in the parson's study, Thord wishes to have his son, Finn, baptized. Who are to be the child's sponsors? Why does Thord ask to have the child baptized on a weekday rather than on Sunday?
3. What evidence is there that the parson is concerned about Thord's feelings for his son? How does he try to warn him?
4. Thord visits the parson before his son's confirmation and again before his marriage. What do both scenes reveal about him as a father?
5. How does the tragic death of his son change Thord? What is implied by the words "I come late"?
6. What is the meaning of the parson's final statement in the story?

TOTAL EFFECT

A great deal of meaning is packed into this simple, spare narrative. On the surface, this seems to be a story about a father's devotion to his only son. But when we examine the different elements of the story, we find that the real subject is the relationship between Thord and his fellow human beings.

The opening sentence of the story tells us that Thord is "the wealthiest and most influential person in the parish." Because of his money and connections, Thord feels that he deserves special attention. In the opening scene, Thord comes to the parson's study in order to make arrangements for the christening of his son, Finn. The child's sponsors are to be Thord's rich relatives. It is significant that Thord asks to have his son baptized by himself, on a weekday, rather than on Sunday, when the other children are to be baptized. We see in this action that Thord is motivated by pride rather than by the religious meaning of the ceremony. The other occasions, his son's confirmation and engagement, also serve to have Finn set apart as special.

The parson sees the dangers in Thord's attitude, and on each occasion tries to warn him. At the end of Thord's first visit, he looks "gravely" into Thord's eyes and hopes that the child will be a blessing to his father. This statement is ironic, for the boy finally becomes a blessing to his father after his death. Thord, shocked by the tragedy of his loss, undergoes a physical and emotional transformation. In the final scene, when he visits the parson's study, he announces his intention to give half his wealth to the poor as a legacy in his son's name. Thord realizes that his devotion to his son has been a form of selfishness. When Thord speaks of doing "Something better," we can assume that he means a life devoted unselfishly to the needs of others.

Study the change in Thord's character. How is it revealed in his appearance? How is it revealed in his attitude toward money?

FOR WRITING

1. Almost everything we learn about the characters in the story is implied through their words and actions. Write an essay analyzing the character of Thord. Take into account each scene of the story.
2. Read the story "War" (page 288). How does each author deal with a father's love for his son?
3. In a brief essay discuss the theme of Björnson's story. Show how this theme is developed in each episode.

*". . . the very best thing in all this world that
can befall a man is to be born lucky."*

LUCK

Mark Twain

It was at a banquet in London in honor of one of the two
or three conspicuously illustrious English military names of
this generation. For reasons which will presently appear, I
will withhold his real name and titles and call him Lieuten-
ant-General Lord Arthur Scoresby, Y.C., K.C.B.,[1] etc., etc.,
etc. What a fascination there is in a renowned name! There
sat the man, in actual flesh, whom I had heard of so many
thousands of times since that day, thirty years before, when
his name shot suddenly to the zenith from a Crimean[2] bat-
tlefield, to remain forever celebrated. It was food and drink
to me to look, and look, and look at that demigod; scanning,
searching, noting: the quietness, the reserve, the noble gravity of his countenance; the simple honesty that expressed
itself all over him; the sweet unconsciousness of his great-
ness—unconsciousness of the hundreds of admiring eyes
fastened upon him, unconsciousness of the deep, loving, sin-
cere worship welling out of the breasts of those people and
flowing toward him.

The clergyman at my left was an old acquaintance of
mine—clergyman now, but had spent the first half of his life
in the camp and field and as an instructor in the military
school at Woolwich. Just at the moment I have been talking

1. **Y.C.:** Yeomanry Cavalry. **K.C.B.:** Knight Commander of the Order of
   the Bath.
2. **Crimean** (krī-mē′ən): In the Crimean War (1854–1856), Russia was
   defeated by England, France, Turkey, and Sardinia.

about a veiled and singular light glimmered in his eyes and he leaned down and muttered confidentially to me—indicating the hero of the banquet with a gesture:

"Privately—he's an absolute fool."

This verdict was a great surprise to me. If its subject had been Napoleon, or Socrates, or Solomon,[3] my astonishment could not have been greater. Two things I was well aware of: that the Reverend was a man of strict veracity and that his judgment of men was good. Therefore I knew, beyond doubt or question, that the world was mistaken about this hero: he *was* a fool. So I meant to find out, at a convenient moment, how the Reverend, all solitary and alone, had discovered the secret.

Some days later the opportunity came, and this is what the Reverend told me:

About forty years ago I was an instructor in the military academy at Woolwich. I was present in one of the sections when young Scoresby underwent his preliminary examination. I was touched to the quick with pity, for the rest of the class answered up brightly and handsomely, while he—why, dear me, he didn't know *anything*, so to speak. He was evidently good, and sweet, and lovable, and guileless; and so it was exceedingly painful to see him stand there, as serene as a graven image,[4] and deliver himself of answers which were veritably miraculous for stupidity and ignorance. All the compassion in me was aroused in his behalf. I said to myself, when he comes to be examined again he will be flung over, of course; so it will be simply a harmless act of charity to ease his fall as much as I can. I took him aside and found that he

3. **Napoleon . . . Solomon:** Famous men noted for their military leadership or wisdom. Napoleon Bonaparte (bō′nə-pärt′) (1769–1821) became Emperor of France; Socrates (sŏk′rə-tēz′) was a Greek philosopher and teacher (470?–399 B.C.); Solomon, King of Israel in the tenth century B.C., was known for his wisdom.
4. **graven image:** an idol carved in wood or stone.

knew a little of Caesar's history;[5] and as he didn't know anything else, I went to work and drilled him like a galley-slave
on a certain line of stock questions concerning Caesar which
I knew would be used. If you'll believe me, he went through
with flying colors on examination day! He went through on
that purely superficial "cram," and got compliments, too,
while others, who knew a thousand times more than he, got
plucked.[6] By some strangely lucky accident—an accident
not likely to happen twice in a century—he was asked no
question outside of the narrow limits of his drill.

It was stupefying. Well, all through his course I stood by
him, with something of the sentiment which a mother feels
for a crippled child; and he always saved himself, just by
miracle apparently.

Now, of course, the thing that would expose him and kill
him at last was mathematics. I resolved to make his death as
easy as I could; so I drilled him and crammed him, and
crammed him and drilled him, just on the line of questions
which the examiners would be most likely to use, and then
launched him on his fate. Well, sir, try to conceive of the
result: to my consternation, he took the first prize! And with
it he got a perfect ovation in the way of compliments.

Sleep? There was no more sleep for me for a week. My
conscience tortured me day and night. What I had done I
had done purely through charity, and only to ease the poor
youth's fall. I never had dreamed of any such preposterous
results as the thing that had happened. I felt as guilty and
miserable as Frankenstein.[7] Here was a woodenhead whom
I had put in the way of glittering promotions and prodigious
responsibilities, and but one thing could happen: he and his

---

5. **Caesar's history:** Julius Caesar (100–44 B.C.) wrote military narratives
   that are still studied by students of Latin as well as by military leaders.
6. **plucked:** British slang, meaning "rejected as candidates."
7. **Frankenstein:** the creator of the famous monster, in *Frankenstein*, a
   novel by Mary Shelley.

responsibilities would all go to ruin together at the first opportunity.

The Crimean War had just broken out. Of course there had to be a war, I said to myself. We couldn't have peace and give this donkey a chance to die before he is found out. I waited for the earthquake. It came. And it made me reel when it did come. He was actually gazetted[8] to a captaincy in a marching regiment! Better men grow old and gray in the service before they climb to a sublimity like that. And who could ever have foreseen that they would go and put such a load of responsibility on such green and inadequate shoulders? I could just barely have stood it if they had made him a cornet;[9] but a captain—think of it! I thought my hair would turn white.

Consider what I did—I who so loved repose and inaction. I said to myself, I am responsible to the country for this, and I must go along with him and protect the country against him as far as I can. So I took my poor little capital that I had saved up through years of work and grinding economy, and went with a sigh and bought a cornetcy in his regiment, and away we went to the field.

And there—oh, dear, it was awful. Blunders?—why, he never did anything *but* blunder. But, you see, nobody was in the fellow's secret. Everybody had him focused wrong, and necessarily misinterpreted his performance every time. Consequently they took his idiotic blunders for inspirations of genius. They did, honestly! His mildest blunders were enough to make a man in his right mind cry; and they did make me cry—and rage and rave, too, privately. And the thing that kept me always in a sweat of apprehension was the fact that every fresh blunder he made always increased the luster of his reputation! I kept saying to myself, he'll get

8. **gazetted** (gə-zĕt′əd): appointed.
9. **cornet** (kôr′nĭt): the fifth commissioned officer in a cavalry troop.

so high that when discovery does finally come it will be like the sun falling out of the sky.

He went right along up, from grade to grade, over the dead bodies of his superiors, until at last, in the hottest moment of the battle of ——— down went our colonel, and my heart jumped into my mouth, for Scoresby was next in rank! Now for it, said I; we'll all land in Sheol[10] in ten minutes, sure.

The battle was awfully hot; the allies were steadily giving way all over the field. Our regiment occupied a position that was vital; a blunder now must be destruction. At this crucial moment, what does this immortal fool do but detach the regiment from its place and order a charge over a neighboring hill where there wasn't a suggestion of an enemy! "There you go!" I said to myself; "this *is* the end at last."

And away we did go, and were over the shoulder of the hill before the insane movement could be discovered and stopped. And what did we find? An entire and unsuspected Russian army in reserve! And what happened? We were eaten up? That is necessarily what would have happened in ninety-nine cases out of a hundred. But no; those Russians argued that no single regiment would come browsing around there at such a time. It must be the entire English army, and that the sly Russian game was detected and blocked; so they turned tail, and away they went, pell-mell, over the hill and down into the field, in wild confusion, and we after them; they themselves broke the solid Russian center in the field, and tore through, and in no time there was the most tremendous rout you ever saw, and the defeat of the allies was turned into a sweeping and splendid victory! Marshal Canrobert looked on, dizzy with astonishment, admiration, and delight; and sent right off for Scoresby, and

---

10. **Sheol** (shē′ōl′): in the Old Testament, a place described as the dwelling place of the dead.

hugged him, and decorated him on the field in presence of all the armies!

And what was Scoresby's blunder that time? Merely the mistaking his right hand for his left—that was all. An order had come to him to fall back and support our right; and instead, he fell *forward* and went over the hill to the left. But the name he won that day as a marvelous military genius filled the world with his glory, and that glory will never fade while history books last.

He is just as good and sweet and lovable and unpretending as a man can be, but he doesn't know enough to come in when it rains. Now that is absolutely true. He is the supremest ass in the universe; and until half an hour ago nobody knew it but himself and me. He has been pursued, day by day and year by year, by a most phenomenal and astonishing luckiness. He has been a shining soldier in all our wars for a generation; he has littered his whole military life with blunders, and yet has never committed one that didn't make him a knight or a baronet or a lord or something. Look at his breast; why, he is just clothed in domestic and foreign decorations. Well, sir, every one of them is the record of some shouting stupidity or other; and, taken together, they are proof that the very best thing in all this world that can befall a man is to be born lucky. I say again, as I said at the banquet, Scoresby's an absolute fool.

CHECK-UP (True/False)

1. At the opening of the story, the Reverend is attending a banquet to honor a former pupil.
2. Scoresby passed his examinations at the military academy by cheating.
3. Scoresby took first prize in mathematics.
4. Scoresby's stunning military victories were actually blunders.
5. During the Crimean War, Scoresby put the entire English army to flight.

FOR DISCUSSION

1. This story has two narrators. What impression do you form of the first narrator? What is his attitude toward Lord Arthur Scoresby?
2. How does Twain convince you that his second narrator, the Reverend, is someone who can be trusted to tell the truth?
3. What are the Reverend's motives for helping Scoresby?
4. Why do you suppose that only the Reverend is aware of Scoresby's "secret"?
5. What is the point of Twain's satire in this story?

TOTAL EFFECT

The *tall tale* was a popular form of humor in American folklore of the nineteenth century. Folk heroes like Paul Bunyan and Pecos Bill performed superhuman feats. Like the tall tale, Twain's story contains elements of outlandish exaggeration. Which events in the Reverend's tale are improbable or comically absurd?

Note that Twain achieves his effects through a combination of exaggeration and comic deflation. Find examples of language in the first paragraph that glorify the figure of Lord Arthur Scoresby. Why do you suppose Twain emphasizes the narrator's reverence for this man? How does the Reverend's tale deflate this image of Scoresby?

Some readers think that Twain's satire is aimed at debunking a military hero. Other readers think that Twain is expressing a cynical attitude toward life. What is your opinion of Twain's intention? Give evidence from the story to support your position.

UNDERSTANDING THE WORDS IN THE STORY (Completion)

Choose one of the words in the following list to complete each of the sentences below. Use a word only once.

conspicuous   gravity
illustrious   countenance
renowned   welling
zenith   singular
demigod   glimmer

1. At high noon the sun is said to be at its _____.

2. Character can be read in a person's _____.

3. An idea is beginning to _____ in your eyes.

4. A person who stands out in a crowd is _____.

5. A _____ seems to be superhuman.

6. Scoresby had enjoyed a (an) _____ career.

7. Tears began _____ up in the eyes of the audience.

8. Despite the _____ of his expression, Scoresby was a fool.

9. Scoresby was _____ for his military victories.

10. The Reverend had a _____ look on his face.

(Matching Columns)

1. veracity		a. authentic
2. preliminary		b. commonly used
3. guileless		c. awaken or excite
4. veritable		d. determine
5. compassion		e. coming before
6. arouse		f. understand; imagine
7. stock		g. truthfulness
8. superficial		h. pity or sympathy
9. resolve		i. innocent
10. conceive		j. on the surface

(Multiple-Choice)

1. The Reverend found, to his *consternation,* that Scoresby had passed his examinations.
   a. pleasure
   b. amusement
   c. dismay
2. Scoresby received *an ovation.*
   a. a prize
   b. a reward
   c. an expression of approval
3. The Reverend found the outcome of the examinations *preposterous.*
   a. ridiculous
   b. frightening
   c. prejudiced
4. Scoresby was given *prodigious* responsibilities.
   a. unusual
   b. huge
   c. professional
5. Scoresby achieved a *sublimity* denied to other men of greater talent.
   a. supreme honor
   b. command
   c. reputation

6. The Reverend gave up a life of *repose.*
   a. calmness
   b. simplicity
   c. idleness
7. The Reverend was in a constant state of *apprehension.*
   a. controlled anger
   b. worried expectation
   c. intense fascination
8. The Russians did not expect a regiment to come *browsing* around.
   a. spying
   b. charging
   c. looking casually
9. Scoresby was responsible for the *rout* of the Russian army.
   a. blunder
   b. disastrous defeat
   c. loss
10. Scoresby was blessed with *phenomenal* luck.
   a. extraordinary
   b. absolute
   c. repeated

FOR WRITING

1. Use a history book or an encyclopedia to learn the details of the Battle of Balaklava, which took place in 1854. Pay particular attention to the Charge of the Light Cavalry Brigade. What aspects of this battle might Twain have had in mind in creating the character of Scoresby and the events in "Luck"?
2. Read the poem "The Charge of the Light Brigade" by Alfred, Lord Tennyson. Compare Tennyson's attitude toward this event with Twain's attitude toward Scoresby's charge in "Luck."

*"Paternal love is not like bread
that can be broken into pieces and
split amongst the children in equal shares."*

WAR

Luigi Pirandello

The passengers who had left Rome by the night express had had to stop until dawn at the small station of Fabriano in order to continue their journey by the small old-fashioned local joining the main line with Sulmona.

At dawn, in a stuffy and smoky second-class carriage in which five people had already spent the night, a bulky woman in deep mourning was hoisted in—almost like a shapeless bundle. Behind her, puffing and moaning, followed her husband—a tiny man, thin and weakly, his face death-white, his eyes small and bright and looking shy and uneasy.

Having at last taken a seat he politely thanked the passengers who had helped his wife and who had made room for her; then he turned round to the woman trying to pull down the collar of her coat, and politely inquired:

"Are you all right, dear?"

The wife, instead of answering, pulled up her collar again to her eyes, so as to hide her face.

"Nasty world," muttered the husband with a sad smile.

And he felt it his duty to explain to his traveling companions that the poor woman was to be pitied, for the war was taking away from her her only son, a boy of twenty to whom both had devoted their entire life, even breaking up their home at Sulmona to follow him to Rome, where he had to go as a student, then allowing him to volunteer for war with an assurance, however, that at least for six months he would not be sent to the front and now, all of a sudden, receiving a wire saying that he was due to leave in three days' time and asking them to go and see him off.

The woman under the big coat was twisting and wriggling, at times growling like a wild animal, feeling certain that all those explanations would not have aroused even a shadow of sympathy from those people who—most likely—were in the same plight as herself. One of them, who had been listening with particular attention, said:

"You should thank God that your son is only leaving now for the front. Mine has been sent there the first day of the war. He has already come back twice wounded and been sent back again to the front."

"What about me? I have two sons and three nephews at the front," said another passenger.

"Maybe, but in our case it is our *only* son," ventured the husband.

"What difference can it make? You may spoil your only son with excessive attentions, but you cannot love him more than you would all your other children if you had any. Paternal love is not like bread that can be broken into pieces and split amongst the children in equal shares. A father gives *all* his love to each one of his children without discrimination, whether it be one or ten, and if I am suffering now for my two sons, I am not suffering half for each of them but double . . ."

"True . . . true . . ." sighed the embarrassed husband, "but suppose (of course we all hope it will never be your case) a father has two sons at the front and he loses one of them, there is still one left to console him . . . while . . ."

"Yes," answered the other, getting cross, "a son left to console him but also a son left for whom he must survive, while in the case of the father of an only son if the son dies the father can die too and put an end to his distress. Which of the two positions is the worse? Don't you see how my case would be worse than yours?"

"Nonsense," interrupted another traveler, a fat, red-faced man with bloodshot eyes of the palest gray.

He was panting. From his bulging eyes seemed to spurt inner violence of an uncontrolled vitality which his weakened body could hardly contain.

"Nonsense," he repeated, trying to cover his mouth with his hand so as to hide the two missing front teeth. "Nonsense. Do we give life to our children for our own benefit?"

The other travelers stared at him in distress. The one who had had his son at the front since the first day of the war sighed: "You are right. Our children do not belong to us, they belong to the Country. . . ."

"Bosh," retorted the fat traveler. "Do we think of the Country when we give life to our children? Our sons are born because . . . well, because they must be born and when they come to life they take our own life with them. This is the truth. We belong to them but they never belong to us. And when they reach twenty they are exactly what we were at their age. We too had a father and mother, but there were so many other things as well . . . girls, cigarettes, illusions, new ties . . . and the Country, of course, whose call we would have answered—when we were twenty—even if father and mother had said no. Now at our age, the love of our Country is still great, of course, but stronger than it is the love for our children. Is there any one of us here who wouldn't gladly take his son's place at the front if he could?"

There was a silence all round, everybody nodding as to approve.

"Why then," continued the fat man, "shouldn't we consider the feelings of our children when they are twenty? Isn't it natural that at their age they should consider the love for their Country (I am speaking of decent boys, of course) even greater than the love for us? Isn't it natural that it should be so, as after all they must look upon us as upon old boys who cannot move any more and must stay at home? If Country exists, if Country is a natural necessity, like bread, of which each of us must eat in order not to die of hunger, somebody must go to defend it. And our sons go, when they are twenty, and they don't want tears, because if they die, they die inflamed and happy (I am speaking, of course, of decent boys). Now, if one dies young and happy, without having the ugly sides of life, the boredom of it, the pettiness, the bitterness of disillusion . . . what more can we ask for him? Everyone should stop crying; everyone should laugh, as I do . . . or at least thank God—as I do—because my son, before dying, sent me a message saying that he was dying satisfied at having ended his life in the best way he could have wished. That is why, as you see, I do not even wear mourning. . . ."

He shook his light fawn coat as to show it; his livid lip over his missing teeth was trembling, his eyes were watery and motionless, and soon after he ended with a shrill laugh which might well have been a sob.

"Quite so . . . quite so . . ." agreed the others.

The woman who, bundled in a corner under her coat, had been sitting and listening had—for the last three months—tried to find in the words of her husband and her friends something to console her in her deep sorrow, something that might show her how a mother should resign herself to send her son not even to death but to a probably dangerous life. Yet not a word had she found amongst the many which had been said . . . and her grief had been greater in seeing that nobody—as she thought—could share her feelings.

But now the words of the traveler amazed and almost stunned her. She suddenly realized that it wasn't the others who were wrong and could not understand her but herself who could not rise up to the same height of those fathers and mothers willing to resign themselves, without crying, not only to the departure of their sons but even to their death.

She lifted her head, she bent over from her corner trying to listen with great attention to the details which the fat man was giving to his companions about the way his son had fallen as a hero, for his King and his Country, happy and without regrets. It seemed to her that she had stumbled into a world she had never dreamt of, a world so far unknown to her and she was so pleased to hear everyone joining in congratulating that brave father who could so stoically speak of his child's death.

Then suddenly, just as if she had heard nothing of what had been said and almost as if waking up from a dream, she turned to the old man, asking him:

"Then . . . is your son really dead?"

Everybody stared at her. The old man, too, turned to look at her, fixing his great, bulging, horribly watery light gray eyes, deep in her face. For some little time he tried to answer, but words failed him. He looked and looked at her, almost as if only then—at that silly, incongruous question— he had suddenly realized at last that his son was really dead . . . gone forever . . . forever. His face contracted, became horribly distorted, then he snatched in haste a handkerchief from his pocket and, to the amazement of everyone, broke into harrowing, heart-rending, uncontrollable sobs.

CHECK-UP (True/False)

1. The people in this story are being evacuated from Rome during wartime.
2. The couple who board the train at the opening of the story have just lost their only son.
3. The characters present different points of view about losing sons in warfare.
4. The old man argues that a parent should be comforted by a son's heroic death.
5. At the end of the story, the old man is overwhelmed by grief.

FOR DISCUSSION

small station of fabriano

1. What is the setting of this story? How does it serve to bring together the different characters?
2. The major conflict in the story is the difference in attitudes toward a specific subject. Tell what the subject of discussion is and briefly give the different points of view of the characters.
3. The climax of the story occurs when the woman asks a "silly" question. What does the old man realize at that moment? Explain his reaction.
4. Why do you suppose the author did not identify his characters by name? Is the story's impact heightened or lessened by the element of anonymity?
5. Do you think the author has chosen a good title for his story? Give reasons to support your answer.

TOTAL EFFECT

The first thing a reader may note about this story is that although its title is "War," there is little physical action to speak of. The story focuses on the feelings and thoughts of people whose lives have been disrupted by war.

The characters are strangers who are brought together because they share the same second-class railroad carriage. The author identifies his characters by prominent physical characteristics rather than by name. Their names, we can infer, are not important. They have a common interest in what the war is doing to their families. The conflict or conflicts in the story take the form of debates between characters, on the matter of enduring loss and grief.

The man whose son has been killed appears to have accepted his loss. His son has died a noble and heroic death. The old man claims that in dying young his son has been spared the "bitterness of disillusion." Just as we are convinced that the old man has found consolation, the woman whose son is leaving for the front asks him if his son is "really dead." This question, the climax of the story, evokes a change in the old man. The phrase "really dead" seems to catch him off guard. He begins to cry uncontrollably. All the arguments with which he has armed himself dissolve as his reason is overcome by emotion.

The aspect of war that this story shows is the profound misery of its victims, who are unable to come to terms with its destruction and sacrifice.

UNDERSTANDING THE WORDS
IN THE STORY (Matching Columns)

1. plight
2. excessive
3. paternal
4. console
5. spurt
6. livid
7. stoically
8. incongruous
9. distorted
10. harrowing

a. ease or help
b. enduring suffering
c. gush forth
d. too much
e. extremely painful
f. not fitting
g. unfortunate position
h. twisted
i. characteristic of a father
j. grayish or colorless

FOR WRITING

Some stories focus on the heroic, glorious aspects of war. Other stories focus on the ironies or destructiveness of war. Choose *two* of the following stories and compare their attitudes toward war.

Eric Knight, "The Rifles of the Regiment" (page 81)
Liam O'Flaherty, "The Sniper" (page 101)
Ernest Hemingway, "Old Man at the Bridge" (page 237)
Mark Twain, "Luck" (page 278)
Luigi Pirandello, "War"

*"The Magi, as you know, were wise men—
wonderfully wise men—who brought
gifts to the Babe in the manger."*

THE GIFT
OF THE MAGI

O. Henry

One dollar and eighty-seven cents. That was all. And
sixty cents of it was in pennies. Pennies saved one and two at
a time by bulldozing the grocer and the vegetable man and
the butcher until one's cheek burned with silent imputation
of parsimony[1] that such close dealing implied. Three times
Della counted it. One dollar and eighty-seven cents. And the
next day would be Christmas.

There was clearly nothing to do but flop down on the
shabby little couch and howl. So Della did it. Which instigates[2] the moral reflection that life is made up of sobs, sniffles, and smiles, with sniffles predominating.

While the mistress of the home is gradually subsiding
from the first stage to the second,[3] take a look at the home. A
furnished flat at eight dollars per week. It did not exactly
beggar description, but it certainly had that word on the
lookout for the mendicancy squad.[4]

In the vestibule below was a letter box into which no

---

1. **imputation** (ĭm'pyōō-tā'shən) **of parsimony** (pär'sə-mō'nē): charge or
   accusation of stinginess.
2. **instigates** (ĭn'stĭ-gāts'): provokes.
3. **first . . . second:** from sobs to sniffles.
4. **mendicancy** (mĕn'dĭ-kən'sē) **squad:** a police squad that picked up beg-
   gars. O. Henry means that the apartment is shabby.

letter would go, and an electric button from which no mortal finger could coax a ring. Also appertaining thereunto[5] was a card bearing the name "Mr. James Dillingham Young."

The "Dillingham" had been flung to the breeze during a former period of prosperity when its possessor was being paid thirty dollars per week. Now, when the income was shrunk to twenty dollars, the letters of "Dillingham" looked blurred, as though they were thinking seriously of contracting to a modest and unassuming *D*. But whenever Mr. James Dillingham Young came home and reached his flat above he was called "Jim" and greatly hugged by Mrs. James Dillingham Young, already introduced to you as Della. Which is all very good.

Della finished her cry and attended to her cheeks with the powder rag. She stood by the window and looked out dully at a gray cat walking a gray fence in a gray backyard. Tomorrow would be Christmas Day, and she had only one dollar and eighty-seven cents with which to buy Jim a present. She had been saving every penny she could for months, with this result. Twenty dollars a week doesn't go far. Expenses had been greater than she had calculated. They always are. Only one dollar and eighty-seven cents to buy a present for Jim. Her Jim. Many a happy hour she had spent planning for something nice for him. Something fine and rare and sterling—something just a little bit near to being worthy of the honor of being owned by Jim.

There was a pier glass[6] between the windows of the room. Perhaps you have seen a pier glass in an eight-dollar flat. A very thin and very agile person may, by observing his reflection in a rapid sequence of longitudinal strips, obtain a fairly accurate conception of his looks. Della, being slender, had mastered the art.

5. **appertaining thereunto:** belonging to.
6. **pier glass:** a long narrow mirror that fits between two windows.

Suddenly she whirled from the window and stood before the glass. Her eyes were shining brilliantly, but her face had lost its color within twenty seconds. Rapidly she pulled down her hair and let it fall to its full length.

Now there were two possessions of the James Dillingham Youngs in which they both took a mighty pride. One was Jim's gold watch that had been his father's and his grandfather's. The other was Della's hair. Had the Queen of Sheba[7] lived in the flat across the air shaft, Della would have let her hair hang out the window someday to dry, just to depreciate Her Majesty's jewels and gifts. Had King Solomon been the janitor, with all his treasures piled up in the basement, Jim would have pulled out his watch every time he passed, just to see him pluck at his beard from envy.

So now Dell's beautiful hair fell about her, rippling and shining like a cascade of brown waters. It reached below her knee and made itself almost a garment for her. And then she did it up again nervously and quickly. Once she faltered for a minute and stood still while a tear or two splashed on the worn red carpet.

On went her old brown jacket; on went her old brown hat. With a whirl of skirts and with the brilliant sparkle still in her eyes, she fluttered out the door and down the stairs to the street.

Where she stopped the sign read: "Mme. Sofronie. Hair Goods of All Kinds." One flight up Della ran—and collected herself, panting. Madame, large, too white, chilly, hardly looked the "Sofronie."

"Will you buy my hair?" asked Della.

"I buy hair," said Madame. "Take yer hat off and let's have a sight at the looks of it."

Down rippled the brown cascade.

---

7. **Queen of Sheba** (shē'bə): in the Bible, a woman famous for her wealth and beauty. She visited King Solomon in order to test his wisdom.

"Twenty dollars," said Madame, lifting the mass with a practiced hand.

"Give it to me quick," said Della.

Oh, and the next two hours tripped by on rosy wings. Forget the hashed metaphor.[8] She was ransacking the stores for Jim's present.

She found it at last. It surely had been made for Jim and no one else. There was no other like it in any of the stores, and she had turned all of them inside out. It was a platinum fob chain simple and chaste in design, properly proclaiming its value by substance alone and not by meretricious[9] ornamentation—as all good things should do. It was even worthy of The Watch. As soon as she saw it she knew that it must be Jim's. It was like him. Quietness and value—the description applied to both. Twenty-one dollars they took from her for it, and she hurried home with the eighty-seven cents. With that chain on his watch Jim might be properly anxious about the time in any company. Grand as the watch was, he sometimes looked at it on the sly on account of the old leather strap that he used in place of a chain.

When Della reached home her intoxication gave way a little to prudence and reason. She got out her curling irons and lighted the gas and went to work repairing the ravages made by generosity added to love. Which is always a tremendous task, dear friends—a mammoth task.

Within forty minutes her head was covered with tiny, close-lying curls that made her look wonderfully like a truant schoolboy. She looked at her reflection in the mirror long, carefully, and critically.

"If Jim doesn't kill me," she said to herself, "before he

---

8. **hashed metaphor** (mĕt′ə-fôr′, -fər): A metaphor is a comparison between two unlike things. O. Henry's metaphor is "mixed" for comic effect. He describes Time as both walking ("tripped by") and flying ("on rosy wings").
9. **meretricious** (mĕr′ə-trĭsh′əs): attractive but cheap and flashy.

takes a second look at me, he'll say I look like a Coney Island chorus girl. But what could I do—oh! what could I do with a dollar and eighty-seven cents?"

At seven o'clock the coffee was made and the frying pan was on the back of the stove hot and ready to cook the chops.

Jim was never late. Della doubled the fob chain in her hand and sat on the corner of the table near the door that he always entered. Then she heard his step on the stair away down on the first flight, and she turned white for just a moment. She had a habit of saying little silent prayers about the simplest everyday things, and now she whispered, "Please, God, make him think I am still pretty."

The door opened and Jim stepped in and closed it. He looked thin and very serious. Poor fellow, he was only twenty-two—and to be burdened with a family! He needed a new overcoat and he was without gloves.

Jim stopped inside the door, as immovable as a setter at the scent of quail. His eyes were fixed upon Della; and there was an expression in them that she could not read, and it terrified her. It was not anger, nor surprise, nor disapproval, nor horror, nor any of the sentiments that she had been prepared for. He simply stared at her fixedly with that peculiar expression on his face.

Della wriggled off the table and went to him.

"Jim, darling," she cried, "don't look at me that way. I had my hair cut off and sold it because I couldn't have lived through Christmas without giving you a present. It'll grow out again—you won't mind, will you? I just had to do it. My hair grows awfully fast. Say 'Merry Christmas!' Jim, and let's be happy. You don't know what a nice—what a beautiful, nice gift I've got for you."

"You've cut off your hair?" asked Jim laboriously, as if he had not arrived at that patent fact yet even after the hardest mental labor.

"Cut it off and sold it," said Della. "Don't you like me just as well, anyhow? I'm me without my hair, ain't I?"

Jim looked about the room curiously.

"You say your hair is gone?" he said, with an air almost of idiocy.

"You needn't look for it," said Della. "It's sold, I tell you—sold and gone, too. It's Christmas Eve, boy. Be good to me, for it went for you. Maybe the hairs of my head were numbered," she went on with a sudden serious sweetness, "but nobody could ever count my love for you. Shall I put the chops on, Jim?"

Out of his trance Jim seemed quickly to wake. He enfolded his Della. For ten seconds let us regard with discreet scrutiny some inconsequential object in the other direction. Eight dollars a week or a million a year—what is the difference? A mathematician or a wit would give you the wrong answer. The Magi[10] brought valuable gifts, but that was not among them. This dark assertion will be illuminated later on.

Jim drew a package from his overcoat pocket and threw it upon the table.

"Don't make any mistake, Dell," he said, "about me. I don't think there's anything in the way of a haircut or a shave or a shampoo that could make me like my girl any less. But if you'll unwrap that package you may see why you had me going awhile at first."

White fingers and nimble tore at the string and paper. And then an ecstatic scream of joy; and then, alas! a quick feminine change to hysterical tears and wails, necessitating the immediate employment of all the comforting powers of the lord of the flat.

For there lay The Combs—the set of combs, side and back, that Della had worshiped for long in a Broadway window. Beautiful combs, pure tortoise shell, with jeweled rims—just the shade to wear in the beautiful vanished hair.

10. **Magi** (mā'jī').

They were expensive combs, she knew, and her heart had simply craved and yearned over them without the least hope of possession. And now they were hers, but the tresses that should have adorned the coveted adornments were gone.

But she hugged them to her bosom, and at length she was able to look up with dim eyes and a smile and say, "My hair grows so fast, Jim!"

And then Della leaped up like a little singed cat and cried, "Oh, oh!"

Jim had not yet seen his beautiful present. She held it out to him eagerly upon her open palm. The dull precious metal seemed to flash with a reflection of her bright and ardent spirit.

"Isn't it a dandy, Jim? I hunted all over town to find it. You'll have to look at the time a hundred times a day now. Give me your watch. I want to see how it looks on it."

Instead of obeying, Jim tumbled down on the couch and put his hands under the back of his head and smiled.

"Della," said he, "let's put our Christmas presents away and keep 'em awhile. They're too nice to use just at present. I sold the watch to get the money to buy your combs. And now suppose you put the chops on."

The Magi, as you know, were wise men—wonderfully wise men—who brought gifts to the Babe in the manger. They invented the art of giving Christmas presents. Being wise, their gifts were no doubt wise ones, possibly bearing the privilege of exchange in case of duplication. And here I have lamely related to you the uneventful chronicle of two foolish children in a flat who most unwisely sacrificed for each other the greatest treasures of their house. But in a last word to the wise of these days let it be said that of all who give gifts these two were the wisest. Of all who give and receive gifts, such as they are wisest. Everywhere they are wisest. They are the Magi.

CHECK-UP (Short Answer)

1. When does the action of the story take place?
2. What is Della's proudest possession?
3. What does Della buy for Jim?
4. What has happened to Jim's watch?
5. What is Jim's gift to Della?

FOR DISCUSSION

1. Which details in the story tell you that the events take place early in this century?
2. This story is famous for its ironic plot. How do the actions of the characters bring about unexpected results? Are these actions consistent with the nature of the characters?
3. What is the tone of the story? Is O. Henry's attitude toward his characters sympathetic? mocking? amused? or something else?
4. Locate the statement in this story that best expresses its theme.
5. Explain the title of the story. What is the "gift" associated with the Magi? What has this gift to do with Jim and Della?

TOTAL EFFECT

Throughout his story O. Henry emphasizes the way money, or the lack of it, affects the lives of Jim and Della. We know the exact amounts of things. They live in a furnished flat that costs eight dollars a week. Della has saved one dollar and eighty-seven cents. Jim's income is twenty dollars a week. Della sells her hair for twenty dollars and spends twenty-one dollars on a chain for Jim's watch. Yet,

O. Henry means to show us that however deprived they may be of domestic comforts and possessions, Jim and Della are rich in what they give each other.

In the last paragraph, O. Henry appears to contradict himself. He refers to Jim and Della as "two foolish children . . . who most unwisely sacrificed for each other the greatest treasures of their house." In the very next sentence, however, he claims that of all gift givers, these two were "the wisest." It is clear that O. Henry is playing on the meaning of *wise* in order to make a point. To those people who attach value chiefly to money and material things, the sacrifice of Jim and Della must seem foolish and wasteful. To others, like the author, Jim and Della are wisest because their gift of love and sacrifice is far more important than any material gift.

The reader knows that far from narrating an "uneventful chronicle," O. Henry succeeds in giving meaning to the story of two ordinary people whose love for one another transforms them into the Magi—the wisest.

How does the title of the story reveal O. Henry's purpose? The Magi were wise men who brought gifts to Bethlehem. Yet, O. Henry's title refers to a single gift. Why?

UNDERSTANDING THE WORDS IN THE STORY (Matching Columns)

1. reflection
2. vestibule
3. prosperity
4. unassuming
5. sterling
6. agile
7. longitudinal
8. depreciate
9. faltered
10. ransacking

a. wealth and success
b. excellent
c. hesitated
d. quick
e. entranceway
f. running lengthwise
g. belittle or lessen
h. searching
i. serious thought
j. modest

(Completion)

Choose one of the words in the following list to complete each of the sentences below. A word may be used only once.

chaste	scrutiny
prudence	inconsequential
mammoth	adornment
laborious	ardent
patent	chronicle

1. Something that is evident or clear is said to be
   _____.

2. An object used to decorate or ornament something is
   a(an) _____.

3. A(n) _____ style is restrained and simple.

4. A narrative or history is known as a(n) _____.

5. Something of little significance is _____.

6. Impulsive people tend to act without _____.

7. A(n) _____ love is intense in feeling.

8. That which calls for hard work is _____.

9. To be subjected to _____ is to be examined carefully.

10. A(n) _____ undertaking is very big.

FOR WRITING

1. Is the surprise ending of O. Henry's story a trick, or is it a logical ending? State your opinion, using evidence from the story to support your position.
2. Discuss O. Henry's use of irony in "The Gift of the Magi."

3. Read the account of the meeting of King Solomon and the Queen of Sheba in 1 Kings 10. Then explain O. Henry's allusion in "The Gift of the Magi."
4. Investigate the custom of giving gifts. Find out which occasions were used in ancient times before the advent of Christianity. Or find out how people in another country, say England, celebrate the giving of Christmas gifts.

More Stories

"Pettigrew was breathing fast.
His finely drawn face began to coarsen . . ."

MASON'S LIFE

Kingsley Amis

"May I join you?"

The medium-sized man with the undistinguished clothes and the blank, anonymous face looked up at Pettigrew, who, glass of beer in hand, stood facing him across the small corner table. Pettigrew, tall, handsome and of fully molded features, had about him an intent, almost excited air that, in different circumstances, might have brought an unfavorable response, but the other said amiably,

"By all means. Do sit down."

"Can I get you something?"

"No, I'm fine, thank you," said the medium-sized man, gesturing at the almost-full glass in front of him. In the background was the ordinary ambience[1] of bar, barman, drinkers in ones and twos, nothing to catch the eye.

"We've never met, have we?"

"Not as far as I recall."

"Good, good. My name's Pettigrew, Daniel R. Pettigrew. What's yours?"

1. **ambience** (ăm′bē-əns): atmosphere; the predominant mood of one's surroundings.

307

"Mason. George Herbert Mason, if you want it in full."

"Well, I think that's best, don't you? George . . . Herbert . . . Mason." Pettigrew spoke as if committing the three short words to memory. "Now let's have your telephone number."

Again Mason might have reacted against Pettigrew's demanding manner, but he said no more than, "You can find me in the book easily enough."

"No, there might be several . . . We mustn't waste time. Please."

"Oh, very well; it's public information, after all, Two-three-two, five——"

"Hold on, you're going too fast for me. Two . . . three . . . two . . ."

"Five-four-five-four."

"What a stroke of luck. I ought to be able to remember that."

"Why don't you write it down if it's so important to you?"

At this, Pettigrew gave a knowing grin that faded into a look of disappointment. "Don't you know that's no use? Anyway: two-three-two, five-four-five-four. I might as well give you my number too. Seven——"

"I don't want your number, Mr. Pettigrew," said Mason, sounding a little impatient, "and I must say I rather regret giving you mine."

"But you must take my number."

"Nonsense; you can't make me."

"A phrase, then—let's agree on a phrase to exchange in the morning."

"Would you mind telling me what this is all about?"

"Please, our time's running out."

"You keep saying that. Our time for what?"

"Any moment everything might change and I might

find myself somewhere completely different, and so might you, I suppose, though I can't help feeling it's doubtful whether——"

"Mr. Pettigrew, either you explain yourself at once or I'll have you removed."

"All right," said Pettigrew, whose disappointed look had deepened, "but I'm afraid it won't do any good. You see, when we started talking I thought you must be a real person, because of the way you——"

"Spare me your infantile catch phrases,[2] for heaven's sake. So I'm not a real person," cooed Mason offensively.

"I don't mean it like that. I mean it in the most literal way possible."

"Are you mad or drunk or what?"

"Nothing like that. I'm asleep."

"Asleep?" Mason's nondescript face showed total incredulity.

"Yes. As I was saying, at first I took you for another real person in the same situation as myself: sound asleep, dreaming, aware of the fact, and anxious to exchange names and telephone numbers and so forth with the object of getting in touch the next day and confirming the shared experience. That would prove something remarkable about the mind, wouldn't it?—people communicating via their dreams. It's a pity one so seldom realizes one's dreaming: I've only been able to try the experiment four or five times in the last twenty years, and I've never had any success. Either I forget the details or I find there's no such person, as in this case. But I'll go on——"

"You're sick."

"Oh no. Of course it's conceivable there is such a person as you. Unlikely, though, or you'd have recognized the true

---

2. **catch phrases:** A catch phrase is a phrase often repeated, such as "a real person."

situation at once, I feel, instead of arguing against it like this. As I say, I may be wrong."

"It's hopeful that you say that." Mason had calmed down, and lit a cigarette with deliberation. "I don't know much about these things, but you can't be too far gone if you admit you could be in error. Now let me just assure you that I didn't come into existence five minutes ago inside your head. My name, as I told you, is George Herbert Mason. I'm forty-six years old, married, three children, job in the furniture business . . . Oh, giving you no more than an outline of my life so far would take all night, as it would in the case of anybody with an average memory. Let's finish our drinks and go along to my house, and then we can——"

"You're just a man in my dream saying that," said Pettigrew loudly. "Two-three-two, five-four-five-four. I'll call the number if it exists, but it won't be you at the other end. Two-three-two——"

"Why are you so agitated, Mr. Pettigrew?"

"Because of what's going to happen to you at any moment."

"Happen to me? What can happen to me? Is this a threat?"

Pettigrew was breathing fast. His finely drawn face began to coarsen, the pattern of his jacket to become blurred. "The telephone!" he shouted. "It must be later than I thought!"

"Telephone?" repeated Mason, blinking and screwing up his eyes as Pettigrew's form continued to change.

"The one at my bedside! I'm waking up!"

Mason grabbed the other by the arm, but that arm had lost the greater part of its outline, had become a vague patch of light already fading, and when Mason looked at the hand that had done the grabbing, his own hand, he saw with difficulty, it likewise no longer had fingers, or front or back, or skin, or anything.

CHECK-UP (True/False)

1. Pettigrew and Mason are old friends.
2. Mason is a man who makes a striking impression.
3. Pettigrew asks to join Mason at his table.
4. Pettigrew asks for Mason's telephone number.
5. Mason won't give Pettigrew his telephone number.
6. Pettigrew writes down his notes.
7. Mason believes that Pettigrew is asleep.
8. Pettigrew believes Mason exists only in a dream.
9. Mason invites Pettigrew to come home with him.
10. Mason's body begins to disappear.

FOR DISCUSSION

1. What details in the description of Mason make him sound like a figure in a dream?
2. Why does Pettigrew believe that Mason does not exist?
3. Why does Pettigrew wish to exchange telephone numbers?
4. Mason insists that he is a real person. Do you agree, or do you think he exists only in Pettigrew's mind?
5. In what way is the ending of the story ironic?

FANTASY

The term *fantasy* embraces many different stories that deal with unreal or fantastic things. A fairy tale, which takes place in an imaginary kingdom and tells about magical events, is one kind of fantasy. Science fiction is another kind of fantasy, although it has become popular enough to be designated a separate category.

Some stories of fantasy are set in the real world, and elements of the fantastic are made to seem commonplace. "Mason's Life," for instance, begins in a recognizable setting—a bar. The conversation between Mason and Pettigrew may strike us as odd, but the characters are convincing as flesh-and-blood creatures. Not until the end of the story, when the figures begin to disappear, do we realize that we have been witnessing a scene that has no natural explanation.

UNDERSTANDING THE WORDS
IN THE STORY (Multiple-Choice)

1. Clothes that are *undistinguished*
   a. have no distinctive character
   b. call attention to the owner
   c. are ill-fitting and unattractive
2. A *blank* face is a face
   a. with ordinary features
   b. without makeup
   c. without expression
3. In a crowd, an *anonymous* face would
   a. call attention to itself
   b. look strained and puzzled
   c. not be noticed
4. A person would most likely have an *intent* look
   a. during sleep
   b. while taking a test
   c. in mowing the lawn
5. The word *air* refers to a person's
   a. beneficiary
   b. manner or appearance
   c. inner feelings
6. To speak *amiably* is to speak
   a. in a friendly way
   b. coldly
   c. proudly
7. In *committing* a telephone number to memory, you
   a. write it down
   b. learn it by heart
   c. practice dialing it

8. A *demanding* individual
   a. makes troublesome requests
   b. demonstrates self-control
   c. exercises patience
9. Behavior that is *infantile* is
   a. unexpected
   b. annoying
   c. childish
10. When someone behaves *offensively,* that person is
    a. acting in a disagreeable way
    b. gaining others' sympathy
    c. doing something dangerous

(Matching Columns)

Match each word in the left column with a word in the right column that is its *opposite*. Use a word only once.

1. literal
2. nondescript
3. incredulity
4. anxious
5. confirm
6. conceivable
7. deliberation
8. agitate
9. coarsen
10. vague

a. strong belief
b. not true to fact
c. to calm
d. clear; definite in shape
e. unbelievable
f. uninterested
g. to make smooth
h. strikingly individual
i. to deny
j. thoughtlessness

FOR WRITING

1. Imagine that Mason and Pettigrew meet again. Describe the circumstances of their meeting and write the dialogue that takes place between them.
2. Write a short essay telling how you were affected by this story. Were you amused? frightened? confused? Or did you experience something else?

*"I got into dry clothes and went down
to supper—and then I made a break
that spoiled my day."*

STOLEN DAY

Sherwood Anderson

It must be that all children are actors. The whole thing
started with a boy on our street named Walter, who had
inflammatory rheumatism.[1] That's what they called it. He
didn't have to go to school.

Still he could walk about. He could go fishing in the
creek or the waterworks pond. There was a place up at the
pond where in the spring the water came tumbling over the
dam and formed a deep pool. It was a good place. Sometimes you could get some good big ones there.

I went down that way on my way to school one spring
morning. It was out of my way but I wanted to see if Walter
was there.

He was, inflammatory rheumatism and all. There he
was, sitting with a fish pole in his hand. He had been able to
walk down there all right.

It was then that my own legs began to hurt, My back too.
I went on to school but, at the recess time, I began to cry. I
did it when the teacher, Sarah Suggett, had come out into
the schoolhouse yard.

She came right over to me.

"I ache all over," I said. I did, too.

I kept on crying and it worked all right.

---

1. **inflammatory rheumatism** (roo′mə-tiz′əm): a painful disease affecting
   the joints and muscles.

"You'd better go on home," she said.

So I went. I limped painfully away. I kept on limping until I got out of the schoolhouse street.

Then I felt better. I still had inflammatory rheumatism pretty bad but I could get along better.

I must have done some thinking on the way home.

"I'd better not say I have inflammatory rheumatism," I decided. "Maybe if you've got that you swell up."

I thought I'd better go around to where Walter was and ask him about that, so I did—but he wasn't there.

"They must not be biting today," I thought.

I had a feeling that, if I said I had inflammatory rheumatism, Mother or my brothers and my sister Stella might laugh. They did laugh at me pretty often and I didn't like it at all.

"Just the same," I said to myself, "I have got it." I began to hurt and ache again.

I went home and sat on the front steps of our house. I sat there a long time. There wasn't anyone at home but Mother and the two little ones. Ray would have been four or five then and Earl might have been three.

It was Earl who saw me there. I had got tired sitting and was lying on the porch. Earl was always a quiet, solemn little fellow.

He must have said something to Mother for presently she came.

"What's the matter with you? Why aren't you in school?" she asked.

I came pretty near telling her right out that I had inflammatory rheumatism but I thought I'd better not. Mother and Father had been speaking of Walter's case at the table just the day before. "It affects the heart," Father had said. That frightened me when I thought of it. "I might die," I thought. "I might just suddenly die right here; my heart might stop beating."

On the day before I had been running a race with my brother Irve. We were up at the fairgrounds after school and there was a half-mile track.

"I'll bet you can't run a half-mile," he said. "I bet you I could beat you running clear around the track."

And so we did it and I beat him, but afterwards my heart did seem to beat pretty hard. I remembered that lying there on the porch. "It's a wonder, with my inflammatory rheumatism and all, I didn't just drop down dead," I thought. The thought frightened me a lot. I ached worse than ever.

"I ache, Ma," I said. "I just ache."

She made me go in the house and upstairs and get into bed.

It wasn't so good. It was spring. I was up there for perhaps an hour, maybe two, and then I felt better.

I got up and went downstairs. "I feel better, Ma," I said.

Mother said she was glad. She was pretty busy that day and hadn't paid much attention to me. She had made me get into bed upstairs and then hadn't even come up to see how I was.

I didn't think much of that when I was up there but when I got downstairs where she was, and when, after I had said I felt better and she only said she was glad and went right on with her work, I began to ache again.

I thought, "I'll bet I die of it. I bet I do."

I went out to the front porch and sat down. I was pretty sore at Mother.

"If she really knew the truth, that I have the inflammatory rheumatism and I may just drop down dead any time, I'll bet she wouldn't care about that either," I thought.

I was getting more and more angry the more thinking I did.

"I know what I'm going to do," I thought; "I'm going to go fishing."

I thought that, feeling the way I did, I might be sitting on the high bank just above the deep pool where the water went over the dam, and suddenly my heart would stop beating.

And then, of course, I'd pitch forward, over the bank into the pool and, if I wasn't dead when I hit the water, I'd drown sure.

They would all come home to supper and they'd miss me.

"But where is he?"

Then Mother would remember that I'd come home from school aching.

She'd go upstairs and I wouldn't be there. One day during the year before, there was a child got drowned in a spring. It was one of the Wyatt children.

Right down at the end of the street there was a spring under a birch tree and there had been a barrel sunk in the ground.

Everyone had always been saying the spring ought to be kept covered, but it wasn't.

So the Wyatt child went down there, played around alone, and fell in and got drowned.

Mother was the one who had found the drowned child. She had gone to get a pail of water and there the child was, drowned and dead.

This had been in the evening when we were all at home, and Mother had come running up the street with the dead, dripping child in her arms. She was making for the Wyatt house as hard as she could run, and she was pale.

She had a terrible look on her face, I remembered then.

"So," I thought, "they'll miss me and there'll be a search made. Very likely there'll be someone who has seen me sitting by the pond fishing, and there'll be a big alarm and all the town will turn out and they'll drag the pond."

I was having a grand time, having died. Maybe, after

they found me and had got me out of the deep pool, Mother would grab me up in her arms and run home with me as she had run with the Wyatt child.

I got up from the porch and went around the house. I got my fishing pole and lit out for the pool below the dam. Mother was busy—she always was—and didn't see me go. When I got there I thought I'd better not sit too near the edge of the high bank.

By this time I didn't ache hardly at all, but I thought.

"With inflammatory rheumatism you can't tell," I thought.

"It probably comes and goes," I thought.

"Walter has it and he goes fishing," I thought.

I had got my line into the pool and suddenly I got a bite. It was a regular whopper. I knew that. I'd never had a bite like that.

I knew what it was. It was one of Mr. Fenn's big carp.

Mr. Fenn was a man who had a big pond of his own. He sold ice in the summer and the pond was to make the ice. He had bought some big carp and put them into his pond and then, earlier in the spring when there was a freshet,[2] his dam had gone out.

So the carp had got into our creek and one or two big ones had been caught—but none of them by a boy like me.

The carp was pulling and I was pulling and I was afraid he'd break my line, so I just tumbled down the high bank, holding onto the line and got right into the pool. We had it out, there in the pool. We struggled. We wrestled. Then I got a hand under his gills and got him out.

He was a big one all right. He was nearly half as big as I was myself. I had him on the bank and I kept one hand under his gills and I ran.

---

2. **freshet:** a sudden overflowing of a stream from a heavy rain or thaw.

I never ran so hard in my life. He was slippery, and now and then he wriggled out of my arms; once I stumbled and fell on him, but I got him home.

So there it was. I was a big hero that day. Mother got a washtub and filled it with water. She put the fish in it and all the neighbors came to look. I got into dry clothes and went down to supper—and then I made a break that spoiled my day.

There we were, all of us, at the table, and suddenly Father asked what had been the matter with me at school. He had met the teacher, Sarah Suggett, on the street and she had told him how I had become ill.

"What was the matter with you?" Father asked, and before I thought what I was saying I let it out.

"I had the inflammatory rheumatism," I said—and a shout went up. It made me sick to hear them, the way they all laughed.

It brought back all the aching again, and like a fool I began to cry.

"Well, I *have* got it—I *have, I have,*" I cried, and I got up from the table and ran upstairs.

I stayed there until Mother came up. I knew it would be a long time before I heard the last of the inflammatory rheumatism. I was sick all right, but the aching I now had wasn't in my legs or in my back.

CHECK-UP (Putting Events in Order)

Arrange the following events in the order in which they occur in the story.

The narrator begins to cry during recess.
Mother puts the big carp in the washtub.
The narrator sees Walter fishing at the pond.
The narrator's mother sends him upstairs to bed.
The narrator tells his family that he has inflammatory rheumatism.
The narrator's father asks him why he left school.
The narrator's legs and back begin to hurt.
The narrator gets his fishing pole and heads for the pool.
The narrator wrestles with the fish.
The narrator gets a bite on his line.

FOR DISCUSSION

1. This story is told by an adult who remembers an episode in his childhood. He opens the narrative by saying, "It must be that all children are actors." How do the events of the story show this to have been true in his own case?
2. How does the narrator convince himself that he has inflammatory rheumatism? What do you suppose is his motivation?
3. Why is the narrator angry at his mother? How does he punish her in his fantasy?
4. In what way is the narrator's day "stolen"?

FLASHBACK

The sequence of events in a story usually follows chronological order. Sometimes an author will interrupt a narrative to relate an action that has already occurred. Such an interruption is called a *flashback.* In "Stolen Day" the narrator tells about a drowning accident that had occurred a year earlier. What causes him to remember the death of the Wyatt child? How does this memory stimulate him to imagine the effect of his own death?

FOR WRITING

A "stolen day" is a day spent shirking one's normal duties and responsibilities. Imagine how you might spend such a day.

THE FUN
THEY HAD

Isaac Asimov

Margie even wrote about it that night in her diary. On the page headed May 17, 2155, she wrote, "Today Tommy found a real book!"

It was a very old book. Margie's grandfather once said that when he was a little boy *his* grandfather told him that there was a time when all stories were printed on paper.

They turned the pages, which were yellow and crinkly, and it was awfully funny to read words that stood still instead of moving the way they were supposed to—on a screen, you know. And then, when they turned back to the page before, it had the same words on it that it had had when they read it the first time.

"Gee," said Tommy, "what a waste. When you're through with the book, you just throw it away, I guess. Our television screen must have had a million books on it and it's good for plenty more. I wouldn't throw *it* away."

"Same with mine," said Margie. She was eleven and hadn't seen as many telebooks[1] as Tommy had. He was thirteen.

---

1. **telebooks:** books transmitted on a television screen.

She said, "Where did you find it?"

"In my house." He pointed without looking, because he was busy reading. "In the attic."

"What's it about?"

"School."

Margie was scornful. "School? What's there to write about school? I hate school." Margie always hated school, but now she hated it more than ever. The mechanical teacher had been giving her test after test in geography and she had been doing worse and worse until her mother had shaken her head sorrowfully and sent for the County Inspector.

He was a round little man with a red face and a whole box of tools with dials and wires. He smiled at her and gave her an apple, then took the teacher apart. Margie had hoped he wouldn't know how to put it together again, but he knew how all right and, after an hour or so, there it was again, large and black and ugly with a big screen on which all the lessons were shown and the questions were asked. That wasn't so bad. The part she hated most was the slot where she had to put homework and test papers. She always had to write them out in a punch code they made her learn when she was six years old, and the mechanical teacher calculated the mark in no time.

The inspector had smiled after he was finished and patted her head. He said to her mother, "It's not the little girl's fault, Mrs. Jones. I think the geography sector[2] was geared a little too quick. Those things happen sometimes. I've slowed it up to an average ten-year level. Actually, the overall pattern of her progress is quite satisfactory." And he patted Margie's head again.

Margie was disappointed. She had been hoping they

---

2. **sector:** section or part.

would take the teacher away altogether. They had once taken Tommy's teacher away for nearly a month because the history sector had blanked out completely.

So she said to Tommy, "Why would anyone write about school?"

Tommy looked at her with very superior eyes. "Because it's not our kind of school, stupid. This is the old kind of school that they had hundreds and hundreds of years ago." He added loftily, pronouncing the word carefully, *"Centuries* ago."

Margie was hurt. "Well, I don't know what kind of school they had all that time ago." She read the book over his shoulder for a while, then said, "Anyway, they had a teacher."

"Sure they had a teacher, but it wasn't a *regular* teacher. It was a man."

"A man? How could a man be a teacher?"

"Well, he just told the boys and girls things and gave them homework and asked them questions."

"A man isn't smart enough."

"Sure he is. My father knows as much as my teacher."

"He can't. A man can't know as much as a teacher."

"He knows almost as much I betcha."

Margie wasn't prepared to dispute that. She said, "I wouldn't want a strange man in my house to teach me."

Tommy screamed with laughter, "You don't know much, Margie. The teachers didn't live in the house. They had a special building and all the kids went there."

"And all the kids learned the same thing?"

"Sure, if they were the same age."

"But my mother says a teacher has to be adjusted to fit the mind of each boy and girl it teaches and that each kid has to be taught differently."

"Just the same, they didn't do it that way then. If you don't like it, you don't have to read the book."

"I didn't say I didn't like it," Margie said quickly. She wanted to read about those funny schools.

They weren't even half finished when Margie's mother called, "Margie! School!"

Margie looked up. "Not yet, mamma."

"Now," said Mrs. Jones. "And it's probably time for Tommy, too."

Margie said to Tommy, "Can I read the book some more with you after school?"

"Maybe," he said, nonchalantly. He walked away whistling, the dusty old book tucked beneath his arm.

Margie went into the schoolroom. It was right next to her bedroom, and the mechanical teacher was on and waiting for her. It was always on at the same time every day except Saturday and Sunday, because her mother said little girls learned better if they learned at regular hours.

The screen was lit up, and it said: "Today's arithmetic lesson is on the addition of proper fractions. Please insert yesterday's homework in the proper slot."

Margie did so with a sigh. She was thinking about the old schools they had when her grandfather's grandfather was a little boy. All the kids from the whole neighborhood came, laughing and shouting in the schoolyard, sitting together in the schoolroom, going home together at the end of the day. They learned the same things so they could help one another on the homework and talk about it.

And the teachers were people. . . .

The mechanical teacher was flashing on the screen: "When we add the fractions ½ and ¼ . . ."

Margie was thinking about how the kids must have loved it in the old days. She was thinking about the fun they had.

CHECK-UP (True/False)

1. This story takes place many years from now.
2. Margie and Tommy are sister and brother.
3. Margie is younger than Tommy.
4. Margie and Tommy are used to reading books on television screens.
5. Margie finds an old book in the attic of her house.
6. Margie enjoys school.
7. Tommy and Margie are taught by mechanical teachers.
8. Margie's schoolroom is next to her bedroom.
9. Margie goes to school all alone.
10. Tommy keeps a diary.

FOR DISCUSSION

1. Why do Tommy and Margie find reading a "real book" a funny experience? What kind of books are they used to reading?
2. Describe the school that Margie attends. How is it different from the schools we know?
3. What problems is Margie having at school? Why does she believe that schools in the "old days" were more fun?
4. Science fiction often predicts future scientific developments. What kind of educational system does Asimov project in this story? What problems does the story suggest may result from the technology of the future?

SCIENCE FICTION

The science-fiction tale is a special kind of fantasy. As a rule, the action is set on some strange world or in the distant future. Consequently, the science-fiction story tends to focus on details of background, such as landscapes, machines, and customs.

Asimov makes this point about "The Fun They Had":

> In a little over a thousand words, I must not only describe the feelings and frustrations in the mind of a little girl, but I must get across, somehow, the entire educational system of a future society, compare it with our own, and do it all without being obvious.[1]

Point out details in the story that describe the schoolroom, classes, and teachers in this society. How does Asimov make these changes sound convincing?

UNDERSTANDING THE WORDS IN THE STORY (Multiple-Choice)

1. Paper that is *crinkly* is
   a. smooth to the touch
   b. full of wrinkles
   c. dusty and stained
2. A *scornful* look indicates
   a. contempt
   b. respect
   c. affection
3. When a grade is *calculated,* it is
   a. estimated roughly
   b. entered in the record book
   c. arrived at by mathematics
4. To make *progress* is to
   a. pass all subjects
   b. complete all homework assignments
   c. improve steadily
5. A computer screen that has *blanked out*
   a. responds to all instructions
   b. shows nothing
   c. flashes messages to the user

1. *Fifty Short Science Fiction Tales,* ed. Isaac Asimov and Groff Conklin (New York, 1963), page 15.

6. A person who looks at you with *superior* eyes
   a. has eyes set high above the nose
   b. gives the impression of being frightened
   c. wears an expression of disdain
7. One speaks *loftily* when one
   a. is proud and haughty
   b. wishes to be heard above a crowd
   c. stands on a platform
8. To *dispute* a point is to
   a. show disrespect for the speaker
   b. question or doubt it
   c. examine it part by part
9. When the County Inspector *adjusted* the machine, he
   a. regulated it to suit the pupil's abilities
   b. inserted new parts to make it more efficient
   c. changed the punch code
10. If one behaves *nonchalantly,* one acts
    a. excitedly
    b. nervously
    c. coolly

FOR WRITING

1. Although Margie lives in the year 2155, her problems at school are very similar to problems students have faced in all generations. Discuss her difficulties and the solutions offered by the society in which she lives.
2. In a brief essay discuss the advantages and disadvantages of the type of education that is depicted in Asimov's story.

*Maud Martha and her family hoped that
the things they loved about their
home would last forever.*

HOME

Gwendolyn Brooks

What had been wanted was this always, this always to
last, the talking softly on this porch, with the snake plant in
the jardiniere[1] in the southwest corner, and the obstinate
slip from Aunt Eppie's magnificent Michigan fern at the left
side of the friendly door. Mama, Maud Martha, and Helen
rocked slowly in their rocking chairs, and looked at the late
afternoon light on the lawn and at the emphatic iron of the
fence and at the poplar tree. These things might soon be
theirs no longer. Those shafts and pools of light, the tree, the
graceful iron, might soon be viewed possessively by different
eyes.

Papa was to have gone that noon, during his lunch hour,
to the office of the Home Owners' Loan. If he had not succeeded in getting another extension, they would be leaving
this house in which they had lived for more than fourteen
years. There was little hope. The Home Owners' Loan was
hard. They sat, making their plans.

"We'll be moving into a nice flat somewhere," said
Mama. "Somewhere on South Park, or Michigan, or in
Washington Park Court." Those flats, as the girls and Mama
knew well, were burdens on wages twice the size of Papa's.
This was not mentioned now.

1. **jardiniere** (järd'n-îr'): a decorative pot for plants.

"They're much prettier than this old house," said Helen. "I have friends I'd just as soon not bring here. And I have other friends that wouldn't come down this far for anything, unless they were in a taxi."

Yesterday, Maud Martha would have attacked her. Tomorrow she might. Today she said nothing. She merely gazed at a little hopping robin in the tree, her tree, and tried to keep the fronts of her eyes dry.

"Well, I do know," said Mama, turning her hands over and over, "that I've been getting tireder and tireder of doing that firing.[2] From October to April, there's firing to be done."

"But lately we've been helping, Harry and I," said Maud Martha. "And sometimes in March and April and in October, and even in November, we could build a little fire in the fireplace. Sometimes the weather was just right for that."

She knew, from the way they looked at her, that this had been a mistake. They did not want to cry.

But she felt that the little line of white, sometimes ridged with smoked purple, and all that cream-shot saffron[3] would never drift across any western sky except that in back of this house. The rain would drum with as sweet a dullness nowhere but here. The birds on South Park were mechanical birds, no better than the poor caught canaries in those "rich" women's sun parlors.

"It's just going to kill Papa!" burst out Maud Martha. "He loves this house! He *lives* for this house!"

"He lives for us," said Helen. "It's us he loves. He wouldn't want the house, except for us."

"And he'll have us," added Mama, "wherever."

"You know," Helen sighed, "if you want to know the truth, this is a relief. If this hadn't come up, we would have gone on, just dragged on, hanging out here forever."

2. **firing:** starting a coal fire.
3. **saffron:** a yellow-orange color.

"It might," allowed Mama, "be an act of God. God may just have reached down and picked up the reins."

"Yes," Maud Martha cracked in, "that's what you always say—that God knows best."

Her mother looked at her quickly, decided the statement was not suspect, looked away.

Helen saw Papa coming. "There's Papa," said Helen.

They could not tell a thing from the way Papa was walking. It was that same dear little staccato walk, one shoulder down, then the other, then repeat, and repeat. They watched his progress. He passed the Kennedys', he passed the vacant lot, he passed Mrs. Blakemore's. They wanted to hurl themselves over the fence, into the street, and shake the truth out of his collar. He opened his gate—the gate—and still his stride and face told them nothing.

"Hello," he said.

Mama got up and followed him through the front door. The girls knew better than to go in too.

Presently Mama's head emerged. Her eyes were lamps turned on.

"It's all right," she exclaimed. "He got it. It's all over. Everything is all right."

The door slammed shut. Mama's footsteps hurried away.

"I think," said Helen, rocking rapidly, "I think I'll give a party. I haven't given a party since I was eleven. I'd like some of my friends to just casually see that we're homeowners."

CHECK-UP (True/False)

1. Maud Martha is unhappy about leaving the old house.
2. The family plans to rent out rooms in the house.
3. Papa wants to move into a better neighborhood.
4. Helen is tired of starting the fire in the house.
5. Papa gets an extension on his loan.

FOR DISCUSSION

1. In this story we see how the members of a family react to the threat of losing their home. How do Mama and Helen react? What defenses do these characters use against disappointment?
2. How does Maud Martha's reaction differ from the reactions of Mama and Helen? What are the things she feels she will miss?
3. What evidence is there that Maud Martha and Helen value different things?
4. How is the problem the family faces resolved?

UNDERSTANDING THE WORDS IN THE STORY (Matching Columns)

1. obstinate		a. arousing suspicion
2. emphatic		b. came out
3. shafts		c. troubles
4. possessively		d. short and abrupt
5. extension		e. slender rays
6. flat		f. as an owner
7. burdens		g. hard to control
8. suspect		h. apartment
9. staccato		i. striking
10. emerged		j. additional time

FOR WRITING

A character may be presented through direct and indirect methods of characterization (see pages 48 and 58). Show how Gwendolyn Brooks develops the character of Maud Martha.

"By degrees she grew aware that her hand had encountered something very soothing, very pleasant to touch."

A PAIR OF SILK STOCKINGS

Kate Chopin

Little Mrs. Sommers one day found herself the unexpected possessor of fifteen dollars. It seemed to her a very large amount of money, and the way in which it stuffed and bulged her worn old *porte-monnaie*[1] gave her a feeling of importance such as she had not enjoyed for years.

The question of investment was one that occupied her greatly. For a day or two she walked about apparently in a dreamy state, but really absorbed in speculation and calculation. She did not wish to act hastily, to do anything she might afterward regret. But it was during the still hours of the night when she lay awake revolving plans in her mind that she seemed to see her way clearly toward a proper and judicious use of the money.

A dollar or two should be added to the price usually paid for Janie's shoes, which would insure their lasting an appreciable time longer than they usually did. She would buy so and so many yards of percale for new shirtwaists for the boys and Janie and Mag. She had intended to make the old ones do by skillful patching. Mag should have another gown.

1. ***porte-monnaie*** (pôrt'môn-nē'): a small pocketbook.

333

She had seen some beautiful patterns, veritable bargains in the shop windows. And still there would be left enough for new stockings—two pairs apiece—and what darning that would save for a while! She would get caps for the boys and sailor hats for the girls. The vision of her little brood looking fresh and dainty and new for once in their lives excited her and made her restless and wakeful with anticipation.

The neighbors sometimes talked of certain "better days" that little Mrs. Sommers had known before she had ever thought of being Mrs. Sommers. She herself indulged in no such morbid retrospection.[2] She had no time—no second of time to devote to the past. The needs of the present absorbed her every faculty. A vision of the future like some dim, gaunt monster sometimes appalled her, but luckily tomorrow never comes.

Mrs. Sommers was one who knew the value of bargains; who could stand for hours making her way inch by inch toward the desired object that was selling below cost. She could elbow her way if need be; she had learned to clutch a piece of goods and hold it and stick to it with persistence and determination till her turn came to be served, no matter when it came.

But that day she was a little faint and tired. She had swallowed a light luncheon—no! when she came to think of it, between getting the children fed and the place righted, and preparing herself for the shopping bout, she had actually forgotten to eat any luncheon at all!

She sat herself upon a revolving stool before a counter that was comparatively deserted, trying to gather strength and courage to charge through an eager multitude that was besieging breastworks[3] of shirting and figured lawn.[4] An all-

---

2. **morbid retrospection** (môr′bĭd rĕt′rə-spĕk′shən): looking back on the past in a way that is psychologically unhealthy.
3. **breastworks:** low walls, here used metaphorically.
4. **figured lawn:** fine fabric decorated with a pattern.

gone limp feeling had come over her and she rested her hand aimlessly upon the counter. She wore no gloves. By degrees she grew aware that her hand had encountered something very soothing, very pleasant to touch. She looked down to see that her hand lay upon a pile of silk stockings. A placard nearby announced that they had been reduced in price from two dollars and fifty cents to one dollar and ninety-eight cents; and a young girl who stood behind the counter asked her if she wished to examine their line of silk hosiery. She smiled, just as if she had been asked to inspect a tiara of diamonds with the ultimate view of purchasing it. But she went on feeling the soft, sheeny luxurious things—with both hands now, holding them up to see them glisten, and to feel them glide serpentlike through her fingers.

Two hectic blotches came suddenly into her pale cheeks. She looked up at the girl.

"Do you think there are any eights-and-a-half among these?"

There were any number of eights-and-a-half. In fact, there were more of that size than any other. Here was a light-blue pair; there were some lavender, some all black and various shades of tan and gray. Mrs. Sommers selected a black pair and looked at them very long and closely. She pretended to be examining their texture, which the clerk assured her was excellent.

"A dollar and ninety-eight cents," she mused aloud. "Well, I'll take this pair." She handed the girl a five-dollar bill and waited for her change and for her parcel. What a very small parcel it was! It seemed lost in the depths of her shabby old shopping bag.

Mrs. Sommers after that did not move in the direction of the bargain counter. She took the elevator, which carried her to an upper floor into the region of the ladies' waiting rooms. Here, in a retired corner, she exchanged her cotton stockings for the new silk ones which she had just bought.

She was not going through any acute mental process or reasoning with herself, nor was she striving to explain to her satisfaction the motive of her action. She was not thinking at all. She seemed for the time to be taking a rest from that laborious and fatiguing function and to have abandoned herself to some mechanical impulse that directed her actions and freed herself of responsibility.

How good was the touch of the raw silk to her flesh! She felt like lying back in the cushioned chair and reveling for a while in the luxury of it. She did for a little while. Then she replaced her shoes, rolled the cotton stockings together and thrust them into her bag. After doing this she crossed straight over to the shoe department and took her seat to be fitted.

She was fastidious. The clerk could not make her out; he could not reconcile her shoes with her stockings, and she was not too easily pleased. She held back her skirts and turned her feet one way and her head another as she glanced down at the polished, pointed-tipped boots. Her foot and ankle looked very pretty. She could not realize that they belonged to her and were a part of herself. She wanted an excellent and stylish fit, she told the young fellow who served her, and she did not mind the difference of a dollar or two more in the price so long as she got what she desired.

It was a long time since Mrs. Sommers had been fitted with gloves. On rare occasions when she had bought a pair they were always "bargains," so cheap that it would have been preposterous and unreasonable to have expected them to be fitted to the hand.

Now she rested her elbow on the cushion of the glove counter, and a pretty, pleasant young creature, delicate and deft of touch, drew a long-wristed "kid" over Mrs. Sommers' hand. She smoothed it down over the wrist and buttoned it neatly, and both lost themselves for a second or two in admiring contemplation of the little symmetrical gloved hand. But there were other places where money might be spent.

There were books and magazines piled up in the window of a stall a few paces down the street. Mrs. Sommers bought two high-priced magazines such as she had been accustomed to read in the days when she had been accustomed to other pleasant things. She carried them without wrapping. As well as she could she lifted her skirts at the crossings. Her stockings and boots and well-fitting gloves had worked marvels in her bearing—had given her a feeling of assurance, a sense of belonging to the well-dressed multitude.

She was very hungry. Another time she would have stilled the cravings for food until reaching her own home, where she would have brewed herself a cup of tea and taken a snack of anything that was available. But the impulse that was guiding her would not suffer her to entertain any such thought.

There was a restaurant at the corner. She had never entered its doors; from the outside she had sometimes caught glimpses of spotless damask and shining crystal, and soft-stepping waiters serving people of fashion.

When she entered her appearance created no surprise, no consternation, as she had half feared it might. She seated herself at a small table alone, and an attentive waiter at once approached to take her order. She did not want a profusion; she craved a nice and tasty bite—a half dozen bluepoints,[5] a plump chop with cress, a something sweet—a crème-frappée,[6] for instance; a glass of Rhine wine, and after all a small cup of black coffee.

While waiting to be served she removed her gloves very leisurely and laid them beside her. Then she picked up a

---

5. **bluepoints:** oysters from the south shore of Long Island.
6. **crème-frappée** (krĕme frä-pā'): a chilled dessert.

magazine and glanced through it, cutting the pages with a blunt edge of her knife. It was all very agreeable. The damask was even more spotless than it had seemed through the window, and the crystal more sparkling. There were quiet ladies and gentlemen, who did not notice her, lunching at the small tables like her own. A soft, pleasing strain of music could be heard, and a gentle breeze was blowing through the window. She tasted a bite, and she read a word or two, and she sipped the amber wine and wiggled her toes in the silk stockings. The price of it made no difference. She counted the money out to the waiter and left an extra coin on his tray, whereupon he bowed before her as before a princess of royal blood.

There was still money in her purse, and her next temptation presented itself in the shape of a matinée poster.

It was a little later when she entered the theater, the play had begun and the house seemed to her to be packed. But there were vacant seats here and there, and into one of them she was ushered, between brilliantly dressed women who had gone there to kill time and eat candy and display their gaudy attire. There were many others who were there solely for the play and acting. It is safe to say there was no one present who bore quite the attitude which Mrs. Sommers did to her surroundings. She gathered in the whole—stage and players and people in one wide impression, and absorbed it and enjoyed it. She laughed at the comedy and wept—she and the gaudy woman next to her wept over the tragedy. And they talked a little together over it. And the gaudy woman wiped her eyes and sniffled on a tiny square of filmy, perfumed lace and passed little Mrs. Sommers her box of candy.

The play was over, the music ceased, the crowd filed out. It was like a dream ended. People scattered in all directions. Mrs. Sommers went to the corner and waited for the cable car.

A man with keen eyes, who sat opposite to her, seemed to like the study of her small, pale face. It puzzled him to decipher what he saw there. In truth, he saw nothing— unless he were wizard enough to detect a poignant wish, a powerful longing that the cable car would never stop anywhere, but go on and on with her forever.

CHECK-UP (Putting Events in Order)

Arrange these events in the order in which they occur in the story.

Mrs. Sommers buys a pair of kid gloves.
Mrs. Sommers examines a pair of silk stockings.
Mrs. Sommers cuts the pages of her magazine.
Mrs. Sommers gets on a cable car.
Mrs. Sommers removes her cotton stockings.
A woman passes a box of candy to Mrs. Sommers.
Mrs. Sommers makes her way to the shoe department.
Mrs. Sommers observes women in expensive, showy clothing.
Mrs. Sommers attends an afternoon performance at a theater.
Mrs. Sommers enters an elegant restaurant.

FOR DISCUSSION

1. What evidence early in the story shows that Mrs. Sommers is a devoted mother? How do you know that she is practical and sensible in her everyday life?
2. Although Mrs. Sommers is not accustomed to self-indulgence, she spends all of the money on luxuries for herself. What accounts for the change in her behavior? How does the author make the change believable?

3. Although we are not given Mrs. Sommers' thoughts at the end of the story, we can infer her state of mind. What impression do you get from the last paragraph of the story?

UNDERSTANDING THE WORDS IN THE STORY (Matching Columns)

1. speculation	a. met unexpectedly
2. judicious	b. ability
3. veritable	c. concentrated thought
4. anticipation	d. using good judgment
5. faculty	e. red or flushed
6. gaunt	f. shocked
7. appalled	g. authentic
8. aimless	h. very thin
9. encountered	i. expectation
10. hectic	j. having no purpose

(Completion)

Choose one of the words in the following list to complete each of the sentences below. A word may be used only once.

acute	profusion
fastidious	craves
preposterous	gaudy
contemplation	decipher
consternation	poignant

1. Furniture that is _____ is brightly colored but in bad taste.

2. The uncaged gerbil caused _____ in the classroom.

3. The student's question revealed a(n) _____ intelligence.

4. The expression on the teacher's face was difficult to
   _____.

5. The bored retiree _____ excitement.

6. The _____ music brought tears to our eyes.

7. We laughed at the _____ ending of the movie.

8. The mathematician was lost in _____ of the problem.

9. Cats tend to be _____ in their eating habits.

10. The table was covered with a _____ of flowers.

FOR WRITING

1. This story appeared in *Vogue* magazine on September
   16, 1897. At that time silk stockings were a great luxury.
   Today, we seldom hear of silk stockings—most hose is
   made of nylon. Nevertheless, Chopin's story has rele-
   vance for a twentieth-century audience. In a brief essay,
   tell why this story has meaning for a contemporary
   reader.

2. The theme of this story might be stated in terms of a
   conflict between responsibility and fantasy. Show how
   this idea is developed in the story.

*". . . I couldn't then imagine how he
had managed to get his job.
I have an idea now."*

SUCCESS STORY

James Gould Cozzens

I met Richards ten years or more ago when I first went
down to Cuba. He was a short, sharp-faced, agreeable chap,
then about twenty-two. He introduced himself to me on the
boat and I was surprised to find that Panamerica Steel &
Structure was sending us both to the same job.

Richards was from some not very good state university
engineering school. Being the same age myself, and just out
of tech, I was prepared to patronize[1] him if I needed to; but I
soon saw I didn't need to. There was really not the faintest
possibility of anyone supposing that Richards was as smart
as I was. In fact, I couldn't then imagine how he had managed to get his job. I have an idea now. It came to me when I
happened to read a few weeks ago that Richards had been
made a vice-president and director of Panamerica Steel
when the Prossert interests bought the old firm.

Richards was naturally likable, and I liked him a lot,
once I was sure that he wasn't going to outshine me. The
firm had a contract for the construction of a private railroad,
about seventeen miles of it, to give United Sugar a sea ter-
minal at a small deepwater Caribbean port. For Richards

---

1. **patronize** (pā′trə-nīz′): to treat in an offensive way as an inferior.

and me it was mostly an easy job of inspections and routine paperwork. At least it was easy for me. It was harder for Richards, because he didn't appear ever to have mastered the use of a slide rule.[2] When he asked me to check his figures I found it was no mere formality. "Boy," I was at last obliged to say, "you are undoubtedly the dumbest man in Santa Clara province. If you don't buck up, Farrell will see you never get another job down here."

Richards grinned and said, "I never want another one. Not a job like this, anyway. I'm the executive type."

"Oh, you are!"

"Sure, I am. And what do I care what Farrell thinks? What can he do for me?"

"Plenty. If he thinks you're any good, he can see you get something that pays money."

"He doesn't know anything that pays money, my son."

"He knows things that would pay enough for me," I answered, annoyed.

"Oh," said Richards, "if that's all you want, when Farrell's working for me I'll make him give you a job. A good one."

"Go to the devil!" I said. I was still checking his trial figures for an extra concrete pouring at the Nombre de Dios viaduct.[3] "Look, stupid," I said, "didn't you ever take arithmetic? How much are seven times thirteen?"

"Work that out," Richards said, "and let me have a report tomorrow."

When I had time, I continued to check his figures for him, and Farrell only caught him in a bad mistake about twice; but Farrell was the best man Panamerica Steel had. He'd been managing construction jobs both in Cuba and

---

2. **slide rule:** an instrument that looks like a ruler with a sliding strip in the center, used for rapid calculation.
3. **viaduct** (vī′ə-dŭkt′): a long bridge carrying a road or railroad over a valley or ravine.

Mexico for twenty years. After the first month or so he simply let Richards alone and devoted himself to giving me the whole benefit of his usually sharp and scornful criticism. He was at me every minute he could spare, telling me to forget this or that and use my head, showing me little tricks of figuring and method. He said it would be a good plan to take some Spanish lessons from a clerk he named in the sugar company's office.

"Spanish?" said Richards, when I told him he'd better join the class. "Not for me! Say, it took me twenty-two years to learn English. People who want to talk to me have to know it, or they'd better bring an interpreter with them."

"All right," I said. "I don't mind telling you the idea is Farrell's. He spoke to me about it."

"Well, he didn't speak to me," said Richards. "I guess he thinks I'm perfect the way I am. And now, if you'll excuse me, I have a date with a beer bottle."

I could easily see that he was coming to no good end.

In January several directors of the United Sugar Company came down on their annual jaunt—nominally[4] business, but mostly pleasure; a good excuse to get south on a vacation. They came on a yacht.

The yacht belonged to Mr. Joseph Prossert, who was, I think, chairman of United Sugar's board then. It was the first time I'd ever seen at close quarters one of these really rich and powerful financial figures whose name everyone knows. He was an inconspicuous,[5] rather stout man, with little hair on his head and a fussy, ponderous[6] way of speaking. He dressed in some dark thin cloth that looked like alpaca.[7] His interest in sugar and in Cuba was purely finan-

---

4. **nominally** (nŏm′ə-nəl-ē): in name only, not real or actual.
5. **inconspicuous** (in′kən-spĭk′yōō-əs): not attracting attention.
6. **ponderous** (pŏn′dər-əs): heavy; labored.
7. **alpaca** (ăl-păk′ə): a glossy cotton or rayon and wool cloth, used for suits.

cial—he didn't know anything about it from the practical standpoint. I really saw him at close quarters, too, for he was delayed on his boat when the directors went up to Santa Inez and Farrell left Richards and me and two or three armed guards to come up that afternoon.

Mr. Prossert was very affable. He asked me a number of questions. I knew the job well enough and could have answered almost any intelligent question—I mean, the sort that a trained engineer would be likely to ask. As it was, I suppose I'd said for perhaps the third time, "I'm afraid I wouldn't know, sir. We haven't any calculations on that," getting a glance of mildly surprised disbelief, when Richards suddenly spoke up. "I think, about nine million cubic feet, sir," he said. He looked boyishly embarrassed. "I just happened to be working it out last night. Just for my own interest, that is. Not officially." He blushed.

"Oh," said Mr. Prossert, turning in his seat and giving him a sharp look. "That's very interesting, Mr.—er—Richards, isn't it? Well, now, maybe you could tell me about——"

Richards could. He knew everything. He knew to the last car the capacity of every switch and yard; he knew the load limits of every bridge and culvert;[8] he knew the average rainfall for the last twenty years; he knew the population of the various straggling villages we passed through; he knew the heights of the distant blue peaks to the west. He had made himself familiar with local labor costs and wage scales. He had the statistics on accidents and unavoidable delays. He had figured out the costs of moving a cubic yard of earth at practically every cut and fill. All the way up Mr. Prossert fired questions at him and he fired answers right back.

When we reached the railhead,[9] a motor was waiting to

8. **culvert** (kŭl'vərt): sewer or drain.
9. **railhead:** the farthest point to which rails for a railroad have been laid.

take Mr. Prossert on. Getting out of the gas car, he nodded absent-mindedly to me, shook hands with Richards. "Very interesting indeed," he said. "Very interesting indeed, Mr. Richards. Goodbye and thank you."

"Not at all, sir," Richards said. "Glad if I could be of service to you."

As soon as the motor moved off, I exploded. "Of all the asinine[10] tricks! A little honest bluff doesn't hurt; but some of your so-called figures——"

"I aim to please," Richards said, grinning. "If a man like Prossert wants to know something, who am I to hold out on him?"

"I suppose you think you're smart," I told him. "What's he going to think when he looks up the figures or asks somebody who does know?"

"Listen, my son," said Richards kindly. "He wasn't asking for any information he was going to use. He doesn't want to know those figures. If he ever does, he has plenty of people to get him the right ones. He won't remember these. I don't even remember them myself. What he is going to remember is you and me."

"Oh, yes?"

"Oh, yes," said Richards firmly. "He's going to remember that Panamerica Steel & Structure has a bright young man named Richards who could tell him everything he wanted to know when he wanted to know it—just the sort of chap he can use; not like that other fellow who took no interest in his job, couldn't answer the simplest question, and who's going to be doing small-time contracting in Cuba all his life."

"Oh, yeah?" I said. But it is true that I am still in Cuba, still doing a little work in the construction line.

10. **asinine** (ăs'ə-nīn'): stupid or silly.

CHECK-UP (True/False)

1. The narrator and Richards both worked for United Sugar.
2. Farrell was construction manager for Panamerica Steel.
3. The narrator impressed Prossert with his intelligence and training.
4. Prossert easily saw through Richards' bluffing.
5. Richards was a poor engineer but a good judge of character.

FOR DISCUSSION

1. This story gives us a picture of two young engineers at the start of their careers. How are they different in attitude and ability?
2. Richards claims he is the "executive type." How does the incident with Prossert demonstrate what he means?
3. In what way is the outcome of the story an ironic reversal of what we expect? Why is Richards a success?
4. Consider the author's attitude toward the characters and events in the story. Do you think his attitude is realistic? pessimistic? scornful? Give reasons for your answer.

FOR WRITING

In a brief essay contrast the personalities of the two young engineers in this story. Include a discussion of ability, training, work habits, and attitude.

"These enemies maneuvered, each preparing to kill. It was to be battle without mercy."

THE SNAKE

Stephen Crane

Where the path wended across the ridge, the bushes of huckleberry and sweet fern swarmed at it in two curling waves until it was a mere winding line traced through a tangle. There was no interference by clouds, and as the rays of the sun fell upon the ridge, they called into voice innumerable insects which chanted the heat of the summer day in steady throbbing unending chorus.

A man and a dog came from the laurel thickets of the valley where the white brook brawled[1] with the rocks. They followed the deep line of the path across the ridge. The dog—a large lemon-and-white setter—walked, tranquilly meditative, at his master's heels.

Suddenly from some unknown and yet near place in advance there came a dry shrill whistling rattle that smote[2] motion instantly from the limbs of the man and the dog. Like the fingers of a sudden death, this sound seemed to touch the man at the nape of the neck, at the top of the spine, and change him, as swift as thought, to a statue of listening horror, surprise, rage. The dog, too—the same icy hand was laid upon him and he stood crouched and quivering, his jaw

---

1. **brawled** (brôld): flowed noisily.
2. **smote** (smōt): drove.

drooping, the froth of terror upon his lips, the light of hatred in his eyes.

Slowly the man moved his hands toward the bushes, but his glance did not turn from the place made sinister by the warning rattle. His fingers unguided sought for a stick of weight and strength. Presently they closed about one that seemed adequate, and holding this weapon poised before him, the man moved slowly forward, glaring. The dog with his nervous nostrils fairly fluttering moved warily, one foot at a time, after his master.

But when the man came upon the snake, his body underwent a shock as from a revelation, as if after all he had been ambushed. With a blanched face, he sprang backward and his breath came in strained gasps, his chest heaving as if he were in the performance of an extraordinary muscular trial. His arm with the stick made a spasmodic[3] defensive gesture.

The snake had apparently been crossing the path in some mystic[4] travel when to his sense there came the knowledge of the coming of his foes. The dull vibration perhaps informed him and he flung his body to face the danger. He had no knowledge of paths; he had no wit to tell him to slink noiselessly into the bushes. He knew that his implacable enemies were approaching; no doubt they were seeking him, hunting him. And so he cried his cry, an incredibly swift jangle of tiny bells, as burdened with pathos as the hammering upon quaint cymbals by the Chinese at war—for, indeed, it was usually his death music.

"Beware! Beware! Beware!"

The man and the snake confronted each other. In the man's eyes were hatred and fear. In the snake's eyes were hatred and fear. These enemies maneuvered, each preparing

---

3. **spasmodic** (spăz-mŏd′ĭk): sudden and uncontrolled.
4. **mystic** (mĭs′tĭk): mysterious.

to kill. It was to be battle without mercy. Neither knew of mercy for such a situation. In the man was all the wild strength of the terror of his ancestors, of his race, of his kind. A deadly repulsion had been handed from man to man through long dim centuries. This was another detail of a war that had begun evidently when first there were men and snakes. Individuals who do not participate in this strife incur the investigations of scientists. Once there was a man and a snake who were friends, and at the end, the man lay dead with the marks of the snake's caress just over his East Indian heart. In the formation of devices hideous and horrible, nature reached her supreme point in the making of the snake, so that those who really paint hell well, fill it with snakes instead of fire. These curving forms, these scintillant[5] colorings create at once, upon sight, more relentless animosities than do shake barbaric tribes. To be born a snake is to be thrust into a place aswarm with formidable foes.

As for this snake in the pathway, there was a double curve some inches back of its head which, merely by the potency of its lines, made the man feel with tenfold eloquence the touch of the death-fingers at the nape of his neck. The reptile's head was waving slowly from side to side and its hot eyes flashed like little murder-lights. Always in the air was the dry shrill whistling of the rattles.

"Beware! Beware! Beware!"

The man made a preliminary feint with his stick. Instantly the snake's heavy head and neck were bent back on the double curve, and instantly the snake's body shot forward in a low straight hard spring. The man jumped backward with a convulsive chatter and swung his stick. The blind, sweeping blow fell upon the snake's head and hurled him so that steel-colored plates were for a moment uppermost. But he rallied swiftly, agilely, and again the head and

5. **scintillant** (sīn'tə-lənt): gleaming; sparkling.

neck bent back to the double curve, and the steaming wide-open mouth made its desperate effort to reach its enemy. This attack, it could be seen, was despairing, but it was nevertheless impetuous, gallant, ferocious. The stick swung unerringly again and the snake, mutilated, torn, whirled himself into the last coil.

And now the man went sheer raving mad from the emotions of his forefathers and from his own. He came to close quarters. He gripped the stick with his two hands and made it speed like a flail.[6] The snake, tumbling in the anguish of final despair, fought, bit, flung itself upon this stick which was taking its life.

At the end, the man clutched his stick and stood watching in silence. The dog came slowly and with infinite caution stretched his nose forward, sniffing. The hair upon his neck and back moved and ruffled as if a sharp wind was blowing. The last muscular quivers of the snake were causing the rattles to still sound their treble cry, the shrill, ringing war chant and hymn of the grave of the thing that faces foes at once countless, implacable and superior.

"Well, Rover," said the man, turning to the dog with a grin of victory, "we'll carry Mr. Snake home to show the girls."

His hands still trembled from the strain of the encounter, but he pried with his stick under the body of the snake and hoisted the limp thing upon it. He resumed his march along the path, and the dog walked, tranquilly meditative, at his master's heels.

---

6. **flail** (flāl): a tool used for threshing the heads of ripened grain. It has a short swinging bar attached to a long handle.

CHECK-UP (True/False)

1. The man in the story becomes aware of the snake's presence when he hears its rattles.
2. The man and the dog try to avoid the snake.
3. The snake attempts to slide into the bushes.
4. The dog assists its master by attacking the snake.
5. The man kills the snake by beating it to death.

FOR DISCUSSION

1. This story deals with the conflict between a man and a snake. Crane creates interest in this conflict by depicting the human being and the animal as instinctive enemies. Locate passages where Crane refers to the ancient antagonism between the two species.
2. Crane describes the struggle dramatically. Which details appear to be an eyewitness observation of the struggle? Which details convey the inner feelings of the foes?
3. *Metaphor* is language that draws an imaginative comparison between unlike things. In this story Crane treats the conflict between a man and a snake in terms of warfare. Find examples of effective comparisons.

UNDERSTANDING THE WORDS IN THE STORY (Matching Columns)

1. wended		a. reflective
2. swarmed		b. held in balance
3. innumerable		c. staring angrily
4. meditative		d. moved in a crowd
5. sinister		e. something made known
6. poised		f. threatening trouble
7. glaring		g. cautiously
8. warily		h. turned pale
9. revelation		i. proceeded
10. blanched		j. countless

(Completion)

Choose one of the words in the following list to complete each of the sentences below. A word may be used only once.

wit confronted
slink repulsion
implacable strife
pathos incur
quaint relentless

1. The prisoner _____ his accuser.

2. We informed him that he would _____ a penalty if his application was late.

3. The creature did not have sufficient _____ to escape from its pursuers.

4. We saw the thief _____ into the shadows.

5. The _____ dripping of the faucet kept me awake.

6. His _____ costume attracted attention.

7. The odor of decay filled him with _____.

8. The angry customer was _____.

9. Our hope is to reduce the bitter _____ between the two factions.

10. The _____ of the child's crying aroused the stranger's sympathy.

(Synonyms and Antonyms)

1. An antonym for *animosity* is (love, hatred).
2. A synonym for *formidable* is (impressive, unimpressive).
3. An antonym for *potency* is (power, weakness).

4. A synonym for *preliminary* is (introductory, concluding).
5. A synonym for *feint* is (false show, intended blow).
6. A synonym for *rally* is (recover, fail).
7. An antonym for *impetuous* is (rash, unhurried).
8. A synonym for *unerring* is (exact, imprecise).
9. An antonym for *anguish* is (torment, joy).
10. A synonym for *resume* is (start again, interrupt).

FOR WRITING

1. An omniscient observer can tell the reader what all the characters see, hear, think, and feel, and can comment on or interpret the action (see page 158). In a short essay tell what Crane accomplishes by using the omniscient point of view in "The Snake."
2. Crane does not give the man in the story a name. What is the purpose of this anonymity? If you wish, discuss this element of anonymity in this and other stories, such as "The Sniper" (page 101), "Old Man at the Bridge" (page 237), and "War" (page 288).

"In his lace-bedecked crib the little Dauphin,
whiter than the cushions upon which he lies,
is resting now with closed eyes."

THE
DEATH OF
THE DAUPHIN°

Alphonse Daudet

The little Dauphin is sick; the little Dauphin is going to die. In all the churches of the realm the Blessed Sacrament[1] is exposed night and day, and tall candles are burning for the recovery of the royal child. The streets in the old residence are sad and silent, the bells no longer ring, and carriages go at a footpace. About the palace the curious citizens watch, through the iron grilles, the porters with gilt paunches talking in the courtyards with an air of importance.

The whole château is in commotion. Chamberlains, major-domos,[2] run hastily up and down the marble staircases. The galleries are full of pages and courtiers in silk garments, who go from group to group asking news in undertones. On the broad steps weeping maids of honor greet one another with low courtesies,[3] wiping their eyes with pretty embroidered handkerchiefs.

In the orangery[4] there is a great assemblage of long-

° **Dauphin** (dō-făn′): a title for the French crown prince.
1. **Blessed Sacrament:** the wafer or bread used in Holy Communion.
2. **Chamberlains, major-domos:** officials in charge of the household.
3. **courtesies:** curtseys.
4. **orangery** (ôr′ĭnj-rē): hothouse.

robed doctors. Through the windows they can be seen flourishing their long black sleeves and bending majestically their hammerlike wigs. The little Dauphin's governor[5] and equerry[6] walk back and forth before the door, awaiting the decision of the faculty. Scullions pass them by without saluting[7] them. The equerry swears like a heathen, the governor recites lines from Horace.[8] And meanwhile, in the direction of the stables one hears a long, plaintive neigh. It is the little Dauphin's horse, calling sadly from his empty manger.

And the king? Where is *monseigneur*[9] the king? The king is all alone in a room at the end of the château. Majesties do not like to be seen weeping. As for the queen, that is a different matter. Seated at the little Dauphin's pillow, her lovely face is bathed in tears, and she sobs aloud before them all, as a linen draper's wife might do.

In his lace-bedecked crib the little Dauphin, whiter than the cushions upon which he lies, is resting now with closed eyes. They think that he sleeps; but no. The little Dauphin is not asleep. He turns to his mother, and seeing that she is weeping, he says to her:

"Madame queen, why do you weep? Is it because you really believe that I am going to die?"

The queen tries to reply. Sobs prevent her from speaking.

"Pray do not weep, madame queen; you forget that I am the Dauphin, and that dauphins cannot die like this."

The queen sobs more bitterly than ever, and the little Dauphin begins to be alarmed.

"I say," he says, "I don't want Death to come and take me and I will find a way to prevent his coming here. Let them

---

5. **governor:** tutor.
6. **equerry** (ĕk'wə-rē): official in charge of horses.
7. **saluting:** here, greeting.
8. **Horace:** a famous Roman poet (65–8 B.C.).
9. *monseigneur* (môN-sĕ-nyœr'): my lord.

send at once forty very strong troopers to stand guard around our bed! Let a hundred big guns watch night and day with matches lighted, under our windows! And woe to Death if it dares approach us!"

To please the royal child the queen makes a sign. In a moment they hear the big guns rumbling through the courtyard; and forty tall troopers, halberds in hand, take their places about the room. They are all old soldiers with gray mustaches. The little Dauphin claps his hands when he sees them. He recognizes one of them and calls him:

"Lorrain! Lorrain!"

The soldier steps forward toward the bed.

"I love you dearly, my old Lorrain. Let me see your big sword. If Death tries to take me you must kill him, won't you?"

"Yes, *monseigneur,*" Lorrain replies. And two great tears roll down his bronzed cheeks.

At that moment the chaplain approaches the little Dauphin and talks with him for a long time in a low voice, showing him a crucifix. The little Dauphin listens with an expression of great surprise, then, abruptly interrupting him, he says:

"I understand what you say, *monsieur l'abbé;*[10] but tell me, couldn't my little friend Beppo die in my place, if I gave him a lot of money?"

The chaplain continues to speak in a low voice, and the little Dauphin's expression becomes more and more astonished.

When the chaplain has finished, the little Dauphin replies with a deep sigh:

"All this that you tell me is very sad, *monsieur l'abbé;* but one thing consoles me, and that is that up yonder, in the paradise of the stars, I shall still be the Dauphin. I know that

---

10. **monsieur l'abbé** (mə-syœ' lä-bā'): a title given to a priest.

the good Lord is my cousin, and that He cannot fail to treat me according to my rank."

Then he adds, turning to his mother:

"Let them bring me my richest clothes, my doublet[11] of white ermine, and my velvet slippers! I wish to make myself handsome for the angels, and to enter paradise in the costume of a Dauphin."

A third time the chaplain leans toward the little Dauphin and talks to him for a long time in a low voice. In the midst of his harangue,[12] the royal child angrily interrupts:

"Why, then, to be Dauphin is to be nothing at all!"

And refusing to listen to anything more, the little Dauphin turns toward the wall and weeps bitterly.

11. **doublet:** a closefitting jacket.
12. **harangue** (hə-răng′): a scolding speech.

CHECK-UP (True/False)

1. The doctors are in agreement about the prince's illness.
2. The grooms have neglected to feed the Dauphin's horse.
3. The king and queen are seated beside the Dauphin's crib.
4. The Dauphin tries to prevent Death from taking him.
5. The royal child learns that he will have no special privileges after death.

FOR DISCUSSION

1. Dramatic irony exists when the reader knows something that a character is not aware of. What is the dramatic irony in this story?

2. What are the Dauphin's illusions about his situation? What defenses does he construct against death?
3. How is the Dauphin stripped of his illusions?
4. What does the Dauphin realize at the end of the story? What thematic idea does this insight stress?

UNDERSTANDING THE WORDS IN THE STORY (Matching Columns)

1. château
2. commotion
3. assemblage
4. flourishing
5. majestic
6. faculty
7. scullions
8. plaintive
9. halberds
10. consoles

a. disturbance
b. kitchen helpers
c. great and splendid
d. axlike weapons
e. gathering of persons
f. sad
g. castle
h. soothes
i. learned body
j. moving dramatically

FOR WRITING

1. Daudet emphasizes the external details of court life. Tell how this emphasis contributes to the idea that wealth and privilege are no protection against death.
2. Compare the theme of this story with the theme of "Father and I" (page 127). What do both stories say about the illusions of childhood?

*Laurie's parents were worried that
Charles might be a bad influence
on their little boy.*

CHARLES

Shirley Jackson

The day my son Laurie started kindergarten he renounced[1] corduroy overalls with bibs and began wearing blue jeans with a belt; I watched him go off the first morning with the older girl next door, seeing clearly that an era of my life was ended, my sweet-voiced nursery-school tot replaced by a long-trousered, swaggering character who forgot to stop at the corner and wave goodbye to me.

He came home the same way, the front door slamming open, his cap on the floor, and the voice suddenly become raucous[2] shouting, "Isn't anybody *here?*"

At lunch he spoke insolently to his father, spilled his baby sister's milk, and remarked that his teacher said we were not to take the name of the Lord in vain.

"How *was* school today?" I asked, elaborately casual.

"All right," he said.

"Did you learn anything?" his father asked.

Laurie regarded his father coldly. "I didn't learn nothing." he said.

"Anything," I said. "Didn't learn anything."

"The teacher spanked a boy, though," Laurie said, ad-

1. **renounced** (rĭ-nounst'): gave up utterly.
2. **raucous** (rô'kəs): harsh and rough.

dressing his bread and butter. "For being fresh," he added, with his mouth full.

"What did he do?" I asked. "Who was it?"

Laurie thought. "It was Charles," he said. "He was fresh. The teacher spanked him and made him stand in a corner. He was awfully fresh."

"What did he do?" I asked again, but Laurie slid off his chair, took a cookie, and left, while his father was still saying, "See here, young man."

The next day Laurie remarked at lunch, as soon as he sat down, "Well, Charles was bad again today." He grinned enormously and said, "Today Charles hit the teacher."

"Good heavens," I said, mindful of the Lord's name, "I suppose he got spanked again?"

"He sure did," Laurie said. "Look up," he said to his father.

"What?" his father said, looking up.

"Look down," Laurie said. "Look at my thumb. Gee, you're dumb." He began to laugh insanely.

"Why did Charles hit the teacher?" I asked quickly.

"Because she tried to make him color with red crayons," Laurie said. "Charles wanted to color with green crayons so he hit the teacher and she spanked him and said nobody play with Charles but everybody did."

The third day—it was Wednesday of the first week— Charles bounced a seesaw onto the head of a little girl and made her bleed, and the teacher made him stay inside all during recess. Thursday Charles had to stand in a corner during story time because he kept pounding his feet on the floor. Friday Charles was deprived of blackboard privileges because he threw chalk.

On Saturday I remarked to my husband, "Do you think kindergarten is too unsettling for Laurie? All this toughness, and bad grammar, and this Charles boy sounds like such a bad influence."

"It'll be all right," my husband said reassuringly. "Bound to be people like Charles in the world. Might as well meet them now as later."

On Monday Laurie came home late, full of news, "Charles," he shouted as he came up the hill; I was waiting anxiously on the front steps. "Charles," Laurie yelled all the way up the hill, "Charles was bad again."

"Come right in," I said, as soon as he came close enough. "Lunch is waiting."

"You know what Charles did?" he demanded, following me through the door. "Charles yelled so in school they sent a boy in from first grade to tell the teacher she had to make Charles keep quiet, and so Charles had to stay after school. And so all the children stayed to watch him."

"What did he do?" I asked.

"He just sat there," Laurie said, climbing into his chair at the table. "Hi, Pop, y'old dust mop."

"Charles had to stay after school today," I told my husband. "Everyone stayed with him."

"What does this Charles look like?" my husband asked Laurie. "What's his other name?"

"He's bigger than me," Laurie said. "And he doesn't have any rubbers and he doesn't ever wear a jacket."

Monday night was the first Parent-Teachers meeting, and only the fact that the baby had a cold kept me from going; I wanted passionately to meet Charles's mother. On Tuesday Laurie remarked suddenly, "Our teacher had a friend come to see her in school today."

"Charles's mother?" my husband and I asked simultaneously.[3]

"Naaah," Laurie said scornfully. "It was a man who came and made us do exercises, we had to touch our toes. Look." He climbed down from his chair and squatted down

---

3. **simutaneously** (sī'məl-tā'nē-əs-lē): at the same time.

and touched his toes. "Like this," he said. He got solemnly back into his chair and said, picking up his fork, "Charles didn't even *do* exercises."

"That's fine," I said heartily. "Didn't Charles want to do exercises?"

"Naaah," Laurie said, "Charles was so fresh to the teacher's friend he wasn't *let* do exercises."

"Fresh again?" I said.

"He kicked the teacher's friend." Laurie said. "The teacher's friend told Charles to touch his toes like I just did and Charles kicked him."

"What are they going to do about Charles, do you suppose?" Laurie's father asked him.

Laurie shrugged elaborately. "Throw him out of school, I guess," he said.

Wednesday and Thursday were routine; Charles yelled during story hour and hit a boy in the stomach and made him cry. On Friday Charles stayed after school again and so did all the other children.

With the third week of kindergarten Charles was an institution in our family; the baby was being a Charles when she cried all afternoon; Laurie did a Charles when he filled his wagon full of mud and pulled it through the kitchen; even my husband, when he caught his elbow in the telephone cord and pulled telephone, ashtray, and a bowl of flowers off the table, said, after the first minute, "Looks like Charles."

During the third and fourth weeks it looked like a reformation in Charles; Laurie reported grimly at lunch on Thursday of the third week, "Charles was so good today the teacher gave him an apple."

"What?" I said, and my husband added warily,[4] "You mean Charles?"

---

4. **warily** (wâr′ĭ-lē): cautiously.

"Charles," Laurie said. "He gave the crayons around and he picked up the books afterward and the teacher said he was her helper."

"What happened?" I asked incredulously.[5]

"He was her helper, that's all," Laurie said, and shrugged.

"Can this be true, about Charles?" I asked my husband that night. "Can something like this happen?"

"Wait and see," my husband said cynically.[6] "When you've got a Charles to deal with, this may mean he's only plotting."

He seemed to be wrong. For over a week Charles was the teacher's helper; each day he handed things out and he picked things up; no one had to stay after school.

"The P.T.A. meeting's next week again," I told my husband one evening. "I'm going to find Charles's mother there."

"Ask her what happened to Charles," my husband said. "I'd like to know."

"I'd like to know myself," I said.

On Friday of that week things were back to normal. "You know what Charles did today?" Laurie demanded at the lunch table, in a voice slightly awed. "He told a little girl to say a word and she said it and the teacher washed her mouth out with soap and Charles laughed."

"What word?" his father asked unwisely, and Laurie said, "I'll have to whisper it to you, it's so bad." He got down off his chair and went around to his father. His father bent his head down and Laurie whispered joyfully. His father's eyes widened.

"Did Charles tell the little girl to say *that?*" he asked respectfully.

---

5. **incredulously** (ĭn-krĕj′ə-ləs-lē): in an unbelieving way.
6. **cynically** (sĭn′ĭk-lē): in a way showing distrust.

"She said it *twice*," Laurie said. "Charles told her to say it *twice*."

"What happened to Charles?" my husband asked.

"Nothing," Laurie said, "He was passing out the crayons."

Monday morning Charles abandoned the little girl and said the evil word himself three or four times, getting his mouth washed out with soap each time. He also threw chalk.

My husband came to the door with me that evening as I set out for the P.T.A. meeting. "Invite her over for a cup of tea after the meeting," he said. "I want to get a look at her."

"If only she's there," I said prayerfully.

"She'll be there," my husband said. "I don't see how they could hold a P.T.A. meeting without Charles's mother."

At the meeting I sat restlessly, scanning each comfortable matronly face, trying to determine which one hid the secret of Charles. None of them looked to me haggard[7] enough. No one stood up in the meeting and apologized for the way her son had been acting. No one mentioned Charles.

After the meeting I identified and sought out Laurie's kindergarten teacher. She had a plate with a cup of tea and a piece of chocolate cake; I had a plate with a cup of tea and a piece of marshmallow cake. We maneuvered up to one another cautiously, and smiled.

"I've been so anxious to meet you," I said. "I'm Laurie's mother."

"We're all so interested in Laurie," she said.

""Well, he certainly likes kindergarten," I said. "He talks about it all the time."

"We had a little trouble adjusting, the first week or so,"

---

7. **haggard:** tired and worn-out.

she said primly, "but now he's a fine little helper. With occasional lapses,[8] of course."

"Laurie usually adjusts very quickly," I said. "I suppose this time it's Charles's influence."

"Charles?"

"Yes," I said, laughing, "you must have your hands full in that kindergarten, with Charles."

"Charles?" she said. "We don't have any Charles in the kindergarten."

8. **lapses:** slips or failures.

CHECK-UP (True/False)

1. When he begins attending kindergarten, Laurie becomes bold and disrespectful.
2. Laurie claims that Charles is his best friend in school.
3. According to Laurie, Charles is the teacher's pet.
4. Laurie's parents are eager to meet Charles's mother.
5. At the P.T.A. meeting, Laurie's mother learns that her son and Charles are the same person.

FOR DISCUSSION

1. Laurie tells a great many stories about Charles's behavior in kindergarten. Whose behavior is he describing? Is it likely that all these stories are true?
2. Why do you suppose Laurie enjoys telling his family stories about Charles?
3. At what point in the story did you begin to suspect the true identity of Charles? Why do you suppose Laurie's parents never catch on?
4. In what way is the outcome of this story ironic?

UNDERSTANDING THE WORDS
IN THE STORY (Matching Columns)

1. era		a. insultingly
2. swaggering		b. something set by custom
3. insolently		c. vigorously
4. deprived		d. disturbing
5. unsettling		e. improvement
6. heartily		f. bold and self-important
7. routine		g. considering carefully
8. institution		h. a noteworthy period
9. reformation		i. habitual
10. scanning		j. denied or dispossessed

FOR WRITING

The narrator in "Stolen Day" (page 314) says: "It must be that all children are actors." Could Laurie be considered an "actor"? Write an essay exploring this question. Refer to specific evidence in the story.

"The Czar rubbed his hands and took a steaming roll. He broke it open and the smile vanished from his face."

ROLLS FOR THE CZAR

Robin Kinkead

This is a tale of the days of the Czars, of ermine and gold and pure white bread.

In Saint Petersburg[1] the Czar held his court with pomp and ceremony that dazzled peasants and ambassadors alike. His Winter Palace covered acres by the side of the frozen Neva.[2] It had pillars of lapis lazuli[3] and of rare stone from the Urals. Its halls held treasures from all the world.

Once a year the Czar paid a visit of state to Moscow, where the rich merchants lived, trade center of the Imperial Domain. Here he would sit in the throne room of the Kremlin,[4] where his ancestors once ruled warring Muscovy.[5]

There was another great man in Moscow—a baker, Markov by name. The master bakers of the city were famous, and Markov was prince among them. His cakes and pastry were renowned throughout all the Russias, but his rolls were

1. **Saint Petersburg:** now called Leningrad.
2. **Neva** (Nē′və, nyĕ-vä′): a river.
3. **lapis lazuli** (lăp′ĭs lăz′yo͞o-lē): a gemstone, azure-blue in color.
4. **Kremlin** (krĕm′lən): the citadel, or fortress, of Moscow.
5. **Muscovy** (mŭs′kə-vē): the Russian Empire.

the best of all: pure white, like the driven snow of the steppes, a crust just hard enough to crunch, the bread not too soft, but soft enough to hold the melted butter.

Merchant princes from the gold rivers of Siberia, chieftains from the Caucasus in high fur hats, nobles from their feudal estates in the country, all came to Moscow to eat Markov's rolls.

The Czar himself was a mighty eater and especially fond of Markov's delicacies. So one day in February, when it came time for a visit to Moscow, he was thinking of Markov and his art, anticipating the rolls. His private car bore the imperial coat of arms. The rest of the train was filled with grand dukes, princes of the blood, and noble ladies. The railroad track ran straight as an arrow five hundred miles through the snow, the white birch forests, and the pines.

The train chuffed into the Moscow station, into a morning of sun and frost. The sun sparkled on the gold domes of churches, it glittered on the cuirasses[6] of a regiment of guards, all men of noble birth. Smoke rose straight up from chimneys. Twin jets of steam snorted from the nostrils of the three horses of the Czar's troika.[7] The Czar had a fine appetite.

The horses' hoofs kicked up gouts of snow as they galloped over the moat and through the gate in the Kremlin wall. The Czar walked up the royal staircase, carpeted in red and lined with bowing servants. He was thinking of the rolls.

He went through the formal greetings with a distracted look, then sat down eagerly at the breakfast table. Not a glance did he give the caviar, the smoked sterlets,[8] the pheasant in aspic. He watched the door. When a royal footman

---

6. **cuirasses** (kwĭ-răs′əs): armor for the breast and back.
7. **troika** (troi′kə): a small carriage drawn by a team of three horses abreast.
8. **sterlets** (stûr′lĭts): sturgeon, a source of caviar.

came through carrying a silver platter loaded with rolls, the Czar smiled. All was well.

The Czar rubbed his hands and took a steaming roll. He broke it open and the smile vanished from his face. A dead fly lay embedded in the bread. Courtiers crowded around to look.

"Bring Markov here!" said the Czar, with one of his terrible glances.

The banquet room was silent in tense horror. Markov came in puffing slightly but bearing himself with the pride of a master artist.

"Look at this, Markov," said the Czar, pointing at the fly, "and tell me what it is."

Markov looked and stood frozen for a moment. Princes, nobles, and servants all leaned forward waiting for doom to strike him. The Czar could bend horseshoes in his bare hands. A word from him and the bleak wastes of Siberia lay waiting.

No man could tell what Markov thought, but they knew that a fly had endangered his life. He reached to the platter and picked up the fly. He put it in his mouth and ate it. Every eye watched him swallow.

"It is a raisin, Sire," he said.

Wrath faded from the Czar's face. He broke out laughing and the nobles relaxed.

"Markov," he said, "we grant you a coat of arms with a fly as the motif.[9] A fly imperiled your life and a fly saved your life."

And the Czar went on with his rolls.

---

9. **motif** (mō-tēf′): main figure in the design.

CHECK-UP (Putting Events in Order)

The Czar walks up the staircase in the Kremlin.
Markov swallows the fly.
The Czar sends for Markov.
The Czar begins laughing.
Markov is granted a coat of arms.
The Czar finds a fly embedded in a roll.
The Czar leaves his court in Saint Petersburg.
Markov identifies the fly as a raisin.
The Czar reaches for a hot roll on a silver platter.
The Czar arrives at the station in Moscow.

FOR DISCUSSION

1. The word *czar* comes from the name *Caesar.* How does this story show that the Russian Czar had unlimited power in his empire?
2. Instead of punishing Markov, the Czar rewards him. Why? What does the Czar find admirable in Markov?
3. Is this story merely an entertaining anecdote, or does it reveal insight into human nature?

UNDERSTANDING THE WORDS
IN THE STORY (Matching Columns)

1. ermine	a. overpowered with brilliance
2. pomp	b. endangered
3. dazzled	c. diverted; turned aside
4. renowned	d. brilliant display
5. moat	e. well known
6. distracted	f. severe; empty
7. embedded	g. violent anger
8. bleak	h. enclosed
9. wrath	i. white fur
10. imperiled	j. deep trench

FOR WRITING

1. Show how the author re-creates the splendor in which the Russian czars lived. Refer to specific details in the story.
2. Analyze the author's use of direct and indirect methods of characterization in depicting the Czar.

*"It was her turn to give
a party . . . but she could not
seem to hit upon anything to celebrate."*

THE
ECLIPSE

Selma Lagerlöf
Translated by Velma Swanston Howard

There were Stina of Ridgecôte and Lina of Birdsong and
Kajsa of Littlemarsh and Maja of Skypeak and Beda of Finn-
darkness and Elin, the new wife on the old soldier's place,
and two or three other peasant women besides—all of them
lived at the far end of the parish, below Storhöjden, in a
region so wild and rocky none of the big farm owners had
bothered to lay hands on it.

One had her cabin set up on a shelf of rock, another had
hers put up at the edge of a bog, while a third had one that
stood at the crest of a hill so steep it was a toilsome climb
getting to it. If by chance any of the others had a cottage built
on more favorable ground, you may be sure it lay so close to
the mountain as to shut out the sun from autumn fair time
clear up to Annunciation Day.[1]

They each cultivated a little potato patch close by the
cabin, though under serious difficulties. To be sure, there
were many kinds of soil there at the foot of the mountain,
but it was hard work to make the patches of land yield anything. In some places they had to clear away so much stone

---

1. **Annunciation Day:** March 25, the day commemorating the appearance
   of the angel Gabriel to Mary (Luke 1:26–38).

373

from their fields, it would have built a cow-house on a mano-rial estate;[2] in some they had dug ditches as deep as graves, and in others they had brought their earth in sacks and spread it on the bare rocks. Where the soil was not so poor, they were forever fighting the tough thistle and pigweed which sprang up in such profusion you would have thought the whole potato land had been prepared for their benefit.

All the livelong day the women were alone in their cabins; for even where one had a husband and children, the man went off to his work every morning and the children went to school. A few among the older women had grown sons and daughters, but they had gone to America. And some there were with little children, who were always around, of course; but these could hardly be regarded as company.

Being so much alone, it was really necessary that they should meet sometimes over the coffee cups. Not that they got on so very well together, nor had any great love for each other; but some liked to keep posted on what the others were doing, and some grew despondent living like that, in the shadow of the mountain, unless they met people now and then. And there were those, too, who needed to unburden their hearts, and talk about the last letter from America, and those who were naturally talkative and jocular,[3] and who longed for opportunity to make use of these happy God-given talents.

Nor was it any trouble at all to prepare for a little party. Coffeepot and coffee cups they all had of course, and cream could be got at the manor, if one had no cow of one's own to milk; fancy biscuits and small cakes one could, at a pinch, get the dairyman's driver to fetch from the municipal[4] bak-ery, and country merchants who sold coffee and sugar were

---

2. **manorial** (mă-nôr′ē-əl) **estate:** The manor was the main house or man-sion on a large, landed estate.
3. **jocular** (jŏk′yə-lər): given to joking.
4. **municipal** (myoo-nĭs′ə-pəl): city.

to be found everywhere. So, to get up a coffee party was the easiest thing imaginable. The difficulty lay in finding an occasion.

For Stina of Ridgecôte, Lina of Birdsong, Kajsa of Littlemarsh, Maja of Skypeak, Beda of Finn-darkness, and Elin, the new wife at the old soldier's, were all agreed that it would never do for them to celebrate in the midst of the common everyday life. Were they to be that wasteful of the precious hours which never return, they might get a bad name. And to hold coffee parties on Sundays or great Holy Days was out of the question; for then the married women had husband and children at home, which was quite company enough. As for the rest—some liked to attend church, some wished to visit relatives, while a few preferred to spend the day at home, in perfect peace and stillness, that they might really feel it was a Holy Day.

Therefore they were all the more eager to take advantage of every possible opportunity. Most of them gave parties on their name-days,[5] though some celebrated the great event when the wee little one cut its first tooth, or when it took its first steps. For those who received money-letters from America, that was always a convenient excuse, and it was also in order to invite all the women of the neighborhood to come and help tack a quilt or stretch a web just off the loom.

All the same, there were not nearly as many occasions to meet as were needed. One year one of the women was at her wits' end. It was her turn to give a party, and she had no objection to carrying out what was expected of her; but she could not seem to hit upon anything to celebrate. Her own name-day she could not celebrate, being named Beda, as Beda had been stricken out of the almanac. Nor could she celebrate that of any member of her family, for all her dear

---

5. **name-days:** The name-day is the feast day of the saint after whom a person is named.

ones were resting in the churchyard. She was very old, and the quilt she slept under would probably outlast her. She had a cat of which she was very fond. Truth to tell, it drank coffee just as well as she did; but she could hardly bring herself to hold a party for a cat!

Pondering, she searched her almanac again and again, for there she felt she must surely find the solution of her problem.

She began at the beginning, with "The Royal House" and "Signs and Forecasts," and read on, right through to "Markets and Postal Transmittances for 1912," without finding anything.

As she was reading the book for the seventh time, her glance rested on "Eclipses." She noted that that year, which was the year of our Lord nineteen-hundred twelve, on April seventeenth there would be a solar eclipse. It would begin at twenty munutes past high noon and end at 2:40 o'clock, and would cover nine-tenths of the sun's disk.

This she had read before, many times, without attaching any significance to it; but now, all at once, it became dazzlingly clear to her.

"Now I have it!" she exclaimed.

But it was only for a second or two that she felt confident; and then she put the thought away, fearing that the other women would just laugh at her.

The next few days, however, the idea that had come to her when reading her almanac kept recurring to her mind, until at last she began to wonder whether she hadn't better venture.[6] For when she thought about it, what friend had she in all the world she loved better than the Sun? Where her hut lay not a ray of sunlight penetrated her room the whole winter long. She counted the days until the Sun would come back to her in the spring. The Sun was the only one she

6. **venture** (věn′chər): dare, take a risk.

longed for, the one who was always friendly and gracious to her and of whom she could never see enough.

She looked her years, and felt them, too. Her hands shook as if she were in a perpetual chill and when she saw herself in the looking glass, she appeared so pale and washed out, as if she had been lying out to bleach. It was only when she stood in a strong, warm, down-pouring sunshine that she felt like a live human being and not a walking corpse.

The more she thought about it, the more she felt there was no day in the whole year she would rather celebrate than the one when her friend the Sun battled against darkness, and after a glorious conquest, came forth with new splendor and majesty.

The seventeeth of April was not far away, but there was ample time to make ready for a party. So, on the day of the eclipse Stina, Lina, Kajsa, Maja, and the other women all sat drinking coffee with Beda at Finn-darkness. They drank their second and third cups, and chatted about everything imaginable. For one thing, they said they couldn't for the life of them understand why Beda should be giving a party.

Meanwhile, the eclipse was under way. But they took little notice of it. Only for a moment, when the sky turned blackish gray, when all nature seemed under a leaden pall,[7] and there came driving a howling wind with sounds as of the Trumpet of Doom and the lamentations of Judgment Day[8]— only then did they pause and feel a bit awed. But here they each had a fresh cup of coffee, and the feeling soon passed.

When all was over, and the Sun stood out in the heavens so beamingly happy—it seemed to them it had not shone with such brilliancy and power the whole year—they saw old Beda go over to the window, and stand with folded

---

7. **leaden pall:** gloomy atmosphere.
8. **Trumpet . . . Day:** the day of God's final judgment, also called *dooms-day*.

hands. Looking out toward the sunlit slope, she sang in her quavering[9] voice:

> Thy shining sun goes up again,
> I thank Thee, O my Lord!
> With new-found courage, strength and hope,
> I raise a song of joy.

Thin and transparent, old Beda stood there in the light of the window, and as she sang the sunbeams danced about her, as if wanting to give her, also, of their life and strength and color.

When she had finished the old hymn-verse she turned and looked at her guests, as if in apology.

"You see," she said, "I haven't any better friend than the Sun, and I wanted to give her a party on the day of her eclipse. I felt that we should come together to greet her, when she came out of her darkness."

Now they understood what old Beda meant, and their hearts were touched. They began to speak well of the Sun. "She was kind to rich and poor alike, and when she came peeping into the hut on a winter's day, she was as comforting as a glowing fire on the hearth. Just the sight of her smiling face made life worth living, whatever the troubles one had to bear."

The women went back to their homes after the party, happy and content. They somehow felt richer and more secure in the thought that they had a good, faithful friend in the Sun.

9. **quavering:** trembling.

CHECK-UP (True/False)

1. Coffee parties were never held on Sundays.
2. Men were often invited to coffee parties.
3. Beda considered holding a coffee party on her name-day.
4. Beda searched through her almanac for a solution to her problem.
5. Beda's neighbors joined her in singing a hymn.

FOR DISCUSSION

1. Describe the setting of the story. What aspect of nature is stressed by these details?
2. What is the chief problem that the women face? How do the coffee parties help the women overcome the problem?
3. How does the author create sympathy for Beda? Refer to specific passages in the story.
4. Why does Beda wish to honor the sun?
5. How did you respond to the ending of the story?

UNDERSTANDING THE WORDS IN THE STORY (Matching Columns)

1. bog
2. crest
3. toilsome
4. profusion
5. despondent
6. recurring
7. perpetual
8. ample
9. lamentations
10. awed

a. high point
b. a great deal
c. more than enough
d. laborious
e. continual
f. inspired with wonder
g. mournful expressions
h. wet, spongy ground
i. happening again
j. discouraged

FOR WRITING

1. Is nature in this story presented as an ally or as an enemy of human beings? Or is it presented as both? Defend your answer with specific references to details in the story.
2. Discuss attitudes toward the sun in "The Eclipse" and "All Summer in a Day" (page 91).

". . . her voice was as gentle as the expression
in her beautiful dark brown eyes."

LOVE

William Maxwell

Miss Vera Brown, she wrote on the blackboard, letter by
letter in flawlessly oval Palmer method.[1] Our teacher for the
fifth grade. The name might as well have been graven in
stone.

As she called the roll, her voice was as gentle as the
expression in her beautiful dark brown eyes. She reminded
me of pansies. When she called on Alvin Ahrens to recite and
he said, "I know but I can't say," the class snickered but she
said, "Try," encouragingly, and waited, to be sure that he
didn't know the answer, and then said, to one of the hands
waving in the air, "Tell Alvin what one-fifth of three-eighths
is." If we arrived late to school, red-faced and out of breath
and bursting with the excuse we had thought up on the way,
before we could speak she said, "I'm sure you couldn't help
it. Close the door, please, and take your seat." If she kept us
after school it was not to scold us but to help us past the hard
part.

Somebody left a big red apple on her desk for her to find
when she came into the classroom, and she smiled and put it
in her desk, out of sight. Somebody else left some purple
asters, which she put in her drinking glass. After that the
presents kept coming. She was the only pretty teacher in the

---

1. **Palmer method:** a method of teaching handwriting, popular earlier in
   this century.

school. She never had to ask us to be quiet or to stop throwing erasers. We would not have dreamed of doing anything that would displease her.

Somebody wormed it out of her when her birthday was. While she was out of the room the class voted to present her with flowers from the greenhouse. Then they took another vote and sweet peas won. When she saw the florist's box waiting on her desk, she said, "Oh?"

"Look inside," we all said.

Her delicate fingers seemed to take forever to remove the ribbon. In the end, she raised the lid of the box and exclaimed.

"Read the card!" we shouted.

Many Happy Returns to Miss Vera Brown, from the Fifth Grade, it said.

She put her nose in the flowers and said, "Thank you all very, very much," and then turned our minds to the spelling lesson for the day.

After school we escorted her downtown in a body to a special matinée of D. W. Griffith's[2] "Hearts of the World." She was not allowed to buy her ticket. We paid for everything.

We meant to have her for our teacher forever. We intended to pass right up through the sixth, seventh, and eighth grades and on into high school taking her with us. But that isn't what happened. One day there was a substitute teacher. We expected our real teacher to be back the next day but she wasn't. Week after week passed, and the substitute continued to sit at Miss Brown's desk, calling on us to recite and giving out tests and handing them back with grades on them, and we went on acting the way we had when Miss Brown was there because we didn't want her to come back and find we hadn't been nice to the substitute. One Monday

---

2. **D. W. Griffith:** a pioneer in the motion-picture industry (1875–1948).

morning she cleared her throat and said that Miss Brown was sick and not coming back for the rest of the term.

In the fall we had passed on into the sixth grade and she was still not back. Benny Irish's mother found out that she was living with an aunt and uncle on a farm a mile or so beyond the edge of town, and told my mother, who told somebody in my hearing. One afternoon after school Benny and I got on our bikes and rode out to see her. At the place where the road turned off to go to the cemetery and the Chautauqua[3] grounds, there was a red barn with a huge circus poster on it, showing the entire inside of the Sells-Floto Circus tent and everything that was going on in all three rings. In the summertime, riding in the back seat of my father's open Chalmers,[4] I used to crane my neck as we passed that turn, hoping to see every last tiger and flying-trapeze artist, but it was never possible. The poster was weather-beaten now, with loose strips of paper hanging down.

It was getting dark when we wheeled our bikes up the lane of the farmhouse where Miss Brown lived.

"You knock," Benny said as we started up on the porch.

"No, you do it," I said.

We hadn't thought ahead to what it would be like to see her. We wouldn't have been surprised if she had come to the door herself and thrown up her hands in astonishment when she saw who it was, but instead a much older woman opened the door and said, "What do you want?"

"We came to see Miss Brown," I said.

"We're in her class at school," Benny explained.

I could see that the woman was trying to decide whether

3. **Chautauqua** (shə-tô′kwə): a program of educational assemblies which flourished during the late nineteenth and early twentieth centuries.
4. **Chalmers:** an automobile. The last year of production of Chalmers cars was 1923.

she should tell us to go away, but she said, "I'll find out if she wants to see you," and left us standing on the porch for what seemed like a long time. Then she appeared again and said, "You can come in now."

As we followed her through the front parlor I could make out in the dim light that there was an old-fashioned organ like the kind you used to see in country churches, and linoleum on the floor, and stiff uncomfortable chairs, and family portraits behind curved glass in big oval frames.

The room beyond it was lighted by a coal-oil lamp but seemed ever so much darker than the unlighted room we had just passed through. Propped up on pillows in a big double bed was our teacher, but so changed. Her arms were like sticks, and all the life in her seemed concentrated in her eyes, which had dark circles around them and were enormous. She managed a flicker of recognition but I was struck dumb by the fact that she didn't seem glad to see us. She didn't belong to us anymore. She belonged to her illness.

Benny said, "I hope you get well soon."

The angel who watches over little boys who know but they can't say it saw to it that we didn't touch anything. And in a minute we were outside, on our bicycles, riding through the dusk toward the turn in the road and town.

A few weeks later I read in the Lincoln *Evening Courier* that Miss Vera Brown, who taught the fifth grade in Central School, had died of tuberculosis, aged twenty-three years and seven months.

Sometimes I went with my mother when she put flowers on the graves of my grandparents. The cinder roads wound through the cemetery in ways she understood and I didn't, and I would read the names on the monuments: Brower, Cadwallader, Andrews, Bates, Mitchell. In loving memory of. Infant daughter of. Beloved wife of. The cemetery was so large and so many people were buried there, it would have taken a long time to locate a particular grave if you didn't know where it was already. But I know, the way I sometimes know what is in wrapped packages, that the elderly woman who let us in and who took care of Miss Brown during her last illness went to the cemetery regularly and poured the rancid water out of the tin receptacle that was sunk below the level of the grass at the foot of her grave, and filled it with fresh water from a nearby faucet and arranged the flowers she had brought in such a way as to please the eye of the living and the closed eyes of the dead.

CHECK-UP (True/False)

1. The narrator associated Miss Brown with flowers.
2. The children loved Miss Brown because she never assigned homework.
3. In Miss Brown's absence, the class misbehaved.
4. Miss Brown recognized the boys who visited her.
5. Miss Brown never returned to teach fifth grade.

FOR DISCUSSION

1. Why did Miss Brown make such a strong impression on the children in her class?
2. Although Miss Brown was very young, she seemed to know instinctively how to handle children. Which details show that she was an understanding teacher?
3. Why is the narrator comforted by the thought of flowers being placed on Miss Brown's grave?

FOR WRITING

Are the children depicted in this story believable? Write a short essay expressing your opinion. Cite evidence from the story to support your answer.

"The effect was enchanting. We all sat silent
and steeped our souls completely
in the picture of paradise."

THE
VAMPIRE

Jan Neruda

The excursion steamer brought us from Constantinople[1] to the shore of the island of Prinkipo[2] and we disembarked. The number of passengers was not large. There was
one Polish family, a father, a mother, a daughter and her
bridegroom, and then we two. Oh, yes, I must not forget that
when we were already on the wooden bridge which crosses
the Golden Horn[3] to Constantinople, a Greek, a rather
youthful man, joined us. He was probably an artist, judging
by the portfolio he carried under his arm. Long black locks
floated to his shoulders, his face was pale, and his black eyes
were deeply set in their sockets. In the first moment he interested me, especially for his obligingness and for his knowledge of local conditions. But he talked too much, and I then
turned away from him.

All the more agreeable was the Polish family. The father
and mother were good-natured, fine people, the lover a

1. **Constantinople** (kŏn′stăn-tə-nō′pəl): the former name for Istanbul, the
   largest city in Turkey, located on the Bosporus (bŏs′pər-əs), a narrow
   strait linking the Black Sea and the Sea of Marmara.
2. **Prinkipo** (prēn-kī-pō′): an island in the Sea of Marmara, West Turkey,
   now known as Büyükada (byōō-yōōk-ə-dä′).
3. **Golden Horn:** inlet of the Bosporous forming the harbor of Istanbul. It
   is about five miles long.

handsome young fellow, of direct and refined manners. They had come to Prinkipo to spend the summer months for the sake of the daughter, who was slightly ailing. The beautiful pale girl was either just recovering from a severe illness or else a serious disease was just fastening its hold upon her. She leaned upon her lover when she walked and very often sat down to rest, while a frequent dry little cough interrupted her whispers. Whenever she coughed, her escort would considerately pause in their walk. He always cast upon her a glance of sympathetic suffering and she would look back at him as if she would say: "It is nothing. I am happy!" They believed in health and happiness.

On the recommendation of the Greek, who departed from us immediately at the pier, the family secured quarters in the hotel on the hill. The hotelkeeper was a Frenchman and his entire building was equipped comfortably and artistically, according to the French style.

We breakfasted together and when the noon heat had abated somewhat we all betook ourselves to the heights, where in the grove of Siberian stone pines we could refresh ourselves with the view. Hardly had we found a suitable spot and settled ourselves when the Greek appeared again. He greeted us lightly, looked about and seated himself only a few steps from us. He opened his portfolio and began to sketch.

"I think he purposely sits with his back to the rocks so that we can't look at his sketch," I said.

"We don't have to," said the young Pole. "We have enough before us to look at." After a while he added, "It seems to me he's sketching us in as a sort of background. Well—let him!"

We truly did have enough to gaze at. There is not a more beautiful or more happy corner in the world than that very Prinkipo! The political martyr, Irene, contemporary of

Charles the Great,[4] lived there for a month as an exile. If I could live a month of my life there I would be happy for the memory of it for the rest of my days! I shall never forget even that one day spent at Prinkipo.

The air was as clear as a diamond, so soft, so caressing, that one's whole soul swung out upon it into the distance. At the right beyond the sea projected the brown Asiatic summits; to the left in the distance purpled the steep coasts of Europe. The neighboring Chalki, one of the nine islands of the "Prince's Archipelago,"[5] rose with its cyprus forests into the peaceful heights like a sorrowful dream, crowned by a great structure—an asylum for those whose minds are sick.

The Sea of Marmara was but slightly ruffled and played in all colors like a sparkling opal. In the distance the sea was as white as milk, then rosy, between the two islands a glowing orange and below us it was beautifully greenish blue, like a transparent sapphire. It was resplendent in its own beauty. Nowhere were there any large ships—only two small craft flying the English flag sped along the shore. One was a steamboat as big as a watchman's booth, the second had about twelve oarsmen, and when their oars rose simultaneously molten silver dripped from them. Trustful dolphins darted in and out among them and dove with long, arching flights above the surface of the water. Through the blue heavens now and then calm eagles winged their way, measuring the space between two continents.

---

4. **Irene . . . Charles the Great:** Irene was Byzantine (bĭz'ən-tēn') empress (752–803). After the death of her husband, in 780, Irene ruled the empire until she was exiled in 802. Charles, also known as Charlemagne (shär'lə-mān') or Charles I (742–814), was King of the Franks and Emperor of the Romans. According to some sources, Irene tried to negotiate a marriage with him.
5. **Prince's Archipelago** (är'kə-pĕl'ə-gō'): nine small islands in the eastern part of the Sea of Marmara, about fifteen miles south of Istanbul. In Byzantine times the islands were used as a place of banishment.

The entire slope below us was covered with blossoming roses whose fragrance filled the air. From the coffeehouse near the sea music was carried up to us through the clear air, hushed somewhat by the distance.

The effect was enchanting. We all sat silent and steeped our souls completely in the picture of paradise. The young Polish girl lay on the grass with her head supported on the bosom of her lover. The pale oval of her delicate face was slightly tinged with soft color, and from her blue eyes tears suddenly gushed forth. The lover understood, bent down and kissed tear after tear. Her mother also was moved to tears, and I—even I—felt a strange twinge.

"Here mind and body both must get well," whispered the girl. "How happy a land this is!"

"God knows I haven't any enemies, but if I had I would forgive them here!" said the father in a trembling voice.

And again we became silent. We were all in such a wonderful mood—so unspeakably sweet it all was! Each felt for himself a whole world of happiness and each one would have shared his happiness with the whole world. All felt the same—and so no one disturbed another. We had scarcely even noticed that the Greek, after an hour or so, had arisen, folded his portfolio and with a slight nod had taken his departure. We remained.

Finally after several hours, when the distance was becoming overspread with a darker violet, so magically beautiful in the south, the mother reminded us it was time to depart. We arose and walked down towards the hotel with the easy, elastic steps that characterize carefree children. We sat down in the hotel under the handsome veranda.

Hardly had we been seated when we heard below the sounds of quarreling and oaths. Our Greek was wrangling with the hotelkeeper, and for the entertainment of it we listened.

The amusement did not last long. "If I didn't have other

guests," growled the hotelkeeper, and ascended the steps towards us.

"I beg you to tell me, sir," asked the young Pole of the approaching hotelkeeper, "who is that gentleman? What's his name?"

"Eh—who knows what the fellow's name is?" grumbled the hotelkeeper, and he gazed venomously downwards. "We call him the Vampire."

"An artist?"

"Fine trade! He sketches only corpses. Just as soon as someone in Constantinople or here in the neighborhood dies, that very day he has a picture of the dead one completed. That fellow paints them beforehand—and he never makes a mistake—just like a vulture!"

The old Polish woman shrieked affrightedly. In her arms lay her daughter pale as chalk. She had fainted.

In one bound the lover had leaped down the steps. With one hand he seized the Greek and with the other reached for the portfolio.

We ran down after him. Both men were rolling in the sand. The contents of the portfolio were scattered all about. On one sheet, sketched with a crayon, was the head of the young Polish girl, her eyes closed and a wreath of myrtle[6] on her brow.

---

6. **myrtle** (mûrt'l): a sweet-smelling, evergreen plant, native to the Mediterranean region and Western Asia. In ancient times it was considered sacred to Venus, the goddess of love and beauty.

CHECK-UP (Multiple-Choice)

1. This story takes place
   a. on the mainland of Greece
   b. on an island off the coast of Turkey
   c. in a suburb of Constantinople
2. The Polish family includes
   a. parents, a daughter and a son-in-law
   b. a mother and two children
   c. six people in all
3. The Greek is
   a. a friend of the hotelkeeper
   b. a tour guide
   c. an artist
4. At the end of the story, it is clear that
   a. the Polish family will leave the hotel
   b. the Greek will sell his sketch to the family
   c. the girl will die
5. The vampire of the story is a
   a. large bat that feeds on blood
   b. person who lives by preying on others
   c. beautiful woman who makes men her victims

FOR DISCUSSION

1. The sense of place is very important in this story. In what way does setting reflect the state of mind of the characters?
2. The characters are identified by nationality rather than by name. In what way does this emphasize the universality of the story's theme?
3. What details are used to foreshadow the end of the story?
4. Who is the vampire of the title? Why is this an appropriate name for the character?
5. Did you find the outcome of the story ironic?

UNDERSTANDING THE WORDS IN THE STORY (Matching Columns)

1. excursion
2. disembarked
3. secured
4. abated
5. grove
6. martyr
7. contemporary
8. exile
9. projected
10. ruffled

a. diminished
b. a banished person
c. one who suffers
d. rippled
e. went ashore
f. protruded
g. a wood
h. a person of the same age
i. travel
j. got hold of

(Multiple-Choice)

1. An *opal* would most likely be found in a(n)
   a. hardware store
   b. art gallery
   c. jewelry shop
2. A person whose character is *transparent* is
   a. difficult to understand
   b. easy to see through
   c. reliable and honest
3. Something which is *resplendent*
   a. is radioactive
   b. shines brilliantly
   c. is painful to look at
4. When two people speak *simultaneously,* they speak
   a. at the same time
   b. in anger
   c. out of turn
5. To *tinge* a cloth is to
   a. bleach it white
   b. tint it with color
   c. moisten it

6. A *veranda* is found
   a. along the outside of a building
   b. in a back yard
   c. on top of a roof
7. *Wrangling* people are
   a. engaged in physical combat
   b. laughing loudly
   c. quarreling noisily
8. The opposite of *ascended* is
   a. came down
   b. disappeared
   c. raised up
9. One would look *venomously* at a
   a. close ally
   b. hated enemy
   c. stranger
10. In screaming *affrightedly* one expresses
    a. severe pain
    b. uncontrollable anger
    c. sudden and great fear

FOR WRITING

1. Analyze the role of setting in this story. Tell what it contributes to mood and theme.
2. This story presents a somber theme: Innocence and love and beauty are no deterrent to death. Show how this theme is developed in the story.
3. Compare "The Vampire" with "The Death of the Dauphin" (page 355). What similarities do these stories possess?

Julia loved racing through The Dark Walk
with the memory of the sun behind her,
but she had never come there at night.

THE
TROUT

Sean O'Faolain°

One of the first places Julia always ran to when they arrived in G_____ was The Dark Walk. It is a laurel walk, very old; almost gone wild, a lofty midnight tunnel of smooth, sinewy branches. Underfoot the tough brown leaves are never dry enough to crackle: there is always a suggestion of damp and cool trickle.

She raced right into it. For the first few yards she always had the memory of the sun behind her, then she felt the dusk closing swiftly down on her so that she screamed with pleasure and raced on to reach the light at the far end; and it was always just a little too long in coming so that she emerged gasping, clasping her hands, laughing, drinking in the sun. When she was filled with the heat and glare she would turn and consider the ordeal again.

This year she had the extra joy of showing it to her small brother, and of terrifying him as well as herself. And for him the fear lasted longer because his legs were so short and she had gone out at the far end while he was still screaming and racing.

° **Sean O'Faolain** (shôn ō-fə-lôn', -lĭn).

When they had done this many times they came back to
the house to tell everybody that they had done it. He boasted.
She mocked. They squabbled.

"Cry babby!"

"You were afraid yourself, so there!"

"I won't take you anymore."

"You're a big pig."

"I hate you."

Tears were threatening so somebody said, "Did you see
the well?" She opened her eyes at that and held up her long,
lovely neck suspiciously and decided to be incredulous. She
was twelve and at that age litle girls are beginning to suspect
most stories: they have already found out too many, from
Santa Claus to the Stork. How could there be a well! In The
Dark Walk? That she had visited year after year? Haughtily
she said, "Nonsense."

But she went back, pretending to be going somewhere
else, and she found a hole scooped in the rock at the side of
the walk, choked with damp leaves, so shrouded by ferns
that she only uncovered it after much searching. At the back
of this little cavern there was about a quart of water. In the
water she suddenly perceived a panting trout. She rushed for
Stephen and dragged him to see, and they were both so
excited that they were no longer afraid of the darkness as
they hunched down and peered in at the fish panting in his
tiny prison, his silver stomach going up and down like an
engine.

Nobody knew how the trout got there. Even old Martin
in the kitchen garden laughed and refused to believe that it
was there, or pretended not to believe, until she forced him
to come down and see. Kneeling and pushing back his tattered old cap he peered in.

"You're right. How did that fella get there?"

She stared at him suspiciously.

"You knew?" she accused; but he said, "The divil a know"; and reached down to lift it out. Convinced she hauled him back. If she had found it then it was her trout.

Her mother suggested that a bird had carried the spawn. Her father thought that in the winter a small streamlet might have carried it down there as a baby, and it had been safe until the summer came and the water began to dry up. She said, "I see," and went back to look again and consider the matter in private. Her brother remained behind, wanting to hear the whole story of the trout, not really interested in the actual trout but much interested in the story which his mummy began to make up for him on the lines of, "So one day Daddy Trout and Mammy Trout . . ." When he retailed[1] it to her she said, "Pooh."

It troubled her that the trout was always in the same position; he had no room to turn; all the time the silver belly went up and down; otherwise he was motionless. She wondered what he ate and in between visits to Joey Pony, and the boat and a bathe to get cool, she thought of his hunger. She brought him down bits of dough; once she brought him a worm. He ignored the food. He just went on panting. Hunched over him she thought how, all the winter, while she was at school he had been there. All the winter, in The Dark Walk, all day, all night, floating around alone. She drew the leaf of her hat down around her ears and chin and stared. She was thinking of it as she lay in bed.

It was late in June, the longest days of the year. The sun had sat still for a week, burning up the world. Although it was after ten o'clock it was still bright and still hot. She lay on her back under a single sheet, with her long legs spread, trying to keep cool. She could see the D of the moon through the fir tree—they slept on the ground floor. Before they went to bed her mummy had told Stephen the story of the trout

---

1. **retailed** (rī-tāld′): told and retold.

again, and she, in her bed, had resolutely presented her back to them and read her book. But she had kept one ear cocked.

"And so, in the end, this naughty fish who would not stay at home got bigger and bigger and bigger, and the water got smaller and smaller. . . ."

Passionately she had whirled and cried, "Mummy, don't make it a horrible old moral story!" Her mummy had brought in a Fairy Godmother, then, who sent lots of rain, and filled the well, and a stream poured out and the trout floated away down to the river below. Staring at the moon she knew that there are no such things as Fairy Godmothers and that the trout, down in The Dark Walk, was panting like an engine. She heard somebody unwind a fishing reel. Would the *beasts* fish him out!

She sat up. Stephen was a hot lump of sleep, lazy thing. The Dark Walk would be full of little scraps of moon. She leaped up and looked out the window, and somehow it was not so lightsome now that she saw the dim mountains far away and the black firs against the breathing land and heard a dog say bark-bark. Quietly she lifted the ewer of water, and climbed out the window and scuttled along the cool but cruel gravel down to the maw[2] of the tunnel. Her pajamas were very short so that when she splashed water it wet her ankles. She peered into the tunnel. Something alive rustled inside there. She raced in, and up and down she raced, and flurried, and cried aloud, "Oh, gosh, I can't find it," and then at last she did. Kneeling down in the damp she put her hand into the slimy hole. When the body lashed they were both mad with fright. But she gripped him and shoved him into the ewer and raced, with her teeth ground, out to the other end of the tunnel and down the steep paths to the river's edge.

---

2. **maw** (mô): here, a large opening.

All the time she could feel him lashing his tail against the side of the ewer. She was afraid he would jump right out. The gravel cut into her soles until she came to the cool ooze of the river's bank where the moon-mice on the water crept into her feet. She poured out watching until he plopped. For a second he was visible in the water. She hoped he was not dizzy. Then all she saw was the glimmer of the moon in the silent-flowing river, the dark firs, the dim mountains, and the radiant pointed face laughing down at her out of the empty sky.

She scuttled up the hill, in the window, plonked down the ewer and flew through the air like a bird into bed. The dog said bark-bark. She heard the fishing reel whirring. She hugged herself and giggled. Like a river of joy her holiday spread before her.

In the morning Stephen rushed to her, shouting that "he" was gone, and asking "where" and "how." Lifting her nose in the air she said superciliously,[3] "Fairy Godmother, I suppose?" and strolled away patting the palms of her hands.

3. **superciliously** (soō'pər-sĭl'ē-əs-lē): disdainfully.

CHECK-UP (Multiple-Choice)

1. The main character of the story is
   a. a high-school student
   b. a preschooler
   c. an adolescent girl
2. The action of the story takes place
   a. during the fall and spring
   b. in early summer
   c. in late winter
3. The trout is discovered by
   a. Julia
   b. old Martin
   c. Stephen
4. Julia rescues the trout by
   a. pouring water into the well
   b. feeding it worms
   c. emptying the trout into a river

FOR DISCUSSION

1. Why does Julia enjoy racing through The Dark Walk? How do you know that she feels possessive about this place?
2. In what way does Stephen serve as a contrast to Julia?
3. Julia becomes preoccupied with the trout. How does the trout interfere with her vacation?
4. How does Julia solve her problem? How might this episode be taken as a sign of her growing up?
5. Julia's mother tells Stephen a make-believe story about the trout. How does this story provide an incentive for Julia to act?
6. Are the games and stories of childhood a preparation for life? Consider the events of O'Faolain's story in your answer.

UNDERSTANDING THE WORDS
IN THE STORY (Matching Columns)

1. lofty	a. trial
2. sinewy	b. arrogantly
3. ordeal	c. jug
4. squabbled	d. tough
5. incredulous	e. steadily
6. haughtily	f. moved swiftly
7. spawn	g. rising high in the air
8. resolutely	h. not ready to believe
9. ewer	i. eggs
10. scuttled	j. quarreled noisily

FOR WRITING

1. You have learned that a character may be *static* or *dynamic* (page 77). Is Julia a static or dynamic character? In your essay cite evidence from the story to support your answer.

2. Children are the central characters in a number of stories, including "All Summer in a Day" (page 91), "Too Soon a Woman" (page 109), "The Wild Duck's Nest" (page 118), "Father and I" (page 127), "Zlateh the Goat" (page 151), "A Game of Catch" (page 168), "The Story of Muhammad Din" (page 179), "Stolen Day" (page 314), "The Fun They Had" (page 322), and "Charles" (page 360). Choose any *three* stories and show how the author makes the characters believable. Give examples of direct and indirect characterization.

*"Seal felt a great joy in the flowers
around him and from this
a brilliant longing to give."*

DIFFICULTY WITH A BOUQUET

William Sansom

Seal, walking through his garden, said suddenly to himself: "I would like to pick some flowers and take them to Miss D."

The afternoon was light and warm. Tall chestnuts fanned themselves in a pleasant breeze. Among the hollyhocks there was a good humming as the bees tumbled from flower to flower. Seal wore an open shirt. He felt fresh and fine, with the air swimming coolly under his shirt and around his ribs. The summer's afternoon was free. Nothing pressed him. It was a time when some simple, disinterested impulse might well be hoped to flourish.

Seal felt a great joy in the flowers around him and from this a brilliant longing to give. He wished to give quite inside himself, uncritically, without thinking for a moment: "Here am I, Seal, wishing something." Seal merely wanted to give some of his flowers to a fellow being. It had happened that Miss D was the first person to come to mind. He was in no way attached to Miss D. He knew her slightly, as a plain, elderly girl of about twenty who had come to live in the flats[1]

1. **flats:** a group of apartments.

401

opposite his garden. If Seal had ever thought about Miss D at all, it was because he disliked the way she walked. She walked stiffly, sailing with her long body while her little legs raced to catch up with it. But he was not thinking of this now. Just by chance he had glimpsed the block of flats as he had stooped to pick a flower. The flats had presented the image of Miss D to his mind.

Seal chose common, ordinary flowers. As the stems broke he whistled between his teeth. He had chosen these ordinary flowers because they were the nearest to hand: in the second place, because they were fresh and full of life. They were neither rare nor costly. They were pleasant, fresh, unassuming flowers.

With the flowers in his hand, Seal walked contentedly from his garden and set foot on the asphalt pavement that led to the block of flats across the way. But as his foot touched the asphalt, as the sly glare of an old man fixed his eye for the moment of its passing, as the traffic asserted itself, certain misgivings began to freeze his impromptu joy. "Good heavens," he suddenly thought, "what am I doing?" He stepped outside himself and saw Seal carrying a bunch of cheap flowers to Miss D in the flats across the way.

"These are cheap flowers," he thought. "This is a sudden gift; I shall smile as I hand them to her. We shall both know that there is no ulterior reason for the gift and thus the whole action will smack of goodness—of goodness and simple brotherhood. And somehow . . . for that reason this gesture of mine will appear to be the most calculated pose of all. Such a simple gesture is improbable. The improbable is to be suspected. My gift will certainly be regarded as an affectation.

"Oh, if only I had some reason—aggrandizement,[2]

---

2. **aggrandizement** (ə-grăn′dĭz-mənt, ə-grăn′dīz′-): exaggeration of personal importance.

financial gain, seduction—any of the accepted motives that would return my flowers to social favor. But no—I have none of these in me. I only wish to give and to receive nothing in return."

As he walked on, Seal could see himself bowing and smiling. He saw himself smile too broadly as he apologized by exaggeration for his good action. His neck flinched with disgust as he saw himself assume the old bravados. He could see the mocking smile of recognition on the face of Miss D.

Seal dropped the flowers into the gutter and walked slowly back to his garden.

From her window high up in the concrete flats, Miss D watched Seal drop the flowers. How fresh they looked! How they would have livened her barren room! "Wouldn't it have been nice," thought Miss D, "if that Mr. Seal had been bringing *me* that pretty bouquet of flowers! Wouldn't it have been nice if he had picked them in his own garden and—well, just brought them along, quite casually, and made me a present of the delightful afternoon." Miss D dreamed on for a few minutes.

Then she frowned, rose, straightened her suspender belt, hurried into the kitchen. "Thank God he didn't," she sighed to herself. "I should have been most embarrassed. It's not as if he wanted me. It would have been just too maudlin for words."

CHECK-UP (True/False)

1. Seal wishes to impress Miss D by giving her flowers.
2. Seal chooses unusual flowers for a bouquet.
3. Seal loses courage when a neighbor spies him picking flowers.
4. Seal fears that his actions will be misunderstood.
5. Seal gives his bouquet to a child.

FOR DISCUSSION

1. At the opening of the story, Seal responds to an impulse. Why does he decide to pick flowers for Miss D?
2. When Seal thinks about his behavior, he becomes indecisive. Examine his reasoning. Are his concerns realistic?
3. In what way is Miss D like Seal? Why do you suppose she is identified by only an initial instead of a name?
4. What does the title of the story refer to?
5. Is the tone of the story light or serious? Explain.

UNDERSTANDING THE WORDS IN THE STORY (Matching Columns)

1. disinterested	a. not boastful
2. flourish	b. behavior that is put on
3. unassuming	c. on the spur of the moment
4. misgiving	d. not evident or openly expressed
5. impromptu	e. a disturbed feeling
6. ulterior	f. foolishly sentimental
7. calculated	g. pretended confidence
8. affectation	h. not influenced by personal motives
9. bravado	i. deliberately intended
10. maudlin	j. to grow or prosper

FOR WRITING

1. Write a short essay discussing the author's use of point of view in this story. Explain how the point of view shifts and what purpose the shift serves.
2. What insight does the author give you into conflicting aspects of human motivation? Discuss the conflict between reason and impulse presented in the story.

About the Authors

Akutagawa Ryûnosuke (1892–1927) is best known to Western readers because of the film *Rashōmon*, based on two of his stories about medieval Japan. Akutagawa studied at the University of Tokyo and read widely in Oriental and Western literature. He wrote poems and essays as well as short stories. His work has been admired for its blend of modern stylistic elements with traditional themes. "The Spider's Thread" recalls the *Jatakas* (jəd'ə-kəz), narratives about Gautama Buddha, the Indian philosopher who founded Buddhism.

Kingsley Amis, who was born in 1922, was one of England's "Angry Young Men," a group of novelists and playwrights who wrote about the frustrations of the working class in the period following the Second World War. His most famous character, the protagonist of *Lucky Jim* (1954), is sometimes called an "anti-hero." Lucky Jim is funny, down-to-earth, and sarcastic—the opposite of the traditional, well-bred English gentleman. *Lucky Jim's Politics*, a nonfiction work published in 1968, is a critical examination of the British welfare state. After Ian Fleming's death, Amis was given the legal right to narrate a James Bond story—*Colonel Sun: A James Bond Adventure* (1968). A versatile author, Amis has also written poetry and mystery stories, including *The Riverside Villas Murder* (1973), whose main character is a thirteen-year-old boy.

Hans Christian Andersen (1805–1875) was born in Odense, a small fishing village in Denmark. His father, a shoemaker, died when Andersen was eleven years old. He left school when he was fourteen and tried to support himself on the stage. He was befriended by a theater director who helped him get a scholarship that allowed him to continue his education and gave him the opportunity to write. During his lifetime Andersen became famous for his fairy tales, although he always considered himself a novelist, poet, and playwright. Some of his best-known tales are "The Ugly Duckling," "The Red Shoes," "The Nightingale," and "The Princess and the Pea."

Sherwood Anderson (1867–1941) was born in Camden, Ohio. When he was fourteen, he left school and worked at a number of different jobs. After he moved to Chicago, he met a number of intellectuals, including Theodore Dreiser and Carl Sandburg. Encouraged by them, he gave up his work in order to write. He felt that his experiences had given him a sense of the aspirations of small-town Americans. One of his most important themes was the impact of industrialization on the long-held values and traditions of rural America. *Winesburg, Ohio* (1919), a collection of stories about the inhabitants of a small Midwestern town, is his most famous work. Its theme of self-discovery and its psychological exploration of the unhappy lives of Winesburg's residents influenced several writers, including Ernest Hemingway.

Isaac Asimov was born in the Soviet Union in 1920. He came to the United States as a child. He has written hundreds of books of science and science fiction. Some of his works convey the theme that advances in technology and space exploration must take human needs into account—or else the advances will really be steps backward. Asimov's many works have helped both science and science fiction come alive for his readers.

Björnstjerne Björnson (1832–1910) was a schoolmate and friend of another great Norwegian writer, Henrik Ibsen. Björnson, the composer of Norway's national anthem, was both a major writer and a patriot. In his stories and folk tales, he described his country's heroes and heroines. The literary language of his day was Danish, not Norwegian, and in his writings he encouraged the use of his native tongue. His output of plays, stories, novels, and other works was immense. In 1903 he received the Nobel Prize for Literature for his understanding of social problems and his interest in spiritual concerns.

Ray Bradbury was born in Waukegan, Illinois, in 1920. He graduated from high school in Los Angeles. He sold newspapers in order to support himself while he was writing. His interest in fantasy and space travel has led him to become a science-fiction writer—but of an unusual sort. He has been more concerned with creating poetic images and examining the impact of technology on everyday life than with describing planetary battles. He believes, in fact, that the exploration of space should result in a better understanding of human nature. His works have attained a wide following. His books include the *Martian Chronicles, The Golden Apples of the Sun,* and *Fahrenheit 451.* Several of his works have been adapted for the screen and for television. During the 1985 season, "All Summer in a Day" was dramatized for a television series called *Wonderworks.*

Gwendolyn Brooks was born in Topeka, Kansas, in 1917, but has spent most of her life in Chicago. The story "Home" is from her book *Maud Martha* (1953), about a young black girl growing up in Chicago. Brooks is considered to be one of America's outstanding poets. Many of her poems are set in the South Side of Chicago, in a black community called Bronzeville. Brooks's second collection of poems, *Annie Allen,* won the Pulitzer Prize in 1950.

Katharine Brush (1902–1952), who wrote novels, sketches, and stories, was born in Middletown, Connecticut. She began writing in the 1920's, and her fiction captured the character and spirit of the Jazz Age. Her short stories have been compared, in their lack of sentiment and their sharpness, with those of F. Scott Fitzgerald, her more famous contemporary. Brush's early short stories appeared in popular magazines.

Morley Callaghan, one of Canada's most distinguished writers, was born in Toronto in 1903. He worked as a reporter on the *Toronto Daily Star.* In the late 1920's he went to Paris, where he met Ernest Hemingway, who encouraged him to write fiction. Callaghan has described his experiences in Europe in *That Summer in Paris,* a memoir published in 1963. His stories have been collected in *A Native Argosy* and *Now That April's Here.* He has written several novels, including *Broken Journey, More Joy in Heaven,* and *The Many-Colored Coat.* Some of his well-known stories are "Luke Baldwin's Vow," "The Snob," and "A Cap for Steve."

Anton Chekhov (1860–1904) was born in Taganrog, a tiny Russian town on the Sea of Azov. While he was in medical school in Moscow, he wrote stories to support himself and his family. He left his profession of medicine when his first collection of stories was well received. He wrote more than a thousand stories during his lifetime. His compassion, which led him to investigate the treatment of prison inmates, is evident in his stories. His themes include the powerlessness of many people in society and the misunderstandings that occur between people. Chekhov was an enormous influence on such authors as Ernest Hemingway and Katherine Mansfield. Chekhov also wrote several great plays, including *Uncle Vanya, The Three Sisters,* and *The Cherry Orchard.*

Kate Chopin (1851–1904) was born in St. Louis, Missouri. After her marriage, she settled in Louisiana, which became the setting for many of her stories. When her husband died, she took over the management of the plantation and the village store. She was encouraged to write in order to support her family. *Bayou Folk*, a collection of stories that appeared in 1894, was well received. These stories are about the Cajuns—the descendants of the French Canadians who had been driven out of Acadia (Nova Scotia)—and the Creoles—the people of French and Spanish origin living near New Orleans. Her best-known work is *The Awakening*, a novel published in 1899.

Arthur C. Clarke was born in Minehead, England, in 1917. His interest in science developed early. At the age of thirteen, he constructed a telescope from an old lens and a cardboard tube. A prolific writer, Clarke has been called "the colossus of science fiction." His collections of short stories include *Across the Sea of Stars, The Other Side of the Sky, The Nine Billion Names of God,* and *Tales of Ten Worlds*. Some well-known novels are *Childhood's End, Earthlight,* and *Islands in the Sky*. In 1969 he was nominated for an Academy Award for the screenplay *2001: a Space Odyssey*, which he wrote with Stanley Kubrick. He collaborated on *First on the Moon,* with the astronauts who made that milestone journey, and on *Mars and the Mind of Man,* with Ray Bradbury and Carl Sagan. As an underwater photographer, Clarke has explored the Great Barrier Reef off Australia and the coast of Sri Lanka (Ceylon), where he has lived for many years.

John Collier (1901–1980) was born in London. His stories are both elegant and sinister. Without sentiment or sensation, they evoke the frailty of human relationships. Probably his most famous work is the short novel *His Monkey Wife; or Married to a Chimp* (1930). The hero finds himself happier with a chimpanzee than with the young woman he had been engaged to. Collier went to Hollywood in the 1930's to write screenplays. His credits include *Elephant Boy,* the film adaptation of Rudyard Kipling's story "Toomai of the Elephants."

James Gould Cozzens (1903–1978) had his first book published when he was a student at Harvard. He received the Pulitzer Prize in 1948 for *Guards of Honor*. His novel *By Love Possessed* (1957) was highly acclaimed and became a best-seller. In his writings Cozzens expresses the belief in the necessity of conforming to society's values and norms. His characters, primarily middle- and upper-class men, represent, to Cozzens, the backbone of contemporary American life. "Success Story" first appeared in *Collier's* magazine.

Stephen Crane (1871–1900) was born in Newark, New Jersey, the youngest of fourteen children. After he left college, he worked as a free-lance journalist in New York City. Crane is known for his realistic works. His first novel, *Maggie: A Girl of the Streets* (1893) is based on his observations of slum life. When he submitted the manuscript to publishers, they refused to print the work. As a result, Crane published the book at his own expense. Two years later, his most famous work, *The Red Badge of Courage*, was a popular success. A novel of great influence on such later writers as Ernest Hemingway and Sherwood Anderson, it broke new ground in American literature with its psychological insights into human nature and its unsentimental treatment of its subject, the experiences of a young soldier in the Civil War. Crane also wrote poetry and short stories. Some of Crane's stories are based on his own adventures. While traveling to Cuba as a war correspondent, his ship capsized. He described the event, in which some of the crew drowned, in his well-known tale "The Open Boat" (1898). Crane spent his last two years in poor health. He died of tuberculosis when he was only twenty-eight.

Alphonse Daudet (1840–1897) was born in Nîmes, Provence, in southern France. He wrote stories, novels, poems, and plays. He is best known for his work *Tartarin de Tarascon* (1872), a sort of French *Don Quixote*, and for his short stories, set in his native Provence. Like Charles Dickens, he mixes satire with compassion. Like Guy de Maupassant, he examines the conflicts that often exist beneath the surface of human relationships. "The Death of the Dauphin" is from a collection of short stories called *Lettres de mon moulin* ("Letters from My Mill").

Mona Gardner (1900–1981), who was born in Seattle, Washington, chose the settings for many of her novels and short stories from the places she visited. She traveled in Hong Kong, Malaysia, Thailand, and elsewhere. One of her novels, in fact, is called *Hong Kong*. Her short stories were published in several magazines, including *The New Yorker*, *Saturday Review of Literature*, and *Reader's Digest*.

Ernest Hemingway (1899–1961) was born in Oak Park, Illinois, a suburb of Chicago. In high school Hemingway wrote for the literary magazine. After graduation he went to work for the Kansas City *Star* as a reporter. In 1918 Hemingway joined the Red Cross ambulance corps on the Italian front. He was wounded by an exploding mortar shell and spent three months in a hospital. He returned to the States and worked on his writing. He came under the influence of Sherwood Anderson, a major literary figure of the early twentieth century. In 1921 Hemingway left for Europe and became one of the American expatriates in Gertrude Stein's circle. He worked as a newspaper correspondent and traveled all over Europe and the Near East. His first book, *Three Stories and Ten Poems*, appeared in 1923. His second book, *In Our Time* (1925), created a stir. In this book he introduced the character of Nick Adams, who was a lightly veiled portrait of the author. Hemingway is often credited with having created a new kind of short story. In *The Cycle of American Literature*, Robert E. Spiller describes the typical Hemingway story: "plotless and episodic, stripped of emotion and chary of language, but bound into a tight and powerful sequence by a receptive and recording sensibility." Hemingway's heroes are detached and impersonal, like the narrator in "Old Man at the Bridge," who witnesses the misery of war's dislocation and loss without registering emotion. Among Hemingway's best-known stories are "The Killers," "The Short Happy Life of Francis Macomber," and "The Snows of Kilimanjaro." His novels include *The Sun Also Rises* (1926), *A Farewell to Arms* (1929), *For Whom the Bell Tolls* (1940), and *The Old Man and the Sea* (1952). Hemingway was awarded the Nobel Prize for Literature in 1954.

O. Henry is the pen name of William Sydney Porter (1862–1910), who grew up in Greensboro, North Carolina. He took the name O. Henry after he had served a term in jail for embezzling money from a Texas bank. In 1902 he moved to New York City and became famous for his short stories. Some of his collections are *The Four Million* (1906), *The Voice of the City* (1908), *Heart of the West* (1907), *The Gentle Grafter* (1908), and *Whirligigs* (1910). The trademark of an O. Henry story is its surprise ending. "The Gift of the Magi" is probably O. Henry's most famous story. Other well-known stories are "The Ransom of Red Chief," "A Retrieved Reformation," "Mammon and the Archer," and "The Furnished Room."

Langston Hughes (1902–1967), who was born in Joplin, Missouri, is associated with the Harlem Renaissance of the 1920's, a cultural awakening of remarkable creativity among black writers and artists. In his novels, short stories, and plays, Hughes describes both the bitterness and the triumph of the black experience in America. His most famous character is Jess B. Semple, whose struggles and achievements Hughes portrays with humor and dignity. Hughes was the first black American to earn a living by writing and public speaking. His enduring themes—the joys of love and the closeness of family life—have universal appeal. His works have been translated into a number of languages.

Shirley Jackson (1919–1965) was born in San Francisco. She is known chiefly for her horror stories. Her novel *The Haunting of Hill House* (1959) was made into a movie called *The Haunting*. In her macabre novels and tales, human life is beset by evil and unpredictability. Her most famous story, "The Lottery," appeared in *The New Yorker* in 1948 and created quite a stir. This story is a chilling tale about modern-day ritual sacrifice. Not all of Jackson's works emphasize the sinister elements in human life, however. Her stories of family life, like "Charles," are amusing. More stories about her family can be found in *Life Among the Savages* and *Raising Demons*.

Dorothy M. Johnson was born in Iowa in 1905 and grew up in Montana. She has written a number of works about the American West. The films *The Man Who Shot Liberty Valence, The Hanging Tree,* and *A Man Called Horse* were based on her stories. Her *Warrior for a Lost Nation: A Biography of Sitting Bull* (1969) is about the life of the Sioux chief and resistance fighter. She is an honorary member of the Blackfoot tribe in Montana.

Rudyard Kipling (1865–1936) was born in Bombay, India, of English parents. He was educated in England but returned to India at seventeen to serve on the staff of a newspaper. He soon began writing short stories and poems. "The Story of Muhammad Din" is from a collection of stories called *Plain Tales from the Hills*, which appeared in 1888. Shortly after Kipling returned to England, he wrote his first novel, *The Light That Failed* (1890). *Captains Courageous* appeared in 1897, and *Kim*, considered his greatest novel, in

1901. Kipling wrote amusing tales for children, including *The Jungle Book* (1894) and *Just-So Stories* (1902). In 1907 Kipling became the first English writer to win the Nobel Prize for Literature.

Eric Knight (1897–1943) was born in Yorkshire, England, the setting for his most famous story, "Lassie Come-Home." This story has also appeared as a novel, a movie, and a television series. Another well-known work, *The Flying Yorkshireman*, contains the humorous adventures of Sam Small, a colorful character. Knight fought in the Canadian Army during the First World War. During the Second World War, he was a major in the United States Army. He lost his life in an airplane crash while he was on an official mission. "The Rifles of the Regiment" appeared in *Collier's* magazine the year before his death.

Pär Lagerkvist (1891–1974) is considered one of the greatest modern Swedish writers. As a young man he visited Paris, where the many exciting discoveries in modern art and literature captured his imagination. His prolific writings—including novels, plays, poems, and short stories—explore the conflicts between good and evil and between religion and science. The outbreak of two world wars within a generation was to him, as to many of his contemporaries, a shattering experience. In the 1950's he wrote a screenplay for the film *Barabbas*, based on his novel by that name. This retelling of a New Testament narrative examines the relationship between human beings and God. Lagerkvist received the Nobel Prize for Literature in 1951.

Selma Lagerlöf (1858–1940) was born in Värmland, Sweden. She wrote novels, short stories, poems, and plays. Her lyrical retelling of Swedish folk legends brings Sweden's heroic sagas and folk tales to life. *Gösta Berling's Saga* (1891) was her first novel. Some of her later works, including the two-part novel *Jerusalem* (1901–1902), are written in a less romantic, more contemporary style. *The Wonderful Adventures of Nils* (1906), a collection of stories, was written to teach children geography. In 1909 Lagerlöf became the first woman to receive the Nobel Prize for Literature.

Katherine Mansfield (1888–1923) was born in Wellington, New Zealand, and began her literary career after she moved to London in 1908. Her short stories are often compared with the stories of

Anton Chekhov. Instead of striving for neat, well-made plots, she is concerned with mood and the revelation of character. Her technique is impressionistic. In stories like "Miss Brill," a single episode illuminates the entire life of a character. Some of Mansfield's best-known stories are "The Garden Party," "A Dill Pickle," "The Fly," and "A Cup of Tea."

William Maxwell was born in Lincoln, Illinois, in 1908. He has said that one reason he became a writer was that, as a child, he loved to read. He taught at the University of Illinois until 1933, when he decided to become a professional writer. Although Maxwell has lived in New York for most of his life, his memories of a Midwestern boyhood remain vivid. His novel *The Folded Leaf* (1945) describes the companionship and conflicts of two teen-age boys growing up in Chicago. His stories have been collected in the volume *Over by the River, and Other Stories* (1977). "Love," which first appeared in *The New Yorker,* is based on an incident in Maxwell's childhood.

Michael McLaverty was born in County Monaghan, Ireland, in 1904. He was headmaster of a secondary school in Belfast for many years. His first novel, *Call My Brother Back*, was published in 1939. "The Wild Duck's Nest" is from a collection called *The Game Cock and Other Stories.* While other Irish writers of his generation—like Liam O'Flaherty and Sean O'Faolain—have been deeply involved in political struggles, McLaverty has focused on the internal conflicts of his characters. The world of his native Northern Ireland— its people and its landscape—fills his novels and short stories.

Jan Neruda (1834–1891) was born in Prague, Czechoslovakia. He wrote essays and poems as well as short stories. In his work *Stories from Malá Strana* (1878), he included recollections of his childhood and keen observations of the Czech people. The stories in this collection, which are *vignettes* (short sketches), are early examples of Czech realism.

Sean O'Faolain was born John Francis Whelan in Cork, Ireland, in 1900. At the age of eighteen, he learned Gaelic and changed his name to the Gaelic form. Like many others of his generation, he became involved in the Irish Civil War. He was educated at University College in Dublin. He studied at Harvard and taught Gaelic there from 1926 to 1929. In 1932 he published *A Nest of Simple Folk*, a partly autobiographical novel that describes the long and painful struggle of the Irish people for freedom. His works include a history of Ireland; a biography of Eamon De Valera, the twentieth-century patriot and prime minister; and an autobiography with the amusing title *Vive Moi!* ("Long Live Me!") His short stories, which are compassionate and subtle, have been compared with those of Guy de Maupassant and Anton Chekhov.

Liam O'Flaherty (1896–1984) grew up on the Aran Islands off the western coast of Ireland. He studied at a Dublin seminary but decided against entering the priesthood. He enrolled in University College, Dublin, and left when the First World War broke out. While fighting in France he was shellshocked. After his discharge, he spent three years traveling, then returned to Ireland. He became involved in politics. He was arrested when he and a group of unemployed workers seized a building in Dublin. He left for England, where he wrote his first novel. His most famous work is *The Informer* (1926), about a man who betrays his friends for money. The novel was later made into a movie. "The Sniper" is one of his best-known stories.

Luigi Pirandello (1867–1936) was not a well-disciplined student when he attended the University of Rome, but he was inspired by one of his professors, from whom he learned about the traditions and customs of his native Sicily. As a young man, Pirandello wrote poetry; later he turned to plays, novels, and short stories. His first play, *Right You Are If You Think You Are* (1916), was a success. Five years later his most famous play, *Six Characters in Search of an Author*, was produced. Pirandello was intrigued by the themes of despair, jealousy, and death. He also explored the contradictions between appearance and reality. In 1934, one year after the dictator Mussolini condemned his plays for their "introspective, moody and unrealistic" style, Pirandello was awarded the Nobel Prize for Literature. "War" is from a collection called *The Medals and Other Stories*.

Edgar Allan Poe (1809–1849), a major American writer, left a substantial legacy of poetry, fiction, and literary criticism. He was born in Boston to traveling actors. His father deserted the family, and Poe's mother died when he was two. He was then taken in by John

Allan, a wealthy tobacco merchant in Virginia, but he was never formally adopted. It was from his foster family that he took his middle name. Poe's relations with his guardian were always strained. When he contracted huge debts at the University of Virginia, John Allan refused to pay them, and Poe had to leave the university. Poe entered the army and spent several months as a cadet at West Point in an effort to please his guardian, but all attempts at reconciliation failed. Finally, Poe turned to writing to earn a living. For a time he lived in Baltimore with his aunt, Maria Clemm, and his cousin, Virginia, whom he married when she was thirteen. During the decade of their married life, Virginia was ill much of the time, and Poe, depressed and given to drink, was unable to keep a job. After her death, he tried unsuccessfully to set up his own magazine. Perhaps seeking to find both financial and emotional security, he courted several wealthy women. The circumstances of his death remain a mystery. On a business trip, Poe stopped off in Baltimore. Several days later he was found lying unconscious on a sidewalk, and he died without regaining consciousness. The despair that marked his life appears in his poems and stories. Some of his best-known stories are "The Fall of the House of Usher," "The Cask of Amontillado," "The Masque of the Red Death," and "The Murders in the Rue Morgue."

Quentin Reynolds (1902–1965) served as a war correspondent in London, Paris, Italy, and the South Pacific during the Second World War. His experiences are described in *The Wounded Don't Cry* (1941). He wrote several biographies (his subjects included Winston Churchill and the Wright brothers) and a number of short stories.

Leonard Q. Ross is a pen name for Leo Calvin Rosten, who was born in Poland in 1908. Rosten came to the United States as a child. After graduating from the University of Chicago, he taught English to adults in night school. His most famous work, *The Education of H*Y*M*A*N K*A*P*L*A*N*, describes the amusing, sometimes frustrating attempts of immigrants to learn the language and culture of their new home, America. Rosten has also written a nonfiction work, *The Joys of Yiddish*, which is a playful examination of the language of Jewish immigrants and of the impact of Yiddish on English.

Saki is the pen name of Hector Hugh Munro (1870–1916), who was born in Burma, where his father served in the police force. After his mother's death he was brought up very strictly by two English aunts. He served for a year with the Burma police, then turned to a career in journalism. Back in England, he produced political sketches called "The Westminster Alice" because they were written in the amusing style of Lewis Carroll's *Alice in Wonderland.* The pen name Saki is taken from *The Rubáiyát* by Omar Khayyám. It means "wine-bearer" or "bringer of joy." Saki is famous for his whimsical, ironical short stories. He delighted in surprising his readers with unexpected endings. Some of his best-known stories are "The Open Window," "Sredni Vashtar," "The Schartz-Metter-klume Method," and "The Interlopers." During the First World War, Saki enlisted as a private in the Royal Fusiliers. He was killed in France on November 13, 1916.

William Sansom (1912–1976) was born in England. He traveled in Europe and lived in several countries on the Continent. Until the Second World War, he worked in banking and advertising. From 1949 to his death, he produced a number of novels and collections of short stories. He also wrote a biography of the French novelist Marcel Proust. In his stories Sansom often focuses on the thoughts and feelings of characters during a single, brief incident in their lives. "Difficulty with a Bouquet" appeared in Sansom's first book, *Fireman Flower and Other Stories.*

Juan A. A. Sedillo (1902–1982) was born in New Mexico, a descendant of early Spanish colonists. He was a lawyer and judge, and held several public offices. While he was practicing law in Santa Fe, an incident took place in his office that inspired Sedillo to write the story "Gentleman of Río en Medio." The tale suggests the compassion that Sedillo felt for the Spanish-speaking people of the Southwest.

Isaac Bashevis Singer was born in Radzymin, Poland, in 1904. His father and grandfather were rabbis. He received his formal education in Warsaw. *In My Father's Court* (1966) is Singer's remembrance of his childhood in Warsaw. In 1935 Singer came to the United States, where he has published a number of novels and short stories. Many of his stories, like "Zlateh the Goat," are about Jewish family life in the small villages of Eastern Europe. Singer writes in Yiddish and then has his works translated into English. His first collection of short stories to appear in English was *Gimpel the Fool* (1957). Many of Singer's tales are topsy-turvy narratives of unexpected events and unlikely characters. Some reflect the mystical elements of the Jewish religion that Singer learned about from his family. In 1978 Singer received the Nobel Prize for Literature.

Max Steele was born in Greenville, South Carolina, in 1922. He has written short stories, novels, and children's books. Steele has taught courses in creative writing and has been awarded several prizes for his books.

Elizabeth Taylor (1912–1975) was born in Reading, Berkshire, England. She began writing when she was very young. After leaving school she worked as a governess and as a librarian. Her first novel, *At Mrs. Lippincote's,* was published in 1946. Many of her short stories have appeared in *The New Yorker, Harper's Bazaar,* and *Harper's* magazine. Her writing is noted for its elegance and craftsmanship.

James Thurber (1894–1961), one of America's finest humorists, was born in Columbus, Ohio. For more than thirty years he contributed hundreds of stories, essays, and articles to *The New Yorker* magazine. He was also a talented cartoonist and illustrated many of his own works. Thurber lost one eye in a childhood accident and was completely blind when he died. In "University Days," he has described, with whimsical humor, his predicament in trying to use a microscope. Thurber used incidents from his childhood to create *My Life and Hard Times,* his most famous collection of stories. In "The Secret Life of Walter Mitty," he created his most memorable character, a man who lives a double life.

Mark Twain is the pen name of Samuel Langhorne Clemens (1835–1910), who grew up in Hannibal, Missouri, a small town on the Mississippi River. He worked on a newspaper, then became a riverboat pilot. He may have taken his pen name from a cry used by the riverboatmen, "By the mark, twain!" This cry meant that the river was two fathoms deep, a safe depth for navigation. After a trip to Europe and Palestine, Twain wrote *Innocents Abroad* (1869), a humorous travelogue that received popular success. His other works include *The Adventures of Tom Sawyer* (1876) *Life on the Mississippi* (1883), and his masterpiece, *The Adventures of Huckleberry Finn* (1884). Many critics consider Twain to be the greatest humorist this country has produced.

Sylvia Townsend Warner (1893–1978) was born in Middlesex, England. She originally planned to study music, but decided, instead, to write. Her first novel, *Lolly Willowes* (1926), became the first Book-of-the-Month-Club selection. She produced novels, short stories, poetry, and biography. Many of her short stories, written in a precise and elegant style, were published in *The New Yorker* magazine. Warner's last book, *Kingdoms of Elfin*, is a collection of stories about mythical creatures living in Europe. "The Phoenix" appeared in a volume of short stories called *The Cat's Cradle Book*.

Richard Wilbur was born in New York City in 1921. He began to write poetry while he was in the army during the Second World War. He has published several collections of poetry. *Things of This World* (1956) received the Pulitzer Prize and the National Book Award. Wilbur has also written verse translations of *The Misanthrope* and *Tartuffe* by the French dramatist Molière. He collaborated on the Broadway musical *Candide* (1957) with Leonard Bernstein and Lillian Hellman. "A Game of Catch" first appeared in *The New Yorker*.

Eva-Lis Wuorio was born in Finland in 1918. She emigrated to Canada when she was eleven. Wuorio's vivid memories of her homeland have enabled her to describe the history, landscape, and customs of Finland evocatively and richly. Her books include two novels about the Second World War: *Code Polonaise*, set in Poland, and *To Fight in Silence*, about the Dutch underground. "You Can't Take It with You" is from a collection of short stories called *Escape If You Can*.

Glossary of Literary Terms

Anecdote   A very short humorous or entertaining incident, often from personal experience.

See page 222.

Character   A person, animal, or thing presented as a person. In order to be believable, a character must have credibility, consistency, and motivation.

See Static and Dynamic Characters.
See Stock Character.
See pages 48, 58, 77.

Characterization   The methods used to present a character in a short story. A writer can create character by *direct* and *indirect* methods.

See Direct and Indirect Characterization.
See pages 48, 58.

Climax   The point of greatest excitement or intensity in a story.

See page 20.

Conflict   A problem or a struggle of some kind. Conflict may be *external* or *internal*. In a story there may be a single conflict or several related conflicts.

See page 4.

Direct and Indirect Characterization   Methods of presenting a character in a short story. In *direct characterization,* a writer *tells* what a character is like by means of direct comment. In *indirect characterization,* a writer *shows* what a character is like by 1) giving a physical description of the character; 2) relating the character's actions and words; 3) revealing the character's thoughts and feelings; and 4) making clear what others in the story think about the character.

See pages 48, 58.

Dramatic Irony   A type of irony in which the reader knows something that a character in the story does not know.

See page 204.

Dramatic Point of View

See Objective Point of View.

Dynamic Character   A character who undergoes an important change.

See page 78.

Euphemism   An inoffensive word or phrase substituted for one that is disagreeable or harsh.

See page 202.

Exaggeration   Overstatement or overemphasis, often with comic effect.

See page 211.

Exemplum   Originally, a narrative inserted into a sermon or other text in order to illustrate a moral. Now used to characterize a story used to teach a lesson or rule of conduct.

See page 257.

Explicit Theme   A direct statement expressing the central meaning of a story.

See page 235.

Exposition   Information essential to understanding the background of a story.

See page 4.

Fantasy   A form of fiction that deals with unreal or fantastic things.

See **Science Fiction.**
See page 311.

First-Person Point of View   The "I" vantage point in which the narrator of a story may be the main character or an observer.

See pages 143, 149.

Flashback   An interruption in a narrative to relate an action that has already occurred.

See page 320.

Foreshadowing   The method of building in clues or hints about what is to come in a story.

See page 15.

Frame Story   The outer story in a narrative that contains a story within a story.

See page 40.

Humor   An amusing or funny element, which is warm and genial rather than critical in tone.

See page 221.

Implied Theme   The central meaning that must be inferred from the characters and events in a story.

See page 240.

Incongruity   A technique of pairing opposites to create unexpected contrast.

See page 212.

Irony   A difference or contrast between appearance and reality. The types of irony include *irony of situation, dramatic irony,* and *verbal irony.*

See **Dramatic Irony.**
See **Irony of Situation.**
See **Verbal Irony.**
See pages 29, 203.

Irony of Situation   A type of irony in which there is a contrast between what is expected and what actually happens.

See pages 29, 203.

Limited Third-Person Point of View   A point of view that focuses on one character's thoughts, feelings, and actions.

See page 165.

Literal Meaning   Meaning based on actual fact, in contrast to figurative or symbolic meaning.

See page 249.

Metaphor   Language that draws a comparison between unlike things.

See page 352.

Mood   The emotional quality in a piece of literature.

See pages 132, 184.

Moral   A lesson intended to teach some rule of conduct about life.

See **Exemplum.**
See pages 209, 257.

Narrator   The person who tells a story.

See pages 143, 149, 158.

Objective Point of View   A third-person point of view in which the observer records events without offering commentary or interpretation. Also called the *dramatic point of view.*

See page 174.

Omniscient Point of View   A third-person point of view in which the narrator is an all-knowing observer who knows what all the characters can see, hear, think, and feel.

See page 158.

Personification   The presentation of an abstract quality or idea as a person.

See page 88.

Plot   The sequence of related events or actions in a story.

See pages 4, 14, 20, 29, 40.

Point of View   The angle from which a story is told.

See pages 143, 149, 158, 165, 174.

Protagonist   The main character in a story.

See page 48.

Resolution   The final part of a story that makes clear the outcome of the conflict.

See page 20.

Revelation   A dramatic moment that reveals something important to a character.

See page 61.

Satire   A literary work that pokes fun at some weakness or vice in human nature or society. Satire can be gentle and lighthearted or bitter and savage.

See page 211.

Science Fiction   A form of fantasy in which the action is set on some strange world or in the distant future.

See page 326.

Sentimentalism   The expression of warm and tender feelings, often used to describe *tone.*

See page 195.

Setting   The time, place, and circumstances that form the background of a story.

See pages 99, 107, 116, 124, 132.

Static Character   A character who does not change in any significant way.

See page 77.

Stereotype

See **Stock Character.**

Stock Character   A character who conforms to a familiar and predictable formula, also known as a **stereotype.**

See page 87.

Suspense   The element that keeps readers guessing about the outcome of events.

See page 14.

Symbol   A person, object, or event that has meaning in itself and that also stands for something else.

See page 249.

Tall Tale   A narrative relating superhuman feats or comically exaggerated and improbable events.

See page 284.

Theme   The central idea or underlying meaning about human nature that is developed in a story. A theme may be expressed directly or indirectly.

See **Explicit Theme.**
See **Implied Theme.**
See pages 229, 235, 240, 248, 257.

Third-Person Point of View   The vantage point of an outside observer who is the narrator of a story. This point of view may be *omniscient, limited,* or *objective.*

See **Limited Third-Person Point of View.**
See **Omniscient Point of View.**
See **Third-Person Point of View.**
See pages 158, 165, 174.

Tone   The attitude a writer takes toward the subject, characters, and readers of a work.

See pages 184, 195, 203, 211, 221.

Total Effect   The central impression or impact a work a literary work has on its readers.

See pages 269, 276, 284, 293, 303.

Verbal Irony   A type of irony in which a writer or character says one thing and means something entirely different.

See page 204.

Verisimilitude   The appearance of reality in fiction.

See page 107.

Glossary

The words listed in the glossary in the following pages are found in the short stories in this textbook. In this glossary, the meanings given are the ones that apply to the words as they are used in the selections. Words closely related in form and meaning are generally listed together in one entry (**adorn** and **adornment**) and the definition is given for the first form. Regular adverbs (ending in *-ly*) are defined in their adjective form, with the adverb form shown at the end of the definition.

The following abbreviations are used:

adj., adjective   *n.*, noun
adv., adverb   *v.*, verb

For more information about the words in this glossary, consult a dictionary.

A

abandoned (ə-băn′dənd) *adj.* Deserted; left behind.
abate (ə-bāt′) *v.* To lessen.
abreast (ə-brĕst′) *adv.* Side by side.
absorbed (ăb-sôrbd′, -zôrbd′) *adj.* Completely attentive; wholly involved in.
abstracted (ăb-străk′tĭd) *adj.* Absent-minded.—**abstractedly** *adv.*
acceleration (ăk-sĕl′ə-rā′shən) *n.* An increase in speed.
acknowledge (ăk-nŏl′ĭj) *v.* To admit.
acute (ə-kyo͞ot′) *adj.* **1.** Sensitive. **2.** Sharp; intense. **3.** Keen; perceptive.
adjust (ə-jŭst′) *v.* To change so as to correct; make fit.
adobe (ə-dō′bē) *adj.* Made of unburnt, sun-dried brick.
adorn (ə-dôrn′) *v.* To add beauty to.—**adornment** *n.*

ă pat/ā pay/âr care/ä father/b **bib**/ch **church**/d **deed**/ĕ pet/ē be/f fife/g gag/h hat/ hw which/ĭ pit/ī pie/îr pier/j judge/k kick/l lid, needle/m mum/n no, sudden/ ng thing/ŏ pot/ō toe/ô paw, for/oi noise/ou out/o͞o took/o͞o boot/p pop/r roar/ s sauce/sh ship, dish/t tight/th thin, path/*th* this, bathe/ŭ cut/ûr urge/v valve/ w with/y yes/z zebra, size/zh vision/ə about, item, edible, gallop, circus/ à *Fr.* ami/ œ *Fr.* feu, *Ger.* schön/ü *Fr.* tu, *Ger.* über/KH *Ger.* ich, *Scot.* loch/N *Fr.* bon.

affable (ăf′ə-bəl) *adj.* Pleasant; good-natured.

affectation (ăf′ĕk-tā′shən) *n.* Artificial behavior used to impress others.

affright (ə-frīt′) *v.* To terrify.—**affrightedly** *adv.*

agile (ăj′əl, ăj′īl) *adj.* Quick and light in movement.

agitate (ăj′ə-tāt′) *v.* To upset; disturb—**agitated** *adj.*

agony (ăg′ə-nē) *n.* Intense suffering.

aimless (ām′lĭs) *adj.* Without purpose.—**aimlessly** *adv.*

air (âr) *n.* One's manner or appearance.

aloof (ə-lōof′) *adj.* At a distance from people; cool and reserved in manner.

alternate (ôl′tər-nāt′, ăl′-) *v.* To take turns.

ambassador (ăm-băs′ə-dər, -dôr) *n.* An official messenger or representative of a country.

amiable (ā′mē-ə-bəl) *adj.* Pleasant; friendly.—**amiably** (ā′mē-ə-blē) *adv.*

ample (ăm′pəl) *adj.* Sufficient.

anguish (ăng′gwĭsh) *n.* Suffering.

animosity (ăn′ə-mŏs′ə-tē) *n.* Hatred; bitter hostility.

anonymous (ə-nŏn′ə-məs) *adj.* Lacking individual features.

anticipation (ăn-tĭs′ə-pā′shən) *n.* Expectation.

antics (ăn′tĭks) *n. pl.* Funny acts.

anxiety (ăng-zī′ə-tē) *n.* Eagerness.

anxious (ăngk′shəs, ăng′shəs) *adj.* **1.** Worried. **2.** Eager.

appall (ə-pôl′) *v.* To fill with fear or dismay.

apparent (ə-păr′ənt) *adj.* Plain; obvious.—**apparently** *adv.*

apprehension (ăp′rĭ-hĕn′shən) *n.* Dread; uneasiness.

apron (ā′prən, ā′pərn) *n.* A paved strip in front of a building.

ardent (är′dənt) *adj.* Warm; passionate.

aristocratic (ə-rĭs′tə-krăt′ĭk) *adj.* Having the manners of the upper class; exclusive or snobbish.

arouse (ə-rouz′) *v.* To stimulate or stir up.

arresting (ə-rĕs′tĭng) *adj.* Striking.

arrogant (ăr′ə-gənt) *adj.* Proud; disdainful.

ascend (ə-sĕnd′) *v.* **1.** To rise gradually. **2.** To go up; climb.

ascetic (ə-sĕt′ĭk) *adj.* Self-denying; strictly self-disciplined.

assail (ə-sāl′) *v.* To attack.

assemblage (ə-sĕm′blĭj) *n.* A collection of people.

assured (ə-shōord) *adj.* Confident.

astray (ə-strā′) *adv.* Away from the right direction.

astride (ə-strīd′) *prep.* With a leg on each side of.

attire (ə-tīr′) *n.* Clothing.
audible (ô′də-bəl) *adj.* Loud enough to be heard.
autopsy (ô′tŏp′sē, ô′təp-) *n.* Examination of a corpse to find the cause of death.
awe (ô) *n.* A feeling of wonder and dread. *v.* To inspire with fear or wonder.
awkward (ôk′wərd) *adj.* Clumsy.

B

beam (bēm) *v.* To smile warmly.
behest (bĭ-hĕst′) *n.* Earnest request.
beleaguer (bĭ-lē′gər) *v.* To lay siege to by surrounding with troops.
blanched (blănchd) *adj.* Turned white.
blank (blăngk) *adj.* Empty; expressing nothing. *v.* To cancel; wipe out.
bleak (blēk) *adj.* Harsh and barren.
blurt (blûrt) *v.* To speak suddenly or thoughtlessly.
bluster (blŭs′tər) *v.* To speak boastfully or noisily.—**blustering** *adj.*
boast (bōst) *v.* To speak with pride.
bog (bôg, bŏg) *n.* Marsh.
bound (bound) *v.* **1.** To bounce. **2.** To enclose.
bounder (boun′dər) *n.* Someone whose behavior is coarse and ungentlemanly.
bountiful (boun′tĭ-fəl) *adj.* Generous; plentiful.—**bountifully** *adv.*
brake (brāk) *n.* An area covered with a dense growth such as bushes.
bravado (brə-vä′dō) *n.* False bravery or show of courage without real confidence.
brink (brĭngk) *n.* Land bordering a body of water.
brisk (brĭsk) *adj.* Lively; energetic.—**briskly** *adv.*
bristle (brĭs′əl) *v.* To react angrily; become tense.

ă pat/ā pay/âr care/ä father/b bib/ch church/d deed/ĕ pet/ē be/f fife/g gag/h hat/ hw which/ĭ pit/ī pie/îr pier/j judge/k kick/l lid, needle/m mum/n no, sudden/ ng thing/ŏ pot/ō toe/ô paw, for/oi noise/ou out/ŏŏ took/ōō boot/p pop/r roar/ s sauce/sh ship, dish/t tight/th thin, path/*th* this, bathe/ŭ cut/ûr urge/v valve/ w with/y yes/z zebra, size/zh vision/ə about, item, edible, gallop, circus/ ä *Fr.* ami/ œ *Fr.* **feu,** *Ger.* schön/ü *Fr.* **tu,** *Ger.* über/KH *Ger.* **ich,** *Scot.* loch/N *Fr.* bon.

broach (brōch) *v.* To bring up; introduce.
brood (brōōd) *v.* To think about in a moody or worried manner.
browse (brouz) *v.* To look over casually.
brusque (brŭsk) *adj.* Blunt; abrupt in speech or manner.—
brusquely *adv.*
bullock (bōōl'ək) *n.* A steer.
burden (bûrd'n) *n.* A heavy weight; trouble.
burn (bûrn) *v.* To throw a ball very hard.
bygone (bī'gôn', -gŏn') *adj.* Past; former.

C

cad (kăd) *n.* An ill-bred man.
calculate (kăl'kyə-lāt') *v.* To reckon; determine by mathematical process.
calculated (kăl'kyə-lā'tĭd) *adj.* Determined or planned beforehand.
capricious (kə-prĭsh'əs, -prē'shəs) *adj.* Unpredictable.
carnal (kär'nəl) *adj.* Referring to the body; earthly, worldly; not spiritual.
cast (kăst, käst) *v.* To give forth; shed.
casual (kăzh'ōō-əl) *adj.* Unplanned; relaxed.
causeless (kôz'lĕs) *adj.* Without basis.
ceremony (sĕr'ə-mō'nē) *n.* A formal or conventional act.—**stand on ceremony.** Behave in an extremely formal way.
changeless (chānj'lĭs) *adj.* Unchanging.
chaos (kā'ŏs') *n.* Confusion; complete disorder.
charger (chär'jər) *n.* A horse trained for battle.
chaste (chāst) *adj.* Simple in style.
château (shă-tō') *n.* Castle.
chronicle (krŏn'ĭ-kəl) *n.* A record.
churl (chûrl) *n.* A miser.
churn (chûrn) *v.* To shake or stir with vigor.
civil (sĭv'əl) *adj.* Polite.
clamber (klăm'ər, klăm'bər) *v.* To climb with effort, using hands and feet.
clasp (klăsp, kläsp) *v.* To hold tightly; grip firmly.—**clasped** *adj.*
clench (klĕnch) *v.* To close tightly.
coarsen (kôr'sən, kōr'-) *v.* To become coarse, rough.
coincidence (kō'ĭn'sə-dəns, -dĕns') *n.* An instance of two things appearing at the same place or time purely by chance.

commit (kə-mĭt′) *v.* To set aside for future use or reference.— **commit to memory.** Memorize.

commotion (kə-mō′shən) *n.* Disturbance.

compassion (kəm-păsh′ən) *n.* Sympathy.

composition (kŏm′pə-zĭsh′ən) *n.* Combination of substances.

composure (kəm-pō′zhər) *n.* Calmness.

compound (kŏm′pound) *n.* An enclosed group of residences.

conceivable (kən-sēv′ə-bəl) *adj.* Believable.

conceive (kən-sēv′) *v.* **1.** To form an idea. **2.** To imagine.

concussion (kən-kŭsh′ən) *n.* A shock; violent jolt from impact.

confirm (kən-fûrm′) *v.* To make certain of; verify.

confront (kən-frŭnt′) *v.* To come face to face with.

consequence (kŏn′sə-kwĕns) *n.* Importance.

console (kən-sōl′) *v.* To comfort.

conspicuous (kən-spĭk′yōō-əs) *adj.* Noticeable; attracting attention.—**conspicuously** *adv.*

consternation (kŏn′stər-nā′shən) *n.* Amazement; confusion; alarm.

contemplation (kŏn′təm-plā′shən) *n.* Thoughtful consideration.

contemporary (kən-tĕm′pə-rĕr′ē) *n.* One of the same time or age.

contempt (kən-tĕmpt′) *n.* Strong disdain; scorn.

contract (kən-trăkt′, kŏn′trăkt′) *v.* To pull together; wrinkle.

convey (kən-vā′) *v.* To make known; communicate.

conviction (kən-vĭk′shən) *n.* Strong belief.

countenance (koun′tə-nəns) *n.* Facial expression.

cower (kou′ər) *v.* To crouch or shrink away in fear.

crave (krāv) *v.* To desire intensely.

cremation (krĭ-mā′shən) *n.* The incineration of a corpse.

crest (krĕst) *n.* Top or peak.

crinkly (krĭng′klē) *adj.* Full of wrinkles or ripples.

crisp (krĭsp) *adj.* Short and forceful; sharp—**crisply** *adv.*

croak (krōk) *v.* To speak in a low, hoarse voice.

croon (krōōn) *v.* To sing softly.

cunning (kŭn′ĭng) *adj.* Shrewd.—**cunningly** *adv.*

curt (kûrt) *adj.* Brief in a rude way.

ă pat/ā pay/âr care/ä father/b bib/ch church/d deed/ĕ pet/ē be/f fife/g gag/h hat/ hw which/ĭ pit/ī pie/îr pier/j judge/k kick/l lid, needle/m mum/n no, sudden/ ng thing/ŏ pot/ō toe/ô paw, for/oi noise/ou out/ŏŏ took/ōō boot/p pop/r roar/ s sauce/sh ship, dish/t tight/th thin, path/*th* this, bathe/ŭ cut/ûr urge/v valve/ w with/y yes/z zebra, size/zh vision/ə about, item, edible, gallop, circus/ â *Fr.* ami/ œ *Fr.* feu, *Ger.* schön/ü *Fr.* tu, *Ger.* über/KH *Ger.* ich, *Scot.* loch/N *Fr.* bon.

D

dashing (dăsh'ĭng) *adj.* Bold; full of spirit.

daunt (dônt, dänt) *v.* To discourage.

dawdle (dôd'l) *v.* To linger; lŏiter.

dawn (dôn) *v.* To begin to be understood.

dazzle (dăz'əl) *v.* To overwhelm or amaze with light or splendor.

decade (dĕk'ād', dĕ-kād') *n.* A ten-year period.

decipher (dĭ-sī'fər) *v.* To interpret.

deft (dĕft) *adj.* Skillful; expert.

deign (dān) *v.* To come down to the level of someone considered to be inferior.

deliberation (dĭ-lĭb'ə-rā'shən) *n.* Thoughtfulness; careful consideration.

deliver (dĭ-lĭv'ər) *v.* To set free.

demanding (dĭ-măn'dĭng, dĭ-män'-) *adj.* Making annoying or difficult demands.

demigod (dĕm'ē-gŏd') *n.* A godlike human being.

dense (dĕns) *adj.* Thick.

deplorable (dĭ-plôr'ə-bəl) *adj.* Wretched; bad.—**deplorably** *adv.*

deposit (dĭ-pŏz'ĭt) *v.* To put down carefully.

depreciate (dĭ-prē'shē-āt') *v.* To lessen or diminish in value.

deprive (dĭ-prīv') *v.* To take away; deny.

despondent (dĭ-spŏn'dənt) *adj.* Dejected.

detachment (dĭ-tăch'mənt) *n.* Separation; standing apart.

devour (dĭ-vour') *v.* To eat greedily.

dictate (dĭk'tāt', dĭk-tāt') *v.* To require.

dilated (dĭ-lā'tĭd, dī'lā'tĭd, dĭ-lā'tĭd) *adj.* Widened.

dint (dĭnt) *v.* To make a dent in.

discard (dĭs-kärd') *v.* To reject or throw aside.

discolor (dĭs-kŭl'ər) *v.* To stain or ruin the color of something; fade.

disdainful (dĭs-dān'fəl) *adj.* Scornful; haughty.

disembark (dĭs'-ĭm-bärk') *v.* To go ashore.

disfigure (dĭs-fĭg'yər) *v.* To spoil; make unattractive.

disinterested (dĭs-ĭn'trĭ-stĭd, -ĭn'tə-rĕs'tĭd) *adj.* Impartial; without self-interest.

dismember (dĭs-mĕm'bər) *v.* To take off the arms and legs.

dispute (dĭs-pyo͞ot') *v.* To argue about; doubt.

dissolve (dĭ-zŏlv') *v.* To form a solution with a liquid.

distort (dĭs-tôrt') *v.* To twist out of shape.

distract (dĭs-trăkt') *v.* To pull in different directions.

distracted (dĭs-trăk′tĭd) *adj.* Inattentive.

diversion (dĭ-vûr-zhən) *n.* Something that draws attention away from the original focus of interest.

dogged (dô′gĭd, dŏg′ĭd) *adj.* Stubborn; determined.—**doggedly** *adv.*

dominant (dŏm′ə-nənt) *adj.* Most important or influential.

dour (dŏŏr, dour) *adj.* Gloomy.

dread (drĕd) *n.* Intense fear; terror.

drivel (drĭv′əl) *n.* Stupid talk.

duly (dŏŏ′lē, dyŏŏ′-) *adv.* Correctly and properly.

E

eaves (ēvz) *n.* Overhang at the lower edge of a roof.

ebony (ĕb′ə-nē) *adj.* Dark-colored.

eclipse (ĭ-klĭps′) *v.* To overshadow; outshine.

edifice (ĕd′ə-fĭs) *n.* A building that is large and impressive.

efface (ĭ-fās′) *v.* To destroy; get rid of.

embed (ĕm-bĕd′) *v.* To fix firmly.

emerge (ĭ-mûrj′) *v.* To come into view.

emphatic (ĕm-făt′ĭk) *adj.* **1.** Definite. **2.** Striking. **3.** With emphasis.—**emphatically** *adv.*

encounter (ĕn-koun′tər, ĭn-) *v.* To come upon.

engulf (ĕn-gŭlf′, ĭn-) *v.* **1.** To surround or to enclose completely. **2.** To overwhelm.

entranced (ĕn-trănsd′, -tränsd′, ĭn-) *adj.* Filled with pleasure.

envelop (ĕn-vĕl′əp, ĭn-) *v.* To encircle or cover completely.

era (ir′ə, ĕr′ə) *n.* A distinctive period of time.

ermine (ûr′mĭn) *n.* Valuable white fur of a weasel.

estimation (ĕs′tə-mā′shən) *n.* Opinion; judgment.

ewer (yŏŏ′ər) *n.* Pitcher.

excessive (ĕk-sĕs′ĭv, ĭk-) *adj.* Beyond a normal limit or amount.

excursion (ĕk-skûr′zhən, ĭk-) *adj.* Of or for a pleasure trip.

executor (ĕg-zĕk′yə-tər, ĭg-) *n.* A person appointed to carry out the provisions of another person's will.

ă pat/ā pay/âr care/ä father/b bib/ch church/d deed/ĕ pet/ē be/f fife/g gag/h hat/
hw which/ĭ pit/ī pie/îr pier/j judge/k kick/l lid, needle/m mum/n no, sudden/
ng thing/ŏ pot/ō toe/ô paw, for/oi noise/ou out/ŏŏ took/ŏŏ boot/p pop/r roar/
s sauce/sh ship, dish/t tight/th thin, path/*th* this, bathe/ŭ cut/ûr urge/v valve/
w with/y yes/z zebra, size/zh vision/ə about, item, edible, gallop, circus/ à *Fr.* ami/
œ *Fr.* feu, *Ger.* schön/ü *Fr.* tu, *Ger.* über/KH *Ger.* ich, *Scot.* loch/N *Fr.* bon.

exile (ĕg′zīl′, ĕk′sīl′) *n.* Someone who is banished from his or her country.

exotic (ĕg-zŏt′ĭk, ĭg-) *adj.* Unusual; fascinating.

expression (ĕk-sprĕsh′ən, ĭk-) *n.* A look.

exquisite (ĕks′kwĭ-zĭt) *adj.* Extremely beautiful.

extension (ĕk-stĕn′shən, ĭk-) *n.* A period of extra time.

extraordinary (ĕk-strôr′də-nĕr′ē, ĭk-, ĕk′strə-ôr′) *adj.* Remarkable; exceptional.

exuberant (ĕg-zōō′bər-ənt, ĭg′) *adj.* Joyful; full of high spirits.

exude (ĕg-zōōd′, ĭg-, ĕk-sōōd′, ĭk-) *v.* To give off in abundant quantity.

exult (ĕg-zŭlt′, ĭg-) *v.* To rejoice.

exultant (ĕg-zŭl′tənt, ĭg-) *adj.* Joyful.

F

fabulous (făb′yə-ləs) *adj.* Legendary.

faculty (făk′əl-tē) *n.* **1.** Power or ability. **2.** Members of a profession.

falter (fôl′tər) *v.* To hesitate.

fanatic (fə-năt′ĭk) *n.* Someone with unreasonable attachment to a cause, often a political or religious extremist.

fastidious (fă-stĭd′ē-əs, fə-) *adj.* Extremely careful in all details.

feint (fānt) *n.* A movement intended to mislead.

fervent (fûr′vənt) *adj.* Eager; with great warmth.—**fervently** *adv.*

flat (flăt) *n.* An apartment.

flaw (flô) *n.* Defect; imperfection.

flicker (flĭk′ər) *v.* To give off light unsteadily.

flounce (flouns) *n.* A piece of pleated or gathered material used to trim a garment; ruffle.

flourish (flûr′ĭsh) *v.* **1.** To wave. **2.** To do well or succeed.

fluent (flōō′ənt) *adj.* Smooth; flowing easily.—**fluently** *adv.*

flush (flŭsh) *v.* To turn red; blush.

flustered (flŭs′tərd) *adj.* Nervous or excited.

foible (foi′bəl) *n.* minor weakness or fault in character.

foresight (fôr′sīt′, fōr′) *n.* **1.** Ability to see or to know beforehand. **2.** Preparation for the future.

formidable (fôr′mə-də-bəl) *adj.* Alarming; dreadful.

forsake (fôr-sāk′, fər) *v.* To desert; abandon.

frail (frāl) *adj.* Physically weak.

G

gall (gôl) *v.* To irritate; annoy.

gasp (găsp, gäsp) *n.* A sudden catching of breath.

gaudy (gô'dē) *adj.* Showy and tasteless.

gaunt (gônt) *adj.* Thin and exhausted; bony.

giddy (gĭd'ē) *adj.* Flighty; lighthearted.

glare (glâr) *n.* A strong blinding light.

glaring (glâr'ing) *adj.* Staring in anger.

glaze (glāz) *v.* To cover a surface with a thin layer of ice.

gleam (glēm) *n.* Brightness; shining light.

glimmer (glĭm'ər) *v.* To appear faintly.

glisten (glĭs'ən) *v.* To shine by reflection.

glossy (glôs'ē, glŏs'ē) *adj.* Smooth and shiny.

glut (glŭt) *v.* To supply with too much.

gnarled (närld) *adj.* Knotty and twisted; misshapen.

governess (gŭv'ər-nĭs) *n.* A woman who works as a teacher in a private household.

grate (grāt) *v.* To make a harsh sound by scraping.

grave (grāv) *adj.* Very serious.—**gravely** *adv.*

gravity (grăv'ə-tē) *n.* Dignity.

grim (grĭm) *adj.* Severe.

grope (grōp) *v.* To reach for uncertainly.

grove (grōv) *n.* Small wood.

gruff (grŭf) *adj.* Rough or harsh in speech.—**gruffly** *adv.*

guileless (gīl'lĭs) *adj.* Simple.

gyrate (jī'rāt') *v.* To turn or revolve.

H

hail (hāl) *v.* To call to in greeting.

halberd (hăl'bərd) *n.* A weapon with an axlike blade used in the fifteenth and sixteenth centuries.

handiwork (hăn'dē-wûrk') *n.* The result of a person's efforts.

harrowing (hăr'ō-ĭng) *adj.* Distressing; tormenting.

haughty (hô'tē) *adj.* Proud and vain.—**haughtily** *adv.*

ă pat/ā pay/âr care/ä father/b bib/ch church/d deed/ĕ pet/ē be/f fife/g gag/h hat/
hw which/ĭ pit/ī pie/îr pier/j judge/k kick/l lid, needle/m mum/n no, sudden/
ng thing/ŏ pot/ō toe/ô paw, for/oi noise/ou out/ŏŏ took/ōō boot/p pop/r roar/
s sauce/sh ship, dish/t tight/th thin, path/*th* this, bathe/ŭ cut/ûr urge/v valve/
w with/y yes/z zebra, size/zh vision/ə about, item, edible, gallop, circus/ à *Fr.* ami/
œ *Fr.* feu, *Ger.* schön/ü *Fr.* tu, *Ger.* über/KH *Ger.* ich, *Scot.* loch/N *Fr.* bon.

headland (hĕd′lǝnd, -lănd′) *n.* A point of high land extending out into a body of water.

headlong (hĕd′lông′, -lŏng′) *adv.* Headfirst; at great speed.

heartily (här′tĭl-ē) *adv.* Enthusiastically.

hectic (hĕk′tĭk) *adj.* Flushed; feverish.

heedlessness (hēd′lĭs-nĭs) *n.* Carelessness.

heighten (hīt′n) *v.* **1.** To be raised. **2.** To make higher.

heir (âr) *n.* A person who inherits.

heirloom (âr′lōōm′) *n.* A treasured possession passed down through generations.

hobble (hŏb′ǝl) *v.* To move with difficulty; limp.

hollowed (hŏl′ōd) *adj.* Having dark circles under the eyes, as from illness or weariness.

humility (hyōō-mĭl′ǝ-tē) *n.* Modesty; humbleness.

hyacinth (hī′ǝ-sĭnth) *n.* A plant with fragrant, bell-shaped flowers.

hypocritical (hĭp′ǝ-krĭt′ǝ-kǝl) *adj.* False; insincere.

I

illustrious (ĭ-lŭs′trē-ǝs) *adj.* Famous.

immovable (ĭ-mōō′vǝ-bǝl) *adj.* **1.** Fixed in one place. **2.** Steadfast.

imp (ĭmp) *n.* A young devil; mischievous spirit.

impending (ĭm-pĕn′dĭng) *adj.* Likely to happen soon.

imperial (ĭm-pîr′ē-ǝl) *adj.* Relating to an emperor.

imperil (ĭm-pĕr′ǝl) *v.* To put in danger.

impetuous (ĭm-pĕch′ōō-ǝs) *adj.* Impulsive.

implacable (ĭm-plā′kǝ-bǝl, -plăk′ǝ-bǝl) *adj.* **1.** Inflexible; unyielding. **2.** Not capable of being calmed or soothed.

improbable (ĭm-prŏb′ǝ-bǝl) *adj.* Doubtful or unlikely.

impromptu (ĭm-prŏmp′tōō, -tyōō) *adj.* Spontaneous; on impulse.

improper (ĭm-prŏp′ǝr) *adj.* Not right; unfit.

inadequate (ĭn-ăd′ĭ-kwĭt) *adj.* Less than is needed.

incompetent (ĭn-kŏm′pǝ-tǝnt) *adj.* Not capable.

incongruous (ĭn-kŏng′grōō-ǝs) *adj.* Unsuitable; not appropriate.

inconsequential (ĭn-kŏn′sǝ-kwĕn′shǝl) *adj.* Of little importance.

incredulity (ĭn′krǝ-dōō′lǝ-tē) *n.* Inability to believe.

incredulous (ĭn-krĕj′ǝ-lǝs) *adj.* Disbelieving.

incur (ĭn-kûr′) *v.* To bring about.

indifferent (ĭn-dĭf′ər-ənt) *adj.* Without particular interest or concern.—**indifferently** *adv.*—**indifference** *n.*

indignant (ĭn-dĭg′nənt) *adj.* Annoyed; angry.

indignation (ĭn′dĭg-nā′shən) *n.* Anger caused by something that is unjust, unfair, or wrong.

indolent (ĭn′də-lənt) *adj.* Lazy.—**indolently** *adv.*

induce (ĭn-do͞os′, -dyo͞os′) *v.* To influence; prevail upon.

indulge (ĭn-dŭlj′) *v.* To allow oneself pleasure or to give in to a desire or whim.

ineffable (ĭn-ĕf′ə-bəl) *adj.* Indescribable.

inevitable (ĭn-ĕv′ə-tə-bəl) *adj.* Certain to happen; not capable of being prevented.

infantile (ĭn′fən-tīl′, -tĭl) *adj.* Immature.

informer (ĭn-fôr′mər) *n.* Someone who gives information against others for reward.

innumerable (ĭ-no͞o′mər-ə-bəl, ĭ-nyo͞o′-) *adj.* Countless.

inscription (ĭn-skrĭp′shən) *n.* The writing carved or engraved on a monument.

insolent (ĭn′sə-lənt) *adj.* Insulting; disrespectful.—**insolently** *adv.*

institution (ĭn′stə-to͞o′shən, -tyo͞o′shən) *n.* An established feature.

intense (ĭn-tĕns′) *adj.* Showing concentration.

intent (ĭn-tĕnt′) *adj.* **1.** Firmly directed; attentive. **2.** Concentrated; intense.

interminable (ĭn-tûr′mə-nə-bəl) *adj.* Endless.—**interminably** *adv.*

intolerable (ĭn-tŏl′ər-ə-bəl) *adj.* Unbearable.

intrusion (ĭn-tro͞o′zhən) *n.* Entry without invitation.

invalid (ĭn′və-lĭd) *adj.* Sickly; physically disabled.

islet (ī′lĭt) *n.* A small island.

J

jaunty (jôn′tē, jän′-) *adj.* Carefree; cheerful.—**jauntily** *adv.*

ă pat/ā pay/âr care/ä father/b bib/ch church/d deed/ĕ pet/ē be/f fife/g gag/h hat/ hw which/ĭ pit/ī pie/îr pier/j judge/k kick/l lid, needle/m mum/n no, sudden/ ng thing/ŏ pot/ō toe/ô paw, for/oi noise/ou out/o͞o took/o͞o boot/p pop/r roar/ s sauce/sh ship, dish/t tight/th thin, path/*th* this, bathe/ŭ cut/ûr urge/v valve/ w with/y yes/z zebra, size/zh vision/ə about, item, edible, gallop, circus/ à *Fr.* ami/ œ *Fr.* feu, *Ger.* schön/ü *Fr.* tu, *Ger.* über/ĸʜ *Ger.* ich, *Scot.* loch/ɴ *Fr.* bon.

jeer (jîr) *v.* To mock; make fun of.
jounce (jouns) *v.* To bounce.
judicious (jōō-dĭsh′əs) *adj.* Wise; sensible.

K

kin (kĭn) *n.* Relatives.

L

laborious (lə-bôr′ē-əs) *adj.* Requiring great effort.
lame (lām) *adj.* Weak.—**lamely** *adv.*
lamentation (lăm′ən-tā′shən) *n.* An expression of grief.
languid (lăng′gwĭd) *adj.* Slow of movement; sluggish.—**languidly** *adv.*
languorous (lăng′gər-əs) *adj.* Dreamy; lazy.
leprous (lĕp′rəs) *adj.* Having the characteristics of leprosy, a disease marked by sores and rotting away of the body.
listless (lĭst′lĭs) *adj.* Without enthusiasm or energy.—**listlessly** *adv.*
literal (lĭt′ər-əl) *adj.* Word for word; concerned with facts.
livid (lĭv′ĭd) *adj.* Pale or ashen.
lob (lŏb) *v.* To throw a ball in a slow high arc.
lodge (lŏj) *v.* To register a charge or complaint.
lofty (lôf′tē, lŏf′-) *adj.* **1.** High; towering. **2.** Overproud; haughty.—**loftily** (lôf′tə-lē) *adv.*
loll (lŏl) *v.* To hang or droop loosely.—**lolling** *adj.*
longitudinal (lŏn′jə-tōōd′n-əl, -tyōōd′n-əl) *adj.* Running lengthwise.
lunge (lŭnj) *v.* To move forward suddenly.
lurch (lûrch) *v.* To stagger; sway suddenly.
luxurious (lŭg-zhōōr′ē-əs, lŭk-shōōr′-) *adj.* **1.** Extremely pleasurable. **2.** Fond of extravagant living.
lyre (līr) *n.* An ancient stringed instrument similar to the harp, used to accompany singing.

M

majestic (mə-jĕs′tĭk) *adj.* Grand and dignified.—**majestically** *adv.*
mammoth (măm′əth) *adj.* Gigantic.

manifold (măn′ə-fōld) *adj.* Varied.

martyr (mär′tər) *n.* One who chooses to suffer for some cause or belief.

massive (măs′ĭv) *adj.* Huge; impressive.

matted (măt′ĭd) *adj.* Covered densely.

maudlin (môd′lĭn) *adj.* Overly sentimental.

maze (māz) *n.* An intricate network or pattern.

mean (mēn) *adj.* Shabby; poor in appearance.

meditate (mĕd′ə-tāt′) *v.* To think quietly and deeply.

meditative (mĕd′ə-tā′tĭv) *adj.* In deep thought.

mirror (mĭr′ər) *v.* To show a reflection of.

misgiving (mĭs-gĭv′ĭng) *n.* A feeling of doubt or worry.

moat (mōt) *n.* A deep ditch surrounding a fortress as protection.

mockery (mŏk′ər-ē) *n.* Ridicule; a scornful action.

mocking (mŏk′ĭng) *adj.* In a scornful manner; expressing ridicule.

moral (môr′əl, mŏr′-) *adj.* Upright; of good conduct.

motionless (mō′shən-lĭs) *adj.* Not moving.

mournful (môrn′fəl, mōrn′-) *adj.* Sorrowful.

muffle (mŭf′əl) *v.* To deaden a sound.

N

necessaries (nĕs′ə-sĕr′ēz) *n. pl.* Whatever is needed, such as food.

negligent (nĕg′lĭ-jənt) *adj.* Unconcerned; careless.

negotiation (nĭ-gō′shē-ā′shən) *n.* Bargaining; the act of coming to an agreement.

nincompoop (nĭn′kəm-pōōp′, nĭng′-) *n.* A stupid person; fool.

nominal (nŏm′ə-nəl) *adj.* Minimal in value.

nonchalant (nŏn′shə-länt′) *adj.* Unconcerned; cool.—**nonchalantly** *adv.*

nondescript (nŏn′dĭ-skrĭpt′) *adj.* Indefinite; without individual or distinctive features.

novelty (nŏv′əl-tē) *n.* A new thing.

ă pat/ā pay/âr care/ä father/b bib/ch church/d deed/ĕ pet/ē be/f fife/g gag/h hat/ hw which/ĭ pit/ī pie/îr pier/j judge/k kick/l lid, needle/m mum/n no, sudden/ ng thing/ŏ pot/ō toe/ô paw, for/oi noise/ou out/ōō took/ōō boot/p pop/r roar/ s sauce/sh ship, dish/t tight/th thin, path/*th* this, bathe/ŭ cut/ûr urge/v valve/ w with/y yes/z zebra, size/zh vision/ə about, item, edible, gallop, circus/ ä *Fr.* ami/ œ *Fr.* feu, *Ger.* schön/ü *Fr.* tu, *Ger.* über/ĸн *Ger.* ich, *Scot.* loch/n *Fr.* bon.

O

oblige (ə-blīj') *v.* To do a service for.

obscure (ŏb-skyо̄о̄r', əb-) *adj.* Not clear; faint.—**obscurely** *adv.*

obstinate (ŏb'stə-nĭt) *adj.* Stubborn; difficult to control.

offensive (ə-fĕn'sĭv) *adj.* Disagreeable; unpleasant.—**offensively** *adv.*

ominous (ŏm'ə-nəs) *adj.* Threatening.

ooze (о̄о̄z) *v.* To leak or flow out slowly.

opal (ō'pəl) *n.* A gem that reflects light in various colors.

oppressive (ə-prĕs'ĭv) *adj.* Burdensome; difficult to bear.— **oppressively** *adv.*

orbit (ôr'bĭt) *n.* Region of activity.

ordeal (ôr-dēl') *n.* A difficult experience.

outmoded (out-mō'dĭd) *adj.* No longer usable; out-of-date.

outset (out'set') *n.* The beginning of something.

ovation (ō-vā'shən) *n.* Triumph; enthusiastic reception.

overwhelm (ō'vər-hwĕlm') *v.* To overcome completely with force or feeling.

P

palpable (păl'pə-bəl) *adj.* Capable of being touched or felt.

parapet (păr'ə-pĭt, -pĕt) *n.* A low protective wall along the edge of a roof.

patent (păt'ənt) *adj.* Obvious.

paternal (pə-tûr'nəl) *adj.* Fatherly.

pathos (pā'thŏs', -thôs') *n.* A feeling of sympathy or pity.

patter (păt'ər) *v.* To move making a series of quick, light taps.

pattering (păt'ər-ĭng) *n.* Light rhythmic sounds in quick succession.

peer (pîr) *v.* To look closely, as with difficulty.

peevish (pē'vĭsh) *adj.* Complaining; irritable.

penetrate (pĕn'ə-trāt') *v.* To get in or through something.

penitent (pĕn'ə-tənt) *n.* One who is sorry for his or her faults or sins.

perpetual (pər-pĕch'о̄о̄-əl) *adj.* Uninterrupted.

persist (pər-sĭst', -zĭst') *v.* To continue to do; refuse to stop.

petulant (pĕch'о̄о̄-lənt) *adj.* Irritable; fretful.

phenomenal (fĭ-nŏm'ə-nəl) *adj.* Remarkable.

phial (fī'əl) *n.* A small bottle for liquids. Also spelled **vial.**

pinched (pĭnchd) *adj.* Thin; withered.

pique (pēk) *n.* Resentment.

plaintive (plān′tĭv) *adj.* Mournful.—**plaintively** *adv.*

plausible (plô′zə-bəl) *adj.* Seemingly true, yet deceptive.

plight (plīt) *n.* Difficult situation.

poignant (poin′yənt, poi′nənt) *adj.* Piercing; painful.

poised (poizd) *adj.* Balanced.

pomp (pŏmp) *n.* Splendor; magnificent display.

portly (pôrt′lē, pōrt′-) *adj.* Stout.

possessive (pə-zĕs′ĭv) *adj.* Pertaining to ownership.—**possessively** *adv.*

potency (pōt′n-sē) *n.* Strength.

potion (pō′shən) *n.* A liquid supposed to have magical qualities.

powder (pou′dər) *v.* To sprinkle; cover as if with powder.—**powdered** *adj.*

precaution (prĭ-kô′shən) *n.* Safeguard; caution taken in advance.

preliminary (prĭ-lĭm′ə-nĕr′ē) *adj.* Introductory or preparatory.

premises (prĕm′ĭs-ĭs) *n. pl.* An area of land and the buildings on it.

preposterous (prĭ-pŏs′tər-əs) *adj.* Absurd.

prime (prīm) *n.* Ideal or best period of life.

procession (prə-sĕsh′ən) *n.* A group moving along in a long line.

prodigious (prə-dĭj′əs) *adj.* Enormous.

profound (prə-found′, prō-) *adj.* Of deep knowledge or intellect.

profusion (prə-fyōō′zhən, prō-) *n.* A great deal; abundance.

progress (prŏg′rĕs′, -rəs) *n.* Steady improvement.

project (prə-jĕkt′) *v.* To extend out.

proprietor (prə-prī′ə-tər) *n.* The owner and operator of a business.

prosperity (prŏs-pĕr′ə-tē) *n.* Financial success.

prosperous (prŏs′pər-əs) *adj.* Successful.

protest (prə-tĕst′, prō-tĕst′, prō′tĕst′) *v.* To object to. *n.* (prō′tĕst′) Objection.

prudence (prōōd′əns) *n.* Caution; good judgment.

punishing (pŭn′ĭsh-ĭng) *adj.* Harsh; rough.

ă pat/ā pay/âr care/ä father/b bib/ch church/d deed/ĕ pet/ē be/f fife/g gag/h hat/ hw which/ĭ pit/ī pie/îr pier/j judge/k kick/l lid, needle/m mum/n no, sudden/ ng thing/ŏ pot/ō toe/ô paw, for/oi noise/ou out/ōō took/ōō boot/p pop/r roar/ s sauce/sh ship, dish/t tight/th thin, path/*th* this, bathe/ŭ cut/ûr urge/v valve/ w with/y yes/z zebra, size/zh vision/ə about, item, edible, gallop, circus/ à *Fr.* ami/ œ *Fr.* feu, *Ger.* schön/ü *Fr.* tu, *Ger.* über/KH *Ger.* ich, *Scot.* loch/N *Fr.* bon.

putout (pŏŏt'out') *n.* A play in baseball that causes a runner or batter to be out.

Q

quaint (kwānt) *adj.* **1.** Old-fashioned. **2.** Unusual in a pleasing way.

quarry (kwôr'ē, kwŏr'ē) *n.* Prey; victim.

quarters (kwôr'tərz) *n.* A place to live in.

quick (kwĭk) *adj.* Hasty and sharp.

quiver (kwĭv'ər) *v.* To tremble.

R

rafter (răf'tər, räf'-) *n.* A sloping beam used to support a roof.

rally (răl'ē) *v.* To revive.

rancor (răng'kər) *n.* Ill will.

ransack (răn'săk') *v.* To search carefully.

rapture (răp'chər) *n.* Extreme joy; complete delight.

ready (rĕd'ē) *adj.* Available.

real property *n.* Landed property.

reckless (rĕk'lĭs) *adj.* Careless.

recoil (rē'koil', rĭ-koil') *n.* The movement of a gun as it springs back when fired.

recollection (rĕk'ə-lĕk'shən) *n.* Something remembered.

recommence (rē'kə-mĕns') *v.* To begin again.

recur (rĭ-kûr') *v.* To return.

reel (rēl) *v.* To stagger or sway.

reflection (rĭ-flĕk'shən) *n.* Careful consideration.

reformation (rĕf'ər-mā'shən) *n.* A change for the better.

refrain (rĭ-frān') *v.* To hold back.

regal (rē'gəl) *adj.* Royal.

relentless (rĭ-lĕnt'lĭs) *adj.* Continuing.

reluctant (rĭ-lŭk'tənt) *adj.* Unwilling.—**reluctantly** *adv.*

remorse (rĭ-môrs') *n.* Regret for some action.

renowned (rĭ-nound') *adj.* Widely honored; famous.

repast (rĭ-păst', -päst') *n.* A meal.

repercussion (rē'pər-kŭsh'ən) *n.* Reflection of sound.

repose (rĭ-pōz') *n.* Rest; peace of mind. *v.* To lie at rest.

repulsion (rĭ-pŭl'shən) *n.* Extreme dislike.

resilient (rĭ-zĭl-yənt) *adj.* Leaping back; able to return to its original shape.

resolute (rĕz'ə-lo͞ot') *adj.* Determined; having a firm purpose. —**resolutely** *adv.*

resolve (rĭ-zŏlv') *v.* To decide.

resplendent (rĭ-splĕn'dənt) *adj.* Brilliant.

resume (rĭ-zo͞om') *v.* To begin again after interruption.

retort (rĭ-tôrt') *n.* A quick reply.

revelation (rĕv'ə-lā'shən) *n.* Something surprising revealed in a dramatic way, as a divine revelation.

revelry (rĕv'əl-rē) *n.* Noisy merrymaking.

reverberate (rĭ-vûr'bə-rāt') *v.* To reecho; resound.

reverie (rĕv'ər-ē) *n.* Daydreaming.

revolt (rĭ-vōlt') *v.* To turn away in disgust or shock.

rogue (rōg) *n.* A mischievous one; rascal.

rouse (rouz) *v.* To cause someone or something to stir or wake up.

rout (rout) *n.* A complete defeat.

route (ro͞ot, rout) *n.* A fixed course.

routine (ro͞o-tēn') *adj.* **1.** Regular. **2.** Lacking in originality or interest.

rude (ro͞od) *adj.* Rough.

ruffle (rŭf'əl) *v.* To ripple.

rummage (rŭm'ĭj) *v.* To search thoroughly.

ruse (ro͞oz) *n.* A trick; an action intended to create a false impression in order to mislead.

S

saber (sā'bər) *n.* A cavalry sword with a curved blade.

salutation (săl'yə-tā'shən) *n.* A greeting.

savor (sā'vər) *v.* To enjoy wholeheartedly.

scan (skăn) *v.* To examine closely.

scorn (skôrn) *n.* A feeling of extreme distaste; contempt.—**scornful** *adj.*

scowl (skoul) *n.* An angry or disapproving look. *v.* To frown in disapproval or anger.

ă pat/ā pay/âr care/ä father/b bib/ch church/d deed/ĕ pet/ē be/f fife/g gag/h hat/ hw which/ĭ pit/ī pie/îr pier/j judge/k kick/l lid, needle/m mum/n no, sudden/ ng thing/ŏ pot/ō toe/ô paw, for/oi noise/ou out/o͞o took/o͞o boot/p pop/r roar/ s sauce/sh ship, dish/t tight/th thin, path/*th* this, bathe/ŭ cut/ûr urge/v valve/ w with/y yes/z zebra, size/zh vision/ə about, item, edible, gallop, circus/ â *Fr.* ami/ œ *Fr.* feu, *Ger.* schön/ü *Fr.* tu, *Ger.* über/ᴋʜ *Ger.* ich, *Scot.* loch/ɴ *Fr.* bon.

scramble (skrăm′bəl) *v.* To move quickly, on hands and knees.

scrutiny (skro͞ot′n-ē) *n.* Close observation or careful study.

scullion (skŭl′yən) *n.* Servant who works in a kitchen.

scuttle (skŭt′l) *v.* To run hurriedly.

seclusion (sĭ-klo͞o′zhən) *n.* Solitude or privacy.

secure (sĭ-kyo͞or′) *v.* To get hold of; obtain.

sedate (sĭ-dāt′) *adj.* Calm; serious.—**sedately** *adv.*

senseless (sĕns′lĭs) *adj.* Meaningless; lacking sense.

sentimental (sĕn′tə-mĕnt′l) *adj.* Showing tender feelings.

serene (sĭ-rēn′) *adj.* Calm and peaceful.—**serenely** *adv.*

shabby (shăb′ē) *adj.* Run down; showing much wear.

shaft (shăft, shäft) *n.* A ray of light.

sheen (shēn) *n.* Shininess.

shift (shĭft) *v.* To move from one position to another.

simultaneous (sī′məl-tā′nē-əs, sĭm′əl-) *adj.* Happening at the same time.—**simultaneously** *adv.*

sinewy (sĭn′yo͞o-ē) *adj.* Strong.

singular (sĭng′gyə-lər) *adj.* Rare; extraordinary.

sinister (sĭn′ĭ-stər) *adj.* Suggesting danger or evil.

skim (skĭm) *v.* To throw a stone or other object so that it bounces lightly along the water's surface.

skinflint (skĭn′flĭnt′) *n.* A miser.

slacken (slăk′ən) *v.* To slow down.

slink (slĭngk) *v.* To sneak.

snag (snăg) *v.* To catch quickly.

sniper (snī′pər) *n.* Someone who shoots at other people from a hiding place.

sodden (sŏd′n) *adj.* Thoroughly soaked.

solemn (sŏl′əm) *adj.* Serious.

solitude (sŏl′ə-to͞od′) *n.* State of being alone.

soothe (so͞oth) *v.* To calm; bring comfort.

sophisticated (sə-fĭs′tĭ-kā′tĭd) *adj.* Mature and experienced in worldly things.

spank (spăngk) *v.* To smack.

spatter (spăt′ər) *v.* To spot or soil, as in a shower of drops.

spawn (spôn) *n.* Eggs.

species (spē′shēz) *n.* A kind or type.

speculation (spĕk′yə-lā′shən) *n.* Deep consideration of some subject; serious thought.

spineless (spīn′lĭs) *adj.* Lacking in courage.

spirited (spĭr′ĭ-tĭd) *adj.* Lively and vigorous.

spontaneous (spŏn-tā′nē-əs) *adj.* Of one's own accord; having no outside cause.

spurt (spûrt) *v.* To come out suddenly and forcibly.

squabble (skwŏb′əl) *v.* To quarrel.

squall (skwôl) *v.* To scream or cry loudly.

staccato (stə-kä′tō) *adj.* Short and abrupt.

staggerer (stăg′ər-ər) *n.* A person who moves unsteadily.

stalk (stôk) *v.* **1.** To advance in a stealthy way. **2.** To walk with a noble bearing.

stall (stôl) *n.* A cubicle in a barn.

start (stärt) *n.* A startled reaction.

state (stāt) *n.* A grand or formal style.

sterling (stûr′lĭng) *adj.* Of the highest quality.

stifle (stī′fəl) *v.* To smother; choke.

stifling (stī′flĭng) *adj.* Suffocating.

stock (stŏk) *adj.* Ordinary. *n.* Supply; supplies of goods kept for sale.—**to take stock.** To make a careful examination.

stoical (stō′ĭ-kəl) *adj.* Enduring; brave.—**stoically** *adv.*

stony (stō′nē) *adj.* Unfeeling; hard and cold.

store (stôr, stōr) *n.* Value.—**set store by.** To regard highly.

strife (strīf) *n.* Bitter conflict.

strive (strīv) *v.* To struggle; put forth great effort.

stumpy (stŭmp′ē) *adj.* Short and thick.

sublimity (sə-blĭm′ə-tē) *n.* Something supreme or impressive.

subside (səb-sīd′) *v.* To settle down.

suburb (sŭb′ərb′) *n.* A residential area lying outside a city.

sufficient (sə-fĭsh′ənt) *adj.* Enough.

suit (so͞ot) *n.* A group of things that make up a set, such as one of the four suits of playing cards.—**to follow suit.** To do the same.

suite (swēt) *n.* A train of followers.

sultry (sŭl′trē) *adj.* Extremely hot and humid.

superficial (so͞o′pər-fĭsh′əl) *adj.* Trivial; obvious.

superior (sə-pîr′ē-ər) *adj.* Behaving as if one is better than others.

supple (sŭp′əl) *adj.* Easily bent.

ă pat/ā pay/âr care/ä father/b bib/ch church/d deed/ĕ pet/ē be/f fife/g gag/h hat/ hw which/ĭ pit/ī pie/îr pier/j judge/k kick/l lid, needle/m mum/n no, sudden/ ng thing/ŏ pot/ō toe/ô paw, for/oi noise/ou out/o͞o took/o͞o boot/p pop/r roar/ s sauce/sh ship, dish/t tight/th thin, path/*th* this, bathe/ŭ cut/ûr urge/v valve/ w with/y yes/z zebra, size/zh vision/ə about, item, edible, gallop, circus/ à *Fr.* ami/ œ *Fr.* feu, *Ger.* schön/ü *Fr.* tu, *Ger.* über/KH *Ger.* ich, *Scot.* loch/N *Fr.* bon.

suppress (sǝ-prĕs′) *v.* To hold back.
survey (sǝr-vā′, sûr′vā′) *v.* To determine the boundaries of land.
suspect (sŭs′pĕkt′) *adj.* Open to suspicion.
suspend (sǝ-spĕnd′) *v.* To hold in a fixed state.
sustain (sǝ-stān′) *v.* To support.
swagger (swăg′ǝr) *v.* To brag; behave in an insolent way.—**swaggering** *adj.*
swarm (swôrm) *v.* To move as a mass.

T

taunt (tônt) *n.* Scornful remark.
tawdry (tô′drē) *adj.* Cheap and showy in a tasteless way.
tentative (tĕn′tǝ-tĭv) *adj.* Uncertain.—**tentatively** *adv.*
throng (thrŏng) *v.* To crowd into; fill completely.
thrust (thrŭst) *v.* To push or shove with force.
tinge (tĭnj) *v.* To color slightly.
toilsome (toil′sǝm) *adj.* Causing difficulty.
tolerable (tŏl′ǝr-ǝ-bǝl) *adj.* Able to be endured; bearable.
tolerance (tol′ǝr-ǝns) *n.* Respect for the beliefs and actions of others.
tone (tōn) *n.* Manner of expression in speaking or writing.
transfix (trăns-fĭks′) *v.* To make motionless, as in amazement or fear.
transparent (trăns-pâr′ǝnt, -păr′ǝnt) *adj.* Able to be seen through.
trellis (trĕl′ĭs) *n.* A frame used as a support for climbing plants.
tumultous (tǝ-mŭl′chōō-ǝs) *adj.* Riotous; disorderly.—**tumultously** *adv.*
turret (tûr′ĭt) *n.* On a tank, a rotating structure with mounted guns.

U

ulterior (ŭl′tîr′ē-ǝr) *adj.* Hidden.
unanimous (yōō-năn′ǝ-mǝs) *adj.* Of one mind; sharing the same views.
unassuming (ŭn′ǝ-sōō′mĭng) *adj.* Modest; not boastful.
uncanny (ŭn′kăn′ē) *adj.* Weird and mysterious; not possible to explain.
undermine (ŭn′dǝr-mīn′) *v.* To weaken.

undistinguished (ŭn'dĭs-tĭng'gwĭsht) *adj.* Not having any noticeable differences.

unenterprising (ŭn-ĕn'tər-prī'zĭng) *adj.* Unimaginative.

unerring (ŭn'ûr'ĭng, -ĕr'ĭng) *adj.* Without a mistake.—**unerringly** *adv.*

unfailing (ŭn'fā'lĭng) *adj.* Constant; reliable.

unique (yōō-nēk') *adj.* Being the only one of its kind.

unorthodox (ŭn'ôr'thə-dŏks') *adj.* Untraditional.

unseemly (ŭn'sēm'lē) *adj.* Unbecoming; not in good taste.

unsettle (ŭn'sĕt'l) *v.* To disturb; upset.

unspeakable (ŭn'spē'kə-bəl) *adj.* Indescribable; objectionable.

upright (ŭp'rīt') *adv.* Erect.

usurer (yōō'zhər-ər) *n.* Someone who lends money at a very high rate of interest.

utter (ŭt'ər) *v.* To speak. *adj.* Total; complete.

V

vague (vāg) *adj.* Indefinite; not distinct.

venison (vĕn'ə-sən, -zən) *n.* Deer meat.

venomous (vĕn'ə-məs) *adj.* Spiteful; poisonous.—**venemously** *adv.*

veracity (və-răs'ə-tē) *n.* Honesty; truth.

veranda (və-răn'də) *n.* A roofed balcony or porch, partly enclosed, along the outside of a building.

veritable (vĕr'ə-tə-bəl) *adj.* Actual; real.—**veritably** *adv.*

vestibule (vĕs'tə-byōōl') *n.* An entrance hall or lobby.

vex (vĕks) *v.* To irritate; pester.

vexation (vĕk-sā'shən) *n.* Annoyance.

void (void) *n.* An empty space.

W

wager (wā'jər) *n.* A bet.

wail (wāl) *v.* To make a sad sound suggesting a cry.

ă pat/ā pay/âr care/ä father/b bib/ch church/d deed/ĕ pet/ē be/f fife/g gag/h hat/ hw which/ĭ pit/ī pie/îr pier/j judge/k kick/l lid, needle/m mum/n no, sudden/ ng thing/ŏ pot/ō toe/ô paw, for/oi noise/ou out/ōō took/ōō boot/p pop/r roar/ s sauce/sh ship, dish/t tight/th thin, path/*th* this, bathe/ŭ cut/ûr urge/v valve/ w with/y yes/z zebra, size/zh vision/ə about, item, edible, gallop, circus/ à *Fr.* ami/ œ *Fr.* feu, *Ger.* schön/ü *Fr.* tu, *Ger.* über/кн *Ger.* ich, *Scot.* loch/N *Fr.* bon.

wary (wâr'ē) *adj.* Cautious; watchful.—**warily** (wâr'ə-lē) *adv.*
waver (wā'vər) *v.* To sway; become unsteady.
well (wĕl) *v.* To rise to the surface.—**well up.** To rise from some inner source.
wend (wĕnd) *v.* To proceed.
whimper (hwĭm'pər) *v.* To cry in soft, broken sounds.
whir (hwûr) *v.* To make a swishing or buzzing sound in moving.
wily (wī'lē) *adj.* Sly.
wit (wĭt) *n.* Mental ability.
wonderment (wŭn'dər-mənt) *n.* Astonishment; surprise.
wrangle (răn'gəl) *v.* To quarrel noisily.
wrath (răth, räth) *n.* Rage; fury.

Z
zenith (zē'nĭth) *n.* Peak; highest point.

Index of Authors and Titles